THE FROZEN CONTRACT

by

Bill Rogers

Published in 2012 by Caton Books

First Edition

Whilst this book is based on factual research, and actual police operations are referred to as background context, all of the characters in this book are fictitious, and any resemblance, if any, to actual persons, living or dead, is purely coincidental. Any references to businesses, organisations, places or localities are intended only to give the fiction a sense of reality and authenticity. The only exceptions are Jim Hulme, Dave Wilson and James Mollison who gave their express permission to be fictionalised in this story. Any behaviour, or character traits, given to these individuals serve the fictional story and do not necessarily bear any resemblance to the real people.

Published by Caton Books
www.catonbooks.com

ISBN: 978-0-9564220-7-1

Cover Design by Dragonfruit
Design & Layout: Commercial Campaigns

Author's Note

I am a fan of Football. As a baby, I was taken by my father a half a mile from our home to watch his beloved Arsenal. They have always held a special place in my heart.

I played for the school first team in Hitchin, and when I moved *Up North* to get married, settle down, and follow a career in education, I enjoyed many seasons playing in the Bolton Sunday League.

It was inevitable that marrying into a family of fanatical Wanderers fans, and living in a neighbourhood teeming with them, I would end up going to Burden Park for my fortnightly fix. That didn't rule out visits to Old Trafford when Bolton were away – my wife is a lifelong Manchester United fan – and to Maine Road to watch City on the odd occasion. Working for the City Council made that obligatory.

So I am a fan of football, not just of one club. Which is why it pains me to see the way in which, between them, television and foreign investors have given with one hand, and taken with the other. Football is so much more accessible these days, yet live attendances – with the exception of those clubs wealthy enough to sustain success – are falling inexorably. Foreign players come and go, at the expense of nurturing home grown talent. The gap between the wealthy and the poor clubs is there for all to see, mirroring the widening gulf in society itself. I have no idea how it will end. But I remain a fan of football.

This novel is clearly an exaggerated version of the game today. But for those who doubt that it has its roots in reality, a good starting point would be: *Football And The Gangsters: How Organised Crime Controls The Modern Game.* By Graham Johnson. Or any of the numerous BBC Panorama Programmes on the subject, and the Channel 4 Dispatches programme of Mon 18 July 2012: *How To Buy A Football Club.* Within weeks of the publication of *The Frozen Contract* 50 players in the Italian Leagues are due to appear before a sporting tribunal accused of involvement in match fixing. Last year 17 players, including internationals, were suspended.

Where there is money to be made, there will be crime. The kudos of owning a football club, and the aura that surrounds the most successful clubs, inevitably attracts greed and hubris. I have, however, worked with several Premiership football clubs in Greater Manchester whose commitment to the Community included the setting up of football academies, classrooms, and pupil referral units, and consistent support for children's hospices. As with all human endeavours, the good far outweighs the bad.

This book was completed before any nominations were made for the post of inaugural Police and Crime Commissioner, [Hereafter referred to as police Commissioner] for Greater Manchester. Whoever the candidates turn out to be, any resemblance to characters in this book is entirely coincidental. I wish the incumbent good fortune; for all our sakes.

Acknowledgements

All of the usual suspects. They know who they are. Additionally, Dave Wilson, whose experience in the Metropolitan Police Flying Squad, with Greater Manchester Police, and as a fledgling author, proved invaluable. Mike Atherton for his brilliant cover design. And Joan for her patience, insight, and support.

Dedication

This book is dedicated to young footballers all over the world who have had to overcome adversity, and are now model professionals, in particular, at this time, to Fabrice Muamba.

And to the memory of all those who were not so fortunate.

Chapter 1

Holt heard the ringtone, pushed back his chair and stood up. There were other apartments more conveniently placed along the canal, closer to the city centre, or down by the Castlefield Arena, but each morning this view from the balcony lifted his spirits. Sunset was for lovers. To be savoured from the pavement cafes on Deansgate, in the new financial centre in Spinningfields, or from the Cloud Bar in the Hilton Hotel. It was how you started the day that mattered.

He went inside and picked up.

'Hello?'

'You are still interested in the Titans?'

The voice was Eastern European, possibly Russian, like all the other calls. He still found it impossible to place.

'I'm interested.'

'Get down there now. Take something warm.'

There was a click. Call over.

Not even a *Do svidaniya.*

The streets were quiet. The first tram of the day gliding silently past redbrick warehouse hotels, a motorised street sweeper sucking up detritus from the night before. He lowered the windscreen visor against the blinding glare of the early morning sun. According to Manchester Radio it wasn't going to last.

Winter pansies spoke of spring in the planters beneath the towering shard of the Beetham Tower. He headed southwest past the Museum of Science and Industry until he hit the motorway. As he took the slip road by Barton Bridge an ominous bank of clouds threatened to blot out the sun.

Salford Titans, plucked from the Championship by foreign buyers, relocated to the banks of the Manchester Ship Canal, manager and players cherry picked with Chinese money. Two years, and the brand new Quanxi stadium later, they were champions of the Premiership, and through the qualifying stages of the Champions League. This region already had eight clubs in the Premiership, more than any other. It didn't need another one. You only had to ask the fans at Old Trafford or the Etihad stadium. Or their nearest neighbours, the Salford Reds Rugby League side, with their own Salford City Stadium less than half a mile away.

There were rumours of corruption and dirty money. The mysterious phone calls he'd been getting had all but confirmed it. It was one reason why Holt had relinquished, mid career, his job as North West crime reporter for the News of The World. The other, was a little matter of redundancy.

There were five cars in the car park. One of them he recognised from his time on the crime desk. It belonged to Gina Burman, a former detective sergeant with Greater Manchester Police, one of the few female Asian heritage officers to make it that far. Her sudden and unexplained departure had come as a surprise to everyone, and a blow to the GMP diversity policy. Now she ran a small private investigation agency. As far as he knew she handled infidelity. Men cheating on their wives, wives cheating on their men, men cheating on men, and women on women. She would never be short of work

He pulled up behind her red Ford Kia, and got out clutching his press pass.

She saw him coming in her wing mirror and lowered the window. A weary smile struggled across a perfectly oval face framed with shoulder length silky black hair shot through with a chocolate brown that matched her eyes.

'Hi Gina,' he said. 'What are you doing here?'

'You first,' she replied.

His attention turned to the squat man in the black puffer jacket and matching jeans, a baseball cap, and a yellow dayglow vest. Having advanced towards them he had stopped in his tracks. Holt watched as he put his hand to his ear, said something into his lapel mike, swore, and started to run back towards the Reception block.

'This is why I'm here,' said Holt, putting his press card back in his pocket, and setting off in pursuit.

He heard her car door slam shut behind him, and the click clack of her heels on the plaza.

Opposite the players entrance stood a truck with trailer van attached. The doors of the van were open. The team's physiotherapist stood on the third rung of the pull down steps. A white cloud drifted ghostlike over the rim of the flat bed, and slithered past him onto the floor where it hung suspended like a blanket of fog. There was a disembodied hum from somewhere near the rear of the truck.

Josh and Gina slipped in behind the silent group of burly men straining to see into the van. The physio turned and stepped slowly down from the ladder, head bowed, shoulders drooping.

Now they could see, behind him, the body of a man slumped on a bench along the left hand wall. He was naked but for a pair of brief, black, designer underpants. The surface of his ebony coloured skin was frosted, with a bluish tinge. His arms bent awkwardly behind his back, his head hung stiffly on his chest, crystals of ice glistened on the trademark ponytail.

Gina gasped. Holt didn't blame her. This was Sunday Okowu-Bello, premiership playboy, flawed genius.

Holt wormed his smart phone from his pocket, cupped it in his hand, pressed the video button, and raised it surreptitiously above the shoulder of the guy in front.

Boots slapped the Yorkshire flags like wet fish on a marble slab. Dean Hardman, Head of Security, sprinted towards them. Holt lowered his hand, and dropped the phone into his pocket.

Hardman placed a foot on the steps, took one look inside the trailer, cursed, and swivelled to face them.

'Shut these doors, and switch off that bloody compressor!' he ordered.

Catching sight of Gina and Josh he stabbed his finger towards them.

'And get those two out here now!'

A phalanx of stewards and security guards turned to face them.

Holt held up both hands in a gesture of submission.

'It's OK,' he said. 'We're going.'

They edged their way along the narrow passage between the wall and the stony faced stadium staff, and out onto the plaza. As soon as they were clear Holt flipped open his smart phone and speed dialled

'Jack, it's Josh...no just listen,' he said. 'I've got the

scoop of the decade. What? Let's just say it involves a premiership footballer, murder, and a novel modus operandi. Yes, I'm serious. There's a video coming over now...initial text to follow shortly. Start the bidding war Jack. Whoever wins, tell them to hold the front page. No, I haven't got time to explain. Watch the video. Read the text. I'll send you the rest as soon as it's done.'

The fingers and thumb of his right hand flew over the keys as he sent the video and began to compose the message.

'Hold the front page?' said Gina.

'I've always wanted to say that. It's not the first time though. I was in Albert Square when the IRA bomb went off.'

'Who's Jack?'

'My agent. I don't have time to set up deals with all the media that's out there. I'm going to be too busy hunting down the stories, staying ahead of the pack, writing them up.'

'What the hell was that van all about?' Gina asked as they reached their cars.

'The Titan's mobile cryotherapy unit,' said Josh Googling furiously. 'All the big clubs have one. Ice packs and ice baths are a thing of the past. Now they just shove them in one of those to bring down their metabolic rate, and repair any tissue damage.'

He filtered the results on his screen.

'Apparently Walt Disney has been in suspended animation since his death in 1966, and Michael Jackson is alive and well and living in someone's cryogenic chamber.'

He clicked another link.

'Here we go,' he said. 'They cool the chamber using liquid nitrogen or CO_2. The temperature can go down as low as -120 degrees Celsius.'

He turned to face her.

'Your turn,' he said. 'What were you doing here?'

'Okowu-Bello,' she said. 'His wife hired me to follow him.'

'Bloody Hell! You pick your jobs. How long had you been waiting for him to reappear?'

She pointed to a midnight blue Aston Martin DB9 parked 50 metres to their left.

'Since he arrived in that, at 11.30pm last night.' She grimaced. 'No wonder his hair was white. That's the end of my lucrative little contract. I suppose.'

'You never know. The grieving widow may want you to handle her insurance claim. Or help her bag another footballer.'

'I think she's had her fill of them. With what she stands to inherit she won't have to go out looking.'

'Makes her a prime suspect though.'

'So why did she have me following him?'

'You're her alibi. I think you'd have noticed if she'd turned up here during the night. Unless you sleep on the job of course?'

She jabbed him sharply in the ribs.

'There's no call for that,' he complained.

'No,' she said, gesturing to his right with a tilt of her chin. 'Looks whose here.'

A golden Bentley with black tinted windows, cruised past, slowing as it reached the hastily constructed barrier. The number plate was already a legend: ***CG2 PC1.***

Charles Grey, OBE, the first Police and Crime Commissioner for Greater Manchester. Mr *One Strike and You're Out.* The zero tolerance right wing candidate elected against all odds. It helped that one of his main rivals had been embarrassed by a daughter allegedly hooked on crack cocaine and arrested by police in a drugs raid, and his second biggest rival had inexplicably dropped out due to family circumstances that had never been satisfactorily explained.

'How come he got here before the senior investigating officer?' Josh wondered.

'Only just,' said Gina as a silver Skoda Octavia screeched to a halt beside them. The passenger window slid down. The driver leant across and craned his neck to stare up at them.

'Holt, how the hell did you get here this fast? And what are you doing here Gina?'

'Surname for me, first name for Burman,' said Josh. And a good morning to you Detective Chief Inspector Caton. You the SIO on this one?'

Caton unbuckled his seat belt, hauled his tall athletic frame from the car, and rested his hands on the roof. 'Don't mess me around Josh,' he said. 'Not today. Just answer the question.'

Josh could see his point. The Force Major Incident Team had been disbanded, and most of Caton's squad had been dispersed across other divisions. And now this. He could do without the aggravation.

'I received a tip off,' he said. 'By phone, about an hour ago. And before you ask, caller withheld his number. Ten to one it's in the canal by now.'

Caton held out his hand palm up.

'Let *me* figure that one out.'

Josh shook his head. 'It wasn't on my cell phone Tom. It was on my land line. You've got my number. Your techies should have no problem checking it out.'

Caton turned to Burman. 'Gina? How come you're here?'

She tucked her hair behind her ear. It was a simple, unconscious, gesture but enough to make Holt wonder if there had been something between these two when she was on the force.

'I was on a job,' she said, 'Tailing someone.'

'Who?'

'Okowu-Bello.'

Caton shook his head in disbelief. 'You two stay here. I'll need to talk to you. In the meantime don't talk to anyone else.'

He climbed back inside the car, started the engine, leaned across to the passenger side, and looked up into Gina's eyes. 'It's a shame you didn't tail him into that trailer,' he said.

'He's got his work cut out,' Josh observed as they watched him drive away. He reached into his car and took his iPad from the man bag tucked beneath his seat. 'There'll be more suspects than there are players in the first team squad.'

He waited for it to load, then began to type furiously.

'Like who?' she said.

He had to raise his voice above the wail of approaching sirens.

'Apart from the jealous wife, the jealous boyfriends, the two allegations of rape that were suddenly dropped, the Titan fans who want to see the back of him, the United and City fans in this soccer mad city who hate his guts? That should be enough to go on with.'

'Not to mention his gambling debts, and the affair he's having with the manager's daughter,' she said.

He looked up sharply.

'You are joking?'

'Do I look as though I'm joking?'

He stopped typing. 'Since your contract has come to an end, how do you fancy taking on another one?'

Her forehead creased with concentration, and tiny wrinkles appeared at the sides of her eyes. If anything he thought it made her even more alluring.

'Are you serious?'

'Deadly. When this breaks the tabloids will be all

over it. I don't have the staff, or the resources, to compete with them, but together we might.'

He raised his hand, palm outwards, cutting off her protest.

'We have local contacts, and local knowledge. I'm an investigative reporter; you're a former police officer, and a private detective who's been closer to Okowu-Bello than anyone. With the money I'll get from today alone I can afford to hire you to work with me for as long as it takes. I'll pay your normal rate, plus a percentage of whatever I make when the bigger story's sold. This could make both of us. '

The wind had whipped up, blowing tiny whirlpools of dust across the plaza. Two tactical aid vans pulled into the car park and headed for the barrier. Their sirens stopped abruptly like a brace of strangled cats. She pulled up her collar, and flicked her hair back into place.

'Or break us both,' she said solemnly. 'You forget, Josh, I've been here before: Manchester, murder, and mayhem.'

A slanting hail began to fall from the leaden sky. They took shelter in his Golf, watching the icy stones bounce on the stadium roof, listening in silence as they peppered the car's bonnet like shot gun pellets.

'I know,' he said. 'Don't you just love it?'

Chapter 2

'Do you know who I am?!'

Oblivious to the elements, Charles Grey stood impotent and angry before the solid yellow semi-circle of stewards, arms linked, across the plaza's narrowest point.

'I don't care who you are.' His head shrank further into his bomber jacket with every hail stone strike. 'Nobody gets through here without Mr. Hardman's say so.'

'Except for me,' said Caton, holding up his ID card.

The Police Commissioner swung round, relief lighting up his fleshy features. He stepped towards Caton, took him firmly by the arm, and drew him to one side. His eyes narrowed as he read the name on the warrant card.

'DCI Caton,' he said. 'I take it you'll be in charge of clearing up this mess?'

Caton eased his arm free, and placed his ID back in his pocket.

'No Sir. I happened to be the Duty Officer. I was sent to secure the crime scene, assess the situation, and advise the appointed Senior Investigating Officer accordingly.'

Grey's brow furrowed as his brain struggled to join the dots.

'Caton. You're the one who sorted out that mess

with the serial killer? Saved the Leader from a humiliating public apology?'

'Yes sir, although I wouldn't put it quite like that.' Behind them Caton could hear the Tactical Aid teams piling out of their vans. 'Now, I really must get on.'

The Commissioner seized his arm again.

'I want you in charge of this. It needs someone with tact and political sensitivity. And it needs to be cleared up fast.'

His tone was conspiratorial, with a whiff of desperation.

Caton placed his left hand on the Commissioner's arm, and gently eased his own arm free.

'That really isn't up me Sir,' he said. 'It's a matter for the Assistant Chief Constable Crime. Please excuse me.'

It took him less than a minute to replace the stewards with a cordon comprising members of the Tactical Aid Team until the uniforms and Police and Community Support Officers arrived. Then he agreed with Dean Hardman, the Head of Security, their re-deployment around the stadium to keep the scene as secure as possible.

'What about the press?' said Hardman. 'With Media City less than two miles away this place will be swarming with TV and radio vans any minute now?'

'Can you allocate them an area beyond the perimeter we've just set up?'

'No problem.'

'Make sure they leave access free for our vehicles to come and go.'

'Right,' he said, turning and jogging away through the light drizzle that now enveloped them all.

'And then the SIO will need a word with you,' Caton shouted after him. Thank God it won't be me, he reflected as he headed towards the van.

'This is a first,' said Jack Benson the Crime Scene Manager, as they waited for the Duty Pathologist to finish his initial examination.

'I think you'll find it was a modus operandi beloved of criminal gangs south of the Thames in the 1950's And 60's,' Caton reminded him. 'Not forgetting New York and Chicago.'

'They were hanging from hooks along with the carcasses in cold storage facilities, and meat refrigerators. Nothing like this.'

'Same result,' said Caton. 'Frozen to death.'

'Unless he was dead when they put him in there.'

'He wasn't,' said Mr Douglas using the bench to support him as he got to his feet. 'At least, not as far as I can tell. We'll have to wait for the post mortem to be certain but if I was a betting man I'd say he was alive when they closed the doors on him.'

'So why didn't he hammer on the walls, and call out?' Benson wondered.

'Because his hands were tied behind his back with plastic cable ties, and he had gaffer tape over his mouth.'

He held out his case for Caton to hold while he carefully descended the stairs. His back had never been the same since that hit and run.

'I don't see any tape,' said Caton.

'It's on the floor. Looks like someone helpfully removed it before we got here.'

He took back his case and shook his head.

'Young man like that, an athlete at the peak of his career.'

It made him sound like a vet that had just put down a race horse.

'I suppose with the complication of the temperature in there you're not even going to try to estimate the time of death?'

He took out a pocket umbrella, pressed the button, and watched it spring into action.

'You know DCI Caton,' he said as he raised it above his head. 'You never disappoint me.'

'How long before you'll know?'

He twirled the umbrella, unintentionally spraying them both with captured droplets of rain.

'When you let us have the data from that van, indicating how long the unit was running for, and at what temperature, that, together with the post mortem analysis of the body, should give us a pretty good idea. Well within the usual parameters.'

'I'll let the SIO know you need that data,' said Caton as Benson made a note.

'Not you then?' The pathologist said.

'I'm just here to hold the fort until he or she arrives.'

'Pity, I enjoy working with you. We've reached an understanding over the years wouldn't you say?'

Without waiting for an answer he turned and left them standing there, staring into the van.

'Don't you want to have look?' said Benson.

'It's not my place. I just have to secure the scene, check the suspects aren't still in the vicinity, and get together the key witnesses. I've done that. Now all I have to do is hand it over.'

'You must be curious though Boss?'

'First off, I'm no longer your boss Jack. Secondly there's no point in my contaminating your scene of crime any more than has already been done. And thirdly...'

He was cut off by the squawk of Benson's radio.

'Excuse me.' Benson said moving away a little and inclining his head to better hear the message.

'Is your phone off Boss?' he said, stepping back alongside him

Caton took his BlackBerry from the holster on his belt, and checked.

'I forgot to switch it back on again.'

'Only Detective Chief Superintendent Gates wants a word with you.' Benson attempted a grin but it came out more like a smirk. 'What with you being the Senior Investigating Officer.'

Caton cursed under his breath. He was about to speed dial when she beat him to it. Benson withdrew to a polite distance, and pretended to go over his checklist.

'Tom. Where the hell have you been?'

She sounded uncharacteristically annoyed, not necessarily with him.

'I'm sorry Ma'am,' he said. 'It was a bit hairy for a moment so I switched my phone off and forgot to....'

'Well I'm afraid it's going to get even hairier. The Chief Constable has just informed me that you're to be the SIO on this one. You've friends in high places apparently.

'Charles Bloody Grey,' he said under his breath.

'I'll pretend I didn't hear that,' she said. 'It won't come as surprise to you that the Chief wants this brought to a speedy and tidy conclusion with the minimum of fuss or publicity.'

'Except for when the investigation has reached a successful conclusion. Then the publicity will no doubt be substantial. And he'll figure prominently.'

'You've been doing this for far too long Tom. You're becoming cynical.'

'I want my team back.'

'Not possible I'm afraid.'

'Then I don't see how I'm going to manage *speedy, tidy,* or *clean,* Ma'am.'

Her voice tightened. 'Are you trying to blackmail

me Detective Chief Inspector?'

'Not at all. You know how long it takes at the best of times to build the kind of rapport you need with a new team. This has the stench of the worst of times... Ma'am.'

He counted six before she spoke. Even then she was thinking out loud, working through the ramifications.'

'The Chief Constable isn't going to like it. It will look as though he's making exceptions. Reversing one of his key reforms.'

'Sounds to me like this is already an exceptional case. Perhaps he might want to check with the Commissioner?'

'I suggest you leave the politics to me Tom. Either that or do us all a favour and go before the Promotion Board like you should have done years ago.'

It's Tom again, he noted.

'So you'll talk to ACC Hadfield?'

She sighed. 'I'll see what I can do. In the meantime you'd better get a sprint on. This case is already all over the Web.'

'Yes Ma'am.'

'And Tom...'

'Yes Ma'am?'

'Watch yourself.'

As if he needed telling. Caton sent a text to Kate letting her know he'd be late this evening, if he made it home at all. He slotted the phone back in its holster, and set off in search of the Head of Security.

'Here you'd better put this on.'

Hardman handed him a waterproof Titan's anorak straight from the club shop. Caton shrugged it on. A size too large, but the bonus was that it covered his knees.

'Who did they design this one for,' he said. 'The Goalie?'

'If you check the back I think you'll find it's number nine.'

'Who's that?'

Hardman grimaced. 'Okowu-Bello.'

'You're having me on?'

'Fraid not.'

'I can't wear this; the press will have a field day.'

Hardman shrugged. 'It's either that, or get even wetter than you already are.'

Caton capitulated. 'It'll do until I get someone to bring my own one down.'

'Don't worry. You can always pretend it was a tribute.'

'It's not just that. Everyone knows I'm a City fan.'

Hardman held out his hand. 'In that case, I'll have it back.'

'So, who found the body?' said Caton, anxious to get on with it.

'Steve Makin, our physio. I asked him to wait in my office. I'll take you.'

'No thanks. Just point me in the right direction. I'd like you to get me a list of everyone who was on duty either during the night or early this morning, up to the time the body was found.'

'Two birds with one stone,' said the Head of Security. 'That information is on the computer in my office. It's on the way.'

As they passed through the players' lounge Caton's phone rang. It was DCS Gates. She didn't bother with the niceties.

'You can have DI Holmes, DS Stuart, and DS Carter. I gather Benson is already on the scene. That's it. The best I could do.'

'Thank you Ma'am,' he said. I'm really grateful.'

She snorted. 'You'd better be. Martin is fuming and it's not gone down well with their current commands. So you owe me Tom...big time.'

He could imagine. Breaking up the Force Major Incident Team, whose focus on Major and Serious Crime had been one of the few components to receive an *Outstanding* classification in the last report of Her Majesty's Inspector of Constabulary, had been one of the most controversial moves made by the new Chief Constable. Now here he was breaking his own rules. Bringing back together detectives who had been scattered across the divisions and tasked to cover Volume Crime and even Road Traffic Accidents. True it was only four of his original team. But Dave Wood was out on his neck after his role in the Bluebell Hollow fiasco, and Sarah Weston had been promoted up to Chief Inspector. He would have liked to have Duggie Wallace as his analyst, but he wasn't going to complain. Not that it would have made any difference.

'This is it.'

Hardman opened the door and stood aside to let him in. A man in an anorak identical to Caton's, purple tracksuit bottoms, and white training shoes, leapt to his feet. In his mid thirties, dark hair cut short, athletic build, medium height.

'Steve, this is Mr Caton,' said Hardman over Tom's shoulder.

Caton held out his hand. 'Detective Inspector Caton,' he said.

The physiotherapist shook it firmly.

Stephen Makin,' he said. 'I'm the club's senior physiotherapist.'

Caton thought he detected a slight tremor in the man's hand. It matched the quaver in his voice and the pallor of his face.

'You'd better sit down Stephen, before you fall down,' said the Head of Security. 'I'll get you that list Mr Caton.'

'Is there somewhere I can talk with Mr Makin in private?' said Caton.

'No problem, it'll only take a second to run that list off, and then I'll leave you in peace.'

In the event it took three minutes by Caton's watch, during which he and Makin sat in uncomfortable silence.

'Here you go,' said Hardman, handing over two sheets of A4. 'That one's the security staff on duty, the other one's the list of other staff who signed in during that period.'

There were twelve names on the first list and seven on the second.

'That's a lot of people,' Caton remarked.

'It's a big place.'

Caton placed the lists on the floor beside him.

'We'll need to speak to every one of these people today. This morning if possible. Can you set that up?'

'I'll do my best. And I'll sort out a couple of rooms you can use. I'm going to need mine back.'

'And I'll need access to all your CCTV footage. Not just this area...the whole of the stadium.'

'It's already in hand,' he said.

He closed the door firmly after him.

Chapter 3

'I still can't believe it. Jesus wept! What kind of people would do something like that?'

The tremor in his hands was even more evident now. It had taken over the whole of his lower arms. There were beads of sweat on his forehead and upper lip.

'Listen Stephen,' Caton said, reaching for his phone. 'We can't do this right now. You're in shock. I need to get a paramedic up here.'

'No. It's alright. He gripped the arms of chair tightly. I'll be fine. Let's just get it over with.'

Caton wavered. 'If you're sure. But you'd better loosen your clothes, try to relax, do some deep breathing or whatever. I don't want you passing out on me. And when we're done you see someone. OK?'

'OK.'

The physiotherapist struggled to remove his anorak and tracksuit top, revealing a purple Titan's sweatshirt. He folded his arms so that his hands were pinioned beneath his armpits.

Caton took out his notebook and a biro. 'Are you sure you're up for this?' he said.

'Yes. You need to get the bastards who did it.'

'Good. Let's start with what time you arrived at the club.'

'That would be about five past six.'

'Do you normally get here at that time?'

'No. Not on a Monday.'

'Then why today?'

'Because we had a couple of players injured on Saturday and I'd arranged for them come in early. The Boss is desperate to get them right for the Champions League on Wednesday.'

'Was Sunday Okowu-Bello one of them?'

'No.'

'What time are you expecting them?'

He looked at his watch. 'Half past eight.'

'Two and half hours to get yourself ready?'

'I like to miss the rush hour traffic. Get a coffee, do some paperwork. And I have to switch on the cryo' unit.'

'How long does it take to set up?'

'No time at all. We have a liquid nitrogen boost system that reduces the pull down time by 500%.'

Caton raised a hand. 'You're losing me.'

'That container holds an eight cubic feet cryogenic chamber. If we use a boost of liquid nitrogen the temperature drops to minus 110 degrees almost instantaneously. Without it, it can take up to an hour.'

'How easy is it to operate it?'

'Very. Setting the right temperature, and length of exposure according the player's condition...the medical bit...that's more complicated. But just switching it on...almost anyone can do that.'

'Who apart from you would know how to?'

He unfolded his arms and sat up straight. The shaking had stopped Caton noticed, and the colour had come back to his cheeks.

'I don't know. Loads of people. The rest of the fitness and medical team obviously. When we first got it we did demonstrations for the directors and medical staff from other clubs. I even showed all of the players how easy it was, to de-mystify it. So they wouldn't be scared of it.'

'Should they be?'

'Too right they should. The timing and temperatures are critical. Do you know how it works?'

Caton nodded. 'In theory. Like an ice bath?'

'Exactly. Only far easier to control. We check their blood pressure beforehand. Kit them up with mouth and ear protectors, gloves and socks, so they don't get frostbite. Then they go inside in shorts or trunks for a maximum of three minutes.'

'Only three minutes?'

'That's all it takes for their skin temperature to drop to between 32 degrees and 5 degrees Celsius. It's like giving the body a shock. All the blood gets drawn towards the vital organs. As soon as they come out it rushes back into the muscles and surrounding tissues, full of nutrients and fresh oxygen.'

'And if they stay any longer than three minutes?'

He folded his arms again, locking them tight.

'After four minutes the fluid in your eyeballs freezes. Five minutes...and you're dead.'

There was silence as each of them pictured Sunday Okowu-Bello struggling to free himself. Knowing exactly how long he had to do it. Knowing exactly what was going to happen if he didn't.

'The door isn't locked while they're in there?'

'No. And there's a panel on the wall showing the temperature and time elapsed. An intermittent tone sounds when they need to leave, and an alarm sounds if the door hasn't opened within ten seconds of that.'

'What if the doors jam?'

'There's even an emergency door on the side.' Not that it's ever been needed.'

'You found the body?'

He nodded, slowly.

'I'd only just arrived. As I drew level with the van I noticed that the stairs were down, and I could hear the generator running. Then I saw the locking bolts were in place across the doors. I slid them back and pulled open the doors...

He didn't finish the sentence. Instead he put his head in his hands, resting his elbows on the arms of the chair.

Caton gave him a moment or two.

'Did you touch the body?'

'No.'

'Who switched off the generator?'

'I did.'

'Did you touch anything else?'

He looked up, uncertain where this was going.

'Just the master switch on the control unit.'

'You didn't touch the settings at all?'

'No. Look, I wasn't thinking straight.'

'Don't worry.' Caton told him. 'You did the right thing.' He looked down at his notes. 'The van and the cab are normally locked?'

'Yes.'

'Where are the keys kept?'

'There are two sets. Both are kept in the desk drawer in my office.'

'Locked away?'

The question took him by surprise.

'No.' Then the implication dawned on him. His head dropped. 'There didn't seem to be a need... until now.'

There's was a sharp rap on the door. Caton turned. Gordon Holmes grinned at him through the glazed panel. He waved him in, and turned back to the physiotherapist.

'That will be all for now Mr Makin. You've been very helpful. I suggest you get yourself checked over.'

Makin stood up. 'I'll be alright.'

'Do it anyway. And I'm afraid you'll have to stay away from your room until my forensics team have dusted it for prints.'

Gordon Holmes stood aside to let him past.

'This is a turn up,' he said, closing the door behind him.

'It's good to have you back Detective Inspector.' Caton told him.

'I don't know how you managed it?'

'Don't ask,' he said pointing to the chair Makin had vacated. 'How much do you know?'

'Sunday Okowu-Bello, frozen to death,' he shook his head in disbelief. 'You couldn't make it up.' He grimaced. 'They should have called him Solomon Grundy.'

Caton looked bemused.

'You know,' Holmes persisted. 'Born on a Monday, died on a Sunday

'Buried,' said Caton.

'What?'

'Buried. Solomon Grundy, he was buried on a Sunday. He died on a Saturday.'

'According to Match of The Day that's exactly what he did.'

'What?'

'Died, on Saturday, against Arsenal.'

Caton decided to give up. There was no point in lecturing Gordon on respect for the dead. He'd seen too many. This was how he coped. How they all did.

'DS Stuart and DS Carter are joining us too,' he said. 'Have you seen either of them?'

'No Boss, but Jack Benson's doing a good job. He's got the tent up, and a mobile incident room in place. Just as well, there's television camera's everywhere.'

Caton handed him the sheets that Hardman had

given him.

'Right. I need you to start interviewing everyone on this list. Why were they here? When did they arrive? Where did they go? What did they do? Did they see or hear anything out of the ordinary. I'll get DS Carter to help when he gets here.'

He passed a hand through the hair on the back of his neck. Kate was right. It needed cutting. It was his turn to grin.

'I'm sorry Gordon. Why am I telling you all this?'

'Because you're worried I might have forgotten it all the minute I left your sight?'

He rubbed his chin the way he always did when beating himself up. Gordon was a brilliant interviewer, Caton reminded himself, but a rubbish poker player.

'Speaking of which, I forgot. I was accosted on the way in by Gina Burman and Josh Holt. They were really antsy. Said to tell you they couldn't hang around all day.'

'They're next on my list,' Caton stood up. 'Gina Burman was tailing Okowu-Bello on behalf of his wife, and Holt had a mysterious phone call telling him to get down here.'

'Bloody Hell!' said Gordon. 'This gets better and better.'

Caton opened the door.

'Welcome back,' he said.

'So you've no idea who this mysterious caller was?'

'None whatsoever,' Holt replied.

It sounded to Caton like a partial truth, obfuscation. It was the *whatsoever* that did it, when a simple *No* would have sufficed.

'But you have a theory?'

Holt shook his head.

This time it was the lack of words. As though he didn't trust his voice not to betray him.

Caton turned instead to his former colleague. Not that Gina had ever been part of his team.

'Tell me again,' he said. 'She wanted you to follow her husband because...?'

She shifted uneasily on her seat. It wasn't that she was nervous, far from it, but it was cramped here in the incident van.

'She had reason to believe that he was cheating on her again.'

'Again?'

'You must know his reputation?'

'Remind me,' said Caton.

'He treated the Manchester club scene like a sweet shop. Before he got married it was a different girl every week. Sometimes more than one at a time...allegedly. He was out of control.'

'Hence the two occasions he was arrested for rape.'

She nodded. 'And released when the girls withdrew their statements. Same with the others for sexual assault.'

'Either he was set up, and they were paid off,' Josh Holt observed. 'Or he was guilty, and they were still paid off.'

Caton ignored him.

'I thought that was supposed to have stopped when he married...what's her name?'

'Donna. Donna Dootson. It did, except that he took to having one mistress at a time. That way it was less public, easier to manage.'

'How long have you been tracking him for?'

'Three weeks.'

'And?'

'As far I can tell he has...had...two mistresses going

at the same time. One was gambling. He spent three nights a week, and several afternoons after training, at the same casino. I thought he might have been meeting a woman there but he wasn't. He played the same two tables over and over again. Blackjack and roulette.'

'Did he ever win?'

'Hardly ever by all accounts. But it didn't seem to matter. Like it was something he had to do. Once I saw him lose a pile of chips betting on red. When he lost he just roared with laughter.'

'Given what he's paid he could afford to lose,' said Holt.

She shook her head. 'That's just it. Apparently he owed hundreds of thousands, and they were pressing him to pay up.'

'How do you know?' Caton asked.

'Because I made friends with one of the croupiers. She told me that on Thursday they refused to give him any credit until he'd settled what was outstanding.'

'How did he take it?'

'Badly. I was watching from the wine bar opposite when he stormed out. He pushed one of the doormen, and kicked out at a smart limousine parked up outside. He was lucky they didn't set on him then and there.'

'That explains why he played so badly on Saturday,' said the ex-reporter. 'Had his mind on other things.'

'You said *two* mistresses,' Caton reminded her.

She paused, less for effect he decided than because of the impact of what she was about to say.

'Ah,' she said. 'That's where it got interesting. It was the manager's daughter.'

'As in the Titans manager?' said Caton

'That's right.'

'Jesus!' Holt exclaimed.

He tried to sound surprised, but Caton could tell from the look on his face, and hers, that he wasn't.

Chapter 4

'You two have been working together,' he said.

She placed a hand on Holt's arm to stop him from responding.

'No Tom,' she said. 'It was a complete co-incidence that we met up here this morning. Though you are right in another sense.'

'How's that?'

'We have agreed to pool information, and work together.'

Holt pulled his arm away.

'For God's sake Gina,' he said. 'You didn't have to...'

'Yes she did,' said Caton cutting him off. 'She knows how it works. This is a murder investigation. If you're going to pool anything you pool it with me first.'

The journalist looked down at the floor.

'Do you understand?' said Caton.

He looked up, and nodded reluctantly.

'And don't think it's a two way street either. I choose what I tell you. You tell me everything. Let's start with the mysterious caller. My guess is that today's call wasn't the first.'

Holt looked at Gina Burman, saw her raised eyebrows, and turned back to Caton.

'You're right,' he said. 'I was going to tell you.'

This time it was Caton's turn to raise them. 'Eventually,' he said.

'No, really, I was. They started about six months ago. Once a fortnight give or take. I'd done a couple of free lance articles on corruption in sport. That's when I started to get these calls. About football corruption. Dropping hints. Making insinuations. No hard facts.'

'Always the same voice?'

'A man. With a heavy accent. So heavy I decided it was partly to disguise it.'

'What kind of accent?'

'Eastern European. Possibly Russian. I'm not an expert.'

'These allegations. Were they about football in general, or The Titans in particular?'

'They were generalised at first, but in the past month or so it was clear he was talking about the Titans.'

'Were any threats made against the club, or any person or persons in particular?'

Holt shook his head. 'They weren't like that. I got the impression the whole point was to help me with my own investigations. He wanted me to be the one to find and dish the dirt.'

'And leave your mysterious source with clean hands?'

'Exactly.'

Caton remained silent until the journalist made eye contact.

'If this is all about protecting your source, and your story, Mr. Holt, I need to know.'

Josh held his gaze as he answered.

'No it's not. I don't know who he is or why he keeps calling me.' He tore his eyes away.

'Because if you're bullshitting me,' said Caton.

'When I find out, and I shall, I'll be charging you with obstructing this investigation at best and, at worst, conspiracy to pervert the course of justice. Do you understand?'

Josh did. But before he could say so the door burst open, and DS Joanne Stuart charged in from the rain.

She scanned the faces staring at her. The Boss looked irritated; Gina Burman – what a surprise to see her there – was trying hard to suppress a smile, and Holt...Josh, that was it... was looked distinctly relieved.

'I'm sorry sir,' she said. 'I had no idea you were in a meeting. Only it's raining cats and dogs out there.'

In here too, Caton was tempted to reply.

'It's all right,' he said. 'As it happens your timing is perfect. Mr Holt, whom I think you know, was just leaving. He is going to go and get me a copy of the meticulous record that I'm sure he's kept of every phone call that he's received relating to his current research, and everything he has on the Titans. Then he's going to take it to the Force Headquarters at Central Park and hand it in at Reception as urgent for my attention.'

Josh Burman levered himself off the bench, and stood up. He waited for Gina to join him.

'Miss Burman is staying here,' Caton continued. 'You see, DS Stuart, she was tailing the victim on behalf of his wife, so I think it only right that she should accompany you when you officially break the news to Mrs Okowu-Bello that her husband is dead.'

It was when the Boss reverted to formal speak that Joanne Stuart knew best to keep her head down. They all did. She stepped aside to allow the journalist access to the doorway.

He turned at the top of the steps.

'I'll be in contact Gina,' he said.

'And I with you Mr Holt,' Caton told him.

It took less than five minutes for Caton to bring Joanne Stuart up to speed, and send her and Gina Burman on their way, and a further five minutes to discuss with Jack Benson the progress the scene of crime officers had made. He raised the hood of his anorak and was about to make his way across to the stadium administration block when he caught sight of Charles Grey.

The Police Commissioner was standing in front of a semi-circle of assorted still and video cameras, and microphones. His driver stood beside him holding a Titans' umbrella over them both. Caton edged forward making sure to stay both out of shot, and the Commissioner's peripheral vision.

'You're saying this was an accident?' Said the BBC's correspondent. He sounded as incredulous as Caton was feeling.

'I'm not saying that exactly,' Grey prevaricated. 'Just that I think that when the truth emerges it will turn out to be a lot less sensational than your questions suggest.'

'Have you seen the video Commissioner?' The Granada TV reporter called out.

'Video? What video?' said Charles Grey, echoing the question on Caton's lips.

'The one showing the body with its arms bound behind its back,' said the man from the BBC.

Caton cursed silently. Charles Grey ignored the question and bumbled on defensively, his arrogance heightened by embarrassment.

'On my personal recommendation Detective Chief Inspector Caton has been placed in charge of this case. You will all be aware of his track record, and I have every confidence that the investigation will be concluded speedily.'

Caton was running out of invectives.

'Can you expand on that Mr. Grey?' someone shouted.

The commissioner held up his hand imperiously.

'I have nothing more to say at this time.' He turned his back on the futile chorus of questions, spotted Caton, and blushed like a little boy caught with his hand in a jar of sweets.

'Detective Chief Inspector,' he hissed. 'What are you doing here? Shouldn't you be taking fingerprints, or interrogating suspects?'

'I was hoping for a word with the press officer,' Caton said pointedly. 'Where is she?'

Grey's jaw began to twitch. 'I don't have time for this,' he said. 'And I wouldn't have thought that you did either.'

He strode away towards his car pursued by a continuous cat call of questions, and a very wet chauffeur.

By the time he reached the stadium Reception Caton had begun to calm down. Grey's impromptu press conference he could safely leave to the Chief Constable whose propensity for anger was well known. The video was another matter. It meant that the victim's wife would already know, thus removing the element of surprise when DS Stuart got there. Impossible then to tell if she was surprised to learn of her husband's death, or play acting. Not only that, but it explained the reaction of the media. He could imagine the headlines and the lurid stories that would follow. Ramping up the pressure on him, and exposing the crime scene to the world at large. There was no way now that he could lure suspects into revealing things about what had happened in that van that only the perpetrators could have known.

'Mr Caton?'

A young woman behind the reception desk stood and beckoned to him. 'I have a message for you.'

Her accent was East European. Her English polished. Chestnut coloured hair cascaded over her shoulders and halfway down her back. She wore a tight black fitted blouse, and a matching pencil skirt, which together accented her hour glass figure. Her eyes were wide, dark, and knowing, her cheekbones high. Full crimson lips turned down slightly at the corners as though mildly disappointed.

'Mr. Lightfoot and Mr. Capper are in Mr Lightfoot's office. They wish to see you urgently.'

'And who is Mr Lightfoot?' Caton wanted to know.

Her eyes widened with surprise.

'Mr Lightfoot is our Chief Executive, and Mr. Capper,' she added just in case. 'Is the Manager and Director of Football here at the club.'

There can't have many people in the world who hadn't heard of Gerry Capper, Caton reflected. Even he, a lifelong City fan, had followed Capper's meteoric rise with interest. After eighteen years of loyal service at Chelsea – fifteen of those in the national side - and a brief spell at Barcelona, he had spent eighteen months completing his coaching awards, and taking a management course. After two successful years learning his trade he was offered the chance to manage the newly acquired Salford Titans Championship side. Two years on, he had led them to the Premiership Trophy and into the Champions League. Lightfoot he had never heard of.

'Please let them know I'll be with them shortly,' he said.

She stood her ground.

'Mr Lightfoot asked me to impress upon you that it is extremely urgent,' she insisted.

'Please inform Mr Lightfoot that I am investigating

a suspicious death. I will be with them as soon as I can.'

He took the slight inclination of her head as assent.

'Mr Hardman is waiting for you in his room,' she said tentatively.

'Please tell him I'm on my way.' He headed towards the lifts. A voice called after him.

'Oh thank God! Detective Chief Inspector. I have to speak with you.'

He was tempted to keep going but the sense of desperation, combined with the use of the formal title, gave him pause. He took a deep breath and turned to find a man his own age and height, dressed in a very smart black suit, and sporting a purple and gold Titans' Tie standing in the doorway of the office immediately behind the reception desk. The man came to meet him, arm outstretched.

'I'm James Mollison, General Manager.'

'I'm sorry,' Caton said shaking his hand and letting go. 'But I haven't...'

'Please,' Mollison said. 'I won't keep you, but we have a problem.'

The way he said *we* implied that it was Caton's problem too.

'Alright. But make it quick.'

Relief flooded the man's face.

'There's a conference for insurance brokers in the Cronus suite from 10 till four this afternoon. And three other seminar rooms have been booked for smaller events. They've already started arriving. Your men are preventing them from coming in.'

'You'd better cancel it,' Caton told him.

'The general manager looked as though he was going to have a fit.

'But the caterers have started preparing the lunches.'

Caton shook his head. 'I'm sorry but...'

Mollison grabbed him by the sleeve.

'Please,' he said. 'Look, the Cronus suite is behind the upper tier on the other side of the stadium. We can re-locate the seminars, and lock the doors linking them with this half of the stadium. There's no need for them to come within a half a mile of your crime scene.

Caton thought about it. The crime scene had already been compromised. All but one of the car parks were outside the inner ring that Benson had set up, and would already be full of cars. Anything he need from them would be on the CCTV. Mollison had a point. This place was more like a small town. Thousands of jobs depended on it. He couldn't wrap it up in cotton wool indefinitely.'

'Very well,' he said. I'll let my people know. But if it causes me a problem I'll hold you personally responsible.'

Mollison let go of his sleeve. Relief swamped his face.

'What about the rest of the people who work in this part of the stadium?' he said.

'Speak to Mr. Benson. If you can come up with a way to get them in and out without breaching the inner cordon I've put in place, I'll go along with that. My warning still applies.'

'What about the First Team squad? They'll be arriving anytime now.'

'Don't push your luck,' said Caton. 'There must be a training ground they can go to? And I want them to stay put when they get here. I'll need to meet with them at some point today.'

'You'll have to speak to Mr Capper about that,' said Mollison.

'Don't worry, I shall, when I'm good and ready.'

Chapter 5

As he stepped out of the lift Caton's phone vibrated. He had a text, from Kate.

Where are U? Thought U said Ud B home be4 I left for Uni?

He checked his watch. She'd probably sent it just before she went into the lecture she had been preparing when they got back from the bridal fair on Sunday afternoon. It was too late to ring and explain now. He sent her a brief text, and promised himself he'd ring her at lunchtime.

The Head of Security was waiting in his office. He looked like someone who had been on the wrong end of a severe bollocking. Caton had a pretty good idea from whom.

'I gather the Manager and the Chief Executive have arrived,' Caton said. 'How are they taking it?'

Hardman ran his hand through the close cropped stubble on his head.

'How do you think?'

'Badly?'

He folded his arms, expelling the air from his lungs in a great sigh.

'Incandescent more like,' he said. 'I reckon I'll be out of a job before the week is over.'

He only had himself to blame. If he was unable to keep the players safe on the premises what was the club paying him for?

'Where were you when the body was found?'

'I was right here. I'd been here for about ten minutes.'

'Where did you park your car?'

'In the section for players and senior staff on the plaza car park.'

'And you walked straight down to the Reception?'

Hardman frowned. He had no idea where this was going.

'Yes.'

'In which case you would have passed by the mobile cryotherapy unit.'

He unfolded his arms and pushed himself back from his desk. Righteous indignation gave force to his words.

'What are you trying to say? Are you saying I had something to do with this?'

You should never answer your own questions, Caton reflected. Especially when they're being asked by a police officer.

'Why would I think that Dean?' he said. 'You saw the body. He had to have been there for quite some time to freeze up like that.'

Hardman visibly relaxed. The "*Dean*" had helped.

'Exactly,' he said.

'But you did hear the hum of the generator? See the steam from the exhaust?'

'The heat from the refrigeration process is vented off through a pipe,' he said. 'It's used to help heat the club Jacuzzi and the hotel swimming pool.'

'But you did hear the hum of the generator.'

This time it wasn't a question.

'OK, I heard the generator. But I assumed Steve

Makin must have switched it on. He often comes in early on a Monday to treat any players with injuries from games held over the weekend.'

He was telling the truth about that at least Caton decided.

'Who told you the body had been found?'

'One of the stewards. He was walking past when Steve Makin opened the doors of the chamber. He called me on his radio while Steve was switching off the generator.'

'That reminds me,' said Caton. 'This isn't a match day. Why were there so many stewards around?'

Hardman relaxed a little more.

'Today was a training day in preparation for the Champions League Game on Thursday.'

It struck Caton as surprisingly early for them to be in, but he couldn't see any point in pursuing it. Not yet anyway.

'So, those members of your security team who were on duty overnight, and this morning. Has DCI Holmes started interviewing them?'

All the tension that had leached away seemed to flood back into Hardman's face, and body.

'Yeah. Just down the corridor. And your Detective Sergeant Carter has joined him.'

Caton heard the waver in his voice. There was something wrong. Something Hardman couldn't bring himself to share.

'But?' he said.

It came out slowly. Like blood seeping from a bandage.

'Three of them are missing.'

'Missing as in?'

'As in we can't find them. And nobody remembers seeing them much after midnight last night.'

'Much, or at all?'

'At all.'

It was like drawing teeth.

'Surely they had to check in at regular intervals?'

'That's just it. They did. Every hour, until seven o'clock. But no one actually saw them.'

He had developed a tick in the corner of his left eye. He dabbed at it as though that would make it go away.

'There's something else you're not telling me,' said Caton.

Hardman looked up. He was trying to find an excuse not to have to say it. Knowing that he had no choice.

'Two of the ones that are missing...their designated outside patrol...it was the West Stand.'

'Where the cryotherapy van is located.'

He nodded his head.

'So either they were taken by the perpetrators,' Caton told him. 'Or they were involved in some way.'

'Taken, no question,' he said. 'There's no way either of them would have been involved. I'd stake my life on that.'

'Given we already have one death, and two missing in action, you'd better be careful what you promise. I need their names, addresses, descriptions and known associates. And I need them now.'

Hardman placed his hand on the plastic wallet that lay between them on the desk, and pushed it towards Caton.

Caton took out the contents and flicked through them. It was all there. Hardman wasn't a complete numpty after all.

'What did you do before you took on this job?' he asked.

Hardman sat up straight. Some of his composure regained.

'I was a warrant officer Class 2, in the SIB,' he said proudly. 'I did seventeen years. Then I worked for an upmarket security firm in the City. Then this.'

The Special Investigations Branch of the Royal Military Police. As a warrant officer Caton knew he would have had scene of crime, and criminal investigation training, and commanded a team of detectives. Definitely not a numpty.'

'Where are you up to with the CCTV?' he said.

'It's ready for you to have look at as soon as.'

'Can you show me where?'

Hardman steeled himself.

'But, we do have a little problem there,' he said.

'How little?'

'I'm not sure yet,'

Caton had had enough. 'What the hell does that mean?' he said.

Hardman held up both hands as though to ward off a direct assault.

'The footage from all of the outside cameras on the West Stand was either wiped, or never recorded. We don't yet know which.' He hurried on before Caton could interject. 'If it was wiped we may be able to recover it. It's all computerised. The files will be there somewhere.'

'And if not.'

Hardman shrugged apologetically, folded his arms, and sat back.

'Who was watching those monitors during the night?'

'Danny Denton. He's waiting in the IT suite. I assumed you'd want to see him next.'

Caton stood up.

'Too right. And I want you with me.'

Sandwiched between the match day police control room, and the press box, the IT suite was smaller than Caton had envisaged. He counted three desk top computers, a half a dozen laptops, one electronic whiteboard, one large TV screen, and five rows of six smaller screens covering one wall.

Hardman saw him taking it in.

'This is just the nerve centre,' he explained. 'There are scores of computers, and screens, and audio visual devices throughout the stadium. Most of them link up through here.'

'What about the CCTV screens?' Caton said. 'Where else are they duplicated?'

'Next door in the police control room, and in the Security Office behind the Reception. Which is where Danny was last night?'

At the mention of his name a spotty, skinny, weasel faced man in his late twenties, with sunken eyes, and a poor attempt at a goatee beard, shifted uneasily in his seat.

'This is Detective Chief Inspector Caton,' Hardman told him.

Danny Denton stood up, and held his hand out tentatively. He was short. Very short. Four nine Caton guessed. Definitely not designed for frontline security. And he had a serious personal hygiene problem. Caton declined to shake his hand.

'If you were downstairs who was in this room last night? he asked.

Denton looked puzzled.

'Nobody,' he replied. 'This room is locked at night. As soon as the cleaners are finished.'

'So you were the only one watching the CCTV screens last night?'

'That's right.'

'And you didn't notice anything out of the ordinary

from the cameras covering the exterior of the West Stand?'

He shook his head vigorously.

'No. And I've found out why. Look I'll show you.'

He sat back down and swivelled to face the computer in front of him. His fingers flew across the key board. Then he swivelled back and pointed at the second row of screens on the wall behind them.

That's the West Stand,' he said triumphantly, 'I've recovered the footage from last night.'

'So it wasn't wiped after all?' said Hardman.

'No. It wasn't wiped because it was never recorded?'

Caton studied the screens. The cameras covering the section where the cryotherapy unit was parked panned slowly from left to right and back again. The black and white images were surprisingly sharp.

'So what are we watching?' said Caton.

'The footage from two weeks ago. Same night, different week. Someone must have programmed the computer to switch off those cameras last night, and play the old footage back instead.'

'And you didn't realise you'd seen it all before?'

'That's just it. I wasn't on nights then, not that I'd have noticed anyway. Bugger-all happens most nights.'

'So who was on duty that night?'

Denton looked at his boss.

Hardman took a deep breath.

'Phil Ratten,' he said. 'He's one of the two that are missing.'

Chapter 6

His shoes sank into the purple carpet. It was an inch thicker up here on the seventh floor. And the colour was beginning to grate. Or maybe it was the cute pink walls that made Caton feel like he was in a high end brothel.

He paused outside the heavy wooden door with its ostentatious gold name plate, knocked, and entered without waiting for a response.

The three of them stood with their backs to the door by the tinted windows. They were deep in animated conversation as though they hadn't heard his knock, or had chosen to ignore it.

Caton closed the door firmly. Loud enough to force them to turn and acknowledge his presence.

'You must be the policeman,' said the shortest of the three. 'About bloody time!'

'And you are?' said Caton, knowing full well, but unable to resist his childish pleasure at the annoyance it provoked.

'Gerry Capper!' said the man in a tone that implied that only a fool or a Martian could be ignorant of the fact. 'I'm the Manager, and Director of Football.' He stabbed a stubby finger towards Caton. 'Well...don't just stand there man, come on in.'

Caton held his ground.

The tallest of the three placed his hand lightly on Capper's shoulder, and stepped forward, hand outstretched.

'Harry Lightfoot, Chief Executive,' he said.

Early sixties, silver hair, expertly cut, framed a square face, dark bushy eyebrows above blue eyes, a strong roman nose, a broad confident mouth, and a firm jaw. He was taller than Caton, six two at a guess, well padded from comfortable living, effortlessly suave in an extravagant one button, Italian cut, double twist wool suit with pleated trousers. Caton knew because Kate had wanted him to get something like it for his going away outfit. No problem, he'd told her. If you can find one in T.K. Maxx. Gerry Capper cut a very different figure. The clothes were every bit as expensive, but he wore them like a shop dummy, as though he didn't really own them. His bowed legs, and partially flattened nose, didn't help.

'Detective Chief Inspector Caton,' Tom replied. 'Senior Investigating Officer. Please accept my commiserations.'

'And this is Max Bentham, our company lawyer,' said Lightfoot. 'Why don't we sit down?'

He led Caton to the long, black, glass topped table with silver chairs that matched the embossed paper on the walls. Caton found himself facing the lawyer. Her smile was guarded.

'Max, as in Maxine,' she said, smoothing her knee length pencil skirt, and sitting down. She undid the three buttons of her pinstriped, anthracite- grey, suit, revealing a white silk, high neck, fitted shirt. There was nothing flirtatious about the way in which she did it. More cool, and composed. In her mid forties, the first sign of wrinkles playing at the corners of her hazel eyes, and thin coral coloured lips, she could equally have been a city banker. She placed her iPhone on the table, folded her hands, and returned his stare.

'You've told my players they can't go anywhere without your say so,' said Capper. 'I'm not having that.'

The manager's face was almost purple with anger. His nose already had those broken veins that suggest injudicious drinking. Once more the Chief Executive placed his hand on Capper's shoulder, reinforcing Caton's judgement of who was really in charge.

'Ease up Gerry,' he said. 'Let's not forget that Sunday is dead and Mr Caton has a murder investigation to conduct.'

Under normal circumstances Caton would have asked what made him think it was murder. The leaked video footage had made that question redundant.

'We've got Bayern Munich on Thursday,' Capper protested. 'They can't just sit around kicking their heels.'

'Your concern is touching Gerry,' said Maxine Bentham acidly.

Capper dropped another place down the pecking order.

'They don't need to,' Caton told him. 'If you can take me to speak to them as a group as soon as we are finished here, I see no reason to interrupt your preparations. I will however, need to interview those who were closest to Mr Okowu-Bello, or who may have information relevant to the investigation.

The manager snorted. Whether with scorn, contempt, or simply because of his obstructed airways it was impossible to tell.

'What am I supposed to do, play three a side?'

'*My* concerns are a little wider,' said Lightfoot. 'Keeping the stadium running. We have over two hundred permanent staff and three thousand temporary including the stewards and catering staff.

And then there's the Press. I need to know what to tell them.'

'And the owners,' the lawyer reminded him. She consulted her iPhone. 'Mr Kang Jong-Cheol has just boarded a flight in Shanghai, and Mr Ying is on his way in as we speak.'

'I can't advise you on what to say,' Caton told them. 'My job is to establish what happened.'

'Somebody killed Sunday!' exclaimed Capper. 'Even a fool knows that's what happened. Your job's to catch the bastard.'

Caton couldn't fault his logic.

'Can any of you think of any reason why somebody would have done this?' he said.

'He was a right handful,' said Capper. 'There were times when I could cheerfully have topped him myself. But not this.'

'Gerry!' said the lawyer sharply.

'Mr Capper is under a lot of stress,' said the Chief Executive. 'This has hit us all hard, but him most of all.'

'You don't need to patronise me,' Capper told him. 'The inspector knows what I mean.'

'Were there any people in particular that he may have upset enough for them want to teach him a lesson?' Caton asked.

'Where do I start?' said the manager. 'Most of his team mates. He was always playing tricks on them. They were always looking to get their own back.' He turned to Harry Lightfoot. 'There was that time he super glued their team shirts to the hangers, and when he dumped a sack of chicken manure in Johnny's Ferrari while he was away on honeymoon. And what about the can of paint he poured in Mal's Jacuzzi. Then there was...'

Caton could see it turning into a litany, and held up his hand.

'Apart from pranks,' he said. 'Were there any really serious grievances. Serious enough for someone to want to kill him.'

'It could still have been a prank, though,' said the lawyer neatly skirting his question. 'One that went badly wrong.'

'I'm not discounting that,' said Caton. 'But right now I need to know if he had made any real enemies.'

He saw the way they looked at each other. There were things unspoken here that he needed to unearth. None of them responded.

'Did he have any financial problems then?'

'We pay him £90,000 a week, and he has sponsorship agreements that net him in the region of £8 million a year,' said Lightfoot. He has an estimated net worth of close to £96 million.'

'That doesn't answer my question,' said Caton. 'He may have it all tied up. His investments could have exceeded his income. And it has been suggested that he was gambling heavily.'

'Suggested by whom?' said the lawyer leaning forward.

'That's not relevant,' said Caton. 'What I want to know is if any of you were aware of it?'

Capper shuffled uneasily in his seat. The others stared at him.

'He came to see me Friday morning,' he said. 'Wanted to know if he could have a month's advance on his wages.'

'Why didn't you tell me?' said Lightfoot.

'Because I didn't think it was important. You know what he's like. You never knew when he was taking the piss.'

'What did you say to him?' Caton asked.

'I told him he had no chance. That if he was really desperate he should have a word with his agent, like all the others do.'

'How did he react?'

'He slammed the door on the way out.'

'You should have told me,' said Lightfoot.

'I understand that he also got into difficulties in his relationships with women?' said Caton watching closely for Gerry Capper's reaction.

'He was married,' said the Chief Executive just a little too quickly.

The manager snorted. This time there was no mistaking his contempt.

'That didn't stop him,' he said. 'Though it was more girls than women if you ask me. One minute it was irate husbands, the next it was fathers, and on a bad day it was the police. I was sick and tired of pouring oil on stormy waters. Max too, you can ask her yourself. What was it Fergie said about babysitting millionaires? I know just how he feels.'

'Were you aware of any resultant threats against Mr Okowu-Bello, Mrs Bentham?' Caton asked.

'Ms Bentham,' she corrected him. 'Probably best if you call me Max like everyone else.'

'Max then,' he said reluctantly. 'Well, were you?'

'Just about every aggrieved partner threatened him in one way or another,' she replied. 'Some with the police, others that one dark night they would smash his knee caps, and put an end to his career. The least inventive of them apparently promised to remove his capacity to father children.'

'Looks like someone's managed all three,' said Gerry Capper.

Caton left with the contact details of the victim's agent, and the promise that a copy of every threatening email, letter, or recorded conversation, would be delivered to the mobile incident room by lunchtime.

As he followed Gerry Capper out of the building by the north stand, and across the plaza towards the training ground, he studied the back of the manager's head. If Capper had been aware of the victim's alleged affair with his daughter there had been no sign of it. What tension there was in that bull head, and those square shoulders, could just as easily have been the stress of dealing with the fallout from Sunday's demise, on top of the normal responsibility of management in the premiership that resulted in more than its fair share of triple bypasses. He wondered how his team mates were taking it. I'll soon find out, he reflected, as they reached the entrance to the Academy building.

Chapter 7

'I've been expecting you.'

Donna Okowu-Bello, nee Dootson, waited in the open doorway. She ushered them in, closed the door behind them, and led them across the wide expanse of hallway into what DS Stuart's mother would have called the drawing room. Only this one was vast. Twice the size, she estimated, of the entire floor plan of her mother's semi-detached in West Didsbury.

'Grab a seat.'

There were four luxurious sofas. Joanne Stuart chose the nearest. Gina Burman sat down beside her.

'Can I get you a drink?' said Donna pointing to the stainless steel and glass topped bar along one wall.

'No thank you,' they chimed in unison.

'Please yourselves,' she said. 'Don't mind if I get myself a top up?'

She tottered over to the bar to replenish her glass with Bombay Sapphire and tonic, ice and a slice of lemon. Joanne Stuart sized her up.

Loose blonde hair, wavy, down to her shoulders, a belted knee length leopard print dress, and six inch black heels that raised her up to six foot nine. Not what most people would wear at home at eleven o'clock in the morning. Least of all when their partner has just been murdered.

'There's no one else here,' Joanne Carter whispered. 'Under the circumstances, you'd think she'd have had someone come round?'

'I'm not sure she has that many friends,' Gina Burman replied. 'She's always been alone when I've been here. The other players didn't get on with him, so I suppose the other WAGs...'

'Right then.' Donna took a slurp, and tottered back to join them. She sat on the sofa opposite, kicked off her shoes, and tucked her legs awkwardly beneath her. Her skirt rose high enough to reveal matching briefs but she didn't seem to notice, or care.

'The tele' beat you to it,' she said. 'The press too. I guess you met them on your way in?'

'I'm really sorry for your loss Mrs Okowu-Bello,' Joanne began.

'Call me Donna,' she said cutting her off. 'That Bello business is such a mouthful. So was he, come to that.' She giggled and had another drink.

DS Stuart couldn't work out if it was grief, hysteria, or relief working its way out. Whichever, it wasn't pretty.

'And you don't need to pussyfoot around me,' she continued, waving her glass in Burman's direction. 'Gina here must have told you, Sunday and me, we haven't been on the best of terms recently. Not exactly *bed*fellows if you follow my drift?'

She waved her glass again, oblivious to the dribble of liquid that landed on the sofa beside her. She had clearly been drinking rather more heavily than either of them had realised.

'I haven't disclosed anything beyond...' the private detective began.

'Oh bugger that,' said Donna sloshing a full measure over the side of her glass. 'You can tell her what you like. This is a murder enquiry after all.'

Now she was slurring her words.

'We don't know that Donna,' Joanne Stuart said.

'Tied himshelf up did he?' She threw her head back and drained the glass. 'He wasn't one for that wasn't Sunday, least not for himself. Had a pair of handcuffs, and a scarf he liked to truss me up with though. Back when he gave a damn.'

If memory served her right Joanne felt sure they been married less than a year. It sounded like her husband had moved on pretty sharpish after the honeymoon.

Donna stared at the empty glass, and then placed it precariously on the arm of the sofa.

'Am I a suspect?' she said.

It took them both by surprise, coming out of the blue like that.

'What makes you say that?' said DS Stuart.

'I'm not stupid you know.' She propped one elbow on the same arm of the sofa to stop herself toppling over. 'I watch Midsummer Murders. Wife hires private dick to follow rich playboy husband. Husband murdered. Who you going to place your bets on? Grieving widow, or new boyfriend, that's who.'

'Do you have one?' said DS Stuart. 'A new boyfriend?'

Her laugh was hollow, the words that followed brittle.

'No, an' d'you wanna know why? Because I still loved him. I still loved that cheatin' bastard.'

Her elbow slipped, sending the glass flying onto the solid oak floor where it smashed into tiny shards. She began to weep uncontrollably.

Gina Burman got to her feet. 'I'll see if I can find a dustpan and brush,' she said. 'She'll cut her feet to ribbons on that.'

'I'll see what's holding up the family Liaison

Officer,' said DS Stuart taking out her mobile phone. 'I'll have to stay here till she arrives. And I need to touch base with Tom...DCI Caton. Keep an eye on her will you?'

Donna sat on the sofa, dabbing at her eyes. Streaks of mascara ran down her cheeks, her lipstick was smudged, and her nose was pink from frequent blowing. It was difficult not to feel sorry for her. Three quarters of an hour, and two pots of coffee, had a least brought a degree of sobriety. Enough for DS Stuart to hold a sensible conversation with her.

'How much had Gina told you about your husband's affair?' she asked.

'That he was seeing someone. That it was serious – in that he was shagging her.' She dabbed her eyes and sniffed several times. 'That she was younger than me. Barely legal.'

Joanne wondered when Donna had started out down that road. She was barely out her teens herself.

'Did she tell you her name?' she asked.

Donna stared across at Gina Bentham who had been listening intently to her replies.

'You *wouldn't*, would you Gina? Are you gonna tell me now?'

Gina Bentham saw DS Stuart shaking her head, and took the hint.

'I'm sorry Donna,' she said. 'I can't.'

'Why not? It's what I paid you for.'

'Because everything changed the moment your husband died,' said DS Stuart. 'Her identity, and her relationship with your husband, is now part of a police investigation. That information will be released only when my boss considers it right to do so.'

'You don't have to worry,' Donna told her. 'I'm not

gonna do anything stupid, like beat up on the slag. There's no point is there? Not now he's dead.'

'Don't worry, when the time's right you'll be the first to know,' said Joanne Stuart.

'Like I said, I don't care anymore.'

'What about your husband's financial situation?'

She looked surprised by the question, but it could just have easily have been the sudden change of direction.

'You are joking?' she said. 'This is Sunday – Okowu-Bello we're talking about. He was minted.'

'Only we understand he was having a bit of a cash flow problem.'

She didn't respond at once. She twisted the sodden handkerchief distractedly around the fingers of her left hand, and then unwound it again. She looked up.

'We did have a row on Thursday night. He arrived home in a foul mood. I'd had a bit of a binge in Harvey Nicks. All the bags were on the sofa. I started to show him them. You know, shoes, dresses, sexy underwear. Normally he takes an interest.'

'And this time?'

'He went off on one. Picked the bags up and flung them across the room. Accused me of bleeding him dry. Said he wanted my credit cards back.'

'Did you give them to him?'

She shook her head. 'I was stunned. I just stood there looking at him. Then I tore into him. Told him what a selfish bastard he was. How he never took me out anymore. How he never told me where he was going, or what he was doing. What was I supposed to do all day? Sit around reading fashion mags and baking cup cakes?'

'What did he say to that?'

'He stormed off slamming the doors as he went.'

'He'd just been told he couldn't have anymore

credit at the casino.' Gina Bentham said. It was the first time she'd interrupted DS Stuart's questions but Joanne decided to let it go.

'That again!' said Donna. 'Why did I have to pick a millionaire addicted to cheating and gambling? Why didn't I marry one into alcohol and cocaine? At least that way we could have done it together.'

The family liaison officer arrived at the same time as the forensics team and DS Nick Carter. He was clutching a search warrant.

'You're looking great, Jo,' he said as they stood in the hallway. 'The old firm back together. Who'd have thought it?'

'What does the warrant cover?' she asked.

'Phone records, computers, mobile phones, personal organisers, and financial statements.'

'I'll let you have the pleasure of telling her,' said Joanne Stuart. 'I'm off. And go easy. She's just a kid really. And I think she actually loved him.'

'She'll get over it,' said Carter. 'When the dust has settled, and the probate's sorted. You know what they say?

'Go on,' she said, knowing that she was going to regret it.

'She, who marries for love without money, has good nights, and sorry days.'

He left them on the doorstep and went inside chuckling to himself.

'Why didn't you tell her about Packer's daughter?' said Joanne Stuart as Gina Bentham drove them back to the city.

'Because the fallout was going to be massive. Sunday was screwing his manager's daughter. All hell was going to break loose. All I had was circumstantial. Mainly time spent together in hotels. I needed absolute proof. Photos, video, something like that. I had it all planned. I only needed another couple of days.

'Planned how?'

Gina glanced across at her former colleague. 'You don't want to know Jo, and I don't want to tell you. In fact I don't have to do I? Why would I want to incriminate myself before the fact? Especially now that it's never going to happen.

'Not this time,' said Joanne. 'But there are going to be other times. You want to be careful Gina; you should know that better than anyone. You could lose your license, or worse.'

But Gina's mind was already somewhere else. She was wondering what Josh Holt would be doing right now, and where exactly that might lead her.

Chapter 8

Caton scanned the room again. Heads down, avoiding his gaze, they shuffled their feet, or picked imaginary fluff from their tracksuit bottoms.

They had taken it badly. Not, he was beginning to realise, because of any great affection for the man. It was more what the manner of his death might mean for the club, the team, and more importantly for them as individuals. He sensed them imagining the normal hounding by the press and paparazzi ramping up to unmanageable levels, and the cruel chants from rival fans on the terraces.

Terraces...he still thought of them as that from the years he'd spent on the Kippax, freezing cold, and wet, before the three tier covered stand was built. There were those who still believed that was the final throw of the gypsy curse that had been cast all those years ago when their camp had been cleared for the stadium to be built. He tried again.

'OK then. Which of you got to know him best?'

The wall of silence held. Several of them glanced at one another before lowering their heads again. It was as though they'd just had a 6–0 thrashing, and were waiting for the manager's excoriation.

'Did any of you socialise with him?'

'Come on lads, speak up,' tried Gerry Packer.

Several of them glanced up, but no one spoke.

'Look,' said Caton with mounting frustration. 'We don't know if this was all about your team mate, Sunday. It could have been about this club. If it was, then any one of you could be next. That's why it's even more important that you help me out here. It's not just about catching Sunday's killers, it's about protecting yourselves.'

That had them paying attention. One or two looked as though they might be about to say something, but it died on their lips. Caton had been here before. Every time he'd addressed a group of witnesses on an estate, or a gang of youths one of whose number had been attacked...or worse. None of them were going to be the first to speak or to say anything of consequence in front of the others. It had been a mistake to think that they might.

'Alright,' he said. 'I understand. It's come as a terrible shock to all of you.'

He walked over to one of the whiteboards on the facing wall, picked up a marker pen, and wrote down a number.

'I don't expect to you to speak up now, but I want you to ring this number if you have any information that you think might help me. Anything at all. In complete confidence. I'll see that each of you gets a copy of my card. And you can always ring CrimeStoppers and leave a message for me, anonymously if you have to. That's 0800,555,111. They're in the phone book, and on the internet.

The Brazilian right midfielder snorted derisively.

'I know what you're thinking,' said Caton. 'That there's no such thing as anonymous anymore. That we can always trace the call and work out who it was from. Well take it from me, we don't. Because the first time that we did it would destroy the credibility of

CrimeStoppers, and we cannot afford for that to happen. And anyway, we can't. It's an independent charity. We have no access to their data. They simply act as a go-between, passing on your information.'

If he had hoped to shame the player he was disappointed. But at least he had made the point.

'Is that it then?' said the manager, who seemed more anxious to get on with the training than to help find his player's killers.

'For now,' Caton told him, loudly enough for all of them to hear. 'But if some of these players don't come to me with information pretty sharpish, I shall be seeking them out, individually, Europe or no Europe.'

It was lunchtime when Caton arrived at the Force Headquarters in Central Park. He was still getting used to it, and it was hard not to be impressed. A symphony in tinted ice blue glass, light grey walls and natural wood; it was modern, sophisticated, chic, and confident, everything that Chester House had never been. Certainly the Headquarters building on Boyer Street had never had three fully grown trees in the atrium. Come to that it didn't have an atrium. Nor had there been expensive murals on the walls, and inspirational quotes from Marie Curie, John Lennon, and Martin Luther King as there were here. The closest Caton had come to seeing anything like this was the Harmony Academy High School he had visited several times during the investigation into the murder of Roger Standing during what Gordon Holmes had christened the Head Case.

As part of the re-organisation specialist services had been moved in here together with the counter terrorism unit. All of the Major Incident Rooms in the nearby, and equally impressive, North Divisional

Headquarters building were already taken, so a meeting room had been hastily turned into one for his investigation. He suspected that he was only here so they could keep an eye on him.

Caton was both delighted and relieved to find that Ged his long time office manager had been seconded from the office of the ACC Crime. He told her so.

'It's a pleasure for me too, Sir,' she confided. 'The top floor is a bit too hothouse political for my taste. And it's great to see most of the old team back together.'

'Don't get too used to it,' he replied. 'This is a one off.'

She grinned. 'In that case we'll have to see how long we can make it last.'

He smiled back. 'You learned a thing or two from the top brass, then?'

'Not as much as I learned from you.'

'Where have you put me?' he asked.

'Over here.'

She led him towards to an area approximately three metres square at the far end of the room. She had done her best to shield him from the noise and distractions of the hive of activity behind them by having light blue portable screens erected along three sides. The remaining side was a floor to ceiling window that looked out over the rest of the UK's first truly urban business park. It was a far cry from the Longsight nick, and Leigh, and all the others he had ever thought of as his second home. Or first home if he was honest with himself, at least until Kate had come along. Ged read his thoughts.

'There are over a thousand people working here,' she said. 'And it cost sixty four million pounds to build.'

She placed copies of the information log and the actions file on his desk.

'No surprise then,' he said. 'That they have to cut one hundred and thirty four million pounds from the budget. It's a good job you went for that post on the Sixth Floor Ged or you'd have been down the road with the rest of them.'

'It's you I have to thank for that Sir.'

There was no mistaking the strength of her gratitude. Caton would have bet a tidy sum that she had bullied the ACC to second her back to work with him just one more time.

'Tell everyone I want a catch up briefing in fifteen minutes,' he told her. 'That should be long enough for me to get through these, and make my own entries.'

'Very good Sir.' She pointed to a small table squeezed between the desk and one of the screens. 'I've put you a kettle there for your hot water. And don't worry,' she said, unable to resist a dig at his meticulous concern for health and safety, equal only to that for political correctness. 'It's been PAT tested.'

He checked his watch. There was just time to try and contact Kate again, before he speed read the logs. Ever since he had broken the news to her about Harry, the son he had not known existed until that fateful meeting in Albert Square, he'd felt a need to let her know, as often as possible, how much he loved her. There was an underlying sense of guilt behind that need, he realised, and gratitude and relief in equal measure. She had taken it so well, despite the disappointment she must have felt that their first child together would be his second, and that there would be another woman in his life with a bond between them that would never go away.

She had welcomed Harry with just the right amount of kindness and compassion the first time he had come to visit. Neither over the top, which would have betrayed itself as false, nor hesitant or wary. But he knew that deep down she was hurting.

Organising the arrangements for the wedding had taken her mind off it. He felt sure that in time she would come to see that he would never allow anything to come between them. But it didn't hurt to keep reminding her that she was uppermost in his thoughts. Even when there was a murder to solve. He made the call.

'Tom!' she said excitedly. 'You don't need to apologise, I've just seen it on the news...and the video on YouTube. It's horrible!'

That was something, coming from a forensic profiler.'

'You seen worse than that.'

'I know, but if he was alive when they put him in there it doesn't bear thinking about.'

'Then don't,' he said. 'You're unlikely to get roped in on this one.'

'Not unless poor Okowu-Bello is the first victim of a serial killer.'

'How likely is that? There can't be that many opportunities to freeze someone to death.'

'True. So, what time do you think you'll be home?'

'I'm sorry Kate, I haven't the faintest idea. You know how it is on day one. There are leads we have to follow while they're still warm. God, that sounds awful given the circumstances.'

'I'm making pasta. I'll leave yours in the chiller. You can heat it up in the microwave when you come in.'

'That's great.'

'And if you're not in by lights out, I'll put your PJs in the spare room.'

'Fine,' he said, not meaning it.

It was an arrangement they had agreed as soon as they'd moved in together in their apartment on New

Islington Wharf. He knew it wasn't fair slipping his freezing cold feet into her nice warm bed in the early hours of the morning, but having to sleep apart had become the worst part of those rare occasions when he had no option but to work through the night. At least he no longer had to worry about the shifts that had helped to end his first marriage almost before it began.

'No it isn't,' she replied softly. 'But you know I'll make it up to you.'

'I can't wait,' he said.

They both knew that wasn't an option.

'Right, so where are we up to?'

They'd swivelled their chairs to face him, or were perched on the edge of their desks. Most of them were familiar faces, some of them new. All of them eager in anticipation of the chase.

He turned and wrote the word *Means* on the white board. Jack Benson raised his hand. He had left his team at the scene for this meeting, and was anxious to get back.

'Preliminary findings from the scene of crime,' he said. 'Suggest that the deceased was placed in the cryochamber by person or persons unknown, at some time between twenty three thirty last night when he was seen entering the reception area by former DC Gina Burman, and six minutes past six this morning, when the body was found.'

'Given the state of the body both the physio and pathologist reckon that he must have been in the chamber for not less than three hours,' said DI Holmes.

'We have some fibres, partial footprints, and deposit from the sole of one or more shoes,' Benson continued. 'But no finger or palm prints of any kind.

It's taking longer than usual because of the amount of ice that's built up and inevitable run off as it melts.'

'Same reason the post mortem isn't scheduled until tomorrow morning,' Holmes chipped in.

Caton started another column on the board with the heading *Opportunity,* and the subheading *Person or persons:*

'With access to the Physiotherapists Office where the keys to the chamber were kept, and from which they are now missing,' DS Stuart proposed.

'Able to switch on the generator and the controls for the cryotherapy,' said DS Carter.

'Hang on,' said Caton as the next hand shot up. He finished writing and turned round.

'With the ability to doctor the CCTV computer software,' offered DS Carter.

'With the ability to overpower or render senseless the victim, and to transport him to the cryotherapy chamber,' said someone at the back.

'With the ability to bribe, threaten, and or remove, three security men,' suggested DS Stuart.

Caton stopped writing and stood tall to stretch his back. 'Are we talking *person* or *persons*?

'Persons...got to be persons,' she replied. 'If only because I doubt one person could lift the victim up the steps unaided. And the Doc said there was no indication that he'd been hauled or dragged.'

'That's a bit premature,' said Holmes. 'He hasn't thawed out yet.'

'Even so.'

Caton started another column with the heading: *Motive*. The suggestions came so thick and fast he was unable to register who was making them and just concentrated on getting them down.

'Revenge in relation to the victims widely reported sexual adventures.'

'Pressure applied to make him settle his gambling debts – taken further than intended.'

'To teach a lesson to others with gambling debts.'

'Fanatical fans from a rival club.'

'Racism.'

'What if he was being paid to fix matches and then didn't deliver?' Asked a Detective Constable at the back.

Holmes swivelled round to face him. 'As a forward I doubt he could do that on his own. A goalie might. It always has been goalies they targeted in the past.'

'Doesn't need to be the match that's fixed,' the DS pointed out. 'Could be something as simple as spot betting on him getting a yellow card, or a red one. Or how many of his passes go straight into touch in the first half?'

'Or if he takes a dive in the penalty area within the first ten minutes,' said Carter helpfully.

'What if he knew something he wasn't supposed to know?' said Joanne Stuart.

Caton's mind whirled with the possibilities. 'That brings us to the big one,' he said, and headed the final column *Suspects*.

'Gina Burman, the last person to see the victim,' chorused several people at once.

'We don't know that for certain, not yet,' Caton reminded them. 'But you're right. However unlikely, she has to be on here until we can eliminate her.'

'The physio, first person on the scene,' said Carter.

'That reporter, Josh Holt, how did he get down there so fast?' someone asked.

'We know that the person responsible for watching the monitors is missing, along with the two security men tasked with patrolling the outer West Stand. They've all got to be on there surely?' said Benson.

'Fanatical fans,' someone called out.

'So who are we looking at in terms of jealous partners or ex partners...or fathers, brothers, uncles?' said Caton.

Joanne Carter raised her hand. 'The wife for one. She stands to gain his entire fortune...less his debts.'

'How did she react to his death?' he asked.

'It was difficult to know Boss. Don't forget she already knew he was dead before we got there. But she was angry about him playing away, and I don't mean football.'

That prompted muted laughter from around the room.

'But she was fuming mad when we told her he'd got himself into some serious debt.'

'She'd hardly have paid Burman to follow him if she'd just lined up some hit men to do him in,' Holmes pointed out.

'She stays on the list until she's eliminated,' said Caton.

'Let's hope it's not *eliminated*, as in another one bites the dust,' muttered Nick Carter.

'There's the Manager, Gerry Capper,' said Holmes sliding off his perch. 'Let's face it; he had a reputation for losing it on the pitch. And he knows his way round the club like the back of his hand. If he knew about Okowu-Bello and his daughter, God knows what he might have done. But did he know? That's what we have to find out.'

'I'd suggest the people he owed money to, but those gambling debts don't make sense,' said one of the DC's. 'Hundreds of thousands wouldn't be a problem surely? Not when he's on £150.000 a week.'

Holmes hitched himself back onto his desk. 'That's before the agent's percentage, his own high rolling life style, his wife's spending sprees, and tax at 50%,' he said.

'They have to be there,' said Caton writing it down. 'It wouldn't be the first time a Premiership footballer got into serious debt.'

He stepped to the side of the board and perused it for a moment.

'Right,' he said. 'Now for the actions.'

The DS tasked with responsibility for the Action Log raised his biro with a flourish.

Caton ticked them off on his fingers.

'I want the search for the missing security men stepped up. That's our number one priority. Then there are Okowu-Bello's sexual partners, and their partners. I want names and dates going back a year for starters. I want chapter and verse from the casino, and we need to see what the analysis of bank statements tell us. We also need to check with local bookmakers, online bookies, and his team mates. Was he into horses, dogs, spot betting? We need to know.'

Gordon Holmes put up his hand.

'Boss, we need someone who knows how that might work, to have a look for any suspicious bets relating specifically to him. Just to see if there's a pattern. And to look at his form over the past six months, and see if that might be relevant. I bet the FA and the Gambling Commission could help with that.'

Caton nodded. 'Good point DI Holmes.'

He did a mental catch up, and carried on.

'I want every serious threat on any of the social networks, by letter, email, or phone, followed up, starting with the most recent. And, starting tomorrow morning, I want every person in the *Suspects* column, invited here to assist us with our enquiries.'

That brought some smirks around the room that he deliberately ignored.

'And now...'

He waited until he had their full attention.

'...I don't have to remind you – a high profile case like this - not a word, not a hint, of what we know, think, or plan to do, leaves this room. I am reminding you because of what happened with the Bluebell Hollow investigation. You all know how pear shaped that went, and the serious consequences for two of our officers.'

Joanne Stuart felt herself blushing. She wished he hadn't mentioned it but she more than anyone understood why he had.

Caton searched their faces one at a time.

'Is that understood?'

'Yes Boss!' they chorused.

Chapter 9

'It's *CrimeStoppers,*' Ged told him. 'Something to do with Mr. Okowu-Bello.'

'I'll take it at my desk,' Caton replied.

He picked up the phone, swivelled in his chair, and looked out over the grassy landscaped patch in front of the Fujitsu building.

'DCI Caton.'

'This is Sam Thornton, at *CrimeStoppers,*' she said. 'We've had a phone call within the last hour or so from someone claiming to have information about your victim.'

'Is it OK if I record this conversation?' he asked.

'Of course.'

He leant forward, and pressed the button on the console.

'OK. Go ahead Sam.'

'This person alleges that he was close to the victim Sunday Okowu-Bello. He claims that the victim was having a longstanding affair with the wife of one of his team mates, at the same time that he was seeing the daughter of the club's manager. This person also claims that the victim had just broken off his liaison with the manager's daughter.'

'Your informant used the word seeing?'

The long pause before she replied, and the change

in the tone of her voice, told him that she was embarrassed.

'What he actually said was, *the bastard was screwing the boss's daughter'*.

For some reason he imagined her turning away and blushing.

'But he used the word *affair* in relation to the team mate's wife?'

'That's right.'

'Did he give you any indication of how long the affair had been going on?'

'I'm afraid not.'

'And that's it? There was nothing more said?'

'No, just that.'

'I don't suppose you could tell me exactly when your received the call?'

'You know I can't do that.'

'How about his accent?'

'Sorry, definitely not.'

'Did you get any sense of his age?'

'Are you testing me Detective Chief Inspector?' she said. What little warmth there had been in her voice had disappeared.

'Absolutely not,' he assured her. 'I'm sorry; I know I shouldn't have asked.'

'No you shouldn't.'

'You can't really blame me for trying though.'

'Oh I can,' she said. 'I most certainly can.'

'Fair enough,' he said. 'And thanks for that. It's been a great help.'

''I'm glad. It's what we're here for. Goodbye Mr Caton.'

'Goodbye Sam.'

Caton stopped the recording and replaced the phone. It amused him the way people used his rank to admonish or distance themselves from him, and reverted to *Mr* to level the playing field. He made a note of the call, and the information it contained for the log, and then sat back and thought about it.

She had been right not to tell him anything that might have revealed the identity of the caller. Even the timing of the phone call would have made it possible to narrow down the potential callers for an unscrupulous officer with access to the phone records of anyone he suspected of informing. Not that Caton would have wanted to know, because that would have it made harder not to reveal the fact that he knew, and risk undermining *CrimeStoppers*.

But there were clues. It was a male caller. And she had been so definite about not giving away anything about an accent that he felt certain there must have been one, and a distinctive one at that. Caton was willing to bet that it was one of Okowu-Bello's team mates. It was a bet he was not expecting to collect. He had a feeling, however, that once he had them inside an interview room they'd be lining up to tell him everything they knew about Sunday Okowu-Bello. Well, almost everything.

'No way.' Gerry Capper told him. 'Not with a match of this importance only two days away. Soon as we've finished on the training ground they're down for either massage or physio, then straight home. You can talk to them on Thursday afternoon.'

'This is a murder enquiry Mr Capper,' Caton reminded him. 'Do you really want the press to know that you're obstructing the police investigation?'

'You wouldn't bloody dare!' Capper bellowed into the phone. 'You gave them the chance to come forward with information. If they didn't have anything to tell you then, what makes you think they will now?'

Caton moved the phone away from his ear, and counted to five.

'Caton! Are you still there?'

'I'm just looking up the number of our Press Office,' Caton told him.

In no time at all they reached a compromise. The four players with the closest connections with the victim would come in to Headquarters. DS Stuart and DS Carter would go and see the rest at the training ground. At this stage, as they were neither suspects, nor witnesses to the crime, they would be classed as witness interviews with written notes made and statements signed where appropriate. No cautions, no taped interviews, and no need for legal representation. No interview was to last longer than fifteen minutes unless there were exceptional circumstances. Neither party was happy but, as Holmes pointed out, that was the definition of compromise.

The first two players were home grown talent, neither of them really close to the victim, with nothing of any value to share. Number three, however, was a fellow Nigerian, and reported to be his closest friend.

'Joseph Azuku,' said Holmes. 'Now I really fancy this one.'

'As a footballer, or a partner?' said Caton.

'As a grass, what else?' Holmes retorted. 'OB's best mate. If there's anything worth knowing he'll know it.'

'OB?' said Caton

Holmes grinned. 'I can't keep saying Okowu - Bello. And I didn't know him well enough to call him Sunday.'

Caton shook his head. 'For a moment there I thought you meant Obi-Wan-Kenobi.'

'That would work. You can be him, and I'll be Darth Vader. Two Jedi knights, one from the Dark Side, that's going to put the wind up him.'

'You're in danger of losing me,' said Caton.

Holmes drew an imaginary light sabre from his belt, and waved it above his head. 'Fear not Master, the Force is with you!'

Before Caton could tell him to grow up there was a knock on the door, and it was already opening.

Joseph Azuku was a handsome and impressive athlete. At six foot three, and fourteen and a half stone, he played centre back for his club, and was rated in the top ten footballers in the world in that position. He pushed the door closed behind him and sauntered towards them

'Do come in Mr. Azuku,' said Caton, without a trace of irony in his voice.

The footballer pulled the chair towards him and straddled it like a rider mounting a horse. He sat facing them with his legs sprawled out in front. His demeanour was wholly insolent, but Caton detected a nervousness that this man was trying far too hard to hide.

Caton, went through the preliminaries, and began the interview.

'It's good of you to spare the time,' he said. 'In view of what happened to your friend, and with such a big game just a few days away.'

Azuku wasn't sure how to respond. They could see him trying to work out if the policeman was being sarcastic. Unable to decide he simply grunted.

'Sunday...he was your friend I take it?' said Gordon Holmes, forcing him to turn his head and acknowledge him.

'Yes, he was my friend,' he replied reluctantly, dragging his heels towards him, and folding his arms.

'Good, so you'll want to do everything you can to help us catch whoever killed him?' said Caton.

He seemed not to know if it was a question or a statement.

'Won't you?' Holmes pressed him.

'Yes,' he muttered.

'Can't hear you,' said Holmes

'Yes,' he said, louder this time.

'Thank you Mr Azuku,' said Caton. 'Let's start with what you know about your friend's relationship with women other than his wife.'

The footballer raised his head, and looked directly into Caton's eyes as though trying to gauge how much he already knew. He ran the tip of his tongue over his upper lip.

'It's difficult,' he said.

'We understand that,' said Caton. 'Given that it involves your manager, and your team mates. But we need to hear it from you. There's no reason for them to know how we found out.'

He thought about it for a moment. If they already knew, what was the harm? But something was clearly puzzling him.

'Team mate,' he said. 'Not team mates.'

'Go on,' said Caton.

'Harvey Best. Sunday had a thing going with Mandy, his missus.'

'How long had this *thing* been going on?'

He shrugged his shoulders. 'Three weeks...a month. Something like that.'

'Does Harvey know?'

'You've gotta be joking. If he did there'd be blood all over the changing rooms.'

'Who else knew apart from you?'

'Search me. Sunday would have been stupid to tell anyone else.'

'But Mandy might have done?'

'She wouldn't just be stupid; she'd have to have had a death wish.'

'Got a temper has he, Harvey?' said Holmes

Azuku unfolded his arms, and thrust them into the pockets of his jeans.

'Got more red cards than anyone in the Premiership. What do you think?'

'We ask the questions!' said Holmes, leaning forward aggressively.

Caton placed a restraining hand on his arm. Azuku was relaxing into this. The more confident he became, the more loquacious and less guarded he would be.

'Is it true that Sunday had recently ended his relationship with Jade?' he asked.

The player's eyes widened. He slowly nodded his head.

'You'se know about that too?'

'How long had they been at it?' asked Holmes.

'Since the summer. Started when the boss an' his wife were sunning themselves in the Bahamas. I told him he was mad.'

'Why was that?' said Caton.

He rolled his eyes. 'Obvious in'it? You don't do it in your own backyard, and definitely not with your boss's precious little baby.'

'How little?'

'Seventeen.'

'Legal then.'

'*Lethal* more like.'

'In what way?'

'As in, teenage crush who don't take no for an answer. As in, Daddy pays your wages. As in, when the shit hit the fan ain't nobody gonna wanna pick up your pieces.'

He spread his arms wide in a dramatic gesture. 'Take your pick. Like I told him. It's insane.'

'When did he tell her it was over?'

'He didn't. She found out about Mandy, and threatened to tell Besty.'

'Why didn't she?'

'Because Sunday said if she did, he'd tell the Boss about him and her, and she was more scared of her dad than you can imagine.'

'Why was that?'

'Because between you an' me the Boss has got a problem.' He raised his right hand to his mouth as though knocking back a slug of whisky. 'If you know what I mean?'

'Ugly drunk is he?' said Holmes.

'Ugly sober if you ask me.' He grimaced. 'You should see him in the dressing room when we've screwed up. Sometimes we pick up more injuries after the game than during it.' He smiled at his own joke.

'Are you saying he's violent towards his daughter?'

He shook his head. 'Not that I know of, but rumour is his wife has had a hard time. Sunday said Mandy told him her mum was too frightened to do what she really wanted.'

'What was that?'

'To leave him.'

'Frightened of him, or of losing the lifestyle?' said Holmes.

Azuku placed hands the size of plates firmly on the table top.

'Of him,' he said. 'Take it from me, she's terrified of him. And I don't blame her.'

Caton waited until the footballer had settled back into his chair again. Then he turned over one of the sheets of paper in the file in front of him.

'What can you tell us about his money worries?' he said.

Azuku crossed his arms for a second time. The brash confidence that he had been displaying disappeared. For the first time he looked seriously shifty. His voice when he spoke was guarded, and his words evasive.

'I don't know what you mean.'

'He had gambling debts didn't he?' Holmes pressed.

Caton saw his pupils expand, and then dilate again, as though momentarily relieved.

'Oh, them,' he said.

'Yes them,' Holmes repeated. 'What do you know about them?'

'Only that he'd overstretched himself a bit.'

'A bit?'

'That's right. Not a problem.'

'Then why did he ask you to help him out?'

'How did you kno...' he stopped himself, and leaned further back in his chair as though he could hide himself there.

'What did you tell him?' Holmes said pressing the point.

'That I'd see him right, but it would cost him.'

'Cost him what?' said Caton

'His pussy wagon.'

'The Aston Martin?' said Holmes.

'No, I'm talking his Ferrari 458, F1.' He shook his head forlornly. 'I should 'a closed the deal while I had the chance.'

Some friend, Caton decided. 'How much would that be worth? he said.

'Couple of hundred grand.'

'Is that what he wanted to borrow?'

'He needed a hundred and eighty didn't he? He

grinned. 'I had to think of the interest I was losing. Anyway, it was more than they would 'ave given him for it.'

'They?'

'Them as own the Casino. Wouldn't want to cross them.'

'How come he couldn't find the money himself, given what you lot get paid?' said Holmes.

The footballer fixed him with the kind of stare he normally reserved for opposing centre forwards.

'You don't know shit,' he said. 'We got agents, and PR men, and lawyers, and tax, and people back home, and now...'

'And Ferraris and Aston Martins, and mansions here and abroad...my heart bleeds for you,' said Holmes leaning forward.

Azuku sat forward on the edge of his seat, hands on the desk, as though ready to propel himself.

Caton tugged at Gordon's sleeve.

'OK, let's calm down shall we?

He waited until Holmes had settled back, and the footballer was once more reclined in his seat, both men with their arms folded like a pair of petulant children.

'It wasn't just the gambling was it?' Caton said, remembering the player's initial reaction when asked about Sunday's money problems. 'Tell me about the people back home.'

Azuku stared back sullenly.

'The people back home,' Caton repeated.

'I don't have to answer no more of your questions,' he replied. 'I'm done with helping you.'

Caton felt Holmes tense beside him.

'No you don't, Mr Azuku,' he said. 'I am suspending this interview. You see if you're not helping us it follows that you're obstructing us, in which case I shall caution you, and hold you here, till we find out why that is. While you think about that DI Holmes and I are going to grab a hot drink. Can I bring you one back Joseph?'

It was a gamble, because there was nothing he could do if the footballer really wanted to leave.

'I'll have a macchiato caldo,' Azuku muttered. 'One sugar.'

Holmes chuckled.

'In your dreams,' he said.

Chapter 10

Holmes was mistaken. No expense had been spared. The self service coffee machines in the atrium catered for tastes unheard of in any of the divisional headquarters. Caton sat cradling his mug of hot water. Holmes had a double shot cappuccino, and the footballer was sipping his macchiato made with hot milk.

'You were going telling us,' said Caton. 'About the people back home.'

Azuku put the cup down on the table and shoved his hands in his pockets.

'It's complicated,' he said.

Gamble won.

'Just do your best Joseph,' Caton told him. 'I'm sure we'll manage to make sense of it.'

He stared up at the ceiling, avoiding their eyes.

'Sunday and me, we both grew up in Lagos. In Ajegunle, a tough district down between the ports. Didn't go to the same school but we played for the same football team when we was kids. An' we both had to learn what it takes to survive on the streets.'

His voice had taken on a different quality, almost dreamlike, and his native accent was suddenly exaggerated.

'It was hard. You either an Area Boy, or you were nott'in. If you be a botty boy you gonn'a get them climbing you.' He looked down at the two policemen for a moment. 'You feeling me?'

'Feeling you?' Holmes sounded disturbed.

Azuku grinned. 'You get me?'

'Botty Boy?' said Caton.

'Born wid' butter in your mouth. Like you say *a silver spoon*. Everyone gonn'a rip you off. No way you gonna survive.'

'I'm feeling you,' said Holmes.

That made the footballer laugh, and broke the tension in the room.

'Sunday and me, we had two things goin' for us. We was big for our age, and we could play football. I mean *really* play football. By the time we was nine sponsors was sniffing round us.'

'Sponsors?' said Caton.

'Guys with money, and an eye for the future. The talent scouts tell them about kids who stand a chance of making it. The sponsors move in like sharks. They give the parents money, get them signing on the dotted line. Then they own you, body and soul. You make good, they gonna' make a lot of money. You don't, they walk away.'

'That's what happened to you and Sunday?'

He nodded.

'It was good. A better road than some of the others for an Area Boy.'

'Such as?'

He raised his eyebrows.

'What d'you think? Hustling, robbing, pimping, running drugs, enforcing. Worse for the girls.'

'So what happened when you made it?'

'Me, I was lucky. My mum, she wouldn't take no money. She had her pride, she was smart. She knew where it would go. She got out of there, took me with her. Ended up in France. She married a local, got

French citizenship. I got signed up by Marseille when I was 17.'

'And Sunday?'

He shrugged his shoulders.

'By the time he got out of there he was tied up like a sacrificial goat.'

'In what way?'

'Twenty percent of everything goes to his sponsors. That's everything. Transfer fees, wages, promos. Everything. And he had to bank the bulk of his money in a bank of their choosin' in Nigeria.'

'And it's all legal?'

He nodded. 'All legal.'

'What if he refused to pay, or fought it through the courts?' said Holmes.

He looked at the detective as though he was mad.

'You are joking?'

'Answer the question please Joseph,' said Caton.

He shook his head, placed his palms firmly on the table, and leaned forward.

'Sunday, he still got family in Nigeria. His mum, his sisters, two brothers, aunts and uncles. OK, so he paid for them to move 7 kilometres to Lekki –smart district on Victoria Island – but that's where some of these sponsors also live.'

'They threatened to harm his family?' said Holmes.

His lips curled into a sneer.

'If you call having your family butchered, *harm*. An' I mean butchered. First they chop off the right hand of your brothers. Then the other one. If you still don't change your mind they rape your sisters and your mother. That's your last chance. After that they disappear them all. Maybe send you bits 'n pieces one at a time.'

He sat back and folded his arms.

'What would you do?'

'If I had his money I'd hire myself some mercenaries, and have the bloody lot taken out.' Holmes proclaimed.

'You don't mean that Gordon,' said Caton.

Holmes scowled.

'D'you wanna bet?' he said.

The footballer had left. There was nothing more he could, or would, tell them.

'He's holding back on something,' Caton mused.

'Whatever it is, my guess is he's involved,' Holmes agreed. 'He just doesn't want to incriminate himself.'

'If Sunday had tried to renege on his deal with his sponsors,' said Caton, changing tack. 'I suppose they could have had him killed, but it doesn't make sense. Why kill the goose that lays the golden egg? And why not start with his family, like Azuku said they would?'

'For all we know they may have done.'

'You're right; we need to check that out.'

'Same problem with his betting debts,' said the DI. 'Why would the Casino, or whoever he owed the money to, have him killed? They'll never get their money back now.'

'To discourage others from welching on their debts? Seems like a hell of risk when a broken leg would have been just as effective.'

'So what does that leave us with Boss?'

Caton ticked them off on his fingers.

'His team mate, Harvey Best, Jade Capper the manager's daughter, Capper himself.'

'Only Best still doesn't know he was being cuckolded according to Azuku.'

'We've only his word for that.'

'And there's nothing to suggest that Capper knew about OB messing with his daughter.'

Caton pushed back his chair and stood up.

'Time to find out,' he said. 'Let's start with Best.'

It had always surprised Caton how much smaller professional footballers were in real life than they appeared to be on the television screen. The reverse seemed true of Rugby players. Harvey best was the exception.

He had to stoop as he entered the room. When he sat down the chair proved too small, and they had to fetch one from the seminar room down the corridor.

'It was horrific what they did to Sunday,' he said, thrusting his hands into the pockets of his Armani bomber jacket. 'I'd help you if I could, but I can't think how.'

'Let us worry about that,' Caton told him. 'We have a few questions we'd like to ask you, and then you're free to go.'

'Fair enough,' the centre back replied.

He sounded relaxed and genuine to Caton, but you could never really tell.

'When did you first meet Sunday Okowu-Bello?' he asked.

'January transfer window last year. He came for trials, the first week in Jan. Joined us on 1st of Feb. We hit it off straight away. I took him for a meal to San Carlo, and showed him round Manchester. The clubs mainly. He reckoned that's what helped to swing it for him. You know...signing up for the Titans.'

'And after he'd signed, would you say you became friends?'

'Yeah, you could say that.'

'What did you like about him?' said Gordon Holmes.

'His sense of humour. He was always playing

tricks on people. I'm a bit like that myself. He liked clubbing. So do me and the missus.'

'Did you often go to clubs together, the three of you?' Said Caton innocuously.

'Not really. Not till he got married, then sometimes the four of us would go to a restaurant, and on to a club.'

'Had you noticed any change in his behaviour lately?'

He took his time thinking about that.

'Yeah. He'd been moody ever since we lost to Chelsea.'

'Remind me. When was that?'

His eyebrows arched again. 'You're not a Titans fan then?'

'Sorry no.'

'Sadly, DCI Caton is a City supporter,' said Holmes. 'That Chelsea game was on Boxing Day, so just under two months?'

Azuku grinned. 'That's right. Was you there?'

Now it was Caton's turn to smile.

'I doubt it. Detective Inspector Holmes is a Red.'

The footballer sat up, and placed his hands, joined at the wrist, on the table top. 'Might as well handcuff me now. I've got no chance. United and City! You're gonna stitch me up between you.'

'Not if you continue to help us,' Caton told him. 'Was it that defeat that explained his change of mood?'

He shrugged his shoulders.

'I dunno. I doubt it though. After all, we was seven points clear of your lot, and cruising.'

He hasn't shared any of his problems with you?'

'No. Never did. Even when people were accusing him of things.'

'*Things*?' Said Holmes. 'Like rape, and sexual assault?'

Best shrugged again, his hands sliding back into his pockets.

'Yeah, like that. Happens to a lot of celebs. Birds looking to make big money out of casual sex. Sex they came looking for in the first place.'

'And he never discussed it with you?'

'No, like I said. Anyway, that was all sorted. Not a problem.'

'Did you ever go to casinos with Sunday?' Said Caton, introducing a subtle change of direction.

'Casinos?' He looked genuinely thrown by it. 'Now and again. Yeah. Nothing regular. We'd have something to eat in the restaurant. Couple of drinks at the roulette table. 'Soft drinks,' he added quickly. '...unless we was injured or had a lay off.'

'When was the last time you went to one together?' said Holmes?

He thought about it.

'About six weeks or so.'

'Not long after his mood changed,' observed Holmes. He and Caton were now taking it in turns to question him, forcing him to look from side to side. The tempo of their questions gaining speed.

'Was he betting heavily?'

'Heavier than me.'

'What does that mean?'

'A grand at a time. Sometimes more.'

'Was he losing?'

He laughed.

'Everybody loses. Eventually.'

'What did he bet on?'

'Roulette mainly. Sometimes blackjack. He was rubbish at poker.'

'Always the same tables?'

'Yeah. Only I didn't stay as long as him. He used to head for the high stakes room, and I'd head home.'

'High stakes? How high?'

'Fifty thousand max.'

'Fifty thousand pounds?'

'S'right.'

He could see that had surprised them.

'S' only a week's wages after tax,' he said. 'Mind you, after your agent 'n accountants have had their cut there's bugger all left.'

'My heart bleeds for you,' said Holmes. 'Did you know he was in over his head?'

He sat up in his chair.

'In over his head?'

'Heavily in debt. Debt he couldn't settle.'

He shook his head, sat back in his chair, and folded his arms again.

'First I've heard of it.'

'He never told you?'

'Not a word. Silly bugger. No wonder he was worried.'

'What do you mean?'

He looked from one to the other, certain they knew what he was talking about.

'You don't mess with that lot.'

'What lot?' Holmes pressed him.

'Come on, you know who. '

'Humour us Harvey,' said Caton.

'You know who,' he said. 'The heavy mob, the big guys, the debt collectors.'

'The Casinos are all legit these days,' Holmes told him. 'They'd have got their lawyers to sue him.'

He tipped his head back, and rolled his eyes.

'And pigs'll fly.'

'I do hope you're not talking about us,' said Holmes.

The footballer laughed.

'Look,' he said. 'If Sunday was in trouble he never

told me. If it was to do with money you need to speak to his agent and his accountant.'

'What if it wasn't that?' said Caton.

Harvey Best stared at him for a moment.

'What d'you mean?'

'What if it wasn't about his debts? What if something else was worrying him?'

'Like what?'

'You tell me.'

He shrugged his shoulders.

'Search me. Like I said. If there *was* anything, he didn't share it with me.'

'What do you think?' said Caton.

'He seemed plausible enough,' replied Gordon Holmes. 'Mild mannered too. Nothing like he is on the pitch.'

'That's what struck me,' said Caton. 'Butter wouldn't melt in his mouth. Given his disciplinary record I expected him to be wound up like a spring.'

'I bet we'd have seen another side to him if you'd told him what his missus was getting up to with his best mate.'

'I don't doubt it. But that's all hearsay.'

'Why didn't you ask him about it?'

'Because if he didn't know, and what Azuku said about his temper is only half true, I'd have ended up being an accessory to GBH on Mrs Best.'

'Fair point. We're still going to have to speak to her though.'

Caton closed his notebook. 'Tomorrow morning,' he said. 'Right after the post mortem. While her husband's busy training.'

'I tell you what though,' said Holmes. 'I still think he was holding something back.'

Caton nodded.

'Me too. Did you notice how he looked concerned when you said Okowu was in over his head, and then relaxed as soon as you told him it was gambling debts?'

Holmes paused in the doorway.

'I was wondering about that,' he said. 'Maybe there was something they were both involved with. Apart from his wife.'

Chapter 11

Caton stood in the hospital car park with his BlackBerry to his ear. It was at least as secure as his Tetra radio and, he reasoned, if it was good enough for the London Rioters it was good enough for him. It also meant that he didn't get hassled over excessive use of his radio, and reminders to utilise text messages to keep down the costs. Gordon Holmes didn't like his radio either. Only that was because he claimed that the frequency they utilised caused brain damage. Caton had told him that in his case it was too late for that.

'Nothing much from the post mortem,' he said. 'It confirmed that he was alive when they put him in there. Seems he'd been tazered before he was bound and gagged. He'd obviously struggled to free himself. He had bruises on his wrists, his back and shoulders. Other than that, nothing.'

'What about the tox' results?' said Holmes.

'Initial indications from toxicology show nothing abnormal. They're running the usual follow up tests but it's unlikely he was drugged *and* tazered. Did you check on our friend?'

'Yep. He's at the stadium.'

'In which case I'll meet you at the house.'

He checked his watch.

'Prestbury. What do you reckon, half an hour?'

'Make it forty minutes,' Holmes told him. 'It's alright for you, I've got to cross the city remember. We're not at Longsight anymore.'

Holmes arrived first. It helped that he knew where all the static cameras were, and favourite haunts of the mobile units.

Caton found him sat in his car outside the gates, surrounded by reporters and paparazzi. Ignoring the questions thrown at him, and the cameras thrust in his face, Caton pressed the intercom, gave their names, and returned to his car.

'Serves you right Lewis,' he said as they crunched their way across the gravelled carriageway towards the imposing front doors.

'Lewis,' said Holmes. 'As in Inspector Robbie Lewis? Morse's sidekick?'

'No you numpty, as in Lewis Hamilton. Formula One's champion risk taker.'

Holmes grinned. 'That's alright then.'

The door opened. A young woman stepped back into the hallway. She waved Caton's warrant card aside.

'Come in,' she said. 'Make it quick, before they focus those bloody telephoto lenses.

Mandy Best had no need of six inch heels. Even in her sensible nude ballet pumps she was as tall as Caton, and towered head and shoulders above Gordon Holmes.

They followed her down the hall, admiring her perfectly toned body moving sinuously inside a pair of tailored jersey trousers, and an equally well fitted white silk blouse.

'More SWAG than WAG,' whispered Holmes.

Caton had no idea what he was talking about.

'Sophisticated Wives And Girlfriends,' he explained. 'Think Carla Bruni, Pippa Middleton, Michelle Obabma.'

She led them into an impressive lounge and turned to face them. Her eyes focused on DI Holmes.

'Pippa isn't married yet,' she said. 'And according to *Hello* Magazine she's currently single. You must be thinking of her sister Katherine?'

Caton took great pleasure in watching Gordon's face flush red.

'Oh no,' he said. 'I'm sure that DI Holmes *was* thinking of Pippa.'

She smiled. 'Then I'm flattered.'

She waited for them to sit down on the sofa.

'I don't suppose you can drink on duty? Can I get you a drink...tea, coffee?

'Please. Tea with milk and one sugar for DI Holmes,' said Caton. 'And I'll just have hot water if that's alright?'

'Of course.'

Her gait was lithe, athletic, and sensuous in an understated way. If she sensed their eyes on her as she left the room it didn't show.

'She's too good for Besty,' Holmes confided. 'You can see what OB saw in her; what she saw in him I can't imagine.'

'You never learn do you,' said Caton. 'For all you know this room could be bugged.'

Holmes scanned the room, decided the Boss was joking, but lowered his voice just in case.

'She doesn't seem too perturbed that Okowu-Bello's dead.'

'Seeming is not being.' Caton reminded him.

'Inscrutable, Holmes,' said Holmes.

She served their drinks, and curled up in a sofa chair facing them. Her hands encircled a highball glass.

'Mineral water,' she said unprompted.

They waited.

She took a sip.

'Why are you here exactly?' she said at last.

'We'd like to talk to you about Mr Okowu-Bello,' said Caton.

'Her expression betrayed no emotion whatsoever. She took another sip. Playing for time Caton decided.

'I'm not sure how I can help you,' she said.

'To be *exact*,' said Holmes. 'To ask about *you* and Sunday Okowu-Bello,'

'I'm sorry?'

She raised her eyebrows in bemusement, but her hands tightening around the glass. The livid knuckles betrayed her.

''For what?' said Holmes.

'I meant I'm sorry, I don't understand.'

Caton looked around for somewhere to put his glass, and finding none placed it carefully on the dark oak floor.

''You have two choices Mrs Best,' he said. 'You can drop the pretence and help us out, or we can ask Mr Best instead.'

He thought her glass might crack. She swung her legs to the floor, sat up, and put the glass down beside her, the mask of innocence replaced by fear.

'No please, you can't do that!'

'This is a murder enquiry Mandy,' Caton told her. 'If we have to we will. We'd rather not, but that's entirely up to you.'

One hand gripped the other tightly as she wrestled with the options. Caton saw it all the time with suspects backed into a hole. There was no need to push. Sooner or later they had to face reality. In Mandy's case it was sooner.

She looked him straight in the eyes.

'I have your word that you won't tell Harvey?' Her tone had shifted from cool, and confident, to desperate pleading.

'Are you sure he doesn't already know?'

She looked from one to the other of them, searching their faces for a clue.

'No!'

He sensed that she was trying as much to convince herself as them.

'How can you be so sure Mandy?' Caton asked.

'Because if he knew he would have...' she choked on the words.

Holmes finished it for her.

'Killed you?'

She looked down at the floor, avoiding their gaze, neither contradicting nor confirming the suggestion. In Caton's experience that was as good as a yes.

'We've been told your husband has trouble controlling his temper,' said Holmes pressing home the advantage.

There were tears welling in the corners of her eyes.

'I know what you're thinking,' she said. 'But you're wrong. Harvey wouldn't have done that, not to Sunday. He'd have blamed me. Had it out with me first.'

'Maybe he did?' Holmes persisted.

She shook head, violently this time, and appealed to Caton.

'No he didn't. That didn't happen. Because he doesn't know!'

Caton was inclined to accept what she said. Partly because she was convincing, but mainly because her husband had shown no sign of having known and, finally, because there wasn't a mark on her, nor a trace of disturbance in this room.

'I believe you,' he said.

He registered her relief. It was in her eyes, her face, and the way her shoulders relaxed as the tension left her. She was mistaken if she thought that was the end of it.

'When did your affair with Sunday begin?' he asked.

She rose, pulled a tissue from a dispenser on the coffee table, returned to her seat, dabbed at her eyes, blew her nose and crumpled the tissue in her palm.

'It wasn't really an affair.'

'You were sleeping together,' said Holmes.

Her face reddened as though he had slapped it. 'Only three or four times,' she said as though that made it alright. 'It was...I don't know...insane. I was going to finish it.'

'I asked when your involvement with him began,' Caton reminded her.

'About a month ago.'

'Who initiated it, him or you?'

She looked puzzled.

Holmes decided to translate.

'Who came on first?'

'I know what Mr. Caton meant,' she told him acidly. 'I just wasn't sure how to answer it.' She twisted the tissue between her fingers. 'I don't think either of us did. It just happened.'

'Where was this?' Caton asked.

'Right here, in this room. Sunday called round out of the blue to see if Harvey wanted a game of golf. I told him Harvey had gone into town. Wouldn't be back till later in the afternoon. We just stood staring at each other. The next minute we were in the bedroom.'

'Wasn't that risky,' said Caton. 'Right here in your own house?'

She shook her head. 'Like I said. It was insane.'

'During the period you were sleeping together did he tell you about anything that might have been bothering him?'

'No, apart from Harvey finding out. But I think I was more worried about that. Sunday seemed to thrive on taking risks.'

'For example?'

'Driving his sports cars at ridiculous speeds – half the time without a seatbelt on. Bungee jumping when his insurance and his contract specifically forbade it. Betting silly money on stupid bets...'

'Such as?'

'Who can eat the most red hot chillies in one minute? Which rain drop will reach the bottom of the window first? Who can make the Boss lose his temper first? Who...'

'Gets to sleep with his daughter first?' said DI Holmes.

Caton gave him a stare that would have frozen a hot tub. He waited anxiously for her reaction. She seemed neither surprised nor troubled by the question.

'Maybe not her,' she replied. 'But definitely with some of the girls that stalked him round the clubs and bars.'

'And you still slept with him?' said Holmes.

For a moment it seemed she was about to remind him yet again that it had been insane. She thought better of it, shook her head sadly, brushed imaginary crumbs from her trousers, and turned instead to Caton.

'Do you have any more questions Chief Inspector? Because if not I need to sort myself out before my husband gets home.'

It was said with the kind of dignity with which she

had greeted them. The interview had come full circle. Caton knew they had lost her. Whatever she might have disclosed when her head was all over the place they had no chance of unearthing it now. Thanks to Gordon.

'That's it for now,' he told her. 'If you think of anything else, anything at all, please contact me.'

He handed her a card with his office number on.

She stood.

'If you don't mind I won't show you out,' she said. 'I wouldn't want the press to see me like this.'

It was said half in jest, but Caton knew that she was right. He held out his hand.

'I'm sorry this was difficult for you, but I'm sure you understand we had no option but to ask you these questions?'

She held back for a moment, then took his hand, and held it.

'You won't tell Harvey?'

'No. We won't tell Harvey. But there are people who know about you and Mr Okowu-Bello. It might be best if you chose the moment to tell him yourself, before they do. Or worse still, before the press does.'

Her hand tightened over his, and he felt her flinch as her mind computed the consequences.

'When you do, it may be best to choose a public place,' he told her. 'Your parents' house, somewhere like that?'

'Thank you,' she said, releasing his hand and turning away.

The gates were already open as they headed down the drive. Coming towards them was a silver convertible. Harvey Best was at the wheel.

'Bentley Arnage drophead coupe,' Holmes

confided. 'Close to two grand, brand new. If you could pick one up second-hand it'd set you back sixty grand plus.'

The footballer slowed down, and stopped alongside them. He wound his window down and gestured for Caton to do the same.

'What the hell are you doing here?' he demanded.

'We just wanted to check if you'd thought of anything else.' Caton told him.

'No I haven't!' He hammered the door frame with the palm of his hand. 'And next time you want to talk to me you can do it through my solicitor!'

The window rose noiselessly as he sped off, scattering the gravel chips behind him.

'Tut tut,' said Holmes. 'That's no way to treat a Bentley.'

'I just hope Mandy's had time to repair her face,' Caton reflected as he slipped into gear.

'Serves her right,' his DI observed. 'If you don't want to get burned, don't go...'

'Enough!' said Caton as they sped away from the crowd of reporters and photographers. 'You made it plain how you felt back there, and closed her down in the process, just as I was beginning to get somewhere.'

'I doubt there was anymore she could tell us,' he replied, having the sense to sound a little chastened.

Caton eased back on the accelerator.

'Well we'll never know now, will we? I'm surprised at you Gordon. It's not like you to screw up.'

Holmes reached under his seat, eased it back, and stretched his legs out.

'I'm sorry boss. It's just that these got-rich-quick, flash-it- around celebrities living in La La land, piss me off big time.'

'That's Los Angeles Gordon, not stockbroker belt Cheshire.'

'You could have fooled me. The point is they don't live in the real world.'

'Caton glanced across at him.

'You're just envious.'

'No I'm not,' he protested vigorously. 'I wouldn't have their life thrown at me.'

'*Methinks he doth protest too much,*' Caton quoted at him.

'*The Lady doth protest too much, methinks,*' Holmes corrected him.

Caton stared at him a fraction too long, and had to correct his steering as they approached a bend.

'Hamlet,' Holmes said. 'It's the only one I know. We did it at school. Hammered it to death, which is why I've never been to see another one.'

'Talking of jealousy,' said Caton. 'It seems she didn't know about Okowu-Bello and Capper's daughter, Jade.'

'It doesn't look like it,' Holmes said, suddenly serious. 'I know I was wrong to bring it up. What if she puts two and two together?'

'We have to break it to him sometime.'

Holmes rubbed his chin with the heel of his hand.

'Assuming he doesn't already know.'

Caton decided to go back to Central Park and check on progress before tackling the Titan's manager and his daughter. His office manager intercepted him at the door.

'Can I have a word Sir?' she said.

'Of course Ged. Your office or mine?'

It was a shared joke given that neither of them had the privacy here that they had enjoyed in the Longsight major incident room.

He led her to his screened off area.

'What's the problem?'

'The Commissioner,' she told him. Charles Grey.'

'What's he done now?'

'Turned up here. He engaged one of the DCs in conversation in the lift and followed him straight in. Mr Wallace came to tell me as soon as he spotted him.'

'What did you do Ged?'

'I asked him to leave.'

'Good for you. How did he react?'

'He put on the charm. Told me he quite understood. I was only doing my job. Wished he had a PA like me.'

'So he left?'

'Yes Sir.' She grimaced. 'But I'm afraid he'd been here long enough to have a good look at the progress board.'

'Bugger!' said Caton. 'It wasn't often he swore but, he felt comfortable doing it in front of Ged. They'd been through a lot together.

'I couldn't have put it better myself Sir,' she said. 'Would you like me to see if I can get the Chief Constable on the phone?'

Caton smiled.

'Mind reader,' he said.

Chapter 12

The Chief Constable was not available. He had to make do with DCS Gates instead. It was probably as well he decided, because neither she nor Martin Hadfield would have been happy with him skipping the chain of command yet again.

'How do you think the rest of us feel Tom?' she said. 'We have to deal with him day to day. As far as policy is concerned he can claim he has a right to interfere. And he does.'

'But not at operational level? Not with a murder enquiry?'

'Certainly not.'

'So you'll have a word with the Chief Constable, ask him to call him off?'

The reply was decidedly frosty.

'That would imply that he had *set him on* in the first place. I shall request that the Chief Constable remind the Commissioner that he has no right to information about an ongoing investigation, and that any knowledge he might have gained from being in the incident room, entry to which he gained surreptitiously, had better not be shared with anyone.'

'Do you think he will?'

There was a familiar pause, intake of breath, and heavy sigh.

'You do know who has the final say in the appointment of the Chief Constable I take it Detective Chief Inspector?'

'Yes Ma'am.'

'Then stop asking silly questions. Just tell your team to avoid him like the plague, keep their mouths shut in his presence, and lock the bloody door behind them.'

'I take it this call is not being recorded for training purposes Ma'am,?'

'Very funny.'

She didn't sound amused.

Neither was Gerry Capper, the charismatic, comfortably remunerated, and highly successful manager of the Titans.

'Sod off!' he said. 'You want to interview my daughter you do it in front of me.'

'We don't actually need your permission to do that, given that your daughter is over seventeen years of age,' Caton told him. 'Unless you are suggesting that your daughter is a vulnerable person?

'What do you mean, vulnerable person?'

'A vulnerable person is one who is a Juvenile – that is under the age of seventeen – mentally disordered, learning disabled, has communication difficulties, or is illiterate.' Holmes helpfully explained.

The full vent of Capper's fury was turned on the detective inspector. His hands were balled into fists. The sinews in his neck stood out like knotted ropes. His face was the colour of ripe tomatoes.

'You bastard!' he shouted. 'I let you into my home and you have the nerve to insult our daughter. Get out! Go on, get out!'

Caton was more concerned that he'd have a heart

attack, than attack his DI. As apparently was the manager's wife.

'Please, Gerry,' she said, taking his arm and tugging him back towards the centre of the room. 'You'll kill yourself.'

'Kill them more like,' he said, whilst not resisting her.

Holmes was about to warn him about threatening police officers, but Caton stayed him with an outstretched palm.

'I have no intention of questioning Jade on her own,' he said. 'Even though I have the right to do so. I would be happy to have your wife, or if you insist even your solicitor, sit on our conversation. All I'm saying is that for her sake, and for yours, it's better that you are not present.'

'Why the hell not? I'm her father.'

'Please Gerry,' his wife pleaded. 'They'll have their reasons.'

Caton could tell by the look she gave him that she knew about Okowu-Bello and their daughter even if her husband didn't.

The manager pulled an android Smartphone from his pocket, pressed a speed dial key, and put it to his ear. He didn't bother to turn away; he wanted them to hear.

'Max,' he said. 'I need you here, now! What do you mean you can't? Listen, I've got the police here, and they want to talk to Jade. I need you with me.' He listened impatiently, and then exploded into action again, gesticulating wildly with his free hand. 'I know you're not a bloody criminal lawyer, but you'll have to do. What? No, I don't want you sending someone else. Get yourself down here. You've got half an hour, then we're looking for another company lawyer!'

He ended the call, and tossed the phone on the coffee table.

'Make yourselves comfortable,' he said, sounding as though it was the last thing he wanted them to do. 'I'm going to have a word with my daughter.'

Before anyone could stop him, he'd marched out of the room, into the hallway, and up the stairs.

'Shall I go after him?' asked Gordon Holmes.

'No,' Caton replied. 'It's his house; he can do as he pleases.'

They stood there awkwardly, in silence, expecting at any moment to hear the sounds of a heated argument echoing through the Edwardian mansion. Apart from a door slammed, there was nothing.

'Please sit down,' implored Margaret Capper. 'Can I get you a drink?'

'That'd be brilliant, 'said Holmes. 'Tea, milk one sugar.'

'Hot water for me,' said Caton. 'Just off the boil if possible.'

She couldn't wait to get out of the room.

'We could always take her back to the Incident Room,' said Holmes.

'She'd be just as scared of him finding out there. And if he doesn't get it out of her while he's upstairs I'm inclined to let him sit in after all.'

Holmes looked askance. 'Are you sure Boss?'

'At least here she's got her mother and us to make sure he doesn't do something we'd all regret. And we get to see his reaction.'

'What if his lawyer won't let her say anything?'

'Why would she, we're not charging her with anything? Anyway, if she's a company lawyer odds are she'll be out of her depth.'

She was.

At first Maxine Bentham advised her to exercise her right to silence.

'Jade is neither a suspect nor has she been charged with anything,' Caton reminded her. 'She is simply a person of interest with regard to the investigation who we think may have information which could prove helpful to the police.'

He turned to Capper's daughter.

'You have the same rights as anyone invited to help the police Jade. If you don't want to you don't have to. But if you don't, it's going to leave us wondering why. Lead us to dig a little deeper. I'm sure you understand?'

Head down, she brushed a tear from the corner of her eye, and nodded.

'If you don't want to do this here, right now, you can always come back with us the interview room, have a cup of tea. Compose yourself?'

Mention of the interview room had the desired effect. It usually did. She looked up, her eyes wide with apprehension.

'No I want to do it here. Please.' She sounded utterly defeated.

Bentham had insisted on both parents being present. It was a small victory that Caton was happy to let him have, if it meant that the girl talked. It had all sorts of potential benefits: he would be able to gauge the father's reaction; the girl would feel safer her father finding out with her mother, the police, and the lawyer present; he would feel less guilty than if the father were to find out later on, and take it out on her.

'Thank you Jade,' he said.

He looked across at Gerry Capper, who was sitting on the edge of the seat of an armchair facing the sofa where Jade sat with the lawyer on one side, and her mother, with her arm around her shoulders on the other. Gordon Holmes had chosen a straight backed chair slightly off to the side where he could watch Capper closely without drawing attention to himself.

'Before we start I want to remind you Mr Capper,' Caton said. 'That Jade and I have both agreed with your lawyer that you can be present.'

Capper was about to protest that it was his home and Caton had a bloody cheek. Caton cut him short with an imperious gesture, his right arm extended palm outwards,.

'We've been through all this,' he said. 'Any interruptions and I'm continuing this back at Headquarters. Do you understand?'

The lawyer nodded her head vigorously, and much to Caton' surprise Capper sank back into the chair, his face reflecting suppressed rage rather than capitulation.

'Then I'll keep this is a short as possible,' said Caton. He didn't add *painless,* because he knew that it would be anything but. Not only for her but for her parents too.

'I want to stress that we have no reason to suspect your involvement in Mr Okowu-Bello's death...'

'I should bloody well think not,' Gerry Capper muttered.

Caton closed his notebook theatrically, and started to rise.

'Alright, I get it,' said Capper. 'No comments.'

'No anything,' Holmes told him.

Caton sat back down, flipped his notebook open, and continued where he'd left off.

'But we are questioning everyone who had significant contact with Sunday over the past six months.'

Capper stared at his daughter, a question forming

on his lips, saw the expression on the lawyer's face, and thought better of it.

'We understand Jade,' Caton continued. 'That you and Sunday had been seeing each other until very recently?'

'There was a gasp, and Capper was out of his seat. DI Holmes, having anticipated it, stood between the manager and his daughter, his hands against the man's chest. Their faces were inches apart. A pair of bulls squaring up to each other. All eyes were on them.

'Best if you take a deep breath and sit back down Mr Capper,' said Caton. For a moment he thought that Capper was going to give Gordon a Glasgow kiss.

'Please Gerry,' said his wife, hugging her daughter closer. 'Let Jade get this over with. Then we can talk, as a family.'

'Mrs Capper's right Gerry,' said Maxine Bentham. 'You're not helping your daughter or yourself.'

Holmes withdrew his arms, and stepped back a pace, giving him back his personal space, diffusing the situation.

Capper turned, and walked to the huge open stone fireplace, where he stood, shoulders hunched, with his back to them all.

'Jade,' said Caton. 'Were you seeing Mr Okowu-Bello?'

She stared at her father's back, then down at her shoes. She nodded her head. Her reply was barely audible.

'Yes.'

'Where did you meet?'

'I'd seen him lots of times at the ground. In the directors' lounge, and the players' lounge. The first time he spoke to me was at the club Presentation Evening in August...when he won the Player of the Year Award. I was asked to present it.'

'What did he say?'

'*Thanks Babe...You look real cool*. Something like that.'

Her father grunted something unintelligible, and kicked the pile of logs in the inglenook.

'And then?'

'When we were leaving he came over to thank me again. Only this time he slipped me a piece of paper torn from a menu. It was his mobile number.'

'So you rang him?'

'I texted him; as soon as I got home.'

'And?'

'He asked did I want to go out with him for dinner, take in a club.'

'You said yes?'

'I said it was difficult. My dad always wanted to know where I was going, who with. And I had to be in by ten.'

Her father swung round to face her.

'Now you know why, you stupid...'

'Mr Capper,' said Caton standing up and interrupting him. 'That's the last time. Any more of that, and we're off to the station, if for no other reason, for your daughter's own protection.'

Capper's face reddened again, shading to purple. His fists clenched.

'What the fuck do you mean? Are you saying she's at risk from me? I'm her father for God's sake!'

'Then start behaving like it sir,' said Holmes with uncharacteristic politeness. 'Take a look at yourself man. I wouldn't trust you near a pit bull like this, let alone another human being.'

Much to Caton's surprise, it seemed to have the desired effect. Capper even glanced at himself in the antique mirror on the wall behind the sofa. What he saw there must have confirmed Gordon's description because he turned and walked towards the bay windows, where he stood looking out across the gardens, and the fields beyond.

'So Jade,' Caton continued. 'How did you manage to meet with him?'

She looked nervously at her father, and then at her mother.

'Sometimes I bunked off college in the afternoons. We'd go to the apartment he had in town.'

Caton and Holmes exchanged glances. It was the first they had heard of an apartment.

'This apartment, Jade, where was it?'

'In the Northern Quarter, in what used to be a warehouse. He said it was his secret pad...his hideaway.'

Holmes made a careful note of the address she gave them.

'Who else knew that you were seeing Sunday?' Caton asked.

'I don't know. I didn't tell anyone.'

'You were never out in public with him?'

'No, he said it was too risky. The press would find out. My father would go mad.'

'He got that right,' muttered Holmes.

Caton glanced at Gerry Capper, concerned that Gordon's aside might set him off again, but he was so still he might have been carved from stone.

'Did you tell your mother?' Caton asked.

'No. Not until after I heard that Sunday was dead.'

Mrs Capper nodded in agreement.

'I found her weeping in her bedroom,' she said. 'It took a while but I finally got her to tell me.'

'And you didn't tell your husband?'

She looked towards the windows.

'No. I prayed that he would never find out.'

'Did you finish the relationship or did he?'

'He did.'

'Did he tell you why?'

'No. He just stopped answering my texts and my voice messages.'

'What did you do?'

'I started waiting outside his apartment when I knew the first team training was over.'

'And did you see him at all?'

'Just the once, about three weeks ago.'

'What did he say?'

'That it was good while it lasted, but it was too risky. He was worried Dad would find out.'

'Did you believe him?'

She looked down at the ground, and shook her head slowly.

'Partly. But I knew the real reason. He'd moved on to someone else.'

'Do you know who?'

She looked up and stared straight into his face.

'No, I don't.'

'One last question,' he said. 'Where were you on the evening before Sunday's body was found?'

'We were all together,' said her mother. 'Jade, Gerry and me. It was my birthday. We went out for dinner at San Carlo. Then we came straight back here.'

'What time did you arrive home?'

'Close to half past eleven.'

'Did any of you go out again?'

'No.'

She said it with conviction, but her glance towards the window told Caton that she could not be sure about her husband. They probably slept in separate rooms. Given what he'd witnessed in this room it made sense.

'Can you confirm that Mr Capper?' he said.

For a moment he thought Jade's father might not have heard, but then he turned slowly, and deliberately, to face them.

'We were all here. All night.'

His anger seemed to have drained away, and left him utterly defeated. Physically he appeared to have collapsed in on himself; his shoulders drooped, and Caton became aware for the first time of a sizeable paunch that he must normally have worked hard to hold in.

'Is that it then?' he said when Caton failed to respond.

Caton looked at his DI who shook his head, closed his notebook, and proceeded to put his biro in his top pocket.

'Thank you all for your time,' Caton told them. 'I'm sorry I had to impose on you like this.' He turned to the lawyer. 'Will you be staying here for a while Ms Bentham?'

'Miss Bentham,' she said without malice. 'And yes, I think I shall.'

'Good,' he said. There was no need to explain. Everyone in room knew exactly what he meant.

A person of interest?' said Holmes as they walked to their cars. 'Where did that come from, *CSI Miami*?'

Caton smiled.

'Close. Mickey Haller. Michael Connelly's fictional lawyer. The one that works out of the back of his Lincoln car.'

'Like me you mean?' said Holmes. 'I seem to spend more time on the road these days than anywhere else.'

'Get yourself a sat nav. You wouldn't get lost so often.'

'And then there was *seeing each other*, nice euphemism that, I must remember to use it.'

Caton leant against the passenger door.

'No point in inflaming the situation further,'

His DI adopted an identical position facing him, his back to his own driver's door.

'Some chat up line he had,' he said.

'Sunday didn't need a silver tongue,' Caton told him. 'Neither would you if you had his money, and celebrity status.'

Holmes rubbed his chin with the back of his hand.

'It's not fair Boss. These girls, like moths to a flame they are. And look what happens to them. They get chewed up and spat out.'

It was not the analogy Caton would have used but he knew what Gordon meant.

'And I'll tell you what I thought was strange,' his DI continued. 'Capper's anger seemed to be directed against his daughter, not his player.'

'Okowu-Bello's dead Gordon. His daughter is the only one he can take it out on.'

'Do you think she'll be alright?'

'While her mother and the lawyer are still there. Hopefully it'll give him time to calm down. In any case, I have the feeling that to him the loss of his daughter's virginity is nothing compared to the loss of his star player. And it's not as though she was under the age of consent.'

'You're forgetting Boss, he's a control freak; it's what makes him a brilliant manager. It also makes him dangerous. You saw how frightened they both were of him. Are you sure he couldn't have done it?'

'Not if his alibi stacks up.'

'How are we supposed to check on that?'

Caton swivelled to his right and pointed to the CCTV cameras on the walls either side of the gates.

'We can start with the footage from those, and the ones on the front of the house.'

Gordon struck his forehead lightly with the heel of his hand, and raised his eyes skywards.

'Duh!' he said. 'I guess that's why you're a chief inspector, and I'm a lowly DI.'

Caton walked round the bonnet of his Octavia, and opened the driver's door.

'That's just one of the reasons,' he said, grinning.

'It wasn't a complete waste of time though?'

'Far from it. We need to take a look at that apartment. It's funny that he was bothered about his debts when he had that squirreled away. He could have sold it to pay off his debts.'

'If he actually owned it.'

'Let's find out,' said Caton. 'And don't forget Gordon. First one there pays the speeding fines.'

Chapter 13

He needn't have bothered. Holmes was a good five minutes behind him.

'You must have taken the last parking space,' he moaned. 'I've had to park down by the canal.'

'Do you good,' Caton told him as he climbed out of the car. 'All that sitting behind the wheel you chuntered on about is beginning to show.'

The apartment block was at the western end of the Northern Quarter. A former Victorian redbrick warehouse, it had now been clad in glass and steel, giving the impression of an exhibit in a futuristic architectural museum. Caton wasn't sure if he loved or hated it.

The desk in the lobby was staffed by a concierge who proved unwilling to give them access without either a search warrant or permission from the operations manager.

'More than your job's worth?' said Holmes

'Exactly,' the man replied. It was a statement of fact without a hint of resentment.

'I'd like you to contact the operations manager and tell him that the police are here, and need to speak with him,' said Caton. 'We'll wait.'

While they waited on a banquette in the visitors' waiting area Caton rang and checked who was in the Incident Room. DS Stuart was available. He gave her the address, and the number of Okowu-Bello's apartment.

'I need you to draw up an application for a search warrant,' he said. 'Stress that it's a murder enquiry, that the apartment is uninhabited, and that we need to be able to search and seize whatever may have a bearing on the investigation. That we can't stipulate exactly what that might be until we see it.'

'Was Okowu-Bello the owner Sir?'

He could see where she was going with this.

'No, it was rented on his behalf.'

'What if the magistrate wants you to see if the owner will consent to you searching without a warrant,' she said. 'Or if he wants us to approach whoever holds the rental agreement first?'

'Make sure he, or she, doesn't,' he said. 'I know you can do it.'

She had a feeling it was more a threat than a vote of confidence.

'I'll try Sir.'

He ignored the implication that she might not succeed.

'When you've got it, bring it straight over,' he said. 'And bring Jack Benson with you.'

'Do you want him to bring the whole of the Scene of Crime team?'

'No, just Jack. He can decide who he wants to join him when he's seen what there is to do. OK Jo?' he said, softening the exchange.

'Yes Sir,' she said, deliberately keeping it formal in the open office where even the walls had ears.

'He's taking his time, this caretaker,' Holmes observed.

'Some caretaker,' said Caton, nodding towards the reception where the concierge was pointing a newcomer in their direction.

He wore a bespoke suit and tie, a fitted pinstriped shirt, and hand tooled brogues. In his late thirties, of mixed race, his hair artistically spiked with gel, he had the air and appearance of a cross between an upmarket car dealer, and a finance manager from Spinningfields.

He approached them with hand outstretched, and a frozen smile that jarred with the wary look behind his black rimmed spectacles. They stood to meet him.

'I'm Bradley Sandon,' he said. 'How can I help you?'

'We need access to Mr Okowu-Bello's apartment,' said Caton. Before Sandon could protest he continued. 'I have a warrant on its way here, But I'd prefer it if you gave your permission. While you make up your mind, I'd like to ask you a few questions.'

Sandon arched his eyebrows.

'Questions?'

'About your tenant.'

'Then I doubt that I can help you. He was just that, a tenant. One of sixty in this these apartments alone, and I oversee two other blocks a similar size to this.'

'Did you ever meet him?'

'I showed him round when he moved in. Saw him coming or going several times. Apart from that I don't think I ever spoke to him.'

'Was it common knowledge that he owned the apartment?'

He looked surprised.

'Owned it? He didn't own it; it was rented on a six month rolling lease.'

'In his name?'

He shook his head, as though it was a stupid question.

'Certainly not. Very few of our tenants are named on the rental contracts.'

'I wonder why that is?' said Holmes looking up from his notebook.

'I couldn't say.'

'Or won't?'

'Couldn't. Next question?'

Caton thought his indignation feigned, but let it ride. The truth might well interest Her Majesty's Revenue and Customs, or wives and husbands cheated on, but it would be unlikely to take this investigation further.

'So whose name is on the contract?' he asked.

'I'd have to check.'

'With whom?'

'With my employer.'

'Who is?'

'Littlemoss Estates, on Deansgate.'

A swanky set of offices set into rooms beneath two soaring brick arches of the former Great Northern Railway viaduct. Caton had walked past them hundreds of times. He and Kate had even window shopped there but could never aspire to buy the kind of properties they offered.

'Then ring them,' he said. 'And find out.'

Reluctantly, Sandon took his cell phone from his inside jacket pocket, and moved out of ear shot.

'Rented,' said Gordon Holmes. 'So he couldn't have sold it even if he wanted to.'

'She's been quick,' Caton observed as Detective Sergeant Stuart hurried towards them, envelope in hand.

'Here you are Sir,' she said handing it to him.

'Well Jo,' he said taking out the warrant and reading it through. 'No problems then?'

'None that I couldn't handle. Jack Benson's right behind me. He's just parking the car.'

'We won't expect him anytime soon then,' said Holmes morosely.

Sandon came back to join them.

'Nutmeg Holdings,' he said. That's the name on the contract.'

'Is there another name?' Caton asked.

'The signature's indecipherable and where the name should have been printed underneath it's just as bad.'

'Address?'

He shook his head.

Holmes was incredulous.

'They let them sign a contract without a legible name or an address?'

'They had a verified direct debit. That was good enough don't you think?'

Jack Benson arrived carrying his work case.

'That was quick,' said Holmes. 'Are you down by the canal?'

'Nope. I caught someone pulling out of a space just up the road.'

'Lucky sod!'

Caton waved the search warrant.

'After you Mr Sandon.'

The four detectives stood in the entrance hall, paper thin gloves on their hands, overshoes on their feet. Sandon had been told to wait in the foyer. Caton looked at the plans of the apartment that Sandon had given him. It was exactly what he had expected. An entrance hall, an open plan lounge and kitchen. Two double bedrooms, ensuite. A loggia, or open balcony, that wrapped around two sides, and provided extensive views across the canal to Saddleworth Moor and the Derbyshire Peaks. No gym of any kind because the apartments boasted a health club, including a 15 metre swimming pool in the basement, and a hot tub on the roof.

'Let's do it,' he said.

The room was dominated by a huge black leather sofa, and a wall mounted, sixty five inch, flat screen TV. Along another wall was a well stocked bar and a wall to ceiling fridge full of beer and champagne. The beechwood, chrome, and black marble kitchen was state of the art. Black and white prints and framed photographs of various sizes were dotted around the remaining walls. Three of them were of artistic female nudes.

'The kitchen looks like it's never been used,' Jack Benson reported. 'If he ate here at all, ten to one it was takeaways. There's nothing in the bins.'

He walked back to the centre of the room.

'Either someone's been in and wiped this place clean, or it could be that he has a regular cleaner.'

'My guess is, it's his knocking shop,' said Holmes. 'It's not as though he actually lives here.'

Jack Benson crossed to the door of the master bedroom, and opened it.

'Right first time, *Holmes*,' he said.

The three of them came up behind him. Together they stared into the room.

'Elementary my dear Benson,' said the DI.

The bed was super king sized. Above it was an equally large mirror. Close to the centre of the room, from floor to ceiling, stood a pole, presumably part of the structure of the former warehouse, painted steel blue.

'No guesses what he used that for,' Holmes quipped.

'I know he was great mover on the pitch I wouldn't have thought he was into pole dancing,' said DS Stuart.

'Only for starters. You want to check your Kama Sutra.'

Caton followed Benson into the double walk-in shower wet room. On hooks there were his and hers towelling robes. Up-market shower products were clustered in one corner.

'Boss, you have got to see this!' Gordon Holmes called out.

He had found a walk-in wardrobe with shelves neatly stacked with see through plastic boxes filled with sex aids. One contained masks, another hand and ankle ties and restraints, another bondage costumes, and yet another kinky underwear. Two boxes were devoted to dildos and vibrators. Six boxes contained commercially produced videos and CDs of varying degrees of porn.

'Nothing for himself,' noted Gordon Holmes. Presumably he didn't have a problem in that department.'

'That's more than can be said for what was going on in his head,' said Joanne Stuart trying to hide her embarrassment among this macho male company. They all seemed to have assumed that she was over the worst of the Bluebell Hollow investigation. All, except for the Boss.

The second bedroom was pristine. It looked as though it had never been used. There was another box of videos in the bottom of an otherwise empty built in wardrobe. This one contained videos with dates and initials scrawled on the stick-on labels.

They checked the loggia last. Apart from two metal

tables, and matching chairs, it was empty. Joanne Stuart leaned over the balcony and pointed.

'Look Gordon,' she said. 'You can see your car from here.'

His reply was unrepeatable.

Caton left Benson to organise a forensic sweep of the apartment, and the seizure, labelling, and transfer of the contents of the boxes. He knew that the private videos were likely to prove the most interesting, but how far they would throw any light on the victim's death remained to be seen. And he was concerned that the undoubtedly salacious content of those videos – not to mention the others – would almost certainly cause a distraction for some members of his team that he could do without. He decided to approach Helen Gates again and see if she'd let him have a few more officers to trawl through them in an adjacent secure office. It was worth a try. But first he still had some questions for the two men waiting impatiently downstairs.

'Has anyone been in that apartment since he died?'

'Just the cleaner as far as I know,' said the concierge. 'The Wednesday following. It was her regular day.'

'Did she go in alone?'

'No I always accompanied her. It was part of the agreement.'

'Was anyone else, to your knowledge, aware that Mr Okowu-Bello used that apartment?'

A look passed between them. It was Sandon who answered for the two of them.

'Not unless he'd told them, or they'd been here with him.'

'Did neither of you feel tempted to tell anyone? A big celebrity like that? It would have been understandable.'

'No way!' said the concierge before Sandon could stop him.

Caton stared at him, and then at the operations manager, waiting for one of them to elaborate.

'Let's just say,' said Sandon. 'He made it worth our while not to.'

'What did he mean by that?' asked Holmes as they stood on the pavement.

'If you'd been there all the time instead of slipping down to the health club for a gawk, you'd know.' Caton admonished.

'I just thought it might provide a lead on prospective witnesses, but there was no one there.'

'Tell that to your wife, see if she believes you.'

Holmes grimaced at the thought. Marilyn was not known for her open-mindedness.

'Seriously though,' he said. 'What did he mean?'

'That Okowu-Bello paid all three of them a retainer to keep their mouths shut.'

'What about the staff downstairs?'

'Apparently, he never used the health club, the spa, or the hot tub.' Holmes smirked. 'He didn't need to. Not with all the exercise he was getting in his apartment.'

Caton clicked the remote on his key fob, opened the car door, and lowered himself into his seat.

'Nutmeg Holdings, said Holmes. 'Very funny.'

'What do you mean?' Anxious to leave, Caton had his hand on the door handle.

'Come on Boss, call yourself a football fan. Oh no, I forgot, you support the Blues.'

'Very funny Gordon, We'll see if you're laughing at the end of the season.' He pulled the door to, and wound down the window

Holmes placed one hand on the roof and leant down to Caton's eye level.

'Nutmeg,' he said. 'The best way to humiliate your opponent. Run at him; when he opens his legs you feint one way, push the ball between them, skip round the side, and collect the ball.'

'Just like we do when we're questioning suspects?'

'Exactly.'

'I'd give you a lift, Gordon,' he said. 'But this one-way system is a nightmare, especially at rush-hour. I'll see you back at the station.'

He wound down the window, started up, and drove away. In his rear-view mirror he could see the forlorn figure of his DI trudging back to his car.

He rebuked himself for being mean to Gordon, and to Joanne Stuart. He knew that his mood had changed of late. He suspected that it had something to do with the way that Kate had been behaving. He couldn't put his finger on it; it was just that she had suddenly become moody. Perhaps it was a delayed response to her finding out about his son, Harry. Or maybe she was having second thoughts about the wedding.

He slowed to a stop, and waited for the lights to change on the ring road. Either way, he decided, they couldn't let it drift on like this. And he'd definitely have to stop taking it out on the team.

Chapter 14

An internet search revealed Nutmeg Holdings as a limited liability company registered in Belize. The owner was none other than Joseph Gideon Jones, Okowu-Bello's agent.

'I told you,' said Holmes. 'They were *nutmegging* Her Majesty's Revenue and Customs.'

Caton read the printout. Companies registered in Belize were free of tax, and reporting requirements. There were no fiscal information exchange agreements with any other countries seeking evidence of criminal activity, or tax evasion. All for a single fee of no more than £1000.

'If I have this correct,' he said. 'Jones, and whoever he represented through Nutmeg Holdings, would have to pay tax on money earned and recorded in the UK, but could deposit any other income in the Belize account without being taxed or having the Revenue find out?'

'Other income such as promotions abroad they never reported; under the counter payments for transfers, other bungs, and bribes; winnings from betting that Okowu-Bello's contract forbade him from engaging in, and God knows what else.'

'I thought Jones was high up the list of people we needed to interview?' said Caton.

'He is, but he was out of the country when Okowu-

Bello died.'

'He must be back by now surely? Get him in Gordon.'

Holmes looked at his watch. 'It's getting late Boss,' he said. Can it wait till the morning?'

Caton checked his own watch. It was already 9pm. The day had moved so fast he'd lost track of the time. Kate would be wondering why he hadn't called her. He didn't know if it was a good or a bad sign that she hadn't rung him herself.

'OK,' he said. 'Let's make it first thing. You get off home to Marilyn. I'll see where the rest of them are up to, and shut up shop.'

There were only three others still working in the incident room. They looked tired, and that only led to poor concentration and sloppy records. He told them to stop what they were doing and go home.

He was in the lift when his BlackBerry rang. It was Martin Hadfield the Assistant Chief Constable, Crime.

'Where are you Caton?'

First names seemed to have gone out of the window since Hadfield's promotion. It was just one of many things that failed to endear him to Caton.

'I'm just leaving Force Headquarters, Sir.' he replied.

'Good. The Underwater Search and Marine Unit have just pulled a body out of the Ship Canal. It has your moniker on it.'

'Because?'

'Does the name Ratten mean anything to you?'

Caton's heart sank. He suddenly felt weary.

'Yes Sir. Phil Ratten. A potential witness, possibly even a suspect, in the Okowu-Bello investigation.'

'Well he won't have anything to say to you now. You'd better get down there. See if you can find out how he ended up floating around like that.'

'Yes Sir.'

'I'm glad I caught you,' Hadfield said cheerfully. 'Better than having to phone you at home.'

Caton doubted that Kate would agree.

'It was only a chilli,' she told him. 'Yours is in the oven.'

She sounded tired but not disappointed, though he could have handled that. This was more like indifference. As though she'd expected it. Caton recognised the signs. It was how his first marriage had started to go down the pan, and this time they weren't even married.

'I'm really, really sorry Love,' he said. 'I'll be as quick as I can.'

'One of your witnesses fished out of the ship canal? I don't think so. We both know that's an all-nighter Tom. Just don't wake me up when you come in.'

'I'll sleep in the spare room,' he said, hoping that she'd tell him not to be so daft. The lift doors opened.

'Fine,' she said. 'I'll see you in the morning.'

Disheartened, he trudged across the vast empty atrium towards the exit, where he swiped his electronic pass, and stepped out into the chill night air.

They stood in a pool of light from the searchlight of the pride of the Underwater Unit, a black and yellow chequered forty two foot trawler. A sergeant, and his two fellow divers, were busy stowing their equipment on board the boat. Their inspector, Dave Wilson, warm in his thick padded anorak and thermal gloves, stood beside Caton as he shivered in the freezing fog curling up from the surface of the water, and over the grassy bank.

'Are you sure you're ready?' said Douglas, the pathologist, kneeling beside the body bag.

'Yes,' said Caton.

Douglas unzipped it slowly from the top, and sat back on his heels.

Caton felt the gorge rising in his throat, and fought to keep it down.

'I did warn you,' said the pathologist.

The head had been severed. An attempt had been made to place it in juxtaposition with the rest of the body, but the fact that the whole of the neck on the left side was missing ruined the intended impression. The face was mangled beyond recognition.'

'How do we know that it's Ratten?' said Caton.

'We don't. Not for sure,' said Wilson. 'But his clothes match those in the description you circulated, and this was zipped in his back pocket.'

He held up a black leather wallet in a clear plastic bag.

'In addition to fifty five quid in notes, and four credit cards, it contains his plastic driving licence, and his Titans ID card.'

'What about his mobile phone?'

Wilson shook his head.

'No luck so far. We've tried with the ROB.'

He saw the puzzled look on Caton's face and pointed to an object just off to their left, the size of a large shoe box, like a miniature helicopter without blades. On either side of the skids was a yellow cylinder that could have been a float or a tank of some kind. In the centre at the front was a glass bubble that Caton suspected was a camera.

'It's a remotely operated vehicle. Great for depths below 50 metres or when it's especially cloudy or dangerous. My lads are freezing cold and knackered. We'll try again in the morning with the Konigsberg MS

1000 sonar rig. If it's there, we'll find it.'

To his left Caton could hear the incessant hum of traffic passing over Barton Bridge. Much closer he could just make out the soft hemispherical glow of the Titan's stadium. To his right, beyond the boat, he would have expected to see the Irlam viaduct, but it too was lost in the mist.

'Where was the body?' he asked.

Wilson pointed towards the far bank, shrouded in white, just 20 metres away.

'Over there. Five metres in from the bank,' He pointed again. 'The head was twenty metres up stream. It must have been caught in the undertow from the boat.'

'Boat?' said Caton.

'The Day trippers on the Merseyside Ferries Canal cruise got more than they were bargaining for. As far as we can tell, he'd been wrapped in a tarpaulin, tied round with rope, and weighted down with a couple of slabs of concrete. Seems the concrete must have ripped the tarpaulin, one of the slabs fell out, and your man floated vertically towards the surface. The captain saw him too late.'

'In my view, it was the propeller that severed his head,' Mr Douglas opined. 'Chewed his face up as well. Can't be a hundred percent sure till I've done the post mortem. Can I zip him up now? It's bloody freezing down here.'

'Go ahead,' said Caton.

'I'm guessing it wasn't suicide then?' said a voice from behind him. He turned to find DI Carter grinning at him.

'Thanks for coming Nick,' he said. 'Sorry to have messed up your evening.'

'No problem. You know how it is with us bachelors.'

Caton did. They were always the ones who got pulled out in the middle of the night. Trouble was, there was every chance they'd have had a drink or two. Then you prayed they didn't race to get there, and attract the attention of a trigger happy traffic patrol.

'Who have we got here then?' Carter asked.

'Philip Ratten, we think. The security man who was in the CCTV suite the night that Okowu-Bello died.'

Carter whistled. 'The man who knew too much,' he said.

'Or tried to stop it.'

Carter shook his head.

'No, they'd have left the body there,' he said. 'Not gone to all this trouble. My guess is they paid him to disappear, but he got cold feet. They decided they couldn't trust him.'

It was a reasonable assumption, but only one of many.

'Did you recover the tarpaulin?' said Caton.

'Over there.' Wilson pointed to a large bundle in the middle of the tow path. 'You're going to need a Range Rover to shift it.'

Caton left Carter to have a look at the victim. He smiled wryly as he heard Carter curse. Squatting down, he began to unwrap the plastic material. It was a piece approximately four metres long by three metres wide that had been cut from a larger piece. He could tell, because the light from his torch picked out white letters, two foot high, stencilled across the dark blue material. 'S KICK RAC

'Let's Kick Racism out of Football,' said Carter coming up behind him.

Caton had already made the connection. It was the message he saw unfurled on the centre spot before every home game in the Barclays Premiership.

'It's going to be easy to find out if this was taken from the Titans' ground,' he said, straightening up. 'I want you to get someone onto that straight away Nick. See to it they're asking the right questions, and preserve any evidence. Then check when the body's arrived at the morgue, and is sufficiently presentable for identification. Then get the wife down there. Make sure she's got a family member with her, and someone from family liaison. I'll stay here and task the tactical aid team, and then I'll see you back at Central Park.'

'Right Boss,' said Carter, before moving swiftly down the tow path.

Caton watched him go with a spring in his step, until he was swallowed up by the swirling fog that closed like a curtain behind him. He was reminded of himself not so long since, when the excitement of the chase subsumed everything. It wasn't that he didn't care anymore. Or that he didn't derive some satisfaction from a successful investigation. He simply didn't feel the kind of high that had always been there when the challenge was greatest, and his skills were in full flow. Perhaps Helen Gates was right. It was time to move up. To drive a desk. So why did the thought of that depress him even more?

It was two thirty in the morning when he entered the apartment. Kate had left the alarm off so as not be woken by thirty seconds of pips. Caton slipped off his shoes, and left them in the hallway. He silent-set the alarm, walked down the corridor, and paused by the master bedroom. The door was ajar. He could hear the steady rhythm of her breathing. Despondently, he entered the spare bedroom, stripped, left his clothes in a heap on the floor, and slid beneath the cold, unwelcoming, duvet.

His sleep was fitful. The familiar nightmare he had

not experienced since he and Kate had moved in together, hovered at the edge of his imaginings. Each time that it threatened to encroach, his subconscious forced it to retreat, bringing him to a state of threshold consciousness where he was able to concentrate on something else, until it came slithering back once more, like a python ready to squeeze the breath from his body.

He awoke exhausted and covered in sweat. He wondered if he'd have been better staying up all night. The six o'clock alarm on his BlackBerry was ringing from somewhere in the pile of dishevelled clothes beside the bed. By the time he found it he was wide awake.

Dressed and showered, he made himself a toasted banana sandwich, a cafetiere of coffee, and a mug of tea for Kate. Role reversal, he reflected. It was usually her up first. He took it through to her, set it on her bedside table, and sat on the bed in the hollow left behind where her legs had curled up to her chest. Her head was cupped in her right hand. Rich copper coloured hair fanned out around it like a halo. Even in sleep, her beauty made his heart ache.

She stirred, opened her eyes, and stared blearily up at him.

'What time did you get in?'

'Around two. I was tempted to join you but you sounded so peaceful.'

'Two? Oh Tom you can't keep that up.'

She levered herself into a sitting position, and let him prop up the pillows behind her. He handed her the tea. She blew across the surface.

'Though I have to say, this makes a nice change.'

'You should have been around when I was working shifts,' he said. Then he saw the look on her face. 'Or maybe not.'

'Or *definitely* not,' she said.

While she drank her tea in silence Caton ate his sandwich, the plate tucked under his chin to prevent the crumbs falling on the bed clothes. Not something that would have troubled him before they met. She had changed him in so many ways, he reflected, ones far more important than this. As, he supposed, he had her.

'Are we alright Kate?' he said tentatively, unsure that he wanted to hear her answer.

She stopped drinking, the mug suspended in mid air. A look of surprise suffused her face.

'You and me,' he repeated. 'Are we still alright?'

Her surprise was replaced by uncertainty, and a hint, he thought, of disappointment.

'I'm not sure what you mean,' she said. '*I* thought we were. Don't you?'

'It's just,' he said, struggling to find the right words. Ones that would avoid any intimation of blame. That would lead to reconciliation rather than all out warfare. 'I'm sure it's just me being...I don't know...paranoid, but I get this feeling I've let you down somehow?'

She placed the mug firmly on the bedside table, and folded her arms. Her eyes searched his.

'And how exactly am I supposed to have made you feel like this?'

He looked away, knowing that she could always read his mind, sometimes it seemed she saw deep inside his soul.

'Perhaps I haven't expressed it that well.'

'Try again,' she said.

He looked directly at her.

'Are you happy Kate?'

She smiled wryly. 'What is happiness?'

'Come on,' he pleaded. 'Don't let's play games. I

need to know. Is there something wrong? Something I've done?'

This time it was her that avoided his eyes. She pushed back the duvet on her left side, and swung her feet out of the bed.

'This isn't the time for a conversation like this Tom,' she said calmly. 'I'm taking a shower.'

He stood up.

'So there *is* something?'

'Just leave it,' she said as she stepped into the ensuite. 'Maybe tonight, over dinner. If you make it on time.'

She closed the door behind her, and turned the lock.

Caton left his plate and half eaten sandwich, on the bed, and headed for the hallway. He no longer felt hungry.

Chapter 15

Detective Sergeant Carter intercepted him on the broad steps leading to the entrance to the Central Park HQ.

'Morning Boss.'

He sounded far too bright and cheery, Caton thought, given they'd both had less than three hours sleep. Carter nodded towards the car park from which Caton had just emerged.

'All right for some.'

Spaces were at a premium. Many admin staff and junior officers had three day passes, and were expected to car share, park and ride, and travel by bus, or on the metro. *Agile working* was the phrase the Command Team used. As temporary incumbents Caton and Holmes were the only members of his team exempt.

'Your time will come, Nick,' he replied. 'All you have to do is pass your inspectors' exams, and sail through the promotions board.'

He waited until they were both inside, had swiped their cards, and were heading for the lifts.

'How did his wife take it?'

Carter grimaced.

'Badly. I think she knew it was coming even before I told her. Not that she admitted as much, but you could tell.'

'Did she identify him?'

Carter nodded.

'From his clothes, and a tattoo on his back. *"Phil and Bev Forever"* And a heart with an arrow through it. Shame really. They'd gone to a lot of trouble to make him presentable. Put a cloth across his neck to hide the fact that it had been severed. She got the shock of her life when they had to turn the body over, and the head stayed where it was.'

The lift doors slid silently open.

'Did you manage to speak with her?'

'Once we'd got her back home, with a strong cup of tea down her. She said she'd got the impression he was into something bad. Something he couldn't see a way out of.'

'But she didn't know what?'

He shook his head.

'Sorry Boss. But she's giving the Family Liaison Officer a list of all the names she can remember her husband having mentioned. Forensics are busy going over the place.'

He held up the anti-static Ziploc evidence bag he had been carrying by his side. Inside, Caton could see a second generation cell phone; the kind without a web browser.

'I've brought his old mobile phone in to see what the techies can tell us.'

Caton held the door of the Incident Room open for him.

'Let's hope the divers manage to find his new one,' he said. 'Did his wife tell you when he changed the phones?'

'She thought a couple of months ago. Let's hope he was already in with the bad boys before he swapped over.'

Caton doubted it. Okowu-Bello's murder had the

hallmark of professionals, even if they had screwed up somewhat with the disposal of Ratten's body. And the first thing people like that did was to secure their mode of communication. But he didn't want to undermine Carter's understandable sense of optimism.

'Well done Nick,' he said.

'Mr Caton!'

Ged strode purposefully towards them.

'Mr Holt would like to speak with you,' she said.

'Put him straight through to my extension,' Caton told her, heading off towards his cubbyhole.

'He's not on the phone Sir, he's here,' she called after him.

He swivelled, and she saw the annoyance on his face.'

'It's alright,' she reassured him. 'I asked him to wait in the foyer. I'm surprised you didn't see him on your way in.'

It transpired that Holt had been in toilets when Caton arrived. He wasn't happy at having to wait for so long.

'Then you should have phoned,' Caton told him.

'It's not the kind of thing you'd want me to share over the phone,' he replied.

'Go on,' said Caton, his interest roused.

Holt looked around nervously. They were seated on plastic yellow chairs at a small table on the fourth floor loggia, overlooking the atrium. Designed for breakout meetings and private conversations it felt exposed, but there was clearly no one able to overhear them.

'You're in the Headquarters building,' Caton reminded him. 'If you're not safe here where are you going to be?'

It didn't seem to reassure him. When Holt spoke his voice was so quiet that Caton had to strain to hear him.

'What do you know about the Nigerian connection?' he whispered.

'That he had to pay his so called sponsors a percentage of his money, and use a Nigerian bank.'

'Had to, as in past tense?' said the investigative reporter.

'What do you mean?'

'That Okowu-Bello stopped paying them four months ago.'

Caton sat up. 'I understood that if he did that they'd take it out on his family back home in Lagos?'

'It seems he had someone else looking after him. They put the frighteners on the Nigerians, but not before the bank his funds were in was declared bankrupt, and the money disappeared.'

Caton nodded thoughtfully. That explained why the footballer had no longer been able to pay his debts.

'Who was this mysterious someone else?' he asked.

Holt looked around again

'That's what I'm working on. But I'm not having much luck at this end. I thought you might have people who could follow it up in Lagos?'

Caton had no doubt the National Crime Agency would be capable of doing so; it was in their remit. He doubted they'd be happy to hear there was an investigative reporter involved.

'That's in then,' he said. 'This is all you've come up with?'

Holt looked disappointed.

'It's obvious it was news to you,' he said. 'Don't tell me it doesn't have a bearing on your investigation?'

'I told you,' Caton replied. 'This isn't a two way street. As a citizen you have an obligation to share with me anything you know that might be relevant to Sunday Okowu-Bello's death. I have no such obligation to you. Worse still, if I was to give you privileged information my job would be on the line. Especially since the phone hacking scandal.'

'Come on Tom,' he said. 'That was completely different. That was about police officers being paid for information, not a reciprocal exchange in pursuit of the same goal.'

'Correct me if I'm wrong,' said Caton. 'But I thought your goal was to get a scoop that would bring you fame and fortune.'

He placed both hands on the table, signalling that the meeting was over.

'That's not fair,' Holt complained. 'I want to help find his murderers as well. The two are not mutually exclusive.'

Caton pushed back his chair, and stood up.

'Good,' he said. 'In that case I look forward to hearing from you when you've more information.'

The reporter shook his head in disgust.

'Don't look a gift horse in the mouth,' he said.

'I won't, so long as it *is* a gift,' was Caton's parting comment.

This time he didn't get as far as the Incident Room. Helen Gates stopped him in the corridor.

'Tom, where the hell have you been?' she said. 'The Chief's been asking for you.'

Caton decided not to waste his time explaining that he'd been up all night.

'Mr Hadfield,' he replied. 'Is there a problem?'

'Not Martin,' she said taking him by the arm, and leading him back towards the lifts. 'Mr Hampson, *the* Chief.'

From the outset, Robert Hampson, the new Chief

Constable, had taken an unchacteristic interest in this investigation. Not least by insisting that Caton be the Senior Investigating Officer. Nevertheless Caton was surprised that he was asking to see him. Hampson had assured all of his officers that he had no intention of becoming involved in day to day operations.

"My job," he had said, "Is about policy, command, and control. I'm here to watch your backs, ensure that you have the resources to do your job, and set you free to do it to the best of your ability. So you forget all that *my door is always open* nonsense. If you have a problem take it up with your commanding officer. Follow the chain of command, and you won't go far wrong."

There were just five of them seated at the conference table. Helen Gates, Martin Hadfield her boss, the Chief Constable, immediately to his left Charles Grey the Police Commissioner, and sitting opposite, Caton himself. He was surprised to see the Commissioner there. His remit was the same as that of the former Police Authority: to hire and fire the Chief Constable, set the budget, and agree policing priorities. Any involvement in operational matters was supposedly prohibited. Hampson was nobody's fool. He immediately picked up on Caton's reaction to the presence of Charles Grey.

'The Commissioner has asked for this meeting,' he said. 'Because the investigation currently being led by DCI Caton, apparently, has very important political ramifications.'

Caton's brow furrowed. It was the first he'd heard of it. The Chief too, if his pregnant pause either side of the word *apparently* was anything to go by. And was there, he wondered, an implied threat in the phrase *currently led by...*? It was interesting that it was

Grey who had asked for the meeting.

'That's correct,' the Police Commissioner interjected to the obvious annoyance of his Chief Constable. 'Such is the fervour for Premiership football in this city, I am concerned that the investigation should be resolved as quickly, and as smoothly, as possible, to avoid civil unrest. And then there is understandable interest from the Football Association, the Sports Minister, and the international dimension, UEFA,' his voice faltered as he became aware that everyone apart from the Chief Constable was staring at him with growing incredulity, and even he was looking fixedly down at the table top. 'With Okowu-Bello being a Nigerian,' he continued. 'And Black.'

Caton had seldom heard so much drivel; even allowing for the fact that the man was a politician.

'With respect,' he said, 'We have no reason to suspect that racism played any part in...'

A scowling Martin Hadfield interrupted, his arm raised high and his hand thrust forward towards Caton, as though on traffic duty.

'Thank you Chief Inspector!' he boomed. 'Let the Commissioner finish.'

Caton had long suspected that Hadfield would do anything to smarm his way to the top. Now it looked as though he was ingratiating himself with the Commissioner. If so, in Caton's view, he'd got it badly wrong.

In the spotlight of their stares Charles Grey looked uncharacteristically sheepish. He had run out of things to say.

The Chief Constable did nothing to lessen his embarrassment; on the contrary, he let him stew a little longer before stepping in.

'I can understand your concern, Commissioner,' he

said. 'Given the understandable media interest in this case, but I'd like to make it clear that I am rather more sanguine about the situation. I see no evidence of heightened tension between the supporters of any of our local clubs.'

From the corner of his eye he saw Charles Grey stiffen at this public contradiction, and decided to soften his response.

'However, I agree that we need to move swiftly to counteract some of the wild rumours circulating. Which brings us to the purpose of this meeting.'

He stared across the table at Caton, an unambiguous message in his eyes, and the expression on his face; *give me something to get this idiot off my back.*

It made Caton feel more like an ally than an underling. Something of a first with the upper echelons. He cleared his throat, took a sip of water from the glass in front of him, and composed himself.

'We are making progress, Sir,' he said. 'We have established that Sunday Okowu-Bello's death was neither accidental, nor suicidal. Forensic evidence is still being gathered and analysed. A number of possible motives have been established. Leads relating to those are being vigorously pursued.'

He was aware that he sounded like the archetypical civil servant, giving nothing away. But then he had no idea how much Charles Grey was entitled to know, and even less idea how much, if at all, he could trust him to keep it to himself. If his impromptu statement to the press on the day that Okowu-Bello's body was found was anything to go by, the less he knew the better.

'These motives,' the Commissioner said. 'What are they exactly?'

Caton looked to his Chief for help. None was forthcoming. He was staring fixedly ahead, avoiding eye contact. And then Caton thought he saw the faintest shake of his head. It was enough.

'Several,' he replied. 'Relate to his relationships with people close to him, and others are financial in nature.'

Charles Grey snorted derisively, but before he could press Caton for a detailed explanation the Police Commissioner intervened.

'You have to understand Charles,' he said, in a tone just this side of patronising. 'That there is a limit to what a senior investigation officer can share with us.'

Grey was not impressed. 'But you're The Chief Constable,' he said. 'Surely...'

'I am not in the habit of involving myself in day to day analysis of the progress of investigations Commissioner,' he said with studied patience. 'That would only serve to undermine the SIO's authority, and slow things down. The proper time and place for detail is if, and when, this investigation comes up for a progress review.'

'And when will that be?'

'Twenty eight days from the onset of the investigation, in line with the recommendations of the Association of Chief Police Officers of England, Wales and Northern Ireland. And only then if the murderer remains undetected.'

'What are we doing here then?' Grey demanded.

The Chief Constable smiled thinly. 'Responding to a request by you Charles, to impress on DCI Caton the need to bring this particular investigation to as speedy a resolution as possible, within the constraints of the Police and Criminal Evidence Act.'

It was a perfect rebuff that caused the Commissioner, a picture of frustration, to slump in his chair.

'What about the latest victim, is he connected?' asked Helen Gates, helping them all out.

'Phillip Ratten,' Caton replied. 'A member of the security firm employed by The Titans. He was on duty the night that Okowu-Bello died. He was supposed to be watching the CCTV screens. He disappeared before we were able to question him. So yes, although there is no similarity in the manner of their deaths, I am convinced that there is a connection.'

'He could have committed suicide, because he'd failed to do his job properly,' muttered the Commissioner.

Nobody took him on. It was so crass that Caton was surprised that he had voiced it.

The Chief Constable decided that he'd had enough, and neatly summed up.

'So we can tell the Media that the investigation is ongoing. That a number of witnesses have come forward, that progress is being made, and that anyone who has any information whatsoever should contact us, or Crime Stoppers, immediately.'

He was already pushing back his chair as Caton started to speak.

'Yes Sir.'

'Hampson was already on his feet.

'Good,' he said. 'Make sure you keep DCS Gates and Commander Hadfield up to speed Caton. We're relying on you to put this to bed PDQ.'

He strode to the door, held it open for the disgruntled Commissioner to pass through, and then pulled it to behind them.

'Pretty damned quick,' Hadfield translated, as though neither of the others had heard it before. 'Is that likely?'

Caton shook his head. 'If I'm honest, it's going to take longer than that.'

'How long?'

'I can't say,' he replied. 'You know how it is Sir.

When nobody's been placed at the scene of either of the murders, and what forensic evidence there is requires us to have someone to match it to, that takes time.'

'We don't have any time,'

'Come on Martin,' said Helen Gates. 'Tom's right. He can't just magic up a result because Grey's got his knickers in a twist.'

'*Commissioner* Grey!' said the Assistant Chief Constable Crime, sounding even more pompous and sycophantic than ever.

Gates turned to face Caton.

'We have discussed your request to involve the National Crime Agency,' she said. 'The Chief Constable didn't want to tell you in front of the Commissioner because Mr Grey was adamant that that they should not be involved. However, that was not his decision to make. When the time is right Mr Hampson will be content for you to do so.'

'But not yet?' said Caton.

'I'm afraid not. He wants to wait until your 72 Hour Review on the Okowu-Bello investigation, to see if there's still a need to involve them. If there is, be assured that he will.'

It was a decision that had clearly sat uncomfortably with Martin Hadfield. 'Just remember,' he muttered. 'That if and when we do, it'll be on a need to know basis only,' he said. 'We're not inviting them to muscle in on your investigation.'

'I understand,' said Caton.

All of the regional forces were still trying to work out where they stood in relation to the United Kingdom's answer to the FBI. The Serious and Organised Crime Agency had lasted less than three years, but the new kid on the block had the support of all the political parties and looked likely to be here to stay. They still had to work out how their role related to that of MI5, but it was only a matter of time before they turned their attention to high profile investigations such as his.

'In the meantime,' said Helen Gates, 'let's see if you can't put it to bed so we don't have to involve them at all.'

'I'll do my best,' Caton replied.

'Make sure you do,' she said, dismissing him with a tilt of her head.

He pushed back his chair and left them to it. They were still going at it hammer and tongs as he closed the door behind him. He made his way down the corridor wondering what the meeting had really been about, and what the hell was going on.

Chapter 16

Caton was two hours into his paperwork when Ged came to tell him that the post-mortem on Phillip Ratten was set for 2pm.

'Thanks Ged,' he said. 'Do you know where DI Holmes has got to?'

'He was in earlier, trying to contact Mr Okowu-Bello's agent,' she replied. 'When he didn't have any luck on the phone he decided to drive out to his home.'

'Where is it?'

'Alderley Edge.'

He might have guessed. The once quiet village in the Cheshire countryside had been popular with stockbrokers and Premiership footballers even before the Beckhams had set up residence. Since then it had doubled in size, even though Posh and Becks had long since left.

'Let me know the minute he calls in,' he told her.

'Two minutes later his phone rang.

'It's Mr Holmes, for you,' Ged told him.

'About time Gordon,' he began.

'He's dead,' said Holmes.

'The agent?'

'Joseph Gideon Jones. He's been shot. It looks like

he took a beating first, then they shot him.'

'Where?'

'In the head.'

'No, I mean where did it happen?'

'At his house.'

'In Alderley Edge?'

'I'm there now. The pathologist's on his way, and SOCO's already here with me.'

'Not Jack Benson I hope?'

After several high profile bungles elsewhere in the force, each resulting in the collapse of an otherwise perfectly sound prosecution, Caton was acutely aware of the need to avoid cross contamination of the different crime scenes. Fortunately, so was DI Holmes.

'Course not,' he said. 'What do you take me for?'

Gordon Holmes had been busy. The house and grounds had already been secured. Two officers, neither of whom Caton recognised, stood by the gates, one of them keeping the record of everyone who entered the property.

Detective Inspector Holmes is in the master bedroom on the second floor Sir,' she told him. 'He said to go straight up.'

He parked beside the other police vehicles, and the mortuary van, on a stretch of gravel like a lay-by, 40 metres from the side of the house.

'The Scene of Crime Manager asks that you keep to the right hand edge of the drive,' a police community support officer advised him. 'There are tyre tracks he wants preserved.'

Caton could see deep parallel ruts in the centre of the gravel leading up to the front of the faux Georgian mansion. Something heavy, and big, like a Range Rover, or a Humvee.

He had to pick his way past several forensics officers gathering evidence on the stairs. He paused on the first floor landing. All of the doors to rooms leading from it were open, and the interiors were in disarray. Either SOCO were getting heavy handed or the place had been ransacked.

One flight up, Joseph Gideon Jones, dressed in black narrow legged trousers, a black silk polo neck, and an oatmeal three-quarter length coat, lay sprawled across a super King-sized bed, beneath a yellow silk canopy that hung from a hoop suspended from the ceiling.

'It wasn't mosquitoes that killed him,' said Gordon Holmes.

That much was evident. The agent's face was a bloody mess. Not quite as bad as that of the unfortunate Phil Ratten, but his jaw was either broken or dislocated, his nose had been flattened, and both eyes were so badly swollen that it was impossible to see if they were closed or open. It was the ugly hole in his head that was the clincher. The half inch, jagged edged cavity, was surrounded by hair matted with blood. More blood, and what looked like watery grey tissue, had pooled beneath and around his head. The front of his coat was a tapestry of burnt sienna, against the grey-brown cloth.

Holmes pulled the curtain of silk a little further back on its hoop to enable Caton to view the body more closely.

'Dr Hope reckons he was still alive when he was shot,' he said.

Jean Hope, the assisting pathologist to Professor Flatman during the Bojangles investigation. All that Caton could remember about her was those serious, penetrating brown eyes behind her surgical mask.

'Has something happened to Mr Douglas?'

'Seminar in Florence,' said Holmes. 'Lucky sod.'

Caton had noticed that Gordon's propensity for swear words seemed to increase in the presence of violent death. He had long ago accepted that it was a more acceptable reaction than some he had come across.

'Was she prepared to hazard an estimate of the time of death?' he asked.

'Somewhere between midnight and five am. Although if his watch is anything to go by...' he pointed at Jones's left wrist where his sleeve had ridden up to expose a smart watch with a black face, red gold case, and black crocodile leather strap. '...I'd say nearer four am.'

Caton bent closer. The glass was cracked, and the hands were frozen at seven minutes to the hour. It was reasonable to assume that Jones had raised his arm early in the attack to defend himself, and the blow had smashed the watch.

'The witching hour,' said Holmes.

Caton straightened up.

'You're confusing that with the median hour for house burglaries,' he said. 'I think you'll find the witching hour is three am.'

'Who says?'

'Father Richard Moore in *The Exorcism of Emily Rose*. When he claims that the witching hour is three am, in direct opposition to three pm, when Jesus Christ was crucified, and also mocking the holy trinity. Three pm is the hour of God's mercy; three am is the devil's hour, the hour of darkness.'

'You watch too many films,' said Holmes.

Far from being a distraction Caton found this banter helpful. It was another way in which they distanced themselves emotionally from the horror of what must have happened in this room. He stepped back to gain a wider perspective.

Scene of Crime had already marked up areas of particular interest. The ensuite bedroom door was open, and he could see a smudge of blood on the white wall tiles, with two thin trails six or seven centimetres long. Drips of blood ran from the ensuite towards the right-hand foot of the bed where they were lost in large sticky stain over a foot in diameter on the carpet. The bed rail was bent back at angle of forty five degrees. Spatters of blood stained the side of the canopy, the counterpane, and the carpet. The victim's body lay backwards across the lower half of the bed. Black stockinged feet dangled over the bottom of the bedstead. His trousers were at half-mast.

'Looks like he took his shoes off in the hall, which is where we found them, made his way up here, and went into the ensuite for a pee. They caught him pulling his trousers up, smashed his head against the wall, and dragged him over to the foot of the bed. That's where they beat him up. Then they pushed him back onto the bed, and shot him in the head.'

'How do you know they didn't shoot him standing up, and he fell back onto the bed?'

'From the blood spatter patterns, and because the bullet was tangled in the counterpane where it had tried to exit.'

He consulted his notes.

'It looks like it was a 9mm hollow point cartridge.'

He spotted the Scene of Crime Manager hovering by the door and called him in.

'Have you got the cartridge with you?' he said.

The officer produced a brown paper evidence bag that had been labelled, but had not yet been sealed. Inside was a cylindrical cardboard box, also labelled, that could easily have contained pills. He removed the lid.

Inside nestled an object that to the untrained eye might have been mistaken for a piece of modern jewellery. A brooch, or a pendant perhaps, in the shape of a flower. Like the ones that Caton had so carefully dissected at Manchester Grammar School. Copper coloured metal, twisted into the shape of petals, surrounded a silvery blue mound. Under any other circumstances Caton would have deemed it beautiful, but pieces of brain matter, and splinters of skull, adhering to the petals spoilt the illusion.

Expanding to more than three times its normal size the hollow point bullet would have fragmented on entry, delivering enormous power that had devastated Jones's brain. It said a great deal, Caton knew, about the person who had pulled the trigger. This kind of bullet was favoured by only three types of person: police, armed services and security services personnel who needed to know that the recipient would be stopped first time, and unable to return fire; hunters of medium to large size game; and serious criminals who wanted to leave a message to others considered a danger to themselves or their organisation.

'Thanks,' he said. He let the officer put the lid back on the box and seal the bag. 'Do you know how they gained entry?'

'There's no sign of forced entry, so unless he let them in himself, they must have had a key. The alarm wasn't on.'

'That was probably the last thing on his mind if he needed a pee.' Holmes pointed out.

'You said *they*?'

The crime scene manager nodded. 'At least two, possibly three. We have footprints on the stairs, in here, and in several of the other rooms. Some of them have blood in the treads, presumably picked up when they were doing what they did in here.'

'It looks as though some of the rooms have been searched.' said Caton.

'The entire house has been ransacked. It must have taken them at least an hour.' He smiled ruefully. 'The Drug Squad couldn't have done a better job.'

'Does it look as though they've taken anything?'

'The only things we can be certain about are his PC, and a lap top. The wires are still dangling from the sockets for the PC, and the monitor screen is still there.'

He pointed across the room to an easy chair on which lay a yellow and black Timberland lap top bag.

'He had an Apple Mac Power Book. The power lead and the charger are still there, but everything else has gone, including the printer.'

'He must have put his bag down there when he went through to the loo,' Holmes surmised.

'Have you found any storage devices? USB flash drives, discs, CDs, hard drive backup hardware?' asked Caton.

'No, and what's more they appear to have taken every shred of paperwork with them. He had an office, with a bank of filing cabinets. The drawers are open, and every one of them is empty.'

'They'll have needed a humongous boot to cart that lot off,' said Holmes.

Caton pictured the tyre tracks in the gravelled drive. Not a Landrover then. Probably something like a Transit van.

'What about his mobile phone?' he asked. 'As an agent I doubt it would ever have left his side.'

'Well it has now,' said his DI. 'The only thing he had on him was his watch.'

'What about other high value goods, like televisions, Blue-ray, DVD and Home Cinema, music systems, iPods, Xbox, Nintendo Wii, iPad?'

'All still here, except for the last one. If he had an iPad or an equivalent tablet, it's gone.'

'Did you find a safe?'

The crime scene manager shook his head. 'But we weren't looking for one. Everything I've described was observed when I was planning the order in which to recommend to you the preservation and collection of evidence. You'll have to ask your search team to look for specifics.'

It could easily have been taken as a rebuke, but it wasn't; it was simply a statement of fact.

The officer caught Caton in the act of trying to read his name tag, and grinned.

'Detective Sergeant Brian Roberts,' he said.

Caton smiled to put him at his ease. 'Fair enough,' he said. 'So tell me, what have you got so far?'

It amounted to quite a lot. Aside from the tyre tracks, the bullet, and the footprint, there was a palm print with what looked like a smear of blood, on the chrome handle of a toilet in a bedroom on the first floor. Even better, the toilet had not been flushed. And as Roberts pointed out, given all the violence that had taken place in the bedroom there was every chance they'd find sweat and saliva belonging to the perpetrators. There was also an anomaly.

'We haven't found any other cameras yet,' said Roberts. 'But there was a camcorder on his desk. Right in the middle, where the computer keyboard would have been.'

'Almost as though they wanted you to find it?' said Caton.

'That's what I thought,' the crime scene manager replied. 'I had it swabbed and tested for prints straight away. It's bagged up, but I set aside something I thought you might want to take with you.'

It turned out to be a transparent evidence bag with a chain of custody record attached. Inside nestled a SanDisk memory card. It was the kind of anomaly that lifted Caton's spirits.

'Dirty beggar,' said Holmes as they made their way towards their cars. 'Not flushing that toilet. And you'd think he'd have had the sense to leave his gloves on.'

'Have you ever tried to undo your flies with gloves on?' Caton replied.

'That's true. Or maybe they know they're not on our radar, so we won't be able to match their fingerprints or their DNA.'

'Until we catch them.'

'So they must be confident that we're not going to.'

Caton opened the boot of his Skoda and sat on the rim while he slipped off his Tyvek coverall, gloves, mask, and over shoes, and placed them in a polythene bag for collection. Then he closed the boot, and opened the driver's door. Holmes was still struggling out of his all-in-one.

'Let's prove them wrong Gordon,' Caton said. 'But first we'd better make sure that Okowu-Bello's accountant doesn't end up like Jones.'

'If he isn't already dead,' Holmes replied.

Caton shook his head.

'You can be a right Job's comforter.'

'Think how relieved you'll be when it turns out he isn't.' Holmes crumpled up his Tyvek and tossed it into his boot.

So much for Gordon having got the message about cross-contamination Caton reflected as he drove away.

Outside the gates the first of the media had arrived. He counted two television video units, six paparazzi, three of whom still had their motorcycle helmets on their heads, and several newspaper journalists he knew by name. They circled his car like piranhas as he nudged his way through them, his eyes fixed firmly on the road ahead.

Chapter 17

Caton arrived back at the incident room to discover that every one of his core team was out. Joanne Stuart had taken his place at Ratten's post mortem. Holmes had stayed behind at the victim's house to task the Tactical Aid search team, and DS Carter had located Okowu-Bello's accountant and was bringing him in for questioning. Caton went straight to his desk and booted up his computer.

He eased the SanDisk from the evidence bag with a pair of plastic tweezers from his murder bag. Despite the fact that that the disk had been dusted and swabbed it was still vital not to give the prosecution any opportunity to cry foul. He slid the disk into the slot on the side of the printer, and waited for the prompt to play the video.

He was presented with a grey shade image typical of CCTV cameras everywhere, with a date and time along the bottom edge. He recognised it instantly as the date on which Okowu-Bello had died. The time showed 2.07am. At first all that he could make out was a flat surface that looked like tarmacadam. The camera panned out as a car entered the picture, and stopped. The camera zoomed in on the license plate and then moved a fraction up and to the left where it captured the face of the driver exiting the car. It was unmistakeably the face of Joseph Gideon Jones, as it would have been before he had been beaten and shot to death. The reason that Caton could be sure was the photographs lining the hallway in the agent's mansion. Photos showing him with various footballers, one with Gerry Packer the Titan's manager, and one in a dress suit shaking hands with a minor member of the royal family.

The camera panned out, and remained fixed on the car which Caton could now see was a Jaguar. No doubt Holmes would be able to tell him the model, price on the road, and full spec. None of which would have been relevant. Suddenly the time skipped a full hour and twenty minutes. Twenty seconds later Jones appeared again. He paused for a moment, turned, and looked back in the direction from which he had come. Then he waved to someone off camera, opened the car door and got in. The car headlights came on; the car reversed, straightened up, and drove away.

Caton sat back and thought about what he had seen. He knew what it was supposed to be telling him, but it didn't feel right. He pressed play again, this time intent on looking for anomalies.

This time when it was finished he was even more certain that the footage was suspect. Nothing in Jones's body language, either arriving or leaving, had indicated any kind of tension. The lights on the Jaguar had not been on when the car arrived, only when it left, which was consistent with the change in lighting conditions between the two sequences, but not with the middle of the night. And there was something else he could not put his finger on.

He got up and walked across the room to where Duggie Wallace, the senior collator, and crime intelligence analyst who had miraculously been returned to his team, was bent over his keyboard.

'If you get any closer to the screen you're going to

go blind Duggie,' Caton told him.

Wallace turned round and looked up at him. He grinned, and pointed to the pair of brand new spectacles perched on his roman nose.

'Too late Boss,' he said. 'I'm half way there already.'

'Well before they go completely I want you to come and have a look at something.'

Wallace spotted it immediately.

'Do they think we're stupid?' he said pointing at the lower half of the screen.

'Clearly I am,' said Caton who hadn't the faintest idea what he had missed.

'No Boss, I wouldn't have expected you to pick it up, but anyone who works with video would spot it straight away.'

He drew his finger along the day date line at the bottom of the screen.

'It's a date switch, intended to make you think this was taken on the night Okowu-Bello was killed.'

'And it wasn't?'

'No way. First of all you can tell from the change in light conditions that the first section was taken in dusk rather than at night. Secondly, this isn't an original recording. Someone has taken a video of a piece of CCTV footage, possibly even two pieces of footage, one for each sequence.'

'How can you tell?'

'They've been very clever, and tried their best to exclude any reflections on the screen on which the footage was being played when they filmed it, but there are several places where the camera they were using moved, and the original footage didn't.' He shook his head. 'They should have used a tripod.'

'And that's it?'

'No. The clincher is the size, font, and positioning of the day and date on this footage. You forget, I saw some of the CCTV footage from the stadium. The font is larger, and it appears lower down the screen. They've switched on the date and time record on their own camera, changed the settings to the night in question, and then filmed the upper three quarters of CCTV footage from the stadium to cut out the original date and time.'

'Why didn't they just delete it before starting to film?'

'Because they couldn't. The original was from a security camera. The date and time would have been embedded to stop people from faking the results.'

Now Caton could see what had been bugging him. The size of the picture was that much smaller than the ones he had seen on the screens in the Titan's CCTV suite.

'So they wanted us to think that Jones had been there that night, when in fact this is almost certainly a separate occasion when he had been at the club?'

Wallace sat back in the chair.

'Almost certainly, but not definitely. On the other hand, why would they have gone to the trouble of pulling this stunt if it had been taken on the night in question?'

'Is there any way we can find out when it was taken.'

'By going back through all of the footage from the CCTV cameras covering that sector of the stadium – assuming we can work out which sector it was. And that's assuming Jones always parked in the same spot.'

Caton couldn't see any point in it. The footage had been planted to try and implicate Jones in his client's murder. Wallace had blown it out of the water. The one thing it had done was help to explain why Ratten had to die. Not only had he been on duty the night that CCTV cameras had mysteriously failed to work, but he had access to the CCTV suite and could easily have created this fake for the murderers. The question was why had he done it, and for whom?

'Thanks Duggie,' he said.

'My pleasure,' said the analyst standing up and stretching. 'They have done you a favour though.'

'Go on.'

'I reckon they've given you a much more accurate indication of the time Okowu-Bello was placed in that van.'

Caton watched him make his way back to his beloved computer. He was right of course. Why would they bother to superimpose a time on that footage unless they already knew when the victim had been murdered?

He was still trying to figure out how, if at all, this helped what was now a multiple murder investigation when the door to the incident room swung open, and Detective Sergeant Nick Carter waved to him from the doorway.

'Lucky for him he was visiting his sister,' said Carter as they walked down the corridor to the temporary interview room. 'He arrived back this morning to find a police car waiting outside. Couple of hours earlier and instead of me it could have been whoever killed the agent.'

'Were there any other cars around when the locals arrived?' said Caton.

'There was a four-by-four halfway down the street that drove off just before the uniforms pulled up. They didn't get the registration but I've already got someone trawling through the traffic cameras in the vicinity to see if we can identify it.'

Caton paused outside the door.

'What have you told him?'

'That we believe he may be in some danger, and we need to speak to him urgently.'

'How's he taken it?'

'He's as nervous as a nun at a penguin cull.'

''That's verging on religious intolerance,' Caton told him. 'You've been spending too much time with DI Holmes.'

Carter grinned. 'Verging,' he said. 'As in verger. That's very good Boss.'

'No,' said Caton. 'I'm serious. Next time try as nervous as a cat on a hot tin roof.'

'How about solar panels?'

Caton sighed. What was it they said about familiarity breeding contempt?

'I want you to join me on this one Nick,' he told him. 'You can take on Gordon's role. But don't overdo it. OK?'

'Trust me Boss,' said Carter as he opened the door.

Angus Macleod jumped in his chair, and twisted round to face them. His appearance took Caton by surprise. It wasn't just the sweat on his brow or the fear in his eyes. He was of South Asian heritage.

Caton could feel Carter's eyes on him, watching for his reaction. It was the price he paid for the standards he expected of his team that his own were a subject of continuous scrutiny.

'I am not going to beat around the bush,' Caton told the accountant when the formalities were over. 'There are three deaths already connected with this investigation, and I do not want you to become the fourth. So if you are ready to be completely honest with us, I promise you that I'll do everything in my power to see that you come to no harm.'

The alternative was left unspoken. The threat implied. MacLeod caved in immediately.

'I'll tell you what I know,' he said. 'But I want my solicitor present.'

It suited Caton. That way they could read him his rights, and have it all on the record. It was pointless hoping he'd tell them more if he wasn't under caution and nothing was recorded, because then none of it would be admissible in court. Swings and roundabouts, that was the Police and Criminal Evidence Act under which they laboured. Swings and roundabouts.

While they waited for the solicitor to arrive Caton caught up on the post mortem results with Detective Sergeant Stuart who had only just returned.

'I can give you the headlines,' she told him. 'But the written report won't be with us till the day after tomorrow.'

'Why's that?' he asked.

She screwed up her nose as though a dirty smell was trapped beneath it.

'Because the attending pathologist was Professor Flatman.'

This explained everything. Not only was he a law unto himself, but his overtly sexist behaviour towards Joanne Stuart at her first autopsy would almost certainly have veered in the opposite direction once he'd learned that she was a lesbian.

'Why didn't Dr Hope do it?'

'Because she isn't yet on the list of Home Office forensic pathologists.'

'Pity,'

'Tell me about it.'

'So what was the verdict?'

She consulted her notebook, looked thoughtful, and put on her serious face.

'Apparently Ratten was murdered.'

Caton managed not to laugh. But she was entitled to let off steam after an hour or so in the morgue with Flatman.

'Thank heavens for that,' said Caton. 'I was wondering how he'd managed to jump in the ship canal with all that concrete in the bottom of his tarpaulin.'

'It wasn't that that killed him, he was dead before he went in. He'd been shot. In the face.'

'So it wasn't the propeller the chewed up his face?'

'Yes and no, but mainly no. There were minor post mortem injuries, presumably caused when his body was moved, wrapped up, and dumped in the river. The most severe of these was decapitation. Professor Flatman was not able to identify the cause but the nature of three successive cuts made at oblique angles would, in his professional opinion, be consistent with the blades of the rapidly spinning propeller.'

She looked up.

'It's just as well he was already dead.'

'It's also good to know that Mr Douglas isn't infallible,' he said.

'Better not let the jury hear you say that,' she responded.

Caton supposed that depended on whether Douglas was appearing for the prosecution or the defence.

'Was the Professor able to determine the calibre of the cartridge?'

She shook her head. 'No. But he says from the nature of the damage it caused it was almost certainly flat nosed rather than round nosed.'

'My bet is a 9 millimetre hollow point bullet,' he said.

'What makes you say that Sir?'

'You won't have heard. Joseph Gideon Jones, Okowu-Bello's agent, is dead. He was shot in the head, with a...'

'9 millimetre hollow point bullet,' she said. 'Blimey, they're going down like flies,'

'You have to understand,' said Angus MacLeod. 'I was acting under instructions.'

If Caton had a hundred pounds for every time he'd heard that sentence he'd have been a rich man. All those who used this defence thought it guaranteed immunity. From Adolf Eichmann excusing his part in the Holocaust, to the teenagers who were the street corner eyes and ears of the drug dealers. Caton had learned that it didn't help to disabuse them of them the notion. Not until they'd dug themselves deep into the midden.

'Go on,' he said.

'Joseph Gideon Jones introduced me to Okowu-Bello when he first arrived in the UK. I work for a lot of footballers. Most of them Joseph's clients.'

He looked nervously at his legal representative. It was the same solicitor who had represented the footballer Marcello Barcello in the Bluebell Hollow investigation. He had given Caton plenty of leeway on that occasion. The solicitor nodded for MacLeod to continue.

'From the outset, the arrangement was that ten percent of his monthly salary was paid by electronic transfer to a bank account in Lagos. The remainder, less ten thousand pounds for day to day expenses, went into a separate Nigerian bank account from which all of his direct debits and credit cards were paid.'

'Who owned the account in Lagos?'

'Sunday's sponsors.'

'The people who signed him up as a youth player in Nigeria?'

'That's right.'

'Isn't that illegal?' said DI Carter. 'For them to claim a continuing right to a percentage of his earnings as a senior player under contract to other clubs?'

He shrugged. 'Lots of things are illegal but they still go on. If FIFA or UEFA, or even the FA had questioned it Sunday would have said it was a private arrangement. Nothing to do with a contract. It was obvious that he had to pay up, or suffer the consequences.'

'Did he tell you that?' said Caton.

'Not in so many words. When I asked him about it he said. '*You don't want to know my friend. Just do it. It's safer this way.*'

The other account. Was he trying to avoid paying tax?'

'No. Like all foreign sportsman and entertainers the tax was deducted at source, by the club.'

Carter looked puzzled, and leaned forward.

'So why did he put it in a Nigerian Bank?'

'He said it was because he wanted to support the economy of his own country.'

Caton picked up on the hesitance with which he said it.

'But it wasn't?'

'No. He'd been ordered to use that bank by his so called sponsors.'

'So let me guess,' said Caton. 'In addition to collecting the ten percent, they were getting a cut back from the bank too?'

'It was a small bank,' said MacLeod. 'They probably had a share in it, in which case they were using his capital to boost their assets and keep their operations liquid.'

'You said it *was* a small bank.'

'Six months ago I received instructions to stop the payments into either account. Instead I was to see that the whole of his salary was paid into a UK account, with two signatories. Sunday, and Joseph Gideon Jones.'

'Told by whom?'

'By his agent.'

'Joseph Gideon Jones?'

'Yes.'

'Did you query that with Sunday?'

He nodded vigorously. 'Of course.'

'What did he say?'

'To go ahead. He didn't look too happy about it though.'

'His sponsors won't have been too happy?' said Carter.

He looked at his solicitor as though expecting a response. When none was forthcoming he responded to the DI's question.

'I don't know anything about that,' he massaged his left hand with his right. 'But that Nigerian Bank, where his money was. It suddenly went into liquidation.'

'What about Mr Okowu-Bello's money?' said Caton?

'It disappeared. He lost it all. I'm still trying to recover it.'

'How much are we talking about?'

The accountant stared down at the desk in front of him. When he spoke it was barely audible. Caton had to ask him to repeat it.

'Twelve million,' he said.

'Pounds?' said Caton wondering if he had heard properly.

MacLeod nodded and looked up.

'That's right. Twelve million, three hundred and seventy seven pounds.

'Bloody hell!' said Carter. 'No wonder he was desperate for cash.'

Chapter 18

'Tell me about Nutmeg Holdings,' said Caton.

The accountant was unable to hide his surprise. It was pointless him trying to pretend that that he didn't know what the detective was talking about.

'That was where the other money went,' he said.

'Other money?'

'Any income outside of his wages.'

'Unearned income?'

'Some of it.'

'What does that mean?'

MacLeod turned to his solicitor.

'Look,' he said. 'This had nothing to do with me. I wanted no part of it. This was between Joseph Gideon Jones, and Sunday Okowu-Bello.'

'Then you have nothing to worry about do you Mr MacLeod?' said Nick Carter.

The accountant began to massage his hand again. A twitch had developed under his left eye. Caton hoped he wasn't having a minor stroke. That was all he needed.

'I want immunity,' the accountant pleaded.

'From what?' said Caton.

'From prosecution.'

'Who said anything about prosecution?' Carter said. 'You haven't been charged with anything.'

Now he looked thoroughly confused. The massaging

had moved to his upper arm fuelling Caton's concern.

'Well, protection then,' he said. 'I want protection.'

'Which is it? Immunity or protection?' said Caton.

'Both,' he replied.

Carter laughed. 'Don't be greedy Angus,' he said.

'That's enough,' said the solicitor making his presence felt for the first time. 'You're badgering my client. Do I need to remind you that he is here voluntarily, assisting you with your investigation?'

'You're quite right,' said Caton. 'And we are very grateful to Mr. MacLeod, aren't we Detective Sergeant Carter?'

'We are indeed,' said Carter.

'Perhaps we should have a little break,' said Caton. 'So that Mr MacLeod can have a chat with you in private, while we go and arrange for some drinks. How would that be?'

'I thought I told you not to overdo it?'

They were making their way back to the interview room, with a tray of hot drinks and a plate of biscuits.

'Sorry Boss,' said Carter. 'I just got a bit carried away.'

Caton shook his head. 'It was scary. Just like DI Holmes had inhabited your body.'

'Now that *is* scary.' Carter pushed a fire door open with his shoulder, adjusting the tray to stop the liquid from slopping over. 'It's not us he's frightened of, is it?'

'No, and I imagine the tax man is the least of his worries. He's holding back on something. Let's hope giving him take up time has paid off.'

The accountant's solicitor had a statement ready.

He launched straight into it.

'My client,' he said. 'Is willing to continue to assist you with your investigation providing that you are willing to provide him with a written notice of immunity from prosecution, under Section 71 of the Serious Organised Crime and Police Act 2005.'

'I can't...' Caton began, but the lawyer had not finished.

'He also requires to be entered into the witness protection programme.'

Caton lifted his mug to his lips and took a long drink of hot water. He placed the mug down carefully, and leaned back in his chair.

'There are a couple of problems with that,' he said. 'In the written notice I would have to specify the offence, or offences, against which your client would be promised that no proceedings would be brought. Furthermore, I would have to satisfy myself, and my superiors, that the information your client is willing to provide would be of such value that it would justify immunity. And that such information, would in all likelihood lead to the successful prosecution of other more serious offences.'

The solicitor was about to respond but Caton held up his hand to signal that there was more.

'I would also have to determine if any such written notice of immunity should emanate from the Director of Public Prosecutions, the Director of Revenue and Customs Prosecutions, or the Director of the Serious Fraud Office.'

Once again the lawyer tried to butt in, and was rebuffed.

'As for witness protection,' Caton continued. 'We would have to be convinced that your client's perceived threat against him is in fact real.'

He folded his arms to signal that he was finished.

'Of course it's real!' the accountant exclaimed. 'Sunday's dead, Jones's dead. What more do you need?'

'Don't forget Phil Ratten,' said Caton watching him closely. 'He's dead too.'

MacLeod's face paled at the news of another murder, but showed no sign of having recognised the name.

'Who?'

'Phillip Ratten,' Carter told him. 'He worked for the security team at the Quanxi stadium.'

'There you are then,' he said,' as though it all made sense. 'You've got to protect me.'

'Look,' said Caton patiently, as though explaining to a child. 'You tell us what you know that you think is placing you at risk, and we'll tell you if that's sufficient for us to arrange witness protection for you.'

'But you said before...you promised...' MacLeod began, but did not finish. It had dawned on him that what these two police officers had said about him being in danger, and about doing their best to protect him, had been said without any witnesses, and without the tape switched on. His word against theirs, and his solicitors.

'And provided,' Caton continued. 'That what you have to tell us turns out to be vital to this investigation, and that you are prepared to give evidence in court on behalf of any subsequent prosecution, then we'll see about that notice of indemnity.'

He held out his hands as though offering a gift.

The accountant looked like a man trapped by indecision.

'Ask your solicitor,' said Caton kindly. 'He'll tell you.'

The two of them went into a huddle, their heads together like conjoined twins. It took less than thirty seconds of furtive whispering for him to make up his mind.

'I'll tell you,' he said.

'Good man,' said Caton. 'Why don't you drink your coffee first, we've plenty of time?'

Carter placed the plate and the four mugs on the trays, and pushed them to one side. Tape or no tape, the last thing they needed was spillage over their notes.

'Let's start with your reply to my question about Sunday's unearned income,' said Caton. 'What did you mean by *some of it*?'

'Those accounts in Belize, Nutmeg Holdings,' he said. 'That's where Jones put the under the table bungs that he and Sunday negotiated every time there was a transfer deal. Then there was money from advertising and other kinds of sponsorship with companies outside of the United Kingdom. They didn't pay any tax on it, or declare it to Sunday's so called sponsors back home in Nigeria.'

'How much are we talking about?' said Caton.

MacLeod shrugged. 'I've no idea. Jones handled all of that himself, but it must have run into millions. Not as much as he had in that Nigerian bank, but more than enough.'

'So why was he so desperate for money to pay back the casinos?'

'Because he needed Jones's approval, and his signature to get at those funds. My guess is Joseph would have tied a lot of it up in investments, and been loath to encourage Sunday's gambling which was spiralling out of control.'

'So they would have argued about that?' said Carter.

The accountant nodded. 'Jones said as much. He

told Sunday to sell one of his cars first. He said Sunday went off on one. He wanted me to try and talk some sense into him.'

'Did you?'

'I tried. He didn't want to know. He just stormed off. Next thing, he was flush with money again, and all sweetness and light.'

Caton was puzzled. 'When was this?'

'About three months ago.'

'Let me get this straight,' said Caton. 'He stops paying his sponsors, loses all of his money in the bank in Nigeria, has to go cap in hand to his agent for spends, and then all of a sudden he has lots of cash, and is building up credit with the bookies and the casinos?'

'That's right.'

'So where was the money coming from?'

'I'm not sure, but it's even stranger than you think.'

'You need to explain that.'

'That UK account that his wages were going into, the one that needed both their signatures? Well there was a regular monthly BACS transfer to an account in Eastern Europe.'

'How large?'

'Fifty thousand pounds.'

'BACS?' said Carter.

'Banks Automated Clearing System. An automatic electronic transfer between banks,' explained Caton. He turned back to MacLeod. 'Where in Eastern Europe?'

'Romania. A numbered account. But I would be surprised if it's the final destination for the payments.'

'Why do you say that?'

'Romania is a country with a tradition for money laundering, but it has come under increasing scrutiny from the World bank, and the country's own regulatory systems. My guess is that the money doesn't stay there long.'

'We need the details of both of the UK accounts, and the BACS transfer details.' Caton told him.

'Of course.'

Caton mulled it over.

'We've been led to understand that Sunday was paying his sponsors because they'd threatened to retaliate against his family back in Lagos if he didn't pay them.'

'That was my understanding,' the accountant agreed.

'So what happened when he stopped paying?'

Macleod shook his head. 'Apart from the bank closing down, and him losing all of his money, I've no idea.'

There was silence in the room as they all tried to make sense of it. It was Angus Macleod who broke the silence.

'What about my immunity?' he said.

Caton folded his arms. He wasn't being defensive; it was just that he wanted to give as little away as possible.

'It's a little early for that,' he replied. 'I think that even your solicitor will agree that what you've given us so far in the way of information doesn't amount to anything that would remotely leave you open to prosecution. Nor does it help us to identify anyone else we could charge with a parking offence let alone murder. If you want immunity, you need to up your game, and give us something meaningful.'

'That's not fair Detective Chief Inspector,' said the solicitor. 'Mr MacLeod has been completely honest with you, and...'

'With all due respect,' said Caton. 'My barber is completely honest with me, but that isn't enough for me to give him immunity from prosecution.'

He closed his notebook and flipped over the cover

of the file in front of him.

'But you've got to protect me,' the accountant pleaded, reaching across the table and grabbing Caton's sleeve.

Caton took hold of his wrist, and eased it free.

'Tut tut,' he said sliding his chair backwards, and standing up. 'Now there's something we can charge you with; assaulting a police officer.'

'They got Sunday off the hook with his sponsors...made them go away,' said MacLeod his voice charged with desperation.

Caton, Carter by his side, stood looking down at him, and waited.

'The East Europeans,' the accountant said. 'They threatened the Nigerian gangsters. Gave them an example of what would happen if they didn't back off.'

'And let them walk off with a cool twelve million?' said Carter sceptically.

He shook his head. 'I don't think that was supposed to happen.'

'I bet it wasn't,' said Caton sitting down again, and signalling Carter to do the same. 'So what was in it for these mysterious East Europeans?'

The accountant shuffled uneasily in his chair. 'There was the fifty thousand pounds a month to start with. Sunday told me it was for his personal security. In return they would provide bodyguards, and deal with any threats to his privacy or safety.'

'Like the Nigerian gang,' said Carter.

'What other threats?' said Caton.

'Stalking, paparazzi, people looking to rob his property, looking to pick a fight with him in town just because of who he was. That sort of thing. They said he could claim it against tax. That's how I found out. He wanted to know if that was true.'

'What did you tell him?'

'That it was, on condition that he could prove that they were actually providing a service?'

'And were they? Aside from seeing off the Nigerian gang?'

'Yes.'

Caton was unable to keep his incredulity from showing in his voice. 'Are you saying That Sunday Okowu-Bello had his own private bodyguards?'

'Yes.'

'They didn't do a very good job then did they?' said Carter.

'Where were they the night that Sunday died?' said Caton.

MacLeod shrugged.

'I have no idea.'

'Did you ever meet them?'

'No, not to speak to, but I saw them on a number of occasions. Following him in their car. Waiting outside when he came to see me. They kept a low profile.'

'I suppose you're going to tell us that you couldn't describe them?'

MacLeod surprised them.

'I can, but only if you're going to protect me.'

He sat back in his chair, folded his arms, and waited.

Chapter 19

'Witness protection?' said Gordon Holmes. 'Not immunity?'

'No,' Caton replied. 'As far as I can tell he's admitted to nothing that might incriminate him. He's organised tax avoidance on behalf of Okowu-Bello perhaps, but that's not a crime.'

'What about the money that was going into the accounts in Belize?' said Carter. 'That's deceit, concealment and subterfuge, so tax evasion surely?'

'He claims that was down to Joseph Gideon Jones, the agent. The accounts are owned by Nutmeg Holdings remember.'

'He wouldn't be asking for immunity if he wasn't up to it in his armpits,' reasoned Holmes.

'Maybe,' said Caton. 'We'll let HMRC figure that one out. In the meantime, let's see if we can make some sense of this.'

He led them over to the four white boards that now took up almost a third of one wall of the incident room.

On each of the first three was a photograph of one of the three victims, with notes highlighting key evidence, unanswered questions, and actions underway. On the remaining board were three columns, headed *The Nigerian Gang*, *Manc Security Ltd* and *The East Europeans.*

'We have a Nigerian gang that had been extorting large sums from Okowu-Bello for years. A shadowy East European organisation that muscles in and takes over that role, whilst dressing it up as a legitimate protection service. And finally, we have an actual security firm responsible for protecting the club and its assets.

'And none of them was able to stop someone from killing Okowu-Bello,' said Holmes, stating the obvious.

'Worse than that,' Caton reminded them. 'That someone had help from within the security firm. They either infiltrated it, or applied sufficient threat to persuade an insider to help them out.'

'Insiders,' said Carter.

They turned to look at him.

'Well it's unlikely that Ratten was the only one involved,' he said. 'It needed someone who knew how to operate the cryogenic unit. And it needed someone who could make sure than none of the other security guards on duty that night stumbled across the killers when they took Okowu-Bello, when they put him in the van, and while they made their escape.'

He pointed to the first of the boards with Okowu-Bello's photo at the top.

'Those two missing security guys for a start. Mark Shawcross & Paul Barlow; we still haven't traced them.'

'We know that at least two of the deaths are connected,' said Holmes. 'Nine millimetre flat nose cartridges. That has all the hallmarks of a professional hit man. Maybe they were contract killings.'

'That would fit the Nigerians and the East Europeans,' said Carter.

'And the motive?' asked Caton.

'That's easy,' said Holmes. 'Revenge for the Nigerians.'

'And what about the East Europeans?' said Caton. 'Wouldn't they be killing the goose that laid the golden egg now that they'd prised Okowu-Bello away from the Nigerians?'

The three of them stood looking at the boards for a full minute without speaking.

'There's something we're missing,' said Caton at last. 'We simply don't have enough information. So this is what I suggest we do. I want the families of Ratten, Shawcross and Barlow interviewed again. We need to know if any pressure had been applied, and by whom. We find out everything we can about the East European security organisation and what the hell happened to the men they had guarding Okowu-Bello. And I'm going to have to get permission to involve the National Crime Agency.'

Holmes pulled a face.

'Are you sure you want to do that Boss? The Chief won't be happy, and you told me the Commissioner was dead set against it.'

'I doubt they're happy that we now have three murders, and we're no further forward in solving the first one,' Caton replied wearily. 'What choice have I got? We don't have the resources to do this ourselves, nor do we have the clout to get Her Majesty's Revenue and Customs off their backsides and taking it seriously. The NCA do. They can also find out about the Nigerian gang, something that would take us forever.'

Holmes rubbed his chin vigorously. 'Good luck with that Boss,' he said.

Caton sat with the phone in his hand wondering how best to set up a meeting with whomever it would take to get permission to involve the National Crime

Agency. He knew he'd get his way eventually because there was no alternative, but Gordon Holmes was right; it wouldn't go down well. There were many among the Association of Chief Police Officers who had celebrated the demise of the Serious and Organised Crime Agency, but Caton was reminded of the old adage *be careful what you wish for, a*nd he wasn't thinking of Eminem, or Gabby La La.

Holmes and Carter continued to stare at the four boards in the vain hope that something would miraculously leap out at them. The funny thing was that sometimes it did. Caton had taught them that. Right now it didn't seem to be working.

'Three months,' said Carter out of the blue.

'What?' said Holmes.

'MacLeod, the accountant, he said that Okowu-Bello was suddenly *"flushed with money"* and *"all sweetness and light"*. When the boss asked him when this was he said *"About three months ago."* '

'So?'

'So that's about when Okowu-Bello's form went out of the window. He'd been the Premiership's leading goal scorer for the past two seasons, then all of a sudden he couldn't score goals for toffee.'

'Probably too busy scoring with the manager's daughter, and his best friend's wife.'

'Bit of a coincidence though. You know what the Boss says about coincidences?'

"The world is full of coincidences",' Holmes quoted, *"But when one turns up in an investigation..."*

Carter finished it for him.

"The odds are it's a clue!"

They laughed all the way back to their desks.

'There's no need for an internal meeting Tom,' Helen Gates informed him. 'The Chief Constable was minded to do it anyway.'

'Without consulting me?' said Caton.

'Don't be naive,' she replied. 'Three murders in as many days. The press and the Home Office on his back. You should be grateful that so far he's kept the wolves away from your door. As for the National Crime Agency they are all ready sniffing around. Best to involve them on our terms.'

Caton knew she was right. In any case, he was getting what he wanted without having to justify it to anyone.

'And don't think it was easy for him,' she continued. 'I told you Grey was dead set against it. Apparently he threw a diva strop when he found out. He tried to forbid Bob from involving them. '

Grey, not Charles Grey, or Commissioner Grey, just his surname. It spoke volumes, Caton reflected, for the low esteem in which the man was held on the Sixth Floor. Just as interesting was the fact that Chief Constable Robert Hampson had miraculously morphed into *Bob*. No doubt a Freudian slip on the part of DCS Gates. She was single, he was married. Was this familiarity, he wondered, encouraged by Robert Hampson, hero worship on her part, or something more?

'Whom do I contact?' he said.

'No need, it's all arranged. Mr Hadfield's office, tomorrow morning, at ten am. And Tom,' she paused to add weight to what was coming. 'To save time we propose to precede it with the seventy two hour review of the Okowu-Bello investigation. We'll start at seven thirty sharp. Breakfast provided. Don't be late.'

Caton cursed silently. Because each death had come hard on the heels of the next he had forgotten all about the seventy two hour review. Now he would have to spend what was left of the day preparing for it. At least it would give him an opportunity to get up to date with the mountain of information that had come in, and he knew it would leave him better prepared for the meeting with the agents from the NCA. Two birds with one stone, as his father used to say. Caton wondered what he would have said if he could have seen him now.

If only.

Chapter 20

It was close to eight in the evening when Caton arrived home. Kate had waited dinner for him. While she applied the finishing touches he went into the study to check his emails. He was halfway through deleting most of them when she appeared in the doorway.

'It'll be on the table in two minutes,' she said. 'Can you come and open a bottle of red?'

As he turned to look up at her she bent, and kissed him with a slow intensity that told him she had been waiting all day to do just this.

They were interrupted by a loud insistent chirruping. They broke off, and stared at the computer screen. The flashing Skype message box said *Harry Calling*.

Kate headed for the door.

'Speak to your son,' she said calmly. 'I'll put yours in the oven.'

She closed the door quietly behind her.

Sometimes Caton felt the whole world was conspiring against him. He minimised the mailbox, opened up Skype, and activated the webcam video.

'Hi Harry,' he said.

His son's face beamed back at him.

'Hi Tom.'

Tom, not Dad. Helen had still not told him. Caton wondered how much longer it would be before Harry worked it out for himself.

'I just thought I'd catch up with you,' said Harry. 'You know, 'bout Wigan, and City, and things.'

'I'd love to,' said Caton. 'But we'll have to keep it short, because Kate's just put my dinner on the table.'

Harry's face fell. Caton suspected that it was the mention of Kate's name more than the fact that he couldn't stay and talk. The boy must still be hankering after him getting back together with Helen. How much more would he want that to happen when he found out they were father and son?

'That was good a good result for Wigan,' he said. 'Did you enjoy the game Harry?'

The smile lit up the boy's face.

'It was massive! Victor Moses was brilliant! He made both the goals, and Mum took me to meet him after the game. I got his autograph.

Having a mum who was part of the club's PR team must be magical for a seven year old, Caton reflected. Not something he would ever be able to match. Not that he'd try.

'Well done Harry,' he said. Though from what I saw on *Match of the Day* you were lucky that Al-Habsi was on form.'

''Bolton's loss, our gain,' said Harry.

'We'll see how you do against us in the cup.'

'Bring it on!' said Harry. The look on his face changed from excitement to something verging on conspiracy. He leaned in to the camera, and lowered his voice to a whisper.'

'Sunday Okowu-Bello,' he said. 'D'you have anything to do with that case Tom?'

Caton knew that Helen had told Harry not to ask about his work, but it was inevitable that the gruesome murder of one of the world's top footballers was going to fire the boy's curiosity.

'A little bit,' he replied, conscious that white lies

were becoming a more frequent part of his repertory now that he had son. 'But I'm not really allowed to talk about it.'

'Wow!' Harry said, his disappointment more than compensated for by the fact that he would be able to tell all of his mates that his Mum's friend was in charge of the case.

'Look, I'm really sorry Harry, but I've got to go. My dinner's getting cold.'

'OK Tom,' said his son. 'Laters.'

'Laters,' said Caton, to a blank screen.

'This is great,' he said, topping up their glasses.

'It's not bad,' Kate replied. 'For a Barolo. It was on offer at Waitrose.'

'Not the wine, the food.'

She shrugged. 'It's only a lasagne.'

'Well you've done something different with it.' He shovelled a forkful into his mouth and made an exaggerated play of savouring it.

She moved a piece around her plate as though her appetite had gone.

'I used some red wine for a change. It would have been even better if it hadn't sat in the oven.'

'Oh come on Kate,' he said. 'It was only a minute or two, and you did tell me to answer it.'

'He's your son,' she said. 'How could you not?'

Caton put down his fork and pushed his plate away.

'This has been brewing for a while,' he said. 'I don't know what's wrong, but don't you think we should get it out in the open?'

'Not now.'

'You said that last time. It's never going to be the right time. Whatever it is, the longer it festers the harder it's going to be. You know that.'

'All right,' she said. 'I didn't want to tell you like this, but if you insist.'

She pushed back her chair and started to rise. Caton could see the tears welling in her eyes.

'If you must know,' she said. 'I'm pregnant.'

She fled into the bedroom, slammed the door shut, and turned the lock.

'Shit!' said Caton to the empty room.

'Come on Kate, open the door, please.'

She had been in there over half an hour. Caton was seated on the floor outside, the bottle of wine, and their glasses, beside him. He had begun by apologising – though he wasn't sure for what exactly – then pleading, and had finally lapsed into silence. She had stopped crying sometime ago. He decided to try again.

'You can't stay in there all night.'

He kicked himself as soon as he'd said it. Of course she could, and it would be just like her to prove it. That stubborn streak was one of the things he found both endearing, and frustrating.

He drained his glass, and filled it up again. The title of a song, vaguely remembered, began to surface in his brain.

I can't give you anything but love, baby.

It was swiftly followed by the tune, and finally the words. Only the first four lines, and the chorus, but it was enough to start him singing it quietly. Over and over again.

He heard her get off the bed, and pad towards the door, heard the lock turn, and her footsteps retreating. He picked up both glasses and the bottle of wine, spilling a little on the wooden floor. Still singing the refrain he nudged the handle down with his elbow, and pushed the door open.

Kate was sitting in the middle of the bed, propped up against pillows piled behind her. Her hair was messed, her eyes red, and there were thin black streaks down her cheeks where the mascara had run. Somehow she managed to look both sheepish, and wary.

Caton placed the glasses and the bottle on the bedside table. He eased himself onto the bed until he was sitting beside her. He took her hands in his. They stared into each other's eyes, conveying silent messages.

'It's bloody brilliant,' he told her.

A smile crept across her face as he took her in his arms, and pulled her to him.

'I love you Kate Webb,' he said. 'And I already love this baby, because it's ours. Because we created it together.'

'I'm sorry,' she said. 'It's just that I wanted so much to give you a baby...for you to be a father...and...' her voice faltered.

'Harry,' he said.

She nodded. 'It's silly, I know.'

'No it's not,' he told her. 'I knew how it would make you feel, make any woman feel. That's why it took me so long to pluck up the courage to tell you. I was still coming to terms with it myself. But I swear I never knew about Harry until I bumped into Helen in Albert Square.'

She squeezed his hand. 'I know. And I know it's been hard for you too.'

He rested his back against the headboard.

'I have to accept that now he's in my life I can't just walk away.'

'I don't want you to,' she began.

He placed a finger gently on her lips.

'Shhh' he said. 'Please let me finish Kate. This is so hard.'

He waited for her nod, and then moved his hand away.

'I can't reject him. When, if, Helen tells him that I'm his father it's only natural that he will want to see me. To spend some time with me. I can't refuse him that.'

He turned to her so that she could the read truth in his face.

'But that will never change the fact that he was not planned. That his mother and I were never truly in love.'

He placed a hand on her stomach. Kate folded both of her hands over his.

'This baby was something that both of us wanted,' he said. 'Born out of our love, and into our lives. Nothing will ever change, or challenge that. I swear that I will never let it.'

She squeezed his hand, leant into his chest, and kissed him softly on his lips. He felt the warmth of her body, and the wetness of her cheeks on his, and his on hers.

Chapter 21

The seventy two hour review was over. While they waited for the representatives of the National Crime Agency to join them Caton took the opportunity to sneak a second bacon croissant. He was pleased that the review had been uneventful, and relieved and surprised that the police commissioner had been absent.

'The Chief had to lay it on the line for him,' Helen Gates had whispered. 'Grey threatened to complain to the Home Secretary. Mr Hampson told him to go ahead.'

'Daring,' said Caton.

'Not much of a dare,' she replied. 'Given how explicit the terms of reference are. Thank God for that amendment in the House of Lords.'

All that mattered to Caton was that the man was off his back, and hopefully off his case as well. It was already obvious that Charles Grey had been the source of leaks to the press. His interest in the investigation was obsessive, almost personal. He assumed that the club must be putting pressure on Grey to justify his seat in the Directors' box.

He drank the last of his coffee and, with the neatly folded napkin beside his plate, wiped a smear of ketchup from his mouth. It was ironic, he reflected, not to mention hypocritical, that a recent memo from the Commissioner himself had reminded all ranks to refuse and report the offer of any gift or consideration, or any kind of inducement or reward, for doing, or refraining from doing, or for having done, or having refrained from doing, anything at all.

The door opened. The first two people to enter the room brought Caton to his feet. Barbara Bryce, former Deputy Director of the now defunct Serious and Organised Crime Agency, scanned the room, saw Caton, and smiled. Behind her Dave Munby, formerly of the Asian Intelligence Section, gave a cheery wave. Ignoring protocol, Munby promptly walked across the room, around the table, past the Chief and his senior colleagues, and enveloped Caton in a bear hug.

'Great to see you Tom,' he said.

'You too Dave,' Caton replied wriggling free. 'Are you still with...?'

'Sally? You bet!' The Agent gave a broad grin and nodded. He reminded Caton of the Churchill dog in the back window of his aunt's Nissan Micra.

'Agent Munby,' called Barbara Bryce from across the room, indicating a vacant chair beside her.

'Catch you later,' said Munby with a knowing wink.

The Chief welcomed his visitors, introduced his staff, and invited Barbara Bates to do the same.

'My name is Barbara Bates,' she said. 'Assistant Deputy Director of the National Crime Agency. On my right is Dave Munby who is Head of the Asian Intelligence Division within the Economic Crime Command. Some of you...'

She looked pointedly in Caton's direction,

'...have worked with both of us before in our former roles with the Serious and Organised Crime Agency.'

She shifted her position to her left to include the short, slim, pale skinned man wearing a suede kippah that matched his slate grey eyes.

'And this is Agent Simon Levi, from the Organised Crime Command. Thank you for inviting us to your splendid new headquarters building.'

The way in which she stressed the word *splendid* left little room for doubt that she was using it as a synonym for luxurious, or lavish, the implication being that the NCA had to make do with a couple of lock-ups under the arches at the Elephant and Castle. Caton knew otherwise. As did the Chief.

'Sorry it's not quite what you're used to,' said Robert Hampson, 'but hopefully our famous Northern hospitality will more than make up for that.'

She smiled it off.

'So, what can we do for you?' she said.

'I think you'll find it may turn out to be of mutual advantage...a two way street.'

Caton couldn't see it. As far he was concerned he had little or nothing to bring to the table. He was here with a begging bowl, and not too proud to admit it. It didn't help to raise their expectations.

'Let's see what you've got then shall we?' said Barbara Bates, reinforcing his disquiet.

Half an hour later Caton had brought them up to speed with his investigation. He had watched for their reactions throughout his presentation but none had been forthcoming.

'Let me see if I have this right,' said Barbara Bates, ticking the points off on her immaculately manicured fingers.

'You have a Premiership footballer of Nigerian heritage, but with French and therefore European citizenship; a member of his club's security team; and his accountant; all of them murdered within three days of each other; and two missing security men '

She was clearly not expecting him to reply. Having witnessed her ability to deal with interruptions during the Chinatown investigation Caton had no intention of doing so.

'So far you have explored: sexual motives involving jealousy and betrayal, and more or less discounted them; punishment for the non-payment of Casino betting debts; revenge and theft by a Nigerian gang who had been extorting money from your first victim ; and the role of some shadowy East European Organisation which you have yet to identify.'

'We were hoping you could help us with...' the Chief Constable started to say.

The Assistant Deputy Director cut him off with an imperious wave of her hand.

'We'll come to that in due course,' she said. Her forehead furrowed as she recapped silently by counting on her fingers of her left hand. She paused as she reached her ring finger, then smiled, and looked up.

'And you appear, understandably, to be uncertain about the role of the club's security firm. Is that a fair summary?'

Not wishing to make the same mistake again Robert Hampson deferred to Caton.

'Well Chief Inspector?' he said.

'I think that covers it Ms Bates,' Caton said, not wanting to make the mistake of patronising her with words such as excellent, or good.

'*Mrs,* Bates,' she replied, though not unkindly. 'Or *Barbara,* since we're among friends.'

Caton glanced at his colleagues. Helen Gates was smiling. Martin Hadfield looked distinctly uncomfortable. The Chief Constable's cheeks had coloured slightly, at the thought of one of his junior officers calling him Robert or, God forbid, Bob. Not that he need worry; Caton had no intention of crossing that barrier. Assistant Deputy Director Bates however, was an entirely different kettle of fish.

'So, how exactly do you think we can help you Tom?'

She had already picked up, Caton realised, on the fact that it was very much a one way street. He was relieved. It meant that he didn't have to pretend to possess information he could trade in return for the Agency's expertise.

'Firstly Barbara,' he said, earning a muttered comment from Martin Hadfield, and a frosty stare from the Chief. 'We don't have the resources to delve into either of these overseas connections. Neither can that be our prime objective at this stage, not with bodies turning up every other day.'

She nodded sagely.

'I can see that.'

'It would be very helpful,' he continued. 'To find out how the Nigerians were made to back off from Okowu-Bello; if they did take any action against his relatives; and what happened to the twelve million pounds that disappeared from his Lagos bank account.'

He paused to make sure that she was following. They all were. Dave Munby was leaning back in his chair with his hands clasped behind his head, but his eyes were alert and focused on Caton. Agent Levi was taking notes.

'As for these Eastern Europeans, we know next to nothing about them. I wondered if either your Organised Crime Command or your Border Command might have something on them.'

'Or equally, our Economic Crime Command,' said Levi, without looking up.

'It was your Economic Crime Command,' Caton

responded. 'That I hoped might be able to look into Okowu-Bello's financial affairs, including the Nutmeg Holdings accounts in Belize. And finally, I wondered if you might use your influence with Her Majesties Revenue and Customs to find out the extent of his debts with the Casino operations?'

He sat back, hoping that he had covered all of the bases.

The Assistant Deputy Director steepled her fingers and pursed her lips.

'You said *either of these overseas connections* Tom. Are you sure you didn't mean *all* of these overseas connections?'

Caton wasn't sure that he understood.

'I'm sorry?' he said.

Munby unclasped his hands and rocked forward. 'What about the Far East connection Tom?' he said.

'The Far East connection?' said the Chief. 'What Far East Connection?'

'I take it you are aware that the Titans are owned by an Asian consortium?' said Munby.

The Chief nodded. 'Chinese,' he said. 'I've yet to meet any of them.'

The agent turned to Caton.

'Our old friends the Manchester and Shanghai Trading Corporation, Tom. Their European Chief Executive, Ying Zheng Xiong, is their domestic contact among the Directors. You'll remember him.'

Caton did. He had never forgotten the moment Zheng Xiong had silently entered the office suite high up in the Beetham Tower. It was a continuing regret that he had been unable to prove the man's complicity in the Chinatown case.

M&STC are nominally the owners,' Munby continued. 'I say *nominally,* because we have reason to believe that they are actually part of a wider Indian and Chinese consortium. Ironic, when you consider that the two countries were engaged in the Sino-Indian war as recently as 1962.'

'What does that have to do with Okowu-Bello's murder, or any of the others come to that?' asked the Assistant Chief Constable, eager to have his presence recognised.

'Good question,' Munby replied. 'It's the one that we have been asking ourselves ever since his death was announced.'

'Why don't you let Simon explain?' said Barbara Bates.

Simon Levi looked up, and pushed his notes aside.

'We were approached six months ago by the Football Association,' he said. 'They had concerns that their due diligence examination into the ownership of the club had failed to uncover the real source of the funds behind the takeover, and therefore the actual owners.'

'Why would that be a concern?' asked Hadfield.

Asking the obvious was in Caton's view the ACC's biggest weakness. It was the main reason why he was never going to make chief officer. And if Barbara Bates' raised eyebrows were anything to go by it was a sure fire way to guarantee that he'd never be invited to apply for a post with the NCA. Better to keep your mouth shut and listen.

'Because unless they are able to identify the actual owner, or owners, they have no way of satisfying themselves that he or she is a fit and proper person to own an English club. Nor do they have any way of knowing if the funds used to secure the purchase are safe in the financial sense, or in an ethical sense.'

'You mean if they're the proceeds of crime?' said Hadfield, digging himself deeper.

'Obviously,' muttered the Chief who was becoming embarrassed, and irritated, by his subordinate's continual interruptions.

'In addition,' the agent continued. 'It is against not only the FA's rules but also the regulations of the Federation of International Football Associations, for someone to own more than one club at the same time.'

'To avoid a conflict of interest.' said Hadfield proving that some people can't take a hint.

'Thank you Martin!' said the Chief, in a tone that made clear that he was doing anything but. He turned to Agent Levi. 'I understand all that, but why is it a matter for the National Crime Agency?'

'Ordinarily it wouldn't be, Robert' replied Barbara Bates. 'But we had an ongoing investigation, inherited from Dave's and my time at SOCA, into the activities of the Manchester and Shanghai Trading Corporation. Ones which your man Tom was instrumental in bringing to our notice at the time.'

'People smuggling, sex slavery, the movement of drugs, and money laundering,' Caton explained for his Chief. 'It was a few years back. Before you joined us Sir.'

Hampson nodded. 'The Chinatown Case. You did a presentation at Bramshill.'

'Yes Sir.'

'And these people are running one of our leading Premiership clubs?'

'Owning the club isn't necessarily the same as running it, Mr Hampson,' said Levi. 'But I take your point. The reality is that the investigation is part of a wider enquiry, in collaboration with the G7 Financial Action Task Force, into a number of clubs in the top two leagues. We don't yet have enough evidence to satisfy the FA or for a criminal prosecution.'

'So what do you have?'

Agent Levi slid his notebook back towards him and flipped the pages back.

'The Owner and president of the Manchester and Shanghai Trading Corporation Kang Jong-Cheol, pronounced Gang Jong-Chul, is the nominal owner of the Titans Football Club. He was represented in the negotiations with the former owners by one Kitjakarn Pratcha, a Malay businessman who is known to us and the FA as something of a rather shady wheeler dealer. We know that he also represents a number of Indian consortia involved with sports at home and abroad. We suspect that the real owners of the Titans are a consortium of Chinese and Indian investors including The Manchester and Shanghai Trading Corporation; the nominal owner with the supposedly clean track record.'

'But why would they invest in a club like the Titans?' asked Helen Gates. 'Not just for the kudos surely? The Titan's weren't even in the Premiership when they took over were they?'

'That was the point, or the major point,' Levi explained. 'If you can pick up, on the cheap, a promising club in the Championship, or even in League One, inject a bit of cash, pick up some decent players on loan from the major clubs, get promoted to the Premiership, and the sell it on, you could stand to make a big profit.'

'*In, up, out!*' said Dave Munby. 'That's how it's sold to prospective buyers. And don't think the Titans are the only ones.'

'And that's illegal?' said Helen Gates.

'Not if the ownership is transparent and that person doesn't own more than one club,' said Dave Munby. 'But it's bad for the FA, bad for the fans, and bad for football.'

'But that's not the only thing that we think is going on here,' said Levi. 'Far from it.'

He was interrupted by a knock on the door,

heralding the arrival of a trolley loaded with fresh cups, stainless steel flasks filled with coffee, tea, milk and hot water, and a plate full of biscuits and pastries.

'No expense spared I see,' said Barbara Bates cheerfully. 'Bags I a Danish whorl.'

Chapter 22

'Money laundering is just one aspect about which we have concerns,' said Simon Levi after they had settled back down. 'There are so many activities through which dirty money can be laundered, from sponsorship deals to transfer fees, food and drink franchises, sales of merchandise through the club shop and worldwide. Even more worrying for the FA, and FIFA, is the role of bookmakers and betting consortia.'

'You're losing me now,' said the Chief Constable whose blood sugar level seemed to have peaked following his third pain au chocolat, and was now nose diving at a perilous speed.

'We have reason to believe the consortium behind the Titans includes a hedge fund with links to a South East Asian betting ring.'

Dave Munby leant forward. 'Simon, do you mind if I have a go at simplifying this?'

The agent waved his hand in a be-my-guest gesture, and sat back.

'OK,' said Munby. 'Let's accept that it was originally their intention to catapult the club into the premiership, and then float it on the open market and when its shares had risen spectacularly, to sell it on at a profit. Even if the club was relegated in its first year there would be the cushion of the parachute money paid out by the league to give them a soft landing.

They could get out at that stage.'

He paused for a drink to moisten his throat.

'However, we think that because of the money laundering potential, and the opportunity to make money through betting scams, they were in it for the long haul.'

'Which is where Sunday Okowu-Bello came in?' said Caton.

Simon Levi nodded encouragingly. At least one of them had cottoned on.

'While it may not be that easy to influence the result of individual games, even from the inside of the club,' said Munby. 'The general trend of performances is another thing.'

'But then you'd have to be able to influence team selection surely?' said Hadfield.

'True, and that's difficult, but not impossible if you've got the manager in your pocket. But even more achievable is rigging spot betting.'

'Spot betting?' said Helen Gates.

'Who is going to score the first goal, the score at half-time, the number of corners, the first person to get a red card, the timing of the first throw in, that sort of thing,' Caton told her.

'That's ridiculous,' she said.

'It's hugely popular, and highly lucrative for those who accept the bets,' said Agent Levi. 'Especially in Pakistan and China where betting is illegal, and in India where it's heavily restricted. That means that it's almost entirely controlled by illegal gangs and organised syndicates.'

'Like those three Pakistani players who were jailed for deliberately bowling no balls to order,' said Barbara Bates. 'As soon as we heard the circumstances of Okowu-Bello's death we had an analysis of his performance, and that of the first team.'

'What did you find?' asked the Chief Constable.

'Having been odds on for the premiership,' said Levi. 'About three months ago the Titans started to perform really badly. That coincided with a fall off in Okowu-Bello's own performance.'

'And that would work for the betting syndicates how exactly?'

'If they had placed, and spread, significant bets against them winning the League title when they were doing well, knowing that their form was going to falter, that could make them a fortune. Not to mention any share dealing they could have planned on the back of that. Selling when the club was doing well, and then buying them back at a lower rate when the form plummeted. Equally, given that Okowu-Bello was leading goal scorer for the club and the League, betting against him scoring, knowing full well that he wasn't going to, would bring them a packet, not to mention raking it in from all of those punters who did bet on him to score every week.'

'So they would be winning both ways; from the fans placing bets with them, and from their bets with other bookies, against the club and the player?'

'Exactly.'

'Completely out of character,' said Caton thoughtfully. 'Okowu-Bello picked up two red cards, one in November, and again in January. That coincided with the initial turn around in his fortunes.'

'Well spotted,' said the Assistant Deputy Director. 'We, and the Financial Action Task Force, are looking specifically at that. We already know there was irregular betting in the Far East. We're trying to track down the source, but the bets were so widely spread that isn't going to be easy.'

'The obvious place to start was with the player,' said Dave Munby. 'We were about to launch an undercover surveillance operation on Okowu-Bello, and then he was murdered.'

There was silence in the room as the four officers from Greater Manchester Police let the implications sink in.

'If the betting syndicates had got wind of that...' Martin Hadfield began. He didn't need to finish. Once again he was stating the obvious.

They chased the issues around for another twenty minutes or so, and then got down to business.

'As I see it, it's a matter of not seeing the wood for the trees,' said Barbara Bates enigmatically. 'We have the resources, remit and connections to concentrate on the wood - the bigger picture - whereas you at GMP have the trees - these murders – to focus on.'

Caton wasn't going to argue with that. It was bad enough hunting down the killers without trying to find out who might be pulling the strings from as far away as the Russian steppes, or the Far East.

She paused to check that they were with her. They were.

'So, how would it be if we continue to pursue the Asian dimension, and do our best to see what we can find out for you about the Eastern European and Nigerian strands?'

'That would be really helpful Mrs Bates,' said Robert Hampson, eschewing her preferred mode of address. 'It would be our first opportunity to demonstrate how well we can work together.'

Caton raised his hand.

'Yes Chief Inspector?' said Hampson, indicating by his tone that whatever Caton had to say it had better be good.

'Not seeing the wood for the trees Barbara,' he said. 'And vice versa. That's still going to be a problem unless we can agree a means of communicating regularly with each other.'

He was aware of the Chief Constable scowling at him for the introduction of a negative premise.'

'Quite right Tom,' Bates replied.

Caton was amused by the speed with which the chief's expression changed to one of approval.

'Dave will be your liaison officer with the Agency,' she said. 'He'll see to it that you get regular updates from himself, and from Simon here, and we'll expect the same of you. As often as necessary, and not less than every seventy two hours. '

'Thank you,' said Caton. It was more than he had expected.

The agents left together, with Dave Munby promising to get in touch as soon as possible for a catch up, as well as to move the business forward. Caton made his way back to the incident room deep in thought. Things were far more complicated than he had envisaged.

His team were even more surprised than he was. When he came to the bit about the gambling syndicates Carter nudged Holmes with his elbow.

'I told you!' he said.

'I wished you'd told me,' said Caton once his DS had explained.

'It was only a hunch Boss,' replied Carter. I hadn't really worked it out.'

'We share hunches in this team,' Caton reminded him. 'Then we can work them out together. It saves time.'

'This is like one of those maddening detective novels,' said Holmes. 'Where there are more suspects than policemen. How the hell are we supposed to follow all these leads?'

'Have you been listening Detective Inspector?' said Caton. 'Tell him DS Stuart.'

Joanne Stuart blushed under Gordon Holmes' withering glare.

'Go on then DS Stuart,' he said. 'Enlighten me.'

'Well,' she began, pausing to check that the Boss wasn't just winding Gordon up, that he really wanted her to explain. Caton winked at her over the DI's shoulder. Gordon was the only one who didn't spot it. Encouraged, she continued.

'Like the Boss said. The NCA will pursue all possible links with the owners, betting consortia and bookmakers, and those elusive East Europeans, and we'll concentrate on the murders. We simply stick to the murders, and follow the evidence, like we're supposed to do.'

'Simply! I'll have to remember that.' Holmes retorted.

'Don't be so grumpy,' said Caton. 'You're always like this when you've missed your beauty sleep.'

'Chance'd be a fine thing,' said Holmes against a background of friendly laughter.

'Excuse me Sir. But this urgent.'

They turned to find Ged clutching a piece of note paper.

'It's a message from CrimeStoppers Sir.'

Caton took the note and, read it twice. Once for meaning, once to order his thoughts.

'It's Jade,' he told them. 'Gerry Capper's daughter. She's been reported missing.'

Chapter 23

'CrimeStoppers?'

'Bizarre.'

'You're telling me.'

'You'd expect the family to be the first to report their daughter missing,' said DS Stuart.

They sat in the Skoda, one hundred metres from the Capper residence. Caton shifted in his seat to make himself comfortable.

'We don't know that they didn't. An anonymous call, a female voice of indeterminate age. It could have been her mother.'

'Why would she do it anonymously? Why not ring you direct?'

'You haven't met the father have you Jo?'

'No. But, if what I've seen of him on the tele is anything to go by, I take your point.'

'Let's not get ahead of ourselves,' he said. 'We don't even know for sure that she's missing.'

He nodded towards the desultory group of paparazzi encamped outside the electronic gates.

'If she was, and the word had got out, there would be a hell of a lot more of these vultures camped on their doorstep.'

'Vultures, isn't that a bit extreme?' she said.

'What would you call them?'

She thought about it.

'Rats? Parasites?'

She pretended to study them more closely.

'No you're right,' she said, as he switched the engine back on, and slipped into gear. 'Vultures does it for me.'

'Jade? Missing? What the hell are you talking about?'

Gerry Capper's face had taken on that worrying purple hue again.

'Your daughter has been reported missing,' Caton told him for the third time. 'We need to satisfy ourselves that she isn't. And if it turns out that our informant is right, I assume that you would want us to find her as soon as possible?'

'Well I'm telling you she isn't!'

'Mrs Capper?' said Joanne Stuart, who had been watching the wife closely throughout.

A shudder passed through Christine Capper, as though shocked to find herself the centre of attention. She stared at DS Stuart, and shrank under her gaze.

'For Christ sake, Chrissie! said her husband. 'Say something.'

She shrank further within herself. It was fear, Caton decided, not shock, which left her speechless. Fear of saying the wrong thing, fear of her husband, probably both.

'It's alright Mrs Capper,' he reassured her. 'Take your time.

'She looked from one to the other of the detectives, at her husband, and then back again.

'I don't know,' she said tentatively.

Her husband snorted his derision. Before he could say or do anything else Caton moved between them.

'How do you mean, Mrs Capper?' he said.

Her eyes sought refuge in his.

'She went to stay with her friend last night,' she said. 'A sleep over. I wasn't expecting her back till later this afternoon.'

It was clear from her expression that she was lying, and that she wanted him to know it.

'Perhaps you could ring her friend, and check?'

'Of course.'

She couldn't get to the phone fast enough. She took it from its cradle, and dialled the number. DS Stuart watched for her husband's reaction leaving Caton to concentrate on the wife. She hugged the phone close to her ear, and turned her body away as spoke.

'Mrs Walker, Jenny, I'm sorry to bother you. Could I speak with Jade? She isn't there? No, no I thought she was staying the night with...I see. My mistake. No, no it's alright. I must have got my wires crossed. Goodbye Mrs Walker...Jenny.'

She replaced the handset and turned to face them. Panic flooded her face.

'She isn't there,' she said. 'She didn't stay the night. She's missing Gerry. Jade is missing!'

'I think you could do with a cup of tea Mrs Capper,' Caton said. 'I think we all could. Mr Capper, could you show me Jade's room please.' The tone of his voice brooked no argument. Christine Capper turned reluctantly towards the kitchen. Her husband led Caton towards the hallway. As Caton reached the door he turned, caught DS Stuart's eye, and nodded towards the phone.

'*Last Number Redial*,' he mouthed silently.

Jade's room was exactly what Caton would have expected of a teenage girl. Not that he'd had a sister, but over the past twenty years he had seen enough of such rooms to last a lifetime. Some involved runaways who had quickly recognised the error of their ways, and had hurried home to mummy. Too many had either ended in, or been occasioned by, a tragedy. He prayed this wasn't going to be one of them.

Clothes were strewn haphazardly about the floor. The bed was made, but Caton sensed the mother's hand in that. There was a dressing table with a three panelled mirror. The surface of the table was cluttered with all the makeup accessories deemed necessary to beautify what at her age should have been a perfect youthful complexion. Jars and pots of foundation, concealer, revealer, eye shadow, blusher, mascara, and eyeliner jostled for space with eyelash curlers, hair straighteners, and make up sponges and brushes. It made Kate's collection look decidedly impoverished.

On the mirrors themselves were pinned step-by-step diagrams cut from fashion magazines. Tucked into the corners were photos of Jade with friends, taken he guessed, in photo booths and with their mobile phones. They smiled back at him. He was touched, as always, by their exuberance, their camaraderie, and the loneliness, and desperate need to be loved and valued, that lurked behind those over-confident smiles. Of them all, he thought Jade's expression the most troubled.

He checked the wardrobes and the drawers. It was impossible to tell if anything was missing. Her father hovered in the doorway as though this was a room into which he had never been allowed to stray.

'Can you ask Mrs Capper to come up?' Caton said.

'Is anything missing Mrs Capper?'

She pointed to the top of the wardrobe.

'Jade has a suitcase that she uses for short stays, it's kept up there.'

Caton looked at the empty space.

'Short stays?'

'Sleepovers and weekends away. That sort of thing.'

She moved to the bed and checked underneath the pillows. 'Her jimjams are gone.' She opened a couple of drawers. 'Her clean knickers and bras are missing too.'

'Does Jade have access to any money Mrs Capper?'

She sat on the bed, and put her head in her hands.

'She has a monthly allowance. Two hundred pounds. I wouldn't know if she'd saved any of it.'

'Chance'd be a fine thing,' muttered her husband as he disappeared onto the landing.

Caton sat down beside her.

'I need you to give me a list of all of her friends and immediate relatives, and any places you think that she might have gone. Don't worry; I'm sure we'll find her soon.'

Before they left Caton actioned an urgent Missing Persons report. Gerry Capper called Dean Hardman and asking him to use as many men as he could to do the same. They heard him instruct his Head of Security to make sure that she wasn't hanging around the stadium, or with any of the players. There was nothing more they could do.

'She knew,' said DS Stuart as they walked down the steps to the drive. 'It was in her voice, and her body language.'

'Of course she knew. Just didn't want her husband to know that she did. She probably made that call to CrimeStoppers using her mobile phone.'

'She'd already rung the Walkers and found out Jade hadn't been there.'

'Probably.'

'That last number dialled?' she said. 'It was Dean Hardman's. The Head of Security at the Titans. Made over an hour and a half ago.'

Caton nodded. 'She wasn't making a call, only pretending to. It was a bluff to fool her husband, and let us know that Jade really is missing.'

'He knew too.'

'How well do you know your Shakespeare?'

'Try me.'

'The lady doth protest too much, methinks.'

'It's from Hamlet. Queen Gertrude talking about the actor playing the queen in the play within a play?'

'Well done.'

He made the mistake of allowing his surprise to show.

'Don't patronize me Sir,' she said.

'Sorry.'

'Apology accepted.' She grinned. 'I went with Abbie to see it at the Library Theatre the week before last, otherwise I'd never have known.'

'Only in this instance it was the father that was protesting too much.'

He was about to hold the passenger door open for her, and thought better of it. He walked round the bonnet, and climbed in beside her.

'Did you see the colour of his face?' she said. 'I thought he was going to explode.'

'Tyrian purple,' said Caton, starting the engine and pulling away.

'Tyrian?'

'From Tyre. A colour whose use was restricted in the Byzantine Empire to dyeing silk worn by the Emperors. It comes from the sebaceous secretions of a predatory snail found in the Easter Mediterranean Sea.'

'You're making it up,' she said.

He grinned.

'No I'm not. Kate wanted me, the best man, and the ushers, to wear bow ties and waistcoats that colour.'

'What did you tell her?'

'That it wasn't in my colourway.'

'You're kidding me! You had your colours done?'

'I went out with a girl who was a colour analyst. She ran day sessions for ten women at a time. According to her, she was doing very well out of it. She insisted on doing mine. Even gave me my very own colourway wallet.'

'You'd never know,' she said.

He glanced across at her to see if she was being serious. Even with the grin that lit up her face he couldn't be sure.

'You wouldn't have dared to say that if I wasn't driving.'

'Probably not.'

'Just one thing,' he said.

'Go on.'

'If I find out you've told anyone, I'll have to kill you.'

DI Holmes, DS Stuart, and Caton himself were seated around his desk, crammed together like sardines in the tiny partitioned bay.

'What do you reckon's going on Boss?' said Holmes.

'I don't know.'

'Worst case scenario she's been taken,' said DI Holmes.

'Because she knows too much, or because she was involved,' said DS Stuart.

'I'm not convinced,' said Caton.

'Maybe it's a way of putting pressure on her father,' she said. 'You saw how stressed out he was.'

Caton looked at his notes. 'I think that's because we were there. I had the feeling the he was angry because someone had reported her missing, not because she was missing.'

'You're saying the father is implicated in her disappearance?' said Holmes.

'That's my intuition. And I think his wife suspects as much.'

'Why the hell would he want her to disappear?'

'That's what we have to find out. But we can't rule out abduction on the basis of my gut instinct.'

'Works most of the time,' said Holmes in a suspiciously ambiguous tone.

Caton gave him the benefit of the doubt.

'It's not infallible though,' he said.

'There's not been any ransom request,' Joanne Stuart pointed out.

'When did you hear of a kidnap victim packing her own case?' Caton found himself saying a little less kindly than he had intended. 'Mind you I suppose she could have been forced to,' he added by way of apology.

DS Carter popped his head around the corner of the screens.

'Excuse me Boss. You asked me to attend the post mortem on Gideon Jones. I've typed up my notes if you want to see them.'

'Come in,' said Caton, 'And sit yourself down.'

'You'll be lucky Nick,' said DS Stuart.

Carter edged into the alcove, handed two sheets of paper across the desk to Caton, and squeezed into a gap between DS Stuart's chair and one of the partitions.

'Whatever you do don't lean on it,' Holmes advised. 'Or you'll end up in Duggie's lap.'

'While I'm reading,' said Caton, 'You can give the others the highlights; it'll save time.'

Holmes and Stuart tried craning their necks round to look at Carter, and gave up.

'He was killed by a single bullet to the left frontal

lobe of the cerebral hemisphere.' He pointed helpfully to the left centre of his forehead. 'Following impact the bullet tumbled, mushroomed and shattered, reducing the brain tissue to mush, before exiting at the rear. In Dr Hope's opinion the significantly larger size of the exit wound, the internal damage caused, and the nature of the exit wound, is consistent with a flat nosed hollow point bullet such as that discovered wedged in the duvet.

'Mush?' said Holmes. 'Jean Hope actually said *mush*?'

'Not exactly, no, but it came to the same thing. The victim's jaw and cheekbone on the left side had both been fractured by heavy blows. Indentations to the skin and bone were consistent with those that would be caused by blows from a fist wearing a metal knuckleduster. Similar indentations were found on the sternum, lower left rib cage - where two ribs had been broken and one sprung - and on the rectus abdominus muscle.'

'Someone punched him in the solar plexus,' observed Holmes.

'And just about everywhere else by the sound of it,' said Joanne Stuart.

'Including his genitals,' said Carter. 'There was severe bruising to his scrotum, and separation of the pubic symphisis,'

'Someone kneed him in the...'

'Thank you DI Holmes,' said Caton without looking up. 'Lady present.'

'The most interesting and anomalous feature was however,'

'Anomalous?' said Holmes.

'The Vaseline,' said Caton, placing the sheets of paper down on his desk.

'Vaseline?' chorused Stuart and Holmes.

'Traces of a petroleum jelly based substance were found at the points of entry and exit, and on the remains of the bullet,' Carter explained. 'According to our firearms team the cavity of hollow point bullets are sometimes filled with Vaseline. The intention being to add weight, and to ensure a dependable expansion of the bullet, and a more efficient transfer of energy. It is a method that originated in Finland, and is especially popular in Russia, and other Eastern European countries.'

'I love it when killers give us a signature,' said Holmes.

'I wonder why there's no mention of Vaseline in the post mortem report on Ratten?' said Joanne Stuart.

'Maybe the fact that he was immersed in water,' said Carter.

'Vaseline is waterproof,' Holmes pointed out.

'I bet there was grease on those propeller blades,' said DS Stuart thoughtfully. 'Maybe Professor Flatman just assumed that's what it was?'

Caton sat back, and folded his arms.

'I'll let you tell him,' he said.

Chapter 24

The meeting was breaking up as Caton's phone rang. He waved them on their way, and then picked up.

'It's Gina Burman, for you Sir,' said Ged.

'Put her through.'

'Tom?'

'Gina.'

'Josh tells me you're looking for Jade Capper?'

'That's right.'

'I know where she is.'

Caton sat bolt upright.

'Where?'

'In a stone cottage just outside Saddleworth. I'm watching the house now.'

'How did you find her Gina?'

'I didn't. I just followed her. It was Josh's idea.'

'You're still working with Holt then?'

'Yes. Is that a problem Tom?'

'Not if you keep me informed, like I asked you to.'

'*Told* us to, actually. Which is what I'm doing right now.'

He kicked himself metaphorically.

'Fair enough. How long as she been there?'

'Since seven o'clock last night.'

'Is she alone?'

'She's got two of her father's hard men with her.'

'His two centre backs?'

She gave a little laugh. Just enough to show she'd got the joke.

'Hardman's security staff. They drove her here in their 4x4. Tinted windows, cow catcher on the front.'

'Tinted windows? So how did you know it was her?'

'I followed her when she left the house last night. She was driving her mother's Rav4. Parked it at the stadium. The 4x4 pulled up alongside. She hopped into the back. One of them opened the tailgate, put her case inside, and climbed into the passenger seat. I tailed them here. No one's left the house since.'

'Are you sure they haven't spotted you?' he said.

'No way. It's what I was trained to do remember?'

Caton did. She had had a reputation as one of the most reliable members of the Force Major Incident Team when it came to surveillance. Before FMIT was disbanded, and she decided to leave under a cloud that had never been satisfactorily explained.

'What are you planning to do?'

'Sit it out until Josh tells me otherwise. He's paying.'

'Has he told you what he thinks is going on?'

'I think he's as much in the dark as I am.'

She paused as though wondering how to phrase her next question.

'What do you think is going on Tom?'

'If I knew I probably wouldn't be able to tell you Gina, you know that.'

'You meant what you said about a one-way street then?'

'You know I did.' He deliberately softened his tone, not so much feigning reasonableness as wanting to convince her of it. 'The best I can do is promise that I'll give you both a heads up when things get exciting, and as much exclusivity as I can get away with without compromising the Force, or my own career.'

'I can tell Holt that?'

'So long as you keep me in the loop the way you've just done.'

'Brilliant!' she said

I hope so, Caton said to himself as he put the phone back in its stand. He doodled on his pad for a minute or two, then picked up the phone and asked Ged to see if she could get hold of DCS Gates. While he was waiting he informed the team of his conversation with Burman, and then brought the murder book up to date. Ten minutes later she returned his call.

'Tom. I've only got two minutes so make it quick.'

'Gina Burman,' he said. 'Why did she leave the Force?'

'Why do you want to know?'

In his experience, whenever people asked that question it meant there was something to hide.

'I just wondered.'

'I don't think so Tom. Idle curiosity is something I've never associated with you. You'd better tell me the real reason.'

He gave it five seconds consideration.

'I take it you know she's working as a private detective?'

'I do.'

'And that she was tailing Okowu-Bello on behalf of his wife?'

'I've read the reports, Tom. Get on with it.'

'Well she's still tied into this investigation. She's working in a private capacity with Josh Holt who seems to think he has future as an investigative reporter.'

'Christ Almighty!' she exclaimed. 'You'll have to put a stop to that.'

'I can't. They can do what they want as private

citizens so long as they don't obstruct my investigation. You know that.'

'Trouble is you'll only find out if they are obstructing it when it's too late.'

'That is why I need the two of them working with me, rather than have them working blind. Gina has just found out where Jade Packer is hiding. That's saved my team, not to mention hundreds of uniformed officers across the Force, hours of wasted effort.'

'Mmm,' she didn't sound convinced.

'I just need to be sure I can trust her,' he said.

There was a long pause before she responded.

'If a word of this gets out, I'll know who it's come from.' It was said with the kind of menace that Caton associated with blackmailers.

'It won't.'

'It had better not. She alleged sexual harassment against a senior officer.'

Caton's mind went into overdrive. He could think of one inspector, a chief superintendent, even a former...'

'Let me guess,' he said. 'Her word against his?'

'Who said it was a man?'

'That narrows it down.'

'I wasn't serious Tom, just giving you some of your own medicine. You were right, his word against hers.'

'They closed ranks, and froze her out?'

'More or less. Except that she read the signs and got out before they had a chance to make things really uncomfortable.' She heaved a sigh. 'I didn't know whether to admire her, or feel sorry for her.'

'From what I've seen I'd say the former. She's kept her self-respect, and is mistress of her own destiny. It was our loss.'

'I agree. But don't let that cloud your judgement. Use her by all means, but don't forget that she's made her choice. Don't tell her anything she couldn't find out for herself, unless you have aspirations to join her on Civvie Street. Where is Packer's daughter anyway?'

He told her.

'What are you going to do about it?'

'Cancel the missing person's search, and leave her there.'

'What if she takes off?'

'Gina Burman will let me know.'

'What about the father?'

'Don't worry,' he said. 'I intend to find out what the hell he's playing at.'

'While you're at it,' she said. 'See if you can't solve a murder or two. The wolves are circling.'

He took his jacket from the back of his chair, shrugged it on, and made for the exit, stopping by Gordon's desk on his way.

'With me,' he said.

'Where are we going Boss?' said Holmes as got to his feet.

'To the Titans' stadium, to have a word with Capper, and his head of security.'

'It's time they changed the name for that place,' said Holmes as he followed Caton to the door. 'The way they're going they should call it the Titanic.'

His laughter echoed around the corridors of the mezzanine, and down into the atrium.

Out in the car park the temperature had dropped. The sky was an ominously uniform blanket of grey that threatened snow. Caton wished he'd left home with his coat.

'Where are we up to with the threat analysis?' he said as they climbed into his car.

'Done and dusted,' said Holmes fastening his seat

belt. 'There were the usual suspects mouthing off on Twitter, and Facebook; fans from rival clubs, and Titans fans who don't like the foreign owners. All of them clowns.'

'What about the arsonists?' said Caton waving to the guard in his glass box as the barrier rose.

'The ones they caught setting fire to the club shop during the riots? They're both inside Thornton Cross Young Offenders. They've still got five months to go before they qualify for parole.'

'What about the organised hooligans?' said Caton.

Every club had them. Some had been going for decades. The very worst attracted members of far right political organisations, anarchists, and nutters. When they weren't warring with rival domestic fans, or their favourite targets the fans of visiting foreign teams, they scrapped with each other.

'They don't come anywhere near the club anymore. It's not just down to the heavy police presence either. Word on the street is that the firm Dean Holden heads up has warned them off.'

Caton found it difficult to believe.

'The Titan's security men scared off those loonies?'

'They're just the tip of the iceberg Boss. We're talking a major Firm here, with a capital F. I thought you knew?'

It had been some time since Caton had worked the streets.

'I thought they'd cleaned up the security industry as far as the Premiership clubs were concerned?' he said.

'They have, in theory. Hardman works for Dedicated International Security Services. Manc Security is just one of their limited companies.'

'I've never heard of them.'

'No reason you should. They've kept themselves

clean. They've only been in the business four years but they've done everything right. They're a Security Industry Association Approved Contractor. Fussy about what they do though.'

'In what way?'

'They provide door supervisors, security guards, CCTV Public Space Surveillance, and close protection. They also provide training for club stewards. They're not interested in any of the other stuff like cash and valuables in transit, or event management.'

'Who owns them?'

'That's where it gets interesting. You remember Harry Lightfoot, the Chief Executive of Titans?'

'He was with Gerry Packer the first time we interviewed him?'

'That's the one. Well, he has a brother-in-law. Frank Moston, ex Royal Marines.'

'How did Lightfoot get that past the Board of Directors?'

'They probably never made the connection. The wife isn't involved in the firm in any way. Doesn't come to any of the matches. How would they know?'

He flipped down the sun visor on his side, and inspected a small cut on his chin.

'They threw in a few sweeteners as well,' he said.

'Such as?'

'They promised discounted security for the Directors own events; weddings, birthdays, anniversaries, bar mitzvahs, bat mitzvahs that sort of thing.'

'That's a corrupt practice.'

He flipped the visor back into place.

'Apparently not. Anyway, it seems there wasn't any competition.'

Caton pulled up to the car park barrier and waited for the security man to check his ID, then he drove into the space to which he had been directed, and switched off the engine. He released his seat belt, and turned to face his DI.

'What does that mean,' he said.

'The other tenders were withdrawn.'

'You are joking?'

'Nope. There we three apparently.'

'And nobody asked why?'

'Probably, but they'd all have had excuses wouldn't they?'

'How did you find out Gordon?'

Holmes undid his seat belt, and checked that he had his phone and his radio.

'From Josh Holt.'

Caton didn't know whether to be annoyed that Holt hadn't contacted him first, or to congratulate his DI on his initiative.

'You spoke to Holt?'

'Given he's been following the fortunes of the club so closely I thought it he might be worth a try.'

'I thought Holt had disappeared off the face of the Earth.'

Holmes grinned. 'Lucky for us he hasn't. And I haven't told you the best of it yet.'

Caton checked his watch. 'Ged rang to tell them we were coming,' he said. 'You'd better tell them we're on the way.'

'According to Holt,' said Holmes. 'Moston and DSSI have a sideline going. They're using *protection* to cream a percentage off the catering services, off the sales of replica shirts and other merchandise, and controlling the supply of tickets onto the black market.'

'Alternative economy,' said Caton

'You said *black*mail,' Holmes retorted.

'OK, said Caton. '*Extortion*, not blackmail.'

'*Alternative economy* then,' said Holmes. 'Holt also thinks Moston is giving kickbacks to both Lightfoot and Packer, to keep them sweet. That still doesn't give them a motive to kill Okowu-Bello or his agent though,' he reflected.

'Not unless the two of them had somehow found out what was going on.' said Caton. 'It seems a bit extreme though. From what you tell me they could easily have bribed or threatened them.'

'According to Holt,' said Gordon Holmes. ''*Extreme*, is their middle name

Chapter 25

'I was just looking out for my daughter. What's wrong with that?' blustered Gerry Packer.

'So why didn't you tell us, instead of letting us waste our time on a wild goose chase?' said Caton. 'Time we should be using to find the people who killed your player, his agent, and one of your staff?'

'How do I know I can trust your lot to keep their mouths shut?'

Holmes looked as though he was going to hit him. Caton could cheerfully have thumped him himself.

'What made you decide to hide her anyway?'

'To protect her from the bloody press! We're not even safe from their cameras inside the house. Why aren't the police doing something about that?'

'From what I've heard, I'd have thought that Mr Hardman here could sort them out for you.'

It was Dean Hardman's turn to look aggrieved. His face reddened. Whether it was in anger or embarrassment it was impossible to tell.

'What do you mean by that?' he said.

'What did you think I meant?'

Caton watched him closely. Hardman didn't seem sure how to reply. That'll be embarrassment then, Caton decided.

'Instead of using your men to secret Jade away, why didn't you use them to see off the press?' he said.

Hardman recovered his composure.

'Because that would be illegal.'

Gordon Holmes gave one of his trademark snorts of derision.

'I beg your pardon?' said Hardman.

'You're welcome,' said Holmes, staring him down.

'It wasn't my fault some idiot decided to ring the police, and report her missing,' said Packer, shifting their attention back to him.

'That's no way to talk about your wife, Mr Packer,' said Holmes.

'And if I hear you've laid a finger on her,' said Caton. 'I'll arrest you for assault as well as obstructing the police.'

'You can't come here accusing me!' stormed the manager. 'I've got rights, and I've got a witness!'

'Oh I don't think Mr Moston would want Mr Hardman to get on the wrong side of the police,' said Caton calmly. 'What do you think Dean?'

He didn't need to reply. His face said it all.

'Did you believe that about hiding her from the press?' said Holmes as they walked back to the car.

'No,' he replied. 'They must be used to that. In fact she's probably milked all the celebrity by association she could get if the number of times she's appeared in the tabloids and the glossy magazines is anything to go by.'

'I didn't know you read the girlie mags,' said Holmes.

'I don't, Kate does. So don't think you can go around spreading rumours.'

'It sounds like Packer is worried about Jade's safety. The question is who does he consider a threat?'

'Maybe she was waiting to confront him at the

stadium that night. Maybe she saw something. Remind me. What was her alibi?'

'She was at home with mummy and daddy. Went to bed early.'

'Why do I find that difficult to believe?'

'There's no way you'll get Packer to change his story.'

'No,' said Caton. 'But the mother might.'

He stopped walking, and turned to look up at the impressive bulk of the stadium, with its twelve lighting towers, twin latticed arches, and gantries suspended from blue steel wires.

'It has something to do with this place,' he said. 'Don't ask me how I know, I just do.'

'It's the only club in the Premiership with a working surplus, and assets twice the value of its debts,' said Holmes. 'That must be worth killing for?'

'The trouble is what little we have so far brings us back to Okowu-Bello, and his financial situation.'

'Still leaves us with a pile of suspects though,' said Homes cheerfully. 'The Casinos, the betting syndicates, the East Europeans about whom we know bugger all, Dedicated International Security Services Ltd.'

'You hadn't finished telling me about them,' Caton reminded him. '*Extreme* Holt said. What did he mean by that?'

They started walking again.

'Frank Moston set it up with three of his buddies. Two from the marines, and an ex-paratrooper who was briefly in the SAS.'

'Why briefly?'

'According to Holt, he was kicked out of the Regiment, and sent back to the paras.'

'Why?'

'Because he'd been caught thieving.'

'I thought they were trained to do that? They call it foraging and requisitioning.'

'Not when it includes the Commanding Officer's wife.' Holmes laughed. 'That's what saved him apparently. To avoid a scandal the CO had him returned to regiment instead of court martialling him for the theft of his other possessions.'

'Where did they get the start up funds from? Their resettlement money?'

'Partly that, but mainly a small number of investors who became silent partners. Holt is still trying to dig a bit deeper, but he reckon's most of it is dirty money.'

'And yet the firm is clean?'

'On the surface. All the staff are police checked and trained to SIA standards. They wear smart suits indoors, and upmarket coats and parkas outdoors. Even their high visibility jackets are bespoke.'

'But they bully and bribe their way into contracts, and make money on the side in the way that Holt described.'

'Exactly.'

'We'd better do some digging of our own then.' said Caton.

They didn't speak again until they were in the car.

'Agatha Christie,' said Holmes, as the engine started.

'What about her?'

'Compared to us, Hercule Poirot and Miss Marple had it easy. No PACE to worry about. They carried out searches without warrants, questioned suspects without cautioning them. The CPS would have gone crazy.'

'They didn't need to prove anything. The perpetrators always confessed.'

'Maybe that's your problem Boss,' he said. 'If you showed a little more empathy for all those murderers and rapists they'd put their hands up straight away, then we wouldn't need to go jumping through all these hoops.'

'If you don't watch your step, the only one jumping around here will be you. Straight back into uniform.'

Gordon reached under his seat, found the bar, pushed his seat back as far as it would go, and stretched his legs out luxuriously.

'No chance,' he said. 'Where would you be without your Holmes, Dr Watson?' His laughter seemed to fill the car.

'Do you know,' said Caton. 'That when you laugh you sound like a cross between a blocked drain, and a demented gorilla?

He pressed the CD button, and turned up the volume. Hoping that *We are the Champions*, would drown him out.

They were on the M602 heading into the city centre when a message came through on Caton's hands free.

'Mr Munby has some information for you Sir,' Ged told him. 'He wants to know if you'd like to meet for a spot of late lunch.'

There were no surprises there. Munby seemed unable to think on an empty stomach. Ray Barnes had been the same. What was it he wondered with these agents? Last time, Caton recalled, it had been an all you could eat buffet in Chinatown. He wasn't going to go through that again. He looked at the clock on the dashboard. It was twenty past three, and he'd had nothing since breakfast. Kate was going to a play at the Contact Theatre with some of her students, and wouldn't be home till around ten o'clock.

'Tell him Katsouris on the corner of John Dalton Street and Deansgate,' he said. 'I'll buy him a late brunch. Better make it ten to four. I've got to drop DI Holmes off and park up.'

'Drop me off where exactly?' said Holmes.

'At the metro stop in St Peter's Square,' Caton told him. 'You'll be back at Headquarters within fifteen minutes,'

'I could be soaked by then,' said his DI despondently as he stared through the windscreen at the glowering sky.

Caton found Munby in the hot food counter queue, eyeing joints of gammon, beef, and turkey waiting to be carved, glistening peri–peri chicken, and three kinds of continental sausage sizzling in a massive iron pan.

'How do I choose between this, eggs Benedict with smoked salmon, or a full English breakfast?' said the Agent. 'It's impossible.'

'Easy,' Caton told him. 'Join me in a vegetarian meze.'

Munby pulled a face, and shuffled forward to second in the queue.

'I'll get you a coffee, and grab a table,' Caton told him.

'That looks good,' said Munby pointing his knife at Caton's hot ciabatta stuffed with halloumi, tomatoes, asparagus, and tapenade. 'I wouldn't trade it for this though.'

Caton dragged his eyes away from the plate heaped with chorizo, chicken, eggs, bacon, beans and fried potatoes.

'You're going to kill yourself,' he said.

The agent grinned.

'What a way to go though,' he spluttered.

'Let's finish our meal, then talk,' said Caton 'That way neither of us has to get our jacket dry-cleaned.'

Caton finished first. He took the opportunity to ring Duggie Wallace and ask him to run some detailed checks on Dedicated International Security Services. He was putting his BlackBerry away as Munby wiped the remaining smears of egg and chorizo oil from his plate with a piece of buttered bread.

'I didn't think you'd get back to me this quickly,' said Caton.

The agent smiled. 'You wouldn't believe the resources we have available to us Tom.' He popped the bread into his mouth, and began to masticate like a contented bull.

He was right. Caton didn't believe it. He had no doubt that whatever Munby had come to share with him had already been at his fingertips at the breakfast meeting. Either he had not been ready to share it in that forum, or he had been ordered not to.

The agent pushed his plate away, wiped his lips with the serviette, and finished his coffee in a single gulp. Caton half expected him to belch.

'We should make this a regular occurrence,' said Munby. 'It would be great for GMP and Agency relations.'

'Terrible for the figure though.'

'I'll worry about that next time round.' He patted his stomach fondly.

'You didn't invite me here just for the food,' said Caton

The agent looked around the deli and leaned forward conspiratorially.

'Not here,' he said.

I know the very place,' said Caton pushing back

his chair. 'The Rylands Library. It's literally over the road.'

'Straight out of *Tinker Tailor Soldier Spy,*' said Munby in a simulated whisper. 'I can just imagine George Smiley meeting a double agent in a place like this.'

They sat in a booth reserved for private study in an alcove forty feet beneath the magnificent stone vaulted ceiling of the Reading Room.

'They built this room thirty feet above street level so the readers wouldn't be disturbed by the sound of the horses' hooves on the cobbles outside,' Caton told him.'

'They knew a thing or two those Victorians. It works for petrol engines too.'

'It beats walking the streets,' said Caton. 'Now can we get on with it Dave. My team are going to wonder where the hell I've got to.'

Munby peered around the column supporting the shelves. A middle aged couple were standing staring up at the huge stained glass theology window. He decided they were out of earshot.

'OK,' he said. 'Let's start with Lagos. That gang that was putting the squeeze on your victim number one? They're out of the picture.'

He sounded to Caton like a remake of a 1950's film about Chicago during the Prohibition.

'What do you mean, *out of the picture*?'

Our sources tell us that their link was severed with...can we refer to him as OB?'

Caton nodded.

'OB, several months before he was terminated.'

'*Terminated*? Do they have a manual of terms for you to use at the NCA?'

'Sshh!' said the agent. 'No names, no pack drill. That includes the name and initials of our organizations OK?'

Caton wondered if it would have been better to do this by email. Then it occurred to him that Munby wouldn't have wanted to leave either an electronic or a paper trail. It was the last time he'd agree to a meeting outside one of their own buildings.

'Sorry,' he said. 'Carry on.'

'They were approached by the representatives of an Eastern European organisation, and made what was allegedly a very reasonable offer. Foolishly, they declined. Even more foolishly, they roughed up one of these representatives, and issued some particularly nasty and inventive threats.'

'What happened?'

'Two of the leaders of the gang, brothers as it happens, disappeared. I say disappeared, but bits and pieces turned up in neat little packages addressed to their trusted lieutenants, together with a mobile phone containing photos of their nearest and dearest.'

'That would do the trick.'

'It did. The terms of the new offer were considerably less favourable.'

'But they accepted them?'

'They snatched their hands off.'

'Did you find out what these terms were?'

Munby paused while the couple he had observed earlier wandered slowly down the centre of the room to the far end, where they turned to look back down the hall, up at the book filled galleries, at the ceiling, and the great stone statues, before disappearing through the doorway leading to the rose pink spiral staircase.

'In exchange for the contract OB had foolishly signed with them, relinquishing the regular payments they received on the back of that, and fifty percent of the contents of OB's bank account, they were allowed to liquidate that account, see the bank fold, and walk away on their own two legs.'

'What about the Bank's board of directors? They wouldn't have just stood by and let it happen surely?'

Munby stifled a laugh.

'You don't understand,' he said. 'In 2004 there were eighty nine banks in Nigeria, many of them with a capital base of less than ten million dollars. By 2006, as part of a finance reform process, this had been reduced to twenty five consolidated banks with good capital and proper regulation. However, that didn't meet the needs of all the small investors and day to day banking in the country. So over nine hundred sub national microfinance banks sprang up, with one hundred and fifty in Lagos alone. Some of them licensed by the Central Bank of Nigeria, others provisionally licensed. Some neither.'

'And the bank where OB's money was kept was one of those?'

'You've got it.'

'It's still possible that the Nigerians decided to take it out on OB and his agent?'

Munby shook his head.

'Firstly, they didn't dare. Secondly, they are busy living the high life on the back of the six million they were allowed to keep, and finding new ways to make it work for them. Expanding their grip on the supply of drugs, prostitutes and guns according to our contacts.'

'Which leaves the East Europeans?'

'Munby took out his BlackBerry, switched it on, and started searching.'

'We get these supplied,' he said as he flicked through the files. 'Still the most secure on the market, and if BlackBerry Messenger was good enough for the rioters it's...are here it is.'

He turned the device around, and it slid across the table so that Caton could see it.

The photo meant nothing, but he thought he recognised the name. Dmitri Izmailov. There were four addresses, one in Belgravia in London, one in Paris, one in Monte Carlo, and one in St Petersburg.

'Make a note,' said Munby. 'Then swallow it.'

Caton raised his eyebrows quizzically.

'I thought we were *supposed* to be sharing information,' he said.

''Not this,' Munby replied. 'We have an ongoing multi-agency investigation into this guy, and his associates. I'm supposed to warn you not to muddy the waters.'

'Come on Dave,' Caton protested. 'I've got three unsolved murders. I can't sit back and wait until I get the all clear from the Agency.'

'I said *supposed,*' said Munby, reaching for his BlackBerry. 'I never showed you this. Tread softly Tom, and watch your back.'

Chapter 26

'The rape that never was,' said Holmes. 'And the bloodbath that accompanied it. Izmailov was at the party.'

Now Caton remembered. It was four years ago. The Russian had never been interviewed. He hadn't been implicated in any of the deaths or the disappearance of Anjelita Andrades. As a result the reason for his visit to Manchester remained a mystery.

'I want everything there is on Izmailov and his associates,' said Caton. 'Soonest.'

Holmes looked doubtful. 'We'll need another analyst,' he said. Duggie Wallace is up to his armpits with the work you gave him to do on that security firm.'

'Then we'll get one,' said Caton.

He had only just managed to convince Helen Gates of the need for yet more staff, when his Blackberry rang. It was Kate. She was angry, and unnerved.

'My car,' she said. 'Some bastard has clamped it!'

'Where was it parked?' he said, wondering if he dare tell her to be more careful.

'On Denmark Road. Between the Manchester Academy, and the Whitworth Gallery.'

'That's free parking?' he said.

'Precisely! Not only that but they left a note under the wiper blade.'

'Did it give a number for you to ring?'

'Did it hell. It said *"Tell Him to Bak Off."*

'Say that again.'

"Tell him to Bak Off." With *a* capital H, capital B, capital O, and Back spelt without the c.'

'And there's nothing else? No phone number on the clamp itself?'

'No, nothing.'

Where are you now Kate?'

'Sat on the bonnet of the car.'

'I'll come and get you,' he said.

'What about the clamp?'

'I'll get our traffic guys to cut it off.'

'Can you do that?'

'It's illegal,' he said. 'The clamp, not them doing it obviously.'

He checked his watch. It was the end of the rush hour. It would still be fairly heavy on Oxford Road and Cambridge Street.

'It'll take me half an hour at least,' he said. 'Why don't you wait in the Gallery café?'

'It closed at 4.30.' she told him.

She would be cold and despondent. Now that her anger had dissipated Caton could hear it in her voice. He tried to visualise the immediate area around her.

'If you walk back down to Stockport Rd and turn left there's a café on the precinct, just after Greggs.'

'Gemini,' she said. 'They do decent fish and chips.'

'Why don't I pick you up there? You can get yourself a coffee.'

'Good idea,' she said. 'And Tom, can you please tell them to take this clamp off as quickly as possible? I have to go out again this evening.'

'I hadn't forgotten,' he said.

As he was opening the car door Caton's BlackBerry told him he had a text. It was from Josh Holt asking him to ring him as a matter of urgency. It would have to wait.

'What the hell is going on Tom?'

Caton sat on the bed watching her put on a fresh skirt and jumper. He had promised to wait while she changed, and then to drop her off at the Contact Theatre. He had been assured her that her car would be freed by the time the play had finished.

'I have no idea,' he said. 'But I'm going to find out.'

It didn't make any sense. He could think of no one who would imagine for a moment that a threat like that would prevent him pursuing the investigation. Even if he did ask to be taken off the case, someone else would carry it forward. Even East European gangsters couldn't be that stupid, could they?

'How?' she said, wriggling into her super stretch legging jeans, a shade of green that perfectly matched her eyes, and complemented her glorious auburn hair.

He couldn't understand why so many women wore them when they accentuated their bow legs or knobbly knees. On Kate they looked dangerously sexy.

'I've asked for the clamp and the note to be tested for fingerprints, and analysis of the footage from the cameras in the area. Something might turn up.'

He didn't sound hopeful.

She sat down on the bed beside him to slip on her ankle boots.

'Isn't that a bit extreme?'

'Not if someone's trying to obstruct a multiple murder investigation.'

'I suppose.'

He put his arm around her, and pulled her towards him.

'Are you OK?' he said.

'I'm fine,'

She kissed him on the cheek, and eased herself free so that she could fasten the straps.

'So long as this isn't going to escalate.'

Tom didn't think that it would. But it was a worry that they had gone to the trouble of linking Kate to him. He didn't need the distraction, which was possibly what they had intended. Either way, now that she was pregnant he couldn't take the risk of anymore shocks or nasty surprises. He would see that it was taken seriously.

'Come on,' she said, jumping up. 'Or I'll be late.'

By the time he'd dropped her off it was close to seven thirty. He decided to go back to the incident room. At least he wouldn't have to worry about Kate waiting for him in an empty apartment.

It was only when he'd reached his desk that he remembered the text from Josh Holt. He tried ringing him. There was no reply. Not even a voice message. So he tried his home number. This time all he heard was a continuous tone. He tried British Telecom who informed him that the line was faulty, in that there was no connection whatsoever. He asked what that meant.

'Either one of our lines is down, or the phone has been disconnected,' he was told.

He tried Gina Burman instead.

''Have you heard from Josh?' he said. 'He wanted to speak to me urgently but he's answering neither of his phones.'

'I've had the same problem,' she replied. 'To be honest I was beginning to worry.'

Caton had a sudden sense of foreboding.

'Where are you now?' he said.

'I've just done a hand over on the JP surveillance,' she said. 'I'm on the A6048 just outside of Oldham, heading into the city centre.'

'Give me Josh's address,' he said. 'I'll meet you there.'

It was a two bedroomed duplex apartment in the faded grandeur of a three storey Edwardian house in Didsbury, just off Lapwing Lane. Perfect for students at the nearby Manchester Met University, or nurses at The Christie Hospital. Not at all what Caton had expected. He imagined Holt living in a city centre apartment, close to where all the action was.

There were two cars parked in the large driveway, and another on the road outside. None of them matched Burman's Ford Kia.

Caton stood reading the names beside each of the bell pushes on the panel beside the front door. There were 4 flats in total. Burman's was on the ground floor. Caton pressed the button and waited. There was no response. He tried again. The third time he tried another of the names. Kylie, on the second floor.

'Hi,' came a young female voice. 'Who is this?'

'This is Detective Chief Inspector Caton, Greater Manchester Police,' he replied. 'I need to get into the building. It's urgent.'

There was a long pause.

'Are you still there?' he said.

'Yes. But how do I know you're who you say you are?'

Caton could see her point, but even with a video phone there would have been no way of proving he was who he said was.

'Is there a security chain on this door?' he said.

'I think so, though I've never had call to use it.'

'Good. If you could come down and put the chain on, I can pass you my identity card through the gap in the door.'

He heard her sigh.

'OK,' she said. 'But you'll have to wait a minute, I was halfway through changing.'

The minute turned out to be nearer three, by which time Gina Burman had joined him on the doorstep.

'What's going on?' she asked.

'I don't suppose you've got a key?' he said.

She looked affronted. 'Holt and I have only been working together for a week,' she said. 'And that's all it is, work.'

The door opened wide. She was in her mid twenties, Caton estimated, wearing a nurse's uniform under a navy blue raincoat. Petite, blond, and pretty. In one hand she held her keys, in the other a bright red shoulder bag.

'The chain's broken,' she explained. 'Someone's snapped off the catch.'

He showed her his ID card. She looked at it, more out of curiosity than concern, and handed it straight back.

'I've got to get to work I'm afraid. I'm on nights.'

'No problem,' he said. 'And thanks.'

Caton and Burman stood aside to let her pass.

'What's your name,' he said. 'In case I need to speak with you.'

She stopped, and looked at him more closely. Then at Gina Burman, then back at him.

'I think I'd like that,' she said with a cheeky smile. 'I'm Cathy. Cathy Rawlinson. Flat 4, but then you already know that.'

She turned, and set off down the drive with an exaggerated sway of her hips.

'I think you've scored,' said Burman.

Caton was already inside the hallway. As she joined him he began hammering on the door to Holt's apartment.

'If he's not answering his phone or the door bell, it's odds on he's out,' Burman pointed out.

Caton examined the lock. 'An A2001 Rim Autobolt,' he observed. 'I won't be opening this with a lock pick, or a credit card.'

'He takes his security very seriously,' said Burman. 'I should really get one of these myself.'

'Yes you should,' he told her. 'A single woman living alone.'

'Are you sure about that?' she said. 'For all you know I might...'

He had already passed her, was down the steps, and heading around the back of the building. She found him standing in a flower bed by a bay window.

'It's a pity his vigilance hasn't extended to the windows,' he said.

It was obvious that the window of the side bay nearest to them had been forced open. Someone had removed the wooden band between the sill and the window, and had then forced the window with a jemmy or a chisel that had left deep gouges in the sill. The lights were on.

'That's the trouble with keeping sash windows,' she said. 'Fashion over safety.'

'You wait here,' he said, turning away.

'Why? Aren't we going in?'

'Have you forgotten so soon?' he said. 'This is a crime scene. If we go hoofing in there we stand to muddy the evidence.' He looked down at his shoes, suddenly aware how true that was.

'Of course I haven't forgotten.' She sounded affronted by the suggestion. 'But what if something's happened to Josh?'

'If it has there's probably not a lot we can about it,' he said.

Caton returned with his murder bag and the piece of carpet from the boot of his car he kept there in case of emergency tyre changes. He placed the carpet beneath the window, and handed Gina a pair of over shoes and a pair of latex gloves.

'Put these on,' he said. 'And try not to touch the window frames with your coat.'

He climbed in first, and helped her to join him. They found themselves in an open plan kitchen and lounge. Whoever had broken in had done them a favour by moving the table and chairs away from the window. Cupboard doors were open, as were most of the drawers. There was a knife block in the middle of the table; all of the knives appeared to be there. Books from the only book case had been left in neat piles on the floor of the lounge. The disc slot on the DVD was open but neither it, nor the television, nor the Zeppelin iPod SoundDock had been taken.

They moved cautiously into the wooden floored hallway from which a flight of stairs led up to the first floor.

To their right, at the end of the landing, the door to the master bedroom was open. The room had been ransacked. The mattress had been upended, and was propped against the wall behind the headboard. The contents of the single wardrobe, and the chest of drawers, were strewn on the floor. What appeared to be the contents of the bedside cabinet were spread out on the base of the bed.

Neither of them spoke.

They walked back onto the landing and turned right into the second bedroom. It had been converted into an office cum study. The contents of two, large, three drawer beechwood filing cabinets, were piled in separate heaps in the middle of the floor. A far more substantial small metal cabinet had been forced open. The drawers were empty. A series of mixed sized raffia baskets held jumbles of headphones, wires, and battery chargers for various electronic devices. None of those devices were in evidence.

The desk itself was empty but for a 22inch flat screen monitor. To the left and right of the monitor black wires snaked from circular holes in the surface of the desk. More wires were evident on the floor beneath the desk. The devices to which they connected had gone. The integrated double drawers gaped open. There was nothing inside.

'They'd give our search teams a run for their money,' Gina Burman observed dryly.

Caton knew she was trying to make light of a situation that was becoming grimmer by the second. He found it interesting that she had said *our* search teams. Emotionally she had still not severed her connection with the force.

'A damn sight neater too,' he replied.

There was only one room left, at the end of the landing. It was a half tiled bathroom with stone coloured synthetic flooring. There was a muted sound of running water.

His own face stared bleakly back from a mirror above a cream ceramic washbasin with chrome taps. Beside it stood a matching WC, and a storage unit. The doors of the unit were open revealing an unremarkable selection of bathroom products.

He stepped a little further into the room. The whole of the right-hand corner, originally hidden behind the door, contained a floor to ceiling multi-power shower unit in a glass enclosure. Caton took a deep breath, and turned to leave the room.

Gina Burman blocked his way. She searched his eyes.

'I want to see,' she said.

'There's no need,' he told her

She shook her head.

'There is. Don't patronise me Tom. It's hardly going to be my first time is it?'

'The first time it's someone close to you Gina.'

She placed a hand on his chest and pushed him back into the room. She turned, put a hand to her mouth, and froze.

Chapter 27

Josh Holt lay on the tiled floor, in the corner where the two walls met. His knees were pulled up to his chest. His hands appeared to cradle the crown of his head. It was a classic defensive position. It had failed him.

The shower was on. A gentle spray washed over him. Pink tendrils swirled around his feet until the inexorable pull of the vortex took them spinning down the plug hole.

What little Caton could see of Holt's head and face told him that the investigative reporter had been systematically beaten. White gashes of flesh and skin were evident among the matted clumps of hair. At least one cheekbone had been gashed and dislocated. Both of the hands were a mangled mess. Pieces of bone showed through where fingers had been shattered.

Either he had all but bled out, in which case there must be another more grievous wound, or it was simply that once his heart had ceased to pump the shower had washed away the bloody residue from the open wounds.

Gina had held up well. Apart from supporting herself with a gloved hand on the bathroom wall, she seemed composed. Had he not other things to worry about Caton would have chided himself for having doubted her. Somehow, he didn't think she would appreciate an apology.

'There's nothing we can do,' he said. 'I need to call it in.'

She nodded, and turned to leave ahead of him.

'Are you going to tell them we came in?' she asked, as they made their way down the stairs.

'There are no *them*,' he said. 'The deaths are all connected. That makes me the senior investigating officer, unless they decide this is the final straw, and pull me off the case.'

He made the calls, and slipped the latch on the front door. The two of them stood in the hallway, with their backs against the wall, waiting.

'While you were watching Jade Packer,' he said. 'What was Josh doing? Whatever it was, it got him killed.'

She looked down at her feet. Caton thought she looked tired. Though whether it was sitting in the car all night in Saddleworth, or the effect of what she'd just seen he had no idea. In all likelihood it was a combination.

'I don't know,' she said. 'Not for certain.'

'You must have some idea, surely. Or you wouldn't have agreed to work with him.'

'You've no idea how secretive he'd become.' She plucked nervously at her jacket as though it had suddenly become too tight. 'But you're right he did drop titbits here and there, to keep me interested.'

'Such as?'

He wanted her to get on with it, but he knew it wouldn't help to push too hard. She was probably busy finding ways to blame herself for what had happened to Holt. He knew he would in her position.

'From what I gathered,' she said. 'It started as an investigation into corrupt practices in soccer. In the Premiership that is.'

'Such as?'

'Illegal bungs to managers, players, and agents; tax evasion; illegal acquisition of clubs; international betting scams. That sort of thing.'

He nodded. 'It figures.'

'Apparently he reckoned Okowu-Bello was in the thick of it, except for the illegal acquisition of clubs. But while Josh was digging he said he'd come across something completely different. He said it was unbelievable, and it was going to make us both rich and famous.'

Caton felt the hairs on the back of his neck stand up. It could have been a post adrenalin effect, but he doubted it.

'Go on Gina,' he said. 'Spit it out.'

She looked up at him, the disappointment etched on her face.

'That's it Tom. That's all he said. I'm sorry.'

'He must have said something else,' said Caton, unable to prevent his frustration showing. 'Think, Gina think.'

She was startled by the intensity with which he said it. She straightened up and began to pace nervously up and down the hallway. Suddenly she stopped and turned.

'There was something else. He said it was going to leave a lot of red faces in Downing Street.'

'Downing Street,' he echoed. The Prime Minister? The Cabinet?'

'Presumably. Not only that he said...' she strained to remember the exact words.

'There will be a few red faces in the Greater Manchester Police Authority too.'

'The Police Authority,' he said. 'Are you sure about that. Not Greater Manchester Police, but the Police Authority?'

'That's what he said.'

She seemed certain of it.

Caton had no idea what it meant, other than that things were going to become even more difficult, and complicated. As though four murders wasn't bad enough.

'He was all right, Josh,' she said, as though continuing the conversation with someone else. 'When he wasn't busy being obsessed with the next big story. He could be thoughtful, and considerate and, unlike most reporters I know, he was never cynical or sexist.'

Caton looked up. She had tears welling in her eyes, and was shaking ever so slightly. Shock and loss. A lousy combination. He put his arm around her, and hugged her close.

'It's all right Gina,' he said, knowing full well that it was anything but.

He led her to the stairs, and sat her down on the third step. Then he sat on the step below. Their feet had already tramped over whatever the perpetrators might have left. A few extra fibres weren't going to make it any worse. His brain was pursuing what Gina had said about the Police Authority when his phone rang. It was Kate. He checked the time. Five minutes past nine.

'Kate,' he said. 'Where are you? The play can't have finished yet?'

'It's the interval,' she replied. 'I've got a text here from Helen. She wants us to have Harry a day early. Something about a Teacher Day.'

Caton cursed inwardly. He had forgotten that it was his turn to have his son for the weekend. But a Friday. What was she playing at? She knew he couldn't have a weekday off, at the best of times. This was the worst of times.

'That's not on Kate,' he said. 'You'll have to tell her

no. Tell her I'll explain when I've got a moment.'

'Why can't you do it now?'

She sounded as though she was struggling not to show how annoyed she really was. Caton didn't blame her. What with the car, and now this.

'Because,' he said. 'I'm at a murder scene.'

He heard the breath leave her body like a sigh.

'Oh Tom,' she said. 'Not another one. Please tell me it's not connected.'

'It's connected.'

'Shit!' she said.

Obscenities had never been a part of her vocabulary when they started going out together. Not even that time when she had been abducted. Over the past few months they had become increasingly evident. It was his fault, he knew. That and the fact that she was pregnant, her hormones all over the place, and that was his fault too.

'Are we likely to become involved?'

He knew that she was talking about the Offender Profiling unit at the University, where she worked.

'No. It's not a serial killer,' he said.

'It doesn't have to be. You know that we're just as skilled in identifying patterns and profiles of professional killings,' she said. 'If that's what they are?'

'I don't want you involved Kate,' he said.

'Because I'm expecting a baby?'

She was no longer bothering to hide her irritation.

'Not just that.'

'Tom, now you're beginning to worry me.'

She had said worry because she didn't frighten easily. But it came to the same thing in the end. In this case he knew that she was concerned for him, not for herself. He, on the other hand, was thinking about her car, and the warning. And how reckless these people had been from the outset.

'There's nothing to worry about,' he told her. 'We'll talk about it when I get home.'

'How long will that be?'

'I have no idea. As soon as I can.'

'I'll tell Helen OK,' she said. 'I can work from home tomorrow. I'll take Harry to The Museum of Science and Industry. He'll like that.'

'You don't have to do that,' he said.

He heard a bell ring in the background. Almost simultaneously, the buzzer to the apartment sounded.

'I've got to go,' she said. 'I hope your guys have released my car.'

Caton hoped so too.

'Make sure you take someone with you when you go to check,' he said, only realising after he'd said it that it gave the lie to his insistence that there was nothing to worry about.

'Don't worry,' she said. 'I'm giving a couple of the students a lift. One of them practices martial arts.'

He couldn't tell if she was joking or not. The buzzer rang again.

'I love you Kate,' he said as he stood up and headed for the door.

She had gone, and he was talking to himself.

'I think we'll find that it was the gun shot that killed him.'

Holt's hands had been prized away, to reveal a jagged hole in the centre of his forehead. It was identical to the entry wound on the head of Okowu-Bello's agent, Dave Munby. The bullet had shattered a tile and fallen to the floor where it had lodged beneath his buttocks.

'It was on a downward trajectory, which is why you couldn't see the exit wound or the shattered tile,' explained Flatman, the pathologist. 'I'm sorry I missed out on Gideon Jones, but from the photographs and what I read of Jean Hope's splendid PM report, I'd say the modus operandi, and in all probability the weapon, were identical.'

'I didn't think you dealt in probability,' said Caton.

Flatman smiled. 'I'm sure you will allow me the occasional lapse.'

'In which case,' said Caton. 'How about the time of death?'

'There are lapses, and lapses,' Flatman replied. 'I can't help you with that one. Not yet anyway.'

'Why not?'

Because he's been dead for some time. And the cooling effect of the constant running water has muddied the waters.' He paused to look down at the body. 'Bloodied the waters too as it happen.'

'Just give me a window, doctor,' said Caton. 'I don't care how wide it is.'

'In that case, let's see. Rigor mortis is well advanced.' He checked his notes for the temperatures he had recorded. Then straightened up as though making a grand pronouncement.

'Sometime last night.'

'How are you defining night?' said Caton.

The pathologist sighed, as though humouring a child.

'Say between 11pm, and 5am in the morning.'

Caton looked at the head wound.

'Could they have used a silencer?'

'Won't know till I've done the post mortem. You could always ask your firearms experts.'

Caton thought about it. The walls were tiled. Maybe the shower was on. The nurse lived in the apartment above. If they'd seen her leave they'd have known they didn't need one. He thanked the pathologist and went into the room Holt had used as an office. The crime scene manager was watching a technician who was under the table examining the wires.

'There's no chance of retrieving any of his data,' said Caton. It was so obvious he hadn't bothered to phrase it as a question.

The technician sat up, and banged his head on the underside of the desk. He backed out, rubbing his skull.

There's always The Cloud,' he said.

'The Cloud?'

'Virtual back up,' he said. 'Don't tell me you don't use one?'

Caton did. He'd just forgotten that's what they called it. As well as backing up his data on the hard drive, it was automatically saved to a secure data centre somewhere in the world that only his broadband provider knew about. In fact it was backed up twice. Because his antivirus provider also backed it up to their own servers.

'You know what they say about data,' said the technician. 'If it's not saved in three different places, it doesn't exist.'

He was right. A burglary or a fire could easily take out the computer, paper copies, and any disks or data keys. This is precisely what had happened here, and in Gideon Jones's house.

'All we have to do is find out who his provider was,' the man said cheerfully. 'And then get a court order to make them release his files, and hey presto, we've got everything the thieves have got. Maybe even more.'

That could take a month at least, Caton reflected ruefully. Even longer depending on who, and how obstructive and difficult, the provider might prove to be.

'On the other hand,' said the man standing up, with a broad grin on his face. 'You could simply plug this into a computer instead.'

He held out his hand. Nestled in his palm was a shiny black device the same shape, and slightly larger than, a mobile phone. Except that this did not have a screen.

'What is it?' said Caton.

'An S1, mini portable, usb 200 gigabyte hard drive. It won't have the whole of his hard drive on it, but given where I found it my guess is this was what they were looking for.'

'Where did you find it?'

The man pointed to the bottom of the integrated drawers.

'He'd Velcroed the protective wallet for this to the underside of the unit. All he had to do was back up his work whenever, and then slip it into the wallet. I'd never have found it if I hadn't use this.'

He pointed to a ten centimetre diameter mirror attached to a long handle on the floor under the desk.

Caton took the hard drive and examined it. It looked innocuous enough, but he wouldn't have swapped it for its weight in gold.

'Chain of evidence,' said the crime scene manager handing him a bag.

Chapter 28

'I am not leaving!'

Gina Burman folded her arms across her chest and clenched her fists. She looked, and sounded, like a petulant child. Caton admired her spirit. He would probably have reacted in much the same way.

'You can't make me.' It was almost an afterthought.

They were standing in the hallway to the apartments, where they had to move at frequent intervals as members of the scene of crime team trekked between the apartment and their vans. Caton took her by the elbow, and led her out into the cold night air.

'You're right,' he said. 'I can't force you to go and stay with your sister. I understand that you want to play your part in bringing Josh's killers to justice. And you probably want to finish the work he'd begun; for him, not you. But when you take a deep breath, and think about it, you'll know it makes sense.'

She turned her head away and watched the ghostly figures of the crime scene officers come and go in their Tyvek suits. Their breath punctuated the still night air with wraithlike clouds of steam. Police tape guarded by a uniformed officer crisscrossed the entrance to the drive. The steady flash of blue light from a patrol car on the other side of the high yew hedge gave the scene an ethereal glow. It was a sight with which she had once been all too familiar.

'They haven't found what they were looking for,' he said. 'If they knew where he lived the odds are that they know you were working with him. Who do you think they are going to visit next?'

She turned and looked at him defiantly.

'Not necessarily. If they've got his computer and hard drive, and all of his disks and papers. She pointed to the evidence bag he was clutching like a winning Euro Lottery ticket. So they'll have everything he's saved on there.'

'Are you willing to risk your life on that assumption?'

'If you really think they'll come looking for me,' she reasoned. 'You can use that against them. I can be the bait.'

His voice hardened.

'Even if I was prepared to go down that road, which I'm not, they wouldn't let me. Not after the last time.'

He saw the recognition in her eyes.

'It was Joanne Stuart wasn't it?' she said.

He nodded. 'Look how that ended. It nearly cost me my career, and Jo her life.'

He didn't need to explain. It was common knowledge. The Police Improvement Agency had even built a case study around it into their training on undercover operations. Eighteen months on, and it was still raw. Not that he would ever forget it. Nor would DS Stuart.

'At best you would be a distraction. At worst...' he looked back towards the house, at the window of the first floor shower room.

'There must be a way,' she said, but it was obvious the fight had gone out of her.

'I want you to follow DS Carter. He'll take you back to our incident room. He and DS Stuart will ask you all the questions you would have asked if you were still in the force. Then one of them will accompany you back to your place, where you can pack whatever you need. Then they'll make sure you reach your sister's, or wherever you decide to stay.'

She passed a hand over her forehead as though wiping something away.

'What about my house?'

'Is anyone else living there?'

She smiled weakly.

'No.'

'So you were winding me up when you took me to task for assuming you were single?'

'Not at all. The fact that I am, didn't excuse you for assuming that I am.'

It was the kind of unassailable logic in which Kate excelled, and for which he never had an answer.

'I already have someone watching your house,' he said. 'We'll keep it under surveillance until we catch them.'

'You're that confident?'

He raised the evidence bag.

'I am now.'

Gordon Holmes was the last to arrive. It was his son Robbie's birthday, and Gordon had promised to take him, and his wife Marilyn, out for meal at Tom and Jerry's. The boy's choice. After that blip where he'd got in with a bad crowd, and had started skipping school, it all seemed to have come good. Robbie was in the Lower Sixth now, studying A Levels, and making his dad proud. Caton had left it as long as possible before calling in his DI.

'How was the meal Gordon?' he asked as Holmes slammed the door of the patrol car, ducked under the tape and stormed up the drive.

'Bangin'!' he said. 'Apparently. Thanks for letting me finish my dessert, and thanks for arranging the taxi.'

'No problem,' said Caton. 'I wouldn't have wanted my DI arrested for drunk in charge, not tonight anyway.'

He studied Gordon closely. 'Are you sure you're up to this?' he said.

Holmes looked seriously affronted.

'The day I can't function after a glass of cava, two glasses of red wine, and a bottle of Grolsch will be a bad day indeed.'

'Seriously,' said Caton lowering his voice. 'I need you to take over here. There are still some important decisions to make. We can't afford any slip ups, and you can't afford to have people talking about you. Not again.'

To his credit Holmes looked suitable chastened. He took a packet of *Fisherman's Friend* from his pocket, popped one in his mouth, and stretched himself up to his full height. He was still considerably shorter than Caton.

'I know Boss, he said. 'I'll do you proud. Trust me.'

All of the key pieces of evidence had been gathered. The body was ready to be transported to the morgue. Witness statements, to the extent that there were any, were already being taken. It was more about maintaining the crime scene, keeping the residents calm, and the press at bay. Together with re-interviewing the most promising witnesses. Not a lot could go wrong, surely?

'Alright Gordon,' he said, taking his arm and heading towards the front door. 'I'll fill you in.'

'Two hundred gigabytes?' observed the forensic computer analyst, turning over the portable hard drive in a gloved hand. 'I hope you're planning to stay the night Sir?'

'Why,' asked Caton, his heart sinking. 'How much will there be on there?'

He sucked the air in between his teeth. It reminded Caton of the used car salesman who had taken his first car in part exchange. He wondered if that was where the expression *'it sucks'* came from.

'The equivalent,' of approximately 145,000 floppy disks, or 120 million A4 pages of continuous text.'

He plugged the hard drive in with a usb connector, and they both watched as data filled a small box on the screen.

'Actually, it's not so bad,' said the analyst. 'He's been selective. Only half a gigabyte used. That shouldn't take you longer than the middle of next week.'

'How long can you stay?' said Caton.

'As long as you like.' He grimaced. 'There's no one waiting at home now the divorce is through, and I need the overtime to pay the maintenance.'

'I shouldn't need you for too long,' Caton told him. 'So long as you can you sort the files in folders by type, and in date order, with the most recent first.'

The analyst looked over his shoulder at Caton leaning forward in an attempt to make sense of it all.

'You mean documents, Pictures, databases, Excel files, and so on?' he said.

'Exactly.'

He turned back to the screen, his fingers already dancing over the keyboard.

'D'you want the good news, or the bad news?'

'The bad.'

'This is password protected.'

'And the good news is what exactly?'

'That I'm guessing he hasn't bothered to encrypt them.'

'Can you crack the password?'

'Eventually, but it would help if you could give me some clues.'

Carter had just left Gina Burman's sister's house forty miles away in Goosnargh, in the Trough of Bowland. He was not best pleased at the thought of having to go back.

'I'm sorry Nick,' said Caton. 'This isn't something I can do over the phone. You need to sit her down, and get her to pick over every aspect of Holt's life that she came in contact with.'

'Such as?'

'His favourite food, drink, hobbies, football team, players, music, TV programmes. I don't know. Use your imagination. What do you use for your passwords?'

'*Todger* - My first dog's name, *HoltsCrystal* – my favourite beer, my date of birth...'

Caton stopped him in his tracks.

'For crying out loud!' he said. 'I didn't ask you to tell me them. Just think about the way you choose yours, and use that to prompt her.'

'OK Boss. I'll ring you back. Can I go home then?'

'I insist you do,' said Caton. 'Just one thing Detective Sergeant.'

'Yes Boss?'

'You called your first dog *Todger*?'

'I was only thirteen at the time,' he said. 'And the dog *was* well endowed.'

'I bet your mum was pleased.'

Carter laughed.

'She thought I'd called him *Dodger*.'

It was fifteen minutes before Carter rang back with the information. Caton had used that time to get as much data as he could on the dead reporter. He had his date of birth, birthday, his parents' full names, his national insurance number, his National Health Number, his driving licence and passport details, and the schools he attended. Gordon Holmes had gleaned as much as he could from the jumble of books and photos, posters, CDs and record albums now strewn around the apartment. The analyst entered it all into the password cracker he was using. It took another twenty minutes before the analyst punched the air.

'Got it!' he proclaimed.

'What was it?' said Caton coming across to see for himself.

'His favourite song, plus his year of birth. *Jarofhearts77*'

'Christina Perri?'

'Must have had a feminine side. Maybe he'd been unlucky in love.'

'Not only in love,' said Caton. 'How long will it take you now?'

'Shouldn't take more than twenty minutes, but I'm happy to hang on for as long as you want. I wasn't joking about needing the overtime.'

Chapter 29

Caton went to get them both a drink from the machine. He had already decided that he had no option but to work through the best part of the night. Not only were the first 72 hours after any murder the most critical, but come morning he would be besieged on all sides. All of the newspapers would be scrambling to get copy for the second and third editions. It wouldn't take them long to tie Josh Holt into the other murders. Half of them would be screaming serial killer, the other half would be dreaming up one conspiracy or another. The top brass here in Central Park would almost certainly have run out of patience. He had until seven in the morning to come up with answers. After that he had no doubt the National Crime Agency would, at best, be piggybacking his investigation or, at worst, taking it over altogether.

He checked his watch. It was twenty seven minutes past midnight. Too late to ring Kate. He decided to send her a text instead. There were two from her that he had missed. The first was to let him know she was home safely. The second that she was going to bed. There was nothing about a meal in the microwave, or that she loved him. Just a solitary X that could have been added by force of habit.

He felt a knot in his stomach. It was hardly surprising given that he hadn't eaten in over eight hours. He also recognised it as the feeling he used to get when he and his first wife had started to drift apart. He was determined not to screw it up a second time. He was beginning to wonder if determination was going to be enough.

He composed, and sent the text. Then he bought a packet of cheesy Wotsits, two packets of crisps, and two Snicker bars, from the dispenser, and stuffed them in his pockets. As he carried the drinks back to the incident room he promised himself that whatever happened he would be there in the morning when she woke up, and stay until Harry had been dropped off.

It took ten minutes for the analyst to explain what he had done, and to highlight what he saw as some of the most interesting folders, then he left Caton to it while he retired to a nearby desk, feet up, to enjoy his snack. Caton didn't think he'd need him again, but thought it better to play safe. In any case, it seemed as though the guy could do with a break in more ways than one, and he never knew when he might need a similarly swift response in the future.

He placed his cup of coffee well away from the keyboard. It was a rare departure from his usual mug of hot water but he needed to stay not simply awake, but alert. He sat down, and drew up his chair.

The analyst had worked a miracle. Aided, Caton surmised, by Josh Holt's own orderly mind. There were six folders. Each of them contained a list of subfolders. Each of the subfolders had files now arranged in date order.

He opened the first of the folders headed *Okowu-Bello*. It contained five sub-folders: *Sex Life; The Nigerian Connection; Finances; Betting; His Form.* Caton opened them in turn, and studied the contents.

He could see from the outset that very little of the information in the first of the sub-folders was new to him. There were the names and details of two teenagers, and a twenty eight year old woman, who would have to be checked out. Holt had already discounted them as having any special significance. Okowu-Bello's relationship with Jade Packer was the last of the entries and the reporter acknowledged the source as Gina Burman. Holt had ended with a succinct summary. It was clear that he saw no link between the footballer's sex life and his murder. Caton agreed. He moved swiftly on to the Nigerian connection.

This was a much slimmer section. Presumably because Holt would have had few if any contacts in Lagos, and no expense account to fund a trip out there himself. The bulk of his information appeared to have come from research on the web, a reporter on the leading Nigerian Newspaper, and Joseph Azuku, Okowu-Bello's fellow countryman and team member who had first set Caton off in that direction. Again there was nothing new, and considerably less than that Caton had been given by the National Crime Agency.

The folder on his finances confirmed everything Caton had discovered about the rise and fall in the dead man's financial position. The loss of the millions held in the Lagos bank, the money secreted in the Belize account, the role of his agent and accountant, and the ups and downs of the player's apparent cash flow. It amazed Caton how much information Holt had managed to glean without the resources he had available through the Force.

Perhaps it was not that surprising Caton reflected, given the number of people completely unrelated to his own financial arrangements that rang to tell him they knew his insurance was due for renewal, his current tracker mortgage was about to run out, his bank rate was going to change, and offering to find him a better deal. Everyone was busy selling commercially obtained personal information. So much for privacy laws.

It looked as though Holt had been excited by the possibility that the player's financial fortunes might be closely linked to his gambling and to the change in his form on the pitch. Caton eagerly opened the next subfolder headed *Betting*.

For the first time he found information that was not only new but promising. Holt had somehow managed to get details of Okowu-Bello's betting patterns, the Casinos and online sites he used, and the full extent of his wins and losses. Over the twelve months leading up to his death the player had become increasingly obsessed with gambling. He had two preoccupations: black jack and roulette at two casinos in the city, and poker online on two different sites. He lost heavily on all of them.

Holt had ruled out revenge from the online bookies because they charged his credit cards every time he played. If they weren't validated he didn't get to play. It was as simple as that. At some point in September he'd exceeded his credit limit on both cards he used, and the cards were stopped. Instead he had upped his gambling in the casinos. Here he was afforded credit. With his salary and occupation it hadn't been a problem. Until he couldn't pay his monthly tab. Then things had turned nasty.

Holt had managed to identify the real owners of the casinos, rather than those on the list of Directors, and the 'firms' they used to collect from debtors. Nothing illegal was alleged but Caton wouldn't have wanted to find himself with the kind of debts the player had run up.

And then, miraculously, in mid October everything had changed. All of his debts were cleared. He was being afforded credit at one of the casinos, although the other had barred him. Holt had cross referenced this with the file on Okowu-Bello's finances. He had asked the same question Caton had asked. If the player had lost 14 million pounds when the Lagos bank had folded, his assets in Belize were tied up and closely controlled, and his monthly outgoings on his mortgage, cars, and life style more than accounted for his monthly salary, how did he suddenly have access to all this money? According to Holt, the answer lay in the next sub-folder.

Caton leaned back in his chair and stretched his arms, his back, and legs. He found himself yawning. He checked his watch. He had been at it for over an hour. It was time for a break, and another coffee. Behind him the analyst had his legs up on the seat of the chair in front of him, and was snoring. It was a gentle rhythmic sound, like a sow suckling piglets. He decided to let him sleep.

The building was eerily quiet. There was just the hum of the snack dispenser, and a door opening and closing somewhere on the ground floor. It was so far removed from the hustle and bustle of a normal working day that Caton found it slightly disconcerting. Like a student who did all his studying against a background of pop songs, and then had to sit his exams in total silence and found it impossible to concentrate. He took his coffee back to the incident room, suddenly grateful for his companion's musical accompaniment.

The file on the player's form was a detailed analysis of Okowu-Bello's performance not just of the current season, but over the previous two years. It was so detailed that it could only have come from one of those in-game performance analysis programmes such as the *Prozone* system Caton had seen demonstrated at the Etihad where his own team employed seven full-time analysts. Most of the clubs in the Premiership used it, or something like it.

Up to ten cameras tracked the movement of every one of the players, and all three officials, throughout the game. It made it possible to analyse in minute detail the performance of both teams, and individual players. Someone had leaked a file to Holt, presumably in return for payment. It made fascinating reading.

Up until the second game in October of the current season Okowu-Bello's performance had remained fairly consistent against all of the indicators used. These included distance travelled during the game, number of passes made, number of passes completed, number of tackles made, number of these that were successful, number of assists, the number of yellow cards, and red cards received, and the number of goals scored.

From that point on until the day he had died his performance had nose dived. Every single indicator had fallen by between thirty and fifty percent. Except for the number of cards he had received. These had risen. The number of yellow cards had tripled compared with the previous twelve months, and he had been sent off twice in just three months making him ineligible to play for a total of six matches. The effect on the team's performance had been equally striking, causing them to falter, and allowing the other two Manchester teams, together with Arsenal, Liverpool and Spurs, to narrow the gap at the top.

Caton sat back, and sipped his coffee. The conclusion was inescapable. It was one that Caton had already wondered about, but which Holt appeared to have nailed down.

The player's form had nosedived at precisely the point at which his financial problems had disappeared. The change in form was completely out of character, and inexplicable. He had picked up no injuries. The player's around him were unchanged. The source of his additional income was unclear.

The reporter had used contacts in the Gambling Commission and the Remote Gambling Association to dig deeper. It transpired that concerns had already been raised about spot betting in relation to Okowu-Bello during individual games. Especially with regard to his yellow cards, and sendings off. There had also been a surge in betting against the Titans winning the Premiership title despite the impressive gap they had opened up. Some of those bets had come from overseas online betting, unregulated and outside the scope of the UK and European regulators. Far more, it was rumoured, had been placed through illegal betting in the Far East.

Caton had had difficulty in seeing how the player accepting payment in return for agreeing to play in a particular way, or to get booked or sent off to order, could have led to his being murdered. Except, that it is, by fanatical fans, and that had already been ruled out. Josh Holt seemed to have found the answer.

Okowu-Bello's form had suddenly returned to normal in the two weeks prior to his death. If anything he had come back stronger than before, scoring five goals in just three matches, and assisting with four more. What if, under pressure from the Directors, his manager, and the rest of the team, he had ceased to co-operate with whoever was behind the betting scam? There had been rumours in the papers that the player had been hauled before the owner's representative, and the manager, and given a warning that if he didn't buck his ideas up he would be sidelined. If the scale of the bets was as great as Holt had been led to believe, Okowu-Bello's decision to renege on the deal could well have signed his death warrant. He was still mulling it over when the door to the incident room burst open, and Gordon Holmes stormed in. He came straight over to where Caton was sitting.

'It's bloody freezing out there!' he proclaimed. He pulled a chair over and slumped in it. 'Who's the Sleeping Beauty?'

Caton told him.

Holmes peered at the computer monitor.

''Is that what was on Holt's portable back up?'

'Some of it, yes.'

'Anything interesting?' He rubbed his hands together, cupped them, and blew into them. His hair was damp, and he smelt of sweat and warm wool.

'If you're staying,' said Caton. 'You'd better go and get yourself a drink. You can bring me another one too. Then you can update me, and I'll tell you what I've found out so far.'

'Nobody heard anything, nobody saw anything.' Holmes handed Caton his coffee, sat down in the chair he had previously vacated, and tore open a bag of *Mystery Flavour* crisps. 'Now it's your turn.'

'Have SOCO turned up anything?' said Caton.

'Some footprints in the flowerbed under the window they forced to get in. Some more muddy prints on the floorboards and the stairs carpet. The usual raft of fingerprints, but nothing to suggest they might belong to the perpetrators. They'll pick up fibres, and hairs, and sweat no doubt. Oh, and they think he might have some metal particles in the wounds on his head and hands.'

'Like Ratten.' Caton observed. 'A knuckle duster.

'Most likely,' said Holmes. He sniffed the open packet, and crammed a handful of the contents into his mouth. 'Chicken Balti curry,' he declared, spraying tiny particles of fried potato onto the desk.

For God's sake Gordon!' said Caton, brushing them onto the floor. 'Haven't you got a home to go to?'

Holmes shook his head. 'Marilyn won't thank me for waking her at this time of the morning. I'll just turn up for breakfast, have a shave, and come straight back in.'

'Don't forget to change your clothes. You smell like a Labrador that's been running round in the rain.'

The DI pointed his packet at the screen, forcing Caton to cover the keyboard with his hands.

'What have you found on there then?' he asked.

Caton told him.

'And you've still got another five folders to go at?' said Holmes when he'd finished.

Caton nodded despondently.

His DI stood, crumpled the crisp packet in the palm of his hand, and tossed it into the nearest wastepaper basket, missing the sleeping analyst's head by a whisker.

'Right then Boss,' he said. 'Email a couple of them to me, and I'll get to work on them. We'll have it done in half the time.'

Chapter 30

It was ten to four when they came together. Their jackets were over the backs of their chairs. Their shirtsleeves were rolled up. Their beards, unshaven in over twenty hours, more vagrant rubble than designer stubble. Caton had thanked the computer analyst and sent him home to bed.

'I want to get this down so the whole team can see it,' he said.

'There's not enough room on the whiteboards,' Holmes replied. 'I'll get some sheets from a flip board in one of the seminar rooms.'

He came back with six sheets, and began to fix them to the only remaining wall with BluTack.

'I don't think you're supposed to use that on these walls,' said Caton foreseeing peeling paint, and repercussions from the Assistant Chief Officer Resources. His DI carried on regardless.

'If you've a better idea?' he replied.

Caton hadn't. It was, after all, a multiple murder investigation. If it came to it, he'd let Gordon use chewing gum.

Holmes stood back, and surveyed his work.

'Do you want to go first Boss?'

Caton pulled up a chair, and made himself comfortable.

'Let's do it in the order Holt used. Headlines and

key issues only, otherwise we'll still be at when the others turn up.'

Holmes held his notes in his left hand, picked up a black felt tip marker with his right, and wrote a heading on the first sheet. *The Titans.*

'Holt had five sub folders,' he began. 'Each containing a single file. The sub folders were *Ownership, Funding, Transfers & Economic Viability, Directors,* and *Management.* In a nutshell, Holt seems to have managed to arrive at the same conclusion the NCA shared with you. The club was bought with money from two sources; one legitimate, the other criminal.'

Caton nodded. 'The legal source,' he said. 'Being profits made by the Manchester and Shanghai Trading Corporation, and the rest from drugs, sexploitation, gambling, people smuggling, and counterfeit goods?'

'Exactly. The Malay businessman,' he had to check his notes. 'Kitjakarn Pratcha, was the link between them and the legal firm that brokered the deal. Their original plan was to make a quick killing when the club was promoted, and sell it on. That way they'd have successfully laundered the dirty money, and made a tidy profit on top of that.'

'So what changed their minds?'

'According to Holt, three things. First of all sales of season tickets, replica shirts, and all the other merchandise, massively exceeded their expectations. So did the sponsorship they managed to attract. Secondly, the Titans were doing so well they decided to give it until the end of this season, then float the club on the Stock Exchange, and sell their shares for hundreds of times what it cost them to buy the club in the first place.'

'And thirdly?' This was the one that interested Caton most.

Holmes finished the notes he had been writing on

the second sheet. He turned and sat down on the edge of a desk.

'Some of the money used to buy the club had come from illegal betting syndicates. All of those illegal activities were so tied up with each other that it was impossible for Holt to disentangle them. According to his sources however, the people behind these syndicates were making more from their gambling operations than the club was from its core activities. It wasn't in their interest for the club to finish up Champions for a second year in a row, or for Okowu-Bello's form to miraculously recover as it did.'

'The opposite of what the majority owners wanted,' said Caton.

'Precisely.'

'Which gave these silent partners a motive for killing Okowu Bello.'

Holmes shook his head.

'Not exactly. According to Holt, Okowu-Bello's death – especially given it was murder – would have voided all bets relating to his form, and potentially those associated with the Titans too. He reckoned they might have wanted to teach him a lesson, to make sure he kept his side of the bargain, but they certainly wouldn't have wanted him dead.'

'Unless there were other players involved,' said Caton. '*Pour encourager les autres.*'

'Come again?' said Holmes.

'To teach them a lesson. It's from Voltaire's *Candide*. Candide witnesses an English Admiral being shot because he hasn't killed enough of the enemy. He is told that the English shoot an Admiral every now and then to encourage the others.'

'That'd work for me.'

Holmes stood up.

'Anyway, it looks like Holt was going to publish all

this as part of his scoop, but he was looking elsewhere for whoever killed Okowu-Bello and the others.'

'Even so,' said Caton. 'If Holt was going to publish, that alone would have been a reason to kill him.'

'What about Ratten, and the Agent?'

'Ratten because he knew who the killers were, and Gideon Jones because he knew that Okowu-Bello had been bribed by the betting syndicate.'

Holmes rubbed his chin. He seemed surprised by the thickness of the stubble, and rubbed it again.

'I don't buy it,' he said. 'They wouldn't want to draw attention to themselves. And let's face it, as far as they're concerned there are far more fish in the sea.'

Caton agreed. If they could buy international cricketers, athletes, and footballers of Okowu-Bello's standing, they could afford to take the hit, and move on.

'Did Holt have any names in relation to this syndicate?'

'Sorry Boss, not a one. You'll have to see what your friends at the National Crime Agency can come up with.'

He stood up and approached the wall. His felt tip pen hovered over the paper.

'There was one name cropped up I think you'll find interesting,' he said. 'Someone who happens to be on the Board of Directors.'

He turned his back, obscuring what was written from Caton's view. Then he turned back, and stepped to one side, his face suffused with a grin. He had underlined the name twice. *Charles Grey*

'*The* Charles Grey?' said Caton, '*Our* Charles Grey?'

Holmes nodded inanely.

'That's the one. GMP's very own inaugural Commissioner of Police.'

'How come we didn't know about this?'

'Presumably because we didn't ask.'

'It would explain why he's been badgering everybody to get it sorted as quickly as possible.'

'He wasn't invited to join the Board until after he was elected.'

'That makes sense. Until he was in a position of influence he wouldn't have had a lot to offer them. As Commissioner they probably thought he could get them preferential treatment.'

'Like lower rates for policing the games?'

Caton doubted it.

'He wouldn't be that stupid, surely?' he said. Then again, he wouldn't put anything past Grey.

'It shouldn't be too difficult to check it out,' said Holmes cheerfully. 'You never know when that might come in handy.'

Caton couldn't have agreed more, but he thought this nothing more than a distraction.

'Was there anything else?' he said.

'No, that's it.' Holmes lumbered over and handed him the felt tip.

'Your turn Boss,' he said.

Caton took the pen, and walked over to the wall. He moved to the next sheet and wrote a new heading; *The Firm.*

'Josh Holt had six sub-folders,' he said, writing them down in turn as he named them. '*Ownership & Management, History, Activities, Links to the Club, Employees,* and *Revenue.* I'll try and keep this brief, not least because if you remember I asked Duggie Wallace to look into this lot and see what he could find out. He can flesh out any gaps.'

'I'll be surprised if there are many,' said Holmes. 'From what I can see Holt didn't leave a stone unturned.'

Caton's reply was sombre. 'It was something hiding under one of those stones that killed him.' He had a quick look at his notes and started writing. As he wrote he talked.

'We already know that Manc Security, headed up by Dean Hardman, is a subsidiary of Dedicated International Security Services Ltd, run by Frank Moston, who is brother in law of Harry Lightfoot, the Titan's Chief Exec. The source of its original funding is unknown. Both firms are Security Industry Accredited, and licensed, and none of the bosses has a criminal record. The same can't be said for some of the staff in the lower echelons. Holt lists seven or eight in Manc Security alone with convictions ranging from threatening behaviour and affray, to Grievous Bodily Harm. Four of them have done time. Several, including Frank Moston had, and Holt suspected may still have, connections with a Far Right organisation in East Lancashire where Moston hails from.'

Caton had not been surprised. The SIA licence was supposed to reflect a rigorous vetting procedure for all of a company's personnel. He regularly came across security staff acting as door men in clubs and pubs, and at events – even GMP functions – whom he personally knew to have criminal convictions. When you were offering low wages, and expecting a visibly threatening presence, it was inevitable. Not the SIA's fault.

'The most interesting part,' he continued. 'Is the file covering their revenue. They have a number of sidelines, according to Holt, not only here at the Titans, but elsewhere too.'

'Let me guess,' said Holmes. 'Flogging tickets on the black...*alternative* market?'

'That's one of them. They seem to have acquired an exclusive arrangement with the players, and other club employees, to sell on the tickets that they get free, for a percentage. Needless to say Manc Security take the bulk of the profit.'

'What are their other little scams?'

Caton turned to face him.

'Not so little Gordon. In return for what they call security, and Holt describes as *protection,* they cream off a percentage of the catering and events income, and sales from the club shop. They also use the official merchandising people to source replica shirts for them which they then sell on to their contacts on the markets.'

'And no one at the Club is aware of any of this?'

'The respective managers, obviously. And Moston will have insisted on giving them a cut to well and truly implicate them. And then there's Harry Lightfoot himself. He must either know, and be turning a blind eye, or is actively encouraging it, because in the end the bulk of the money ends up back with his brother-in-law.'

'Who will no doubt be a silent partner in DISS. What about the owners? The Chinese?'

'Holt doesn't mention them. My guess is if they ever found out all hell would break loose. After all, the security firm is stealing from them.'

Only when he'd said the words did it occur to Caton that this was something he might be able to use. It wouldn't be something he'd want to discuss in an interview room, on tape. It would have to be deniable. But if it came to it perhaps just the suggestion that someone might let the owners know...

'Is that it Boss?'

Holmes was looking at his watch, impatient to get home and change. Caton checked his own. It was already five o'clock. He glanced at the windows. It was still dark outside, but the Pennine hills were now visible as a mysterious shadowy mass stretching along the horizon.

'That's it,' he said, lobbing the felt tip to his DI.

'I don't know about you but I'm gagging for a drink,' said Holmes placing the pen down on the table beside him. 'How about I go and get them, and then see if we can't wrap it up before the search party arrives?'

Chapter 31

'Right,' said Holmes. '*East European Mobsters*.' He stood back and admired his handiwork.

'Isn't that a bit dramatic Gordon?'

'That's the title Holt gave it,' he said, waving his notes in his defence.

'Fair enough.'

Caton took a sip of his coffee. It was hot, and strong. He'd had that much coffee he doubted he would ever sleep again.

'He kept this one simple,' said Holmes. Just four files: *What, Who, Where, So What*. Perhaps he was getting tired of it all, I know I am.'

He stabbed the first one with his pen.

'A predominantly Russian organised crime network, with links to politicians and oligarchs. They're finding it increasingly difficult to invest their ill gotten gains in the motherland, so they're over here buying up real estate.'

Caton had read in last week's Sunday papers that over a thousand low income families were having to move out of Kensington and Chelsea because of changes to the benefit rules, and foreign investors, led by Russians, were queuing up to buy the empty properties. It was happening in Manchester too.

'And guess whose leading the charge?' said Holmes waving his felt tip in the air?'

'Your old friend Dimitri Izmailov?'

'Shame I never got round to interviewing him,' said Holmes. 'But after Anjelita withdrew her accusation there wasn't any point.'

'Agent Munby named him in connection with this investigation,' Caton reminded him. 'I asked for a detailed check to be run on him. Why haven't I got it?'

Holmes spread his arms wide, palms uppermost. He was a picture of innocence.

'Search me,' he said. 'You also asked for a detailed check on the security firm remember? Duggie Wallace is probably up to his eyes in it.'

'That's why I asked for an extra analyst. Have you seen anybody new in here?'

'Sorry Boss. I've been out and about like you. Even if I'd been here I probably wouldn't have noticed.'

Caton rubbed his eyes. 'What else have you got?' he said wearily.

Holmes consulted his notes again.

'Holt reckons this mob is a regular United Nations. The Russians run it, but they've got links across most of the Eastern European states, especially those in the former Soviet Union. He came up with two names he reckoned were trusted lieutenants of Izmailov's.' He held his notes up close as he wrote the names on the sheet of paper.

'Evegeny Kozlov he has down as his bodyguard and chief enforcer, and a Polish Russian called Stasik Sakovich as his main man here in the North West.'

'Polish Russian?'

'Polish mother, Russian father'. Holmes read verbatim from his notes.

'Pavel Lermontov – Stasik's father - was a Russian military adviser to the Polish Government during the dying years of the Communist era. During this period he married his Polish girlfriend. Following his death whilst leading a

strike breaking operation in Gdansk, his pregnant wife reverted to her maiden name, Sakovich.'

He put the notes down.

'I wouldn't mind knowing where Holt got his information from,' he said.

'Read the Levenson Inquiry Report into phone hacking,' Caton told him. 'That'll give you a clue.'

He stared at the headings on the wall above Gordon's head.

'I take it that the *Where* includes Manchester,' he said. 'Tell me about the *So What*.'

'That's easy,' said Holmes. He listed them off on his fingers before turning to write them down as bullet points.

'Laundering money for the oligarchs through the City of London; buying up real estate; arms dealing; gathering information to be used as leverage in legal and illegal business dealings; softening up targets for East European entrepreneurs; and theft through computer hacking.'

Caton recalled the three Russian hackers who had been jailed for eight years back in 2006. They had extorted over two billion pounds from nine major bookmakers and casinos by threatening to interrupt their betting sites during major sporting events. They proved they could do it by a series of denial of service attacks in which they had hijacked the firms' domain name systems. An easy way to get rich providing you didn't get caught.

'So they're not interested in supplying or dealing in drugs, or bringing in women and girls for the sex trade?'

'Not according to Holt's contacts,' said Holmes over his shoulder as he continued to jot them down. 'They leave marijuana smuggling to the Vietnamese, people trafficking and brothel based prostitution to the Albanians, and Heroin to the Turks, with some help from the Kurds and the Albanians, and cocaine and its derivatives to the British villains who deal direct with the South American and South African suppliers. Some of the other Russian groups dabble in those activities, but more so elsewhere in mainland Europe.'

He stood up and turned round.

'They're into the more Hi-Tec stuff over here. It means they tend to stay under the radar of the Serious and Organised Crime Agency.'

Yet Dave Munby had given Caton Izmailov's name, albeit surreptitiously. That must mean that he was a person of interest to the National Crime Agency.

'I don't see what any of this has to do with Okowu-Bello, or the Titans?' he said.

Gordon Holmes beamed another one of his daft grins.

'Saved the best for last,' he said. 'So did poor old Josh Holt. It seems that Izmailov approached Frank Moston with a proposal to purchase Dedicated International Security Services lock stock and barrel. It was a very decent offer apparently. Moston was interested. He invited Izmailov to a meeting with Harry Lightfoot. Izmailov left empty handed.'

Caton sat up straight.

'Did Holt think that Izmailov had Okowu-Bello killed simply to get back at Lightfoot and Moston?'

Holmes came and sat on the chair beside Caton's.

'Sorry Boss,' he said. 'But that's the lot. Whatever Holt was thinking he didn't share it with us.' He yawned loudly, and stretched his arms. 'Is that it then?' he said. 'Can we go now?'

Caton reached behind him, and picked up his notes.

'Not quite,' he said tapping the papers in his hand.

'I'm not sure what this has to do with anything, but you could say he really did leave the best till last.'

He held out his hand for the felt tip, stood up, and approached the wall. On the final wall he wrote the name *Charles Grey*, and underlined it three times.

'Bloody Hell!' said Holmes when Caton had finished. 'You want to think twice before leaving that up there.'

'I know,' said Caton. 'For now, this is between you and me. I'm going to take that sheet down and lock it in my drawer until I've worked out where we go with it'.

He scanned it again, taking in the key points. The section headed *Early Years* was innocuous enough. Grey had grown up in Blackburn. His parents ran a corner shop and post office. His father was one of the few Conservatives on the local council. Charles attended a local comprehensive where he was poor at sport, but excelled academically. His schoolmates described him as *'a bit of a loner.'* He went off to University in Bradford to study Computer Science. It was during his time there that he allegedly became involved in activities that led Holt to name his next section as *The Nasty Years*.

It seemed that the reporter had managed to find former fellow students who recollected Grey having been part of a small clique of Far Right students who took it upon themselves to disrupt the many student demonstrations pushing for equal rights for women, ethnic minorities, and gays and lesbians. Caton remembered such a group causing trouble at the Anti-Apartheid demos in Manchester and the 20,000 strong day of action in February 1988 by the North West Campaign for Lesbian and Gay rights against the bringing in of Rule 28. Charles Grey would have been too old for the latter but not the former. Perhaps their paths had crossed? One thing was sure, Grey had never been arrested.

After Uni he worked for a few years in a variety of IT firms around Nelson and Colne and Burnley, before branching out on his own. With an original investment of £50,000, the source of which Holt had been unable to identify, he set up a computer consultancy, and an online retail store. Within ten years he had an annual turnover of £8 million, and the company was valued at £46 million. Charles Grey had arrived. His business serviced public corporations and Government departments, as well as selling to the public. Holt thought the consultancy side of his business largely smoke and mirrors. Many were the projects for which he had been paid, that had subsequently failed to produce the benefits promised. Nevertheless, his business had continued to thrive. He received the Queen's Award for Enterprise, and in 2000, an OBE for services to Charity. The loner had become a silver tongued blagger. There were rumours of continuing links with his erstwhile Far Right pals, but Holt had not been able to substantiate any of them. That brought him to *Political Awakening*.

In 2001 Grey sold the business, became a fulltime politician and charitable fundraiser. Careful to distance himself from any one political party he got himself elected onto Manchester City Council as an Independent. In 2003 he was given an OBE for services to charity. Unimpressed, Holt had typed *Other Buggers' Efforts*! Grey's political campaigning centred around pushing for a zero tolerance approach to policing, primarily through turning what he described as a *'touchy feely'* neighbourhood policing approach into a hard edged one. Unpopular though these views were with both the Labour and Liberal Council members, and the Chief Constable, many of the electorate loved them. It had come as no surprise when he announced his candidacy for the post of first Police Commissioner for Greater Manchester. This segued neatly to the final heading.

Election hanky panky. Caton was surprised at Holt's choice of words. He thought him too young to be familiar with the phrase. Then Gordon had reminded him of Madonna's track on her *Breathless* soundtrack album. How could he have forgotten that?

This section was short. Just three paragraphs. It was obvious that Holt had only just begun researching this particular issue. As far as Caton could tell all he had was based on rumour and conjecture.

The history was well known. There had been only two other candidates besides Grey. A former Green Party Member of Parliament, and a female Independent councillor and businesswoman who was already on the Greater Manchester Police Authority. According to the bookies, from the outset the former MP, and Charles Grey, were neck and neck, and the woman was a close outsider.

With only a month to go to polling the female contender withdrew, citing personal and family reasons. There were rumours of her having dabbled with drugs in her student days, and beyond. It then emerged that her daughter had been arrested in possession of crack cocaine, and on suspicion of dealing drugs.

With two weeks to go the former MP was outed in the tabloids as an adulterer. He had allegedly cheated on his wife with her chief bridesmaid on the night before the wedding. In Caton's experience it was not that uncommon, but it was enough to see his standing plummet in the polls. And he withdrew. Charles Grey won by default in what was a very disappointing turn out. Except, according to Holt, among white working class voters in Bolton, Oldham, Salford and Manchester, who would not normally have turned out in such numbers in any elections.

Caton could see where Holt was going with this. Even if he hadn't, the reporter had left little doubt in his even shorter concluding section; *Things to Do.* These he had set down as series of short bullet points.

- *Look for links between CG and Manc Security*
- *Look for links between Manc Security and Neo-Nazis*
- *Talk to Izmailov – Gina can do this. A woman's touch!*
- *Go to Burnley. [Me]*
- *Talk to both the other candidates. I'll take the former MP; Gina can talk to the female.*
- *Tell Jack to sow the seeds for an auction with the newspapers. Won't be long now.*
- *Tell Caton about the Russians. Not too much!*

Caton should have been angry that Holt was planning to feed him just enough to keep him happy and off his back, whilst pursuing what he clearly saw as the most fruitful line of enquiry. Not that fruitful in his sense necessarily meant productive in terms of the murder investigation. Caton was beginning to feel however that it was. In any case, how could he be angry with a dead man? One who had just saved him a mountain of work and set him off in new direction?

Holmes jolted him out of his reverie.

'Penny for them Boss?'

'I was just wondering how much I can afford to tell the others in the morning,' he replied.

'It *is* morning!' said Holmes. He stood and stretched. 'I'm off now if that's alright with you?'

Caton glanced at the clock on the wall. It was ten past six.

'Off you go,' he said. 'And thanks Gordon; I couldn't have done it without you.'

'Too bloody true!' hooted Holmes as headed for the door.

Caton eased the final sheet of paper from the wall, folded it four times, and placed it in the bottom drawer of his desk, which he then locked. When he switched off the lights a faint orange glow filled the room. Through the windows he could see the pink undersides of fluffy clouds in a blue sky tinged red, where dawn heralded a glorious sunrise.

'I hope that's an omen,' he said to the empty room as he pulled the door closed behind him.

Chapter 32

'God, you look awful!' said Kate.

Caton threw his jacket over the back of the chair and started to undress.

'Thanks a bunch,' he said kicking off his shoes and standing on the toes of alternate feet to ease off his socks without bending down.

'I hope this isn't going to become a habit?' she said. 'You and me, passing like ships in the night?'

He stepped out of his trousers, folded them along the crease, and laid them over the seat of the chair.

'I didn't plan it,' he replied. 'Look at me. I'm knackered, and I've got be back in there in less than two hours.'

Kate sat up, pushed back the duvet, and swung her legs out of the bed.

'Oh Tom, you can't! You're going to kill yourself.'

'No I'm not.'

He gathered up his shirt and underpants, and tossed them in the direction of the Ali basket.

'I'm going to have a shower.'

As he entered the ensuite bathroom she called after him.

'In that case I'd better get you some breakfast. What would you like? Cereal, porridge, a fry up?'

But he had already turned on the power jets and didn't hear a word she'd said.

'I left it is a long as I could,' she said, pushing the door open with one elbow. 'I went for cereal, juice, and a fry up.'

Tom lay diagonally across the bed, wrapped in his navy blue bathrobe. His hair was still damp. His eyes were closed, and his breathing was shallow. She was tempted to let him sleep, but she knew he would not thank her for it. She placed the tray on the dressing table and sat down beside him. He looked like a small boy when he slept like this. She brushed the hair away from his forehead and kissed him lightly on his lips. He stirred a little and tried to turn over. She shook his shoulder gently.

'Tom, wake up.'

Reluctantly he opened one bleary eye, and then the other.

'What time is it?'

'Seven thirty.'

'Bugger!' he said levering himself up. 'They'll be expecting me in half an hour.'

'They call you *Boss* don't they?' she said, her hand on his chest, restraining him. Ring and re-schedule the meeting. You've been up all night, you've had no sleep. They'll understand.'

'But...'

'No buts. If it was them instead of you, you'd be telling them to take the morning off.'

She stood, and brought the cereal bowl from the tray.

'Here, get this down you. I'll bring you a cup of tea in a minute. And when your precious meeting's over I suggest you come back home and get some sleep.'

Fat chance of that, he told himself as he scooped up a bite sized piece of shredded wheat.

He'd managed to reschedule for nine o'clock, and had warned Gordon that on no account should he discuss anything they'd discovered with any of the others. When he did arrive he was directed to the reception desk where there was a message.

'Chief Superintendent Gates wants you to go directly to her office, Sir. I understand that the Chief Constable is with her.'

This was the last thing he needed. Whatever it was wasn't going to involve a pat on the back.

'Come in Tom, and close the door,' said Helen Gates.

The use of his first name, and the apologetic tone of her voice, confirmed his fears. This was the way they told you a relative had died, or that you were about to be made redundant.

Robert Hampson sat in an easy chair looking distinctly uncomfortable. His hands were folded in his lap and he was staring out of the window at the Fujitsu building opposite.

Caton made a point of standing, like a schoolboy waiting to be reprimanded.

'Sit down, for God's sake Tom,' said Gates, confirming her discomfort.

When he was seated, she looked at him intently.

'You look dreadful,' she said. 'Like you've been up half the night.'

'The whole night, actually Ma'am,' he replied.

'Working the investigation?' said the Chief Constable, finally meeting his gaze.

'Yes Sir.'

'Then you'll be relieved to hear that I have decided to hand it over to the National Crime Agency.'

'But...' Caton began

Hampson silenced him with an imperious wave of his hand.

'Hear me out,' he said. 'This is no reflection on the work you've done so far. No one could have done more. That's the point. This investigation has developed so rapidly, and in so many different directions, that it now requires resources way beyond those available to a team such as yours. The NCA has the resources to take it on. You will continue to be involved as our liaison with them.'

Caton sat there taking it in. He was about to suggest that the best solution might be to increase the resources available to his team, when Helen Gates leaned forward, radiating appeasement.

'When the time comes to charge the perpetrators you'll get to do it,' she said. 'You can take it all the way to trial.'

'I thought the Police Commissioner was adamant that the NCA should not be involved?' said Caton.

The Chief Constable unfolded his hands and clutched the arms of his chair. His tone was resolute.

'This is an operational decision,' he said. 'It is *my* decision.'

'In which case,' said Caton, more calmly than he felt. 'There's something you need to know.'

Robert Hampson stood with his hands clasped behind his back staring out of the window.

'Who else knows about this?' he said.

'Nobody apart from Detective Inspector Holmes and me,' Caton told him.

The Chief Constable turned to face him.

'What about DS Burman?'

'Gina Burman no longer works for us,' Helen Gates reminded him.

He nodded his head. 'Of course not. '*Ms* Burman then. Does she know?'

'I don't think so,' said Caton.

'Find out,' he said, crossing to his chair, and sitting down. 'What were you proposing to do with this DI Caton?'

'Follow the evidence Sir. Holt was killed because of something he had discovered. The NCA has its own investigation going into Asian betting scams, and we know they already have an interest in Ismailov and his connection with the East European Mafia. Perhaps you could encourage them to intensify their efforts on our behalf? But it's clear that Holt was most interested in a possible link between Mr Grey, the Titan's Security firm, and Neo-Nazi groups in East Lancashire.'

'Based on what?'

'I will only know that when I've retraced his steps. Spoken to his contacts. Visited the places he mentions.'

Hampson looked unconvinced.

'It's what any investigating officer would do at this point.' Caton rammed it home. 'It's what the NCA will do if you hand it over to them.'

The Chief Constable raised his head and looked at Helen Gates. For a moment neither of them moved nor spoke. Then she slowly shook her head. Hampson turned towards Caton.

'That cannot happen,' he said. 'Whatever's going on here, it's our problem. If it turns out to be a red herring, best that nobody finds out that we gave it any credence in the first place. If it isn't...' he drew a deep breath. '...best that we are the ones who found out about it.'

'I agree Sir,' said Caton, carefully suppressing any vestige of triumph that might otherwise have crept into his voice.

He had known all along that this was one piece of dirty washing that they wouldn't want aired in public unless it had to be. He also suspected that both Helen Gates and the Commissioner were secretly hoping that there might just be enough truth in it to rid them of Charles Grey.

'I will see to it that the National Crime Agency increase their involvement in the ways you requested,' The Chief Constable was saying. 'And you, and DI Holmes, will pursue this particular avenue as speedily and as discretely as possible.'

'Only DI Holmes and me, Sir?'

'Nobody else. That's an order. And nobody else outside this room must learn of this until you've completed your inquiries and reported back to me. Is that clear Caton?'

'Not even Mr Hadfield Sir?'

As soon Caton said it he knew that he was pushing his luck. The narrowing of the Chief Constable's pupils, and the colour that came to his cheeks, confirmed it. For a moment he seemed dumbstruck. He breathed out slowly, and folded his arms.

'No one,' he said.

Caton had a feeling that he had been about to say *especially not ACC Hadfield*.

'Very good Sir,' he said. 'There is just one thing. The press conference regarding the discovery of Mr Holt's body? I'm not really in any state to...'

'That goes without saying,' the Chief Constable replied. 'Helen will handle it, won't you Helen?'

'Of course Sir,' she replied, though her demeanour was anything but happy.

'You'd better get on with it then,' she said to Caton.

As he reached the door, she called after him.

'And get yourself a driver. There's no way you should be behind a wheel in that state.'

He breathed a sigh of relief as he hurried down the corridor towards the stairwell. The outcome could have been so different. As it was, the clock was ticking and the stakes had never been higher. Holmes would have to carry out the checks on Charles Grey, the election shenanigans, and the potential involvement of Manc' Security and their owners – Dedicated International Security Services. That would leave him free to get over to Oldham and look into Holt's suspicions about the Commissioner's Neo-Nazi past. None of that could appear in the log book, at least not in those terms. Nor would he even allude to them at the briefing. That was going to tricky. But first, there was something else he had to arrange.

Chapter 33

Kate stood watching Harry as he raced against the clock to build a tower taller than himself. It had been a stroke of genius to bring him to the Museum of Science and Industry. There was more than enough in the twelve galleries to keep a boy like him occupied for several days, or a girl come to that. And all of it free.

Well not quite all of it. The 4D sensory theatre with its moving seats, blasts of air and water sprays had been worth every penny. The hardest part for Harry had been choosing between blasting off into space and walking on the moon, or Maid Marian's whirlwind journey attempting to escape the clutches of the evil Sheriff of Nottingham. In the end Robin Hood had won. Kate had to admit, she'd secretly enjoyed it immensely herself. Well, not so secretly. Her shrieks and screams had probably given that away, and it was a toss-up as to who had squeezed the other's hand the hardest.

'Look Kate! Look!'

As Harry turned to see if she was looking his elbow caught the fragile tower. For a moment it swayed drunkenly, and then imploded.

'Don't worry Harry,' she said. 'You did a great...' She needn't have bothered. Harry had already moved on to the next challenge. It must be wonderful to be that age, she mused. Nothing seemed to faze him. Not even the fact that his mother had a new man in her life. He had mentioned it when they were having breakfast in the cafe.

'Mum's out with her new boy friend,' he said. It was a casual remark made with a mouth full of Eccles cake.

'Do you like him?'

'He's alright I suppose.' He had a slurp of coke. 'I don't see much of him.'

She and Tom had known about Helen's new man for some time. In one sense it was a good thing because it had lessened Kate's lingering fears that Helen had designs on Tom, not just as an occasional father and childminder, as a husband. On the other hand Tom had been mithered about the fact that this Jack had no time for Harry. Kate had told him it wasn't his responsibility, but it was clear that he felt bad about it. She placed a hand on her stomach. She hoped it would change when their child was born.

It would only be a matter of time before Harry put two and two together, and worked out that he was Tom's son. Tom had tried again and again to persuade Helen to tell him before he worked it out for himself. But she was adamant. She probably feared that it would make Harry's attitude to her new bloke even worse. The longer she left it the harder it would become.

Kate switched her awareness to Harry, now busy applying papier-mâché to the huge group sculpture of a locomotive in the sculpture hall. But it was something else that caught her attention. A man she had vaguely been aware of earlier in the day. In the booking hall, and again in the cafe. Now here he was again, admiring, or pretending to admire, the children's work before moving off towards the exit.

He was in his forties, medium height, and medium build, in a brown leather jacket over a plain white tee shirt, blue jeans, and sensible brown shoes. His lightly gelled black hair was cut fashionably short. His face was pleasant enough, more homely than handsome, and the smile on his face as had studied the children's work had seemed to her a little too fixed. More studied than genuine.

What had really alerted her to his presence was the fact that he seemed not to have a child with him. The profiler in her immediately began to compute the possibilities.

Inevitably, her first thought was paedophile. A single man wandering around galleries and workshops specifically geared towards children. She wouldn't be surprised if he was already on the radar of whoever was staffing the CCTV screens somewhere in the complex. Then he might simply be a teacher planning a visit for his class. Or he could be following someone. A child to whom he was denied access perhaps. There was a flutter in her stomach. Her feet suddenly felt cold. And her hands. Or us. He could be following us.

She thought about the clamp on the wheel of her car, and the message tucked under the wiper blade.

"Tell Him to Bak Off."

She closed the gap between Harry and herself, and took her iPhone from her bag.

Caton cursed under his breath, and counted to five before he replied

'You *are* being followed,' he said. 'I organised it.'

'Why the hell didn't you tell me?!'

'Because I didn't want to worry you.'

'Well you have'.

'I'm sorry Kate.'

She took a deep breath, and held it, willing relief to lessen the resentment that had welled inside her.

'Next time, if there is a next time, you discuss it with me first,' she said.

'If I had you wouldn't have agreed.'

'You're probably right, but it would have been my choice.'

'I know. All I can say in mitigation Kate is that you and Harry are the two most important people in my life. I'd do anything to protect you.'

'I know,' she said. 'And I you. But I don't own you, and you don't own me. You have to let me make up my own mind.'

He knew that she was right.

'In future, I will,' he said. 'I promise.'

'Good. So you'll call him off?'

'If you insist.'

There was a long pause. She could tell there was a *but* coming.

'But he isn't only there for you and Harry,' said Tom.

'What do you mean?' she said. Then the penny dropped. 'If someone is watching us this is your opportunity to catch them? You're using Harry and me as bait!'

'That's not fair. You were going to be there anyway. He's watching your backs. If someone is following you wouldn't you want to know? Wouldn't you want us to stop them, before...?'

He'd already said too much.

There was silence on the other end of the phone.

'Kate, say something.'

When she did it was calm and controlled. Too calm, too controlled.

'Will I see you tonight?' she said.

'Of course you will.'

'Good. We need to talk about this.'

'I know.'

'Bye Tom.'

'Kate...'

But she had already rung off.

Caton thrust the BlackBerry into his pocket. He knew that he had made a complete mess of it, but there was nothing he could do about that right now. He fished out his car keys. He reckoned it would take him forty minutes to reach the first of the addresses in Burnley taken from Holt's file. He hoped it wasn't going to be a wild goose chase.

Chapter 34

'What are you then, the Met's Special Demonstration Squad?'

Graham Smith was anything but the stereotypic Neo-Nazi extremist. No tattoos, no shaven head, no flag of St George emblazoned across his tee shirt, no bovver boots. He wore a smart three button navy sports jacket over designer jeans, and an open-necked blue cotton shirt. His black hair, short shag cut, was peppered with grey. Given his age, mid fifties, and heavy build, he had kept his weight under control.

'If I was, I wouldn't have shown you my ID,' Caton told him.

'Could have been a trick. A double bluff.'

Caton shook his head, and put his ID away.

'As far as I know the SDS no longer exist.'

'Good riddance to bad rubbish.' Smith moved onto the top step, and pulled the door of the office block to behind him. 'What do you want then?'

'Just to ask you a few questions.'

Smith grinned, and launched into a dramatic tirade.

'Why are you harassing me when you should be out there saving white teenage girls groomed by rings of middle aged Asian men? Arresting Asian car crash gangs ripping off insurance companies? Smashing the immigrant drug dealers feeding Strawberry Quick to kids at the school gates?'

'Enough!' said Caton.

Smith folded his arms across his chest. The sleeves of his jacket rode up revealing a steel and yellow gold Rolex Oyster on his left wrist. He laughed.

'Isn't that what you expected?' he said.

Caton hadn't known what to expect. The only clue that Holt had left behind was the man's name, and this address, asterisked and underlined as a potential informant. The PNC search had come up blank, so no police record, and his phone number was ex-directory.

'Look Mr Smith,' he said. 'I didn't come here with any expectations, other than to ask for your help.'

'My help?'

'In relation to a murder investigation. A number of murders in fact. And before you ask, you are not a suspect.'

At least, not yet he told himself.

Smith seemed genuinely taken aback, and then his pupils widened.

'Are we talking about that that reporter, Holt?'

'What do you know about Mr Holt?'

'I've just seen it on the news.'

The press conference Helen Gates was going to give. He'd forgotten all about that. Smith was still talking.

'He was supposed to be coming to see me and now he's dead.'

He uncrossed his arms, turned, and pushed the door open.

'You'd better come in,' he said.

'Can I get you a drink?'

'Water will be fine,' Caton told him.

They were in Smith's office on the third floor. It was as well appointed as any Caton had been in, apart from the one high up in the Betham Tower belonging to Ying Zheng Xiong, the European Chief Executive of the Manchester and Shanghai Trading Corporation, and Managing Director of the Titans.

'You've done well for yourself,' Caton remarked as Smith poured them both a glass of water from a blue glass bottle he had taken from a large fridge wedged between two bookcases.

'Insurance.'

Smith handed him a glass.

'There's lots of folk round here who can't get credit, can't get a bank account, can't afford insurance. They go to a loan shark. Get ripped off big style. Four thousand percent interest. Four hundred quid loan, and they're paying it off for the rest of their lives.'

He had a drink and raised his glass towards Caton.

'You'd know all about that.'

Caton did. On the beat he'd known people turn to dealing drugs, shoplifting, even prostitution, just to pay off debts like those. Failing to pay up each month was not an option. Banks took your property. Loan shark enforcers started with your limbs, and moved on from there.

'So you formed what exactly, a Credit Union?'

'Next best thing. I gave loans to those I knew would pay me back. I charged lower rates than the banks. Word spread. I had people with a bit of money, and who could have gone to the banks, who came to me instead. Then I was in profit.'

'Not entirely altruistic then?'

'Couldn't afford to be. But you could say I was using some of the profits I made from the better off to support the poor.'

'Proper Robin Hood.'

'If you say so.'

'I don't suppose the loan sharks were very happy?'

'They weren't, but back then my friends were a damn sight nastier than theirs.'

'You said insurance though, not money lending.'

'That's right. Eventually a proper Credit Union was formed. Then the Government of the day started regulating financial businesses. I switched to insurance. Cars, mainly. Business premises too.'

Caton wondered if that might link him to Dedicated International Security Services. Now was not the time to pursue it. He put his glass down on the floor beside his chair.

'What can you tell me about Josh Holt?' he said.

Smith finished his drink, and put his glass down on the desk.

'Not a lot. He phoned me. Told me he was working on a story involving Charles Grey. Hoped I'd be willing to talk to him in confidence. Said there could be some money in it.'

'Could be?'

'Depending on what I told him.'

'How did he know to contact you?'

'I asked him that, of course I did. He said he'd done some research around Grey's early years, his school days, and his time at Uni. That's how he came across my name.'

'When did you first meet Charles Grey?'

'Only at Uni. Not that we were on the same course. He was studying History and Politics; I was doing Economics.'

'So how did your paths cross?'

Smith tilted back in his chair, as though transporting himself back into his past.

'We had three things in common. Football, politics, and getting pissed in the Student's Union.'

Caton had already marked Smith down as a chameleon. A survivor. But it wouldn't hurt to humour him.

'Let me guess,' he said. 'Leeds United, The National Front, and Tetley's Yorkshire Bitter?'

Smith grinned broadly. Caton noticed for the first time that his teeth had been whitened. The effect was startling. He shook his head.

'Burnley, The student arm of the British Democratic Party, and Double Diamond.'

'Charles Grey was a member of the British Democratic Party?'

It hardly came as a complete surprise given the man's far right policies, but Caton was amazed that it had never emerged in the run up to his election as Police Commissioner that he had been a member of such an extreme and controversial group.

'Student arm,' Smith corrected him. 'There were only seven of us. We kept it clandestine. Well, the rest of the student body was so far left of centre our lives would have been hell.'

He smiled at a private joke.

'You could say we are a bit like the Cambridge Five, only they were Communists, and we were Nationalists.'

'So which one would Charles Grey have been?' said Caton.

Smith thought about it.

'Bit of a tossup really. Could have been Kim Philby, or Edmund Blunt. Grey reckoned he was the intellectual.'

'In what way?'

'Well, he reckoned he'd developed a theoretical model by which nativism, and authoritarianism, combined to bring about the perfect culture, and the perfect society.'

'You are going to have to help me with this.'

Smith sat up, and placed his hands on the desk.

'Britain for the British. Send everyone else packing, together with anyone who doesn't accept the authority of the Nationalist Government.'

Caton grimaced. 'I think you'll find Hitler beat him to it,' he said. 'You said the group was clandestine. What did it actually do?'

'We met together in the back room of a pub in Leeds whose landlord was a hardcore Neo Nazi. We argued, and plotted, and planned, but apart from attending a few meetings of the BDP, and the odd rally or two, all we did was spout hot air. Grey put together some leaflets on the centrality of cultural identity, the evils of mass immigration, effective ways to repatriate non whites. Like I said he was the one who saw himself as the new Oswald Mosley.'

'What did you do with the leaflets?'

'Circulated them. They weren't signed of course, though they did have the name he'd dreamt up for us printed on them. *Students For Britain*.'

He shook his head again. SFB. 'We were more like sad fat bastards.'

'I don't suppose you still have any copies?'

He shook his head.

'No. I left that behind me when I left Uni. It was just a phase. You know how it is?'

Caton did. Though his student activism had been the anti-apartheid movement. Quite the opposite of this man's brief flirtation with virulent racism.

'In any case, I had another reason to turn my back on all of that.'

He placed a finger and thumb on the top of a photograph frame on his desk, and swivelled it through 180 degrees. The face that smiled at Caton was of a charming middle aged woman of Asian heritage.

'Ayanna,' Smith said proudly. 'It means innocent.

We have three children. Two girls and a boy. Ironic isn't it?'

'Does she know?'

Smith turned the photo back to its original position, and stared at the image of his wife.

'About Students For Britain? No, and I don't want her to.'

He looked up and searched Caton's eyes.

'There's no reason she should,' Caton told him.

'That's the only reason I agreed to talk with Holt,' Smith said. 'To find out how much he knew, and to try to make sure he kept my name out of it. Same reason I'm talking to you.'

'Have you had any contact with Grey since you left University?'

'No. I came across his name from time to time in the press, on the radio and tele, but we never met and I never had any hankering to do so.'

Throughout their conversation something had, been bugging Caton.

'Why do you think none of this came out when he was running for the post of Commissioner of Police?'

Smith smiled thinly.

'Two reasons. Firstly, like I said, we kept it clandestine. We never formerly joined the BDP or put our heads above the parapet. So our names were never on any list. We were never arrested. We didn't even use our real names when we were together in public.'

'And the second?'

He took a deep breath, and folded his arms.

'Shortly after Grey's name was put forward, I had a visit.'

'A visit?'

'From two of our little group.'

'What did they want?'

'To warn me off. They said if anything leaked out

about Charles Grey and the SFB I would regret it, whether they could prove it came from me or not.' His fists clenched. 'They knew about Ayanna, and the children. They said I wouldn't want them to find out. Or anything to happen to them.'

'What did you say?'

'I told them that I didn't give a toss about Charles Grey. That there was no way I would be as stupid as to talk about those days. And that if anything did happen to any of my family I would come after them. Then I called security, and had them shown the door.'

Caton assumed that the remaining three of their little cabal would also have been paid a visit.

'Can you write me down the names of the other members of your group?' he said. 'And underline the ones that threatened you?'

Smith took a sheet of paper from the printer on his desk, and a biro from his desk drawer, and began to write. When he had finished he underlined two of the names, then stared at the list as though surprised by what he saw. He shook his head sadly, and handed Caton the sheet of paper.

Caton stared at the names. He was surprised and excited to discover that he recognised the two that had been underlined, but it was the third that really leapt out at him.

Chapter 35

'Are you aware that your hands are shaking?'

Caton studied them. Gordon was right. Both of his hands were trembling. It was barely perceptible. Like the first signs of Parkinson's.

'No Gordon I wasn't,' he said. 'And I've got a splitting headache.'

'You know what that is?' said Gordon cheerfully.

It felt like a really nasty hangover. Dear God, he thought, don't let it be meningitis.

'Withdrawals.'

'Withdrawals?' Caton protested. 'Chance would have been a fine thing. When in the last five days have I had a moment chance to drink at all, let alone to excess?'

Gordon smirked, and raised his mug.

'Not alcohol Boss, caffeine. You hardly ever touch coffee, and last night you must have had at least a gallon. You can't just stop you know, you have to let yourself down gently.'

The relief was palpable. Caton nodded his head, and immediately regretted it.

'That explains it,' he said. 'Have you got any analgesics?'

Gordon stood up. 'Ged usually has a stash, I'll ask her. I'll bring you a coffee too, that'll help.'

'Make it quick,' said Caton. 'I feel dreadful.'

'It explains the irritability too,' said Holmes as he departed.

'I'm not irritable,' Caton called after him.

The little blacksmith inside his head recommenced pounding on his skull with his hammer.

'Shawcross and Barlow,' said Holmes. 'The Titan's missing security men. Surprise surprise. I wouldn't have had them down as university material.'

'Turns out they weren't, said Caton. 'Neither of them graduated. But this is the real shocker.' He pointed to the only other name that Smith had underlined. 'Frank Moston.'

'How did he get to head up Dedicated International Security Services with a background like that?'

'Because they were a tightly knit group, and they stayed off everyone's radar,' Caton told him. 'Plus they were only active for a couple of years.'

'It explains why our revered Commissioner's been panicking about our investigation. He must have known if we kept digging we'd eventually make the connection between him and them.'

'There's more to it than that though isn't there? What did you find out about the reasons why his rivals so conveniently dropped out of the race?'

Gordon consulted his notes.

'Neither of the candidates was willing to talk with me.'

'Not even when you told them it was a multiple murder investigation?'

'Even more so when I told them that. Let's face it, it's understandable. They'd be thinking about the publicity they would get when a case like that came to trial.'

Caton had another sip of coffee to help wash down the paracetemol. He grimaced at the taste.

'You should have promised them we'd try to keep their names out of it.'

'I did. They were far too canny to fall for that. Since when was one of our promises a guarantee?'

Caton knew he was right. In their situation he'd probably have done the same thing.

'So where does that leave us?' he said.

'It's clear from Holt's notes that he suspected someone of deliberately getting the female candidate's daughter hooked on crack, and then informing on her via CrimeStoppers. I checked. The caller was male, anonymous, and the call was made from a phone box in Gorton.'

Caton resisted the urge to nod. If he remembered rightly Shawcross lived in Gorton.

'What did the drugs team have to say?'

'They've all been scattered to the wind since the force was re-organised. But I did track down one of them who's still working in what is now "E" Division. She said they'd thought at the time it was odd the call coming from Gorton, because the girl and her mother both lived in West Didsbury. She also said the girl had no previous, and no known contacts with the regulars on the drugs scene down there. The girl also denied knowing where the stash of drugs they found in her car had come from. They were inclined to believe her, but the evidence was overwhelming. Then all of a sudden a witness came forward claiming he'd seen them planted in the car.'

'Let me guess, just after her mother agreed to withdraw from the election?'

'You've got it.'

'What happened to the girl?'

'She was given a twelve month suspended sentence

for possession, and a hundred and fifty days community service.'

'Poor kid.'

Caton shook his head. He was relieved to find that it had stopped hurting.

'And she lost her place at University,' said Holmes.

'What about the other candidate? Stuart Beresford wasn't it?'

'Holt's research panned out. Beresford had been having an affair for over twenty years. He even had a child by his mistress, out of wedlock. It's never become public knowledge, and as far as I could tell neither the child nor the wife knows anything about it.'

'So they leaked the part about him cheating with her bridesmaid, and threatened to reveal the rest. He backed off, and they kept their side of the bargain?'

'It looks like it.'

'I wonder how the extortionists found out about it in the first place.'

'Not too difficult I should imagine, if you happen to own a security firm.'

Holmes rubbed his chin again.

'What do we do now?'

'Push harder on the search for Shawcross and Barlow.'

'What if they're dead?'

'We still need to find them.'

'Speak to Frank Moston.'

'And there's the other strand Holt was pursuing.'

'The Russians?'

'East Europeans.'

'Whatever. I thought the National Crime Agency was dealing with that?'

'Holt wanted Gina Burman to pay Dimitri Ismailov a visit. I'd like to see him for myself. Face to face.'

Holmes smiled.

'You're in luck. While you were up in Burnley I took the liberty of getting Carter to find out where Izmailov might be. You'll never guess. He isn't at his address in Mayfair. He isn't back in Russia. He isn't...'

'Stop messing around Gordon; just tell me where he is.'

Holmes looked at his watch. 'Half an hour ago he was in the Northern Quarter at Vince Varden's place.'

The name was familiar.

'Vince Varden?'

'The Robert Thornton affair. Varden was the guy at whose apartment Thornton met Anjelita Covas?'

Now he remembered. He may not have been there at the beginning of the investigation but he would never forget how it had ended.

'The very one. Do you want me to find out where he is right now?'

Caton had already covered a fair few miles on urban motorways today. He decided to let his DI drive. As he buckled his seat belt he said.

'What's a strawberry Gordon?'

Holmes gunned the engine and eased towards the barrier.

'A small, sweet, pink, heart shaped fruit.'

'No, it was something Graham Smith said. Urban street slang?'

'A girl who prostitutes herself for drugs, usually crack.'

The barrier began to rise.

'No. It sounded like a drink he claimed they were giving kids at the school gates.'

Holmes grinned, and nodded his head in recognition. He drove out onto the road, and sped towards the roundabout.

'*Strawberry Quick*. Supposedly it's a strawberry coloured, strawberry flavoured, methamphetamine. Like those pop rocks that sizzle in the mouth. It's an urban legend that started in the States. Some Wally in another police force got hauled over the coals recently for warning schools about it. Nearly started a panic.'

'So there's nothing to it?'

'There have been some seizures of coloured and flavoured crack, but there's no evidence it's being targeted at kids.'

'Let's hope it stays that way.'

'Tell you what; it puts a new spin on that old adage.'

'Go on then,' said Caton. 'Surprise me.'

He grinned again.

'Never,' he said. 'Take sweets from a stranger.'

Dimitri Ismailov sat at the head of the only occupied table in the softly lit casino restaurant. He was a tall man, with a relatively small head on top of broad shoulders, and a barrel chest. His nose was straight, almost aquiline. His forehead was pronounced, his cheeks and jawbone strong. He had short dark hair, and piercing eyes the colour of graphite. Ismailov was flanked on either side by two large shaven-headed men. The sinews of their bull necks strained at black polar neck tee shirts. Sixteen stone of muscle appeared to have been packed into each of their shiny black suits. That didn't include the other bulges beneath their jackets to which their right hands had gravitated the moment he and Holmes had entered the room. The fourth person at the table, slight by comparison with the others but with all the signs of a confident self-made man, leaned across and whispered something to Ismailov.

'That's right Mr Varden.'

Gordon Holmes held up his identification card.

'It's us again. Greater Manchester Police. This is Detective Chief Inspector Caton. We'd appreciate a word with Mr Ismailov.'

Ismailov smiled thinly, and waited for them to take a chair each from the adjacent table, and sit down.

'What word would that be Detective Chief Inspector?' he said.

'I wondered if you could tell me what has brought you to Manchester, Mr Ismailov,' said Caton.

'Dimitri, please,' he replied.

'Dimitri.'

'Ismailov smiled sagely.

'Many things bring me here. I love your city. It is so much more compact, comfortable, relaxed than London. More like St Petersburg without the snow. I like your restaurants, your clubs, and I like your women.'

He looked across at Vince Varden, sharing a private joke.

'More than that surely?' said Caton.

'Of course. I come to see my friend, Vincent. And I have business interests here.'

'Business interests?'

He lifted a small shot glass, drained it, and then had a sip of coffee.

'Let me get you a drink,' he said raising his right hand.

A waiter appeared at his shoulder as if by magic.

'A drink for my friends,' he said. 'And the same again for us.'

'I don't think we'll be staying that long Dimitri,' Caton told him.

'How long does it take to have drink with a friend?'

Caton addressed the waiter. 'I'll have a glass of

water please, and my colleague will have...'

'The same,' said Holmes.

Caton stared at him.

His DI shrugged. 'I'm on duty,' he said.

'Water!' Ismailov proclaimed. No wonder your policemen look so miserable Vincent.'

'You were about to tell us about your business interests Dimitri,' said Caton.

Ismailov placed both hands on the table palm down. He looked like a chief Executive about to address a meeting of the Board.

'I have property here. I buy property for myself, my friends, and my business partners. It's what I do. Invest.'

Caton had no doubt where the money was coming from. The same corrupt sources that had fuelled the buying up of much of the most fashionable and wealthy property in London.

'What sort of property?' said Caton, taking the glass of water the waiter handed to him.

Ismailov folded his arms, and sat back.

'I have been patient, and polite,' he said. 'I think it is time you told me why you ask me these questions, don't you Chief Inspector?'

He was right. Caton had found it surprising that he had waited this long. Unless he had known all along.

'We are investigating a murder.'

Ismailov raised his eyebrows.

'*A* murder?' he said.

Of course he knew.

'A number of murders.'

'And this concerns me how exactly?'

It was a good question. One to which Caton would love to have known the answer. He didn't. All he had was conjecture. He was beginning to wonder why he had come.

'Because one of the victims spoke of receiving anonymous messages from someone with a Russian accent.'

'The eyebrows rose again.

'He spoke from the dead?'

Vince Varden chuckled openly. There were the beginnings of a smile on the lips of one of the bodyguards. Caton ignored the question. Instead he watched closely for their response to his.

'He also left some comprehensive notes of research he had done, in which your name appears. I wondered if you could explain that?'

The expression froze on Ismailov's face. He fought to keep it neutral while his mind raced. Caton's words had also wiped the smile from the face of the bodyguard; his colleague looked puzzled and concerned. The briefest of glances passed between them. Someone had messed up. Perhaps it was the two of them.

Ismailov raised his shot glass, and downed the contents in one. He set down the glass, and waited for the warmth to suffuse his body.

'Had I the name of your victim, and a copy of the notes, then maybe I could help. Otherwise...'

He turned his palms face upward in a gesture of innocence and incomprehension.

'Josh Holt, an investigative reporter,' he said.

Ismailov turned to Vince Varden.

'Holt, Vince, you know this name?'

Varden stared back at his friend, studiously avoiding Caton's eyes, and shook his head.

'No Dimitri. Sorry.'

Ismailov looked Caton square in the eyes, and smiled. It was the smile he'd seen countless times on the lips of hardened criminals convinced of their own omnipotence. Too often they were proved correct.

'Neither do I. Sorry Detective Chief Inspector. Unless of course you can show me those notes?'

Caton slid back his chair, and stood. Holmes followed his lead.

'Thank for your co-operation Mr Ismailov,' Caton said.

'You are welcome,' Ismailov replied. 'And like I said, it is Dimitri to my friends. Next time bring those notes with you. You can show them to my solicitor.'

Caton placed his chair back where he had found it, and together he and Gordon started to leave.

'Goodbye Tom,' the Russian called after them.

'Do svidaniya, Mr Ismailov,' Caton replied.

'Do svidaniya?' said Holmes as they stood on the pavement.

'Till we meet again,' Caton told him. 'And we will.'

They started walking back to the car.

'I didn't tell him your first name,' said Holmes.

'I know. It wasn't the only thing he already knew was it?'

'No. He knew straight off why we were there. He's in it up to his armpits. Look how worried he was when you mentioned Holt leaving those notes.'

'Much good they do us.'

'He's probably guessed as much, or we'd have pulled him in for questioning.'

Gordon was right again. Still, they had shaken his tree, and there was no telling what might fall out.

Chapter 36

As they slowed approaching the junction with the Regent Road a car overtook, and screeched to a halt in front of them, causing Gordon to brake hard. Caton looked in his wing mirror. Another identical grey BMW 3 Series had pulled up inches from their bumper.

'What the Hell!' exclaimed Gordon, reaching for the seatbelt release.

Caton put his hand on Gordon's.

'It's alright,' he said.

The nearside passenger door of the car in front opened. Agent Simon Levi of the NCA Organised Crime Directorate emerged. He straightened up, closed the door, and walked towards them. As Levi approached Caton lowered his window. The Agent bent down until their eyes were level. His breath smelt of garlic and dyspepsia.

'I would like to sit in the back please,' he said.

Caton nodded, and Gordon Holmes released the door locks. Levi climbed in, and leaned forward.

'We're causing an obstruction,' he said 'Follow the car in front. We'll park up on the industrial estate. Then we can talk.' He settled back and waited for the cars to set off.

The atmosphere in the car was icy. It was obvious that Levi was inwardly seething. Caton thought he knew why.

They pulled into the industrial estate and parked in parallel bays.

'What the fuck did you think you were doing?!' said the agent leaning forward, his head between the two front seats.

'Conducting a multiple murder investigation.' Caton told him calmly.

'*We* were handling the East European connection. It was agreed.' More garlic, with a hint of bile.

'I just needed to see him for myself.'

'Your being *needy* has just compromised an undercover officer.'

Caton half turned in his seat.

'I'm sorry,' he said. 'I had no idea.'

'No you bloody didn't!'

'The waiter?'

'Amongst others.'

I still don't see how I've compromised them exactly?'

'A detective chief inspector and his dozy inspector sidekick ...'

'Hang on!' Holmes interjected.

Levy ploughed on.

'Blundering in with their size nines. What's he supposed to think, apart from bloody hell I'm under investigation?'

'It didn't exactly come as surprise to him,' said Caton. 'If anything our turning up will have strengthened your guys' positions.'

Levy snorted.

'How the hell d'you to work that one out?'

'If we had people working undercover why would we jeopardise that by showing our hand?'

The agent thumped the top of Caton's seat in sheer frustration.

'That's my bloody point! You idiot.'

'The Boss is right though,' said Gordon. 'If anything it'll have drawn suspicion away from your man.'

'It'll make him take even greater precautions,' retorted Levy. 'That's what you've gone and done.'

'Someone like Ismailov' said Caton. 'His precautions are always in place. If they weren't, you'd have arrested him long before this. How long have you had people undercover?

'That's none of your business either.'

'OK,' said Caton. 'We're supposed to be working together. I've apologised. There's no harm done. Let's stop pissing in the snow. How about if we help each other out instead?'

Levy sat back in his seat.

'How do you propose we do that?'

'An exchange of information. I tell you what I've found out. You tell me what you know.'

There was silence while Levy thought about it.

'You go first,' he said.

Caton told him about the meeting with Graham Smith.

'So we are about to pay a call on Frank Moston,' he said.

The name appeared to mean nothing to the Agent.

'Managing Director of Dedicated International Security Services, which just happens to own Manc Securities.'

Recognition dawned on the agent's face.

'Shawcross and Barlow,' he said.

'Exactly. All three of whom we now believe were members of a far right organisation in their student days. They may still be for all we know.'

'So?'

'I wouldn't want to mess up any undercover operation you might be running into Neo-Nazi groups.'

The agent smiled broadly.

'You're out of touch,' he said. 'Neither we nor MI5 have the time or resources to monitor individual home grown white supremacists. We deal, together with your counter terrorism units, with targets who are considered a serious threat to national security. In the main those are Islamist extremists.'

This was news to Caton.

'I'd have thought the killing of seventy one young Norwegians by Anders Breivik would have been a wakeup call?'

The agent shrugged.

'One delusional psychopath does not a conspiracy make. There's no equivalent to al-Qaeda going on here. The far right is a disparate group of individuals decrying Islamification, stoking up fear about sharia law, demanding our lads be brought home from Afghanistan, and calling for forced repatriation and justice for white victims of racist attacks.'

'Isn't that disturbing enough? 'If you're not monitoring them who is?'

'The Confidential Intelligence Unit,' he replied. Reporting to ACPO.'

Caton recalled an article last summer in *Brief*, the GMP Force magazine.

'They only have a hundred officers at their disposal,' he said. 'And the Association of Chief Police Officers is hardly an operational agency.'

The agent shrugged.

'That's how it is,' he said.

In Caton's view, given major political gains the far right had made in France, Denmark and the Netherlands, the threat from the far right had been massively underestimated. Breivik may have been a lone wolf, but his motivation had been fuelled by the writings and speeches of the far right. In some towns in Italy there were already brown shirts patrolling the streets. All it needed was someone able to build a populist far right political brand. Something akin to the Jobbik Party in Hungary.

'Even so, can you get me whatever you have on these?' he said.

He took out his pocket book and read out the names he had been given by Smith, omitting Charles Grey's.

Levy wrote them down.

'What about those notes the reporter left?' he said.

Caton smiled. Either they'd had a listening device in there, or the waiter had reported like lightning to his handler.

Caton shook his head. 'I'll copy them to you, but you'll be wasting your time. There's bugger all there.'

There was a grunt from the rear seat.

'Your turn,' said Caton

Levi took his time. No doubt deciding just how much to tell, and how much to leave out.

'We've had our eye on Ismailov for some time,' he said at last.

'How long is some time?'

'Look,' said the agent, his irritation showing. 'Do you want hear this or not?'

Caton raised his hands in defeat.

'Right then,' Levi began. 'The Serious and Organised Crime Agency had been building a database on a number of Russian and former Russian States expats for a couple of years before we replaced them. Dimitri Ismailov was one of them. They had nothing specific on him, just loads of evidence of unsavoury connections in Eastern Europe. Arms dealers, sex traffickers, money launderers. Europol has had increasing demands from our counterparts in Russia to help them build a case on the proceeds of crime, and corruption, being laundered in the rest of Europe. In particular, the French Riviera, Paris, and London.'

'And Manchester,' muttered Gordon Holmes.

Levi let it go.

'Ismailov has been splashing the cash big time. Not his cash in the main, but for some of the lesser known oligarchs and Russian mafia names.'

He leaned forward.

'How much do you know about the oligarchs?'

'Only what I read in the press, or see on TV,' said Caton. 'We don't move in the same circles.'

'The term was coined for those businessmen who used their wealth and influence to get Boris Yeltsin elected back in 1996. In return they got to influence policy – especially domestic economic policy. Including Government contracts. They landed oil, steel, and media business. Their wealth spiralled. As often as not they were taxed at low rates or allowed to evade it altogether. When Putin came to power all that changed. He tightened up the laws and chased them for tax and corruption. Most of them fled. Some to England. Those who stayed, and toed the line, got richer still. Their current combined wealth is estimated at close to 480 billion US dollars.'

Holmes whistled.

'They could buy a country with that.'

'They're having a good shot at buying ours,' Levi observed dryly. 'Our problem with Ismailov is that the only money we've been able to track him investing over here is from those new purportedly *clean* oligarchs. Everything else is just highly suspicious. In particular the company he keeps.'

'Those bodyguards for example?' said Caton.

'They all have an army of professional thugs,' Levi replied. 'When I say professional I mean ex KGB, Stasi, Serbian and Albanian war veterans. Not that you can blame them. The number of kidnappings and assassination attempts is becoming a major pain in the arse for us, and for the Met.'

'So you've got nothing for us. In relation to the murders?' said Caton trying hard to hide his frustration.

Levi sat back, enjoying the moment.

'I wouldn't say that,' he said. 'Two East Europeans on the Border Agency watch list came into this country at Hull a month ago. They were spotted talking with Ismailov in a box at the Titans versus Spurs match in London a fortnight ago.'

'Why didn't the Border Agency pick them up when they came in?' asked Holmes.

'Because Watch list means exactly that. There were no international arrest warrants out for them.'

'Why are they on the list?' asked Caton.

'Because they're suspected of being guns for hire.'

'Hit men?'

'Assassins. Whatever you want to call them. They were stopped and searched at the port. They were clean. We were informed, and the Met were informed.'

'Where did they go? Surely they were followed?'

Levi shook his head.

'I told you we don't have the resources. A hire car was waiting for them. It was returned to Heathrow the following day by somebody else.'

Caton twisted in his seat and turned to look back at the agent.

'And you're telling us this because?'

For the first time Levi looked uncomfortable. On the back foot.

'Because when your murders began we wondered if these two might have had something to do with it. The fact they'd been at that Titans game was a bit of a coincidence.'

Caton was furious.

'And you didn't think to tell me?'

The agent shrugged. 'You have to admit there wasn't an obvious connection. There still isn't. It wasn't a lot to go on. But we have been looking for them. They haven't left the country. At least not by any of the normal routes.'

Private yachts, private jets. Caton could think of all manner of ways they could have been smuggled out. If they were still here it would only be because their work was not finished. If it was them. He took out his note book.

'Their names?' he said.

'Hashim Dalca, he's Albanian, five feet six, thirteen stone, black hair cropped short. Branimir Petrovic, Serbian, five feet eight, fourteen stone blonde hair cropped short. His body is covered in tattoos. On the back of his neck he has a cross, over double eagles, topped by a crown. On his chest is a man holding an automatic rifle, on his back is an icon of the Madonna and Child.'

'Not troubled by double standards then?' said Holmes.

'And you're actively looking for them?' said Caton.

'We've pulled out all the stops. I'll fax you their photos over. You'll want to circulate them.'

'Better late than never,' Holmes muttered.

Levi opened his door. 'That's in then,' he said.

He got out and slammed the door. As he drew level with Caton's window he bent down and signalled for him to lower the window.

'And don't think all is forgiven,' he said. 'Barbara

Bryce the Deputy Director will be speaking to your Chief Constable about this.'

He straightened up and walked to his car. Gordon Holmes wound down his own window, and shouted after him.

'Size elevens actually!'

It was a pyrrhic victory, but it still felt good.

'What are we going to do now Boss?' said Holmes. 'Wait to see what Levi comes back with on those names you gave him?'

'No way,' said Caton. 'We have addresses for both of them. You and I are going to pay them a visit.'

'Just the two of us?'

Caton was surprised by Gordon's wariness.

'You don't think we can handle it?'

'We're going to see them in case they can shed any light on the whereabouts of their erstwhile right wing loony partners Shawcross and Barlow,' said Holmes.

Caton was impressed. '*Erstwhile*?' he said. His DI carried on regardless.

'What if the two of them are actually holed up in one or other of these addresses?'

'That had occurred to me.'

'Aside from the fact that they may not be willing to come quietly; have you forgotten what happened to their colleague Ratten?'

Caton was wondering where this was leading.

'I'm not likely to have forgotten,' he said.

'Nor are they. Which is presumably the reason they're in hiding? Less from us than from than Dalca and Petrovic. With us they get locked up. With hit men the clue is in the name.'

'Which is why I don't expect them to resist arrest. But if it'll make you feel better I'll request a tactical firearms team.'

'Good,' said Gordon, who was pleased that Caton

had finally got it. 'Because if we happen to turn up at the same time as whoever killed Okowu, Ratten, Gideon-Jones, and Josh Tatnell, I don't think our bare hands and quick wits are going to be enough, do you?'

Caton could see his point.

Chapter 37

Caton was growing impatient. It had taken forty minutes to obtain the necessary permission to mobilise two tactical firearms teams, and another hour to get them to each of the addresses. In fact the team assigned to Holmes had yet to arrive.

Caton had taken the decision to have DI Holmes and DS Stuart visit the home of Alex Patterson, the first of the names Graham Smith had provided. He and DS Carter were waiting at the end of the street where Derek Moody lived. It had stood to reason that they would have to visit them simultaneously; otherwise there was a risk of having them warn one another. It was just unfortunate that they lived thirty miles apart, and that Patterson lived the furthest away, in Leeds.

'It's still relatively early, Boss,' said Nick Carter. 'What if they're out at work?'

'Then we'll find out where they work, and visit them there. And if they're out of work, we'll wait. But if Shawcross and Barlow are holed up here they're hardly likely to be popping down to the shops are they?'

His phone rang. It was Gordon Holmes.

'Boss, they're here. We're ready to go.'

''Tell them it's not the Iranian Embassy,' said Caton. 'We have no idea if there are guns involved, and I don't want dead witnesses, and the Independent Police Complaints Commission crawling all over this investigation.'

He opened his door, got out, and signalled to the Firearms Incident Commander who exited his unmarked car, followed by two armed officers. They came to meet him.

'November One and Two are in position on Parker Avenue,' said the Incident Commander. 'It runs parallel to this one at the back of the property. Our only problem is if there two or more of them, and they decide to take off in opposite directions through the adjacent properties. Just as well it's a detached house. Fewer issues with neighbours.'

'Right,' said Caton. 'Let's do it.'

There were two vehicles on the drive, a bright Yellow Renault convertible, and a brand new Lexus 4X4. With luck someone was home. The two firearms officers took up position on either side of the door, their backs to the wall. Caton and Carter stood side by side directly in front of it as Caton rang the bell.

It was opened almost immediately. Caton could tell from the terrified expression on the woman's face that she must have seen them coming.

'Police,' he said, holding up his ID. 'There's no need to be frightened, but you need to tell me who else is in the house apart from you?'

'N...no one,' she stuttered. 'My husband's away on business, in Cyprus.'

'That would be Mr Moody?'

'That's right, Doug.'

She caught sight of the armed officer on the left and shrank instinctively into the hallway. Caton followed her.

'Do you mind if we take a look for ourselves?' he said. It didn't sound like a question, it wasn't meant to.

It took less than a minute for them to establish that she was telling the truth about being the only one there. Caton was about to delve a little deeper into her husband's whereabouts when his phone rang. It was Gordon again.

'We were too late,' he said. 'There's one down here, we think it's Patterson. And there have definitely been others staying here. Unmade beds, damp towels, pots in the sink; left in a hurry by the look of it.'

Caton nodded to Carter to keep an eye on Mrs Moody, and walked out of hearing range.

'How did he die?' he asked.

'Bullet in the head. The same as Munby and Holt. He'd been beaten first. '

'They wanted information.'

'About the whereabouts of his guests.'

'No doubt he provided it.'

'I'd put money on it.'

'There has to be something there,' said Caton. 'Is there a computer?'

'There's a PC in the kitchen diner, and a printer.'

'Check the web search history first,' he said. 'Call Jack Benson and ask him to set the wheels in motion, Pathologist, forensics, SOCO...'

'I've done that.'

Holmes sounded peeved that Caton thought it necessary to remind him.

'Good,' said Caton. 'I'll be with you as soon as we've finished here. It shouldn't take long.'

'And Boss,' said Holmes. You need to know, he's still warm.'

Caton never reached the house. One of the first things Holmes had done was to put out a PNC alert on the silver VW Touran owned by Alex Patterson. He was just about to join the M621 for Leeds when Gordon called.

'Boss, that VW's licence plate has been picked up twice by automatic recognition cameras on the M62. The first time travelling east, and then five minutes ago just this side of Goole, heading towards Hull.'

Caton swerved back across the hatched area into the inside lane, followed by the astonished driver of the unmarked vehicle travelling behind him. Their manoeuvre caused a lorry to brake hard, and released a torrent of flashing headlights, and furious hooting.

Whoever was driving Patterson's vehicle, he calculated, was twenty five minutes in front of them. He used his radio to tell the tactical aid team to pull ahead, switch on their flashing blue lights, and turn on their siren if they needed to. Having crossed into another Force area there was no way he would be able to deploy their weapons, but there was no way he was going to send them back until someone – hopefully Helen Gates - had persuaded the Humberside Force to mobilise their own firearms team to support him.

'Another message from DI Holmes,' said Nick Carter, his phone stuck to his ear. 'They've found Google searches on the computer for ferries from Hull, including sailing times.'

'Tell him we're already on our way,' said Caton, and to let the NCA and the Border Agency know.'

They touched speeds in excess of a hundred and ten miles an hour, stretching Caton's car to its limit.

It had taken them thirty five minutes to cover the fifty five miles to the port of Hull. They were finally forced to stop behind a line of traffic at a standstill. Ahead they could just make out the flashing lights of blues and twos.

The Tactical Firearms Team didn't wait to be told to switch on their own lights and sirens, forcing the stationary vehicles to pullover. As they approached the head of the line a police officer waved them on past the police vans, and an ambulance, and onto a ramp over a bridge that led to a roundabout where the A63 met the A1033. Both lanes were blocked by police traffic cars. The reason was clear to see.

A silver VW Touran had mounted the sill surrounding the vast area of sand, shale and shrub at the centre of the roundabout. The radiator grill was impaled on one of the steel posts of a black and white directional sign. There were deep black gouges along the left hand door panels. The passenger window was shattered. The driver's door hung open.

The unmarked car pulled over and stopped, its lights still flashing. Caton followed suit. He and Carter got out of the car, their ID's held high. A traffic cop came over to them.

'Are you the ones from Manchester,' he said. Wanted us to stop this vehicle?'

'Yes,' said Caton. 'Have you detained the occupants?'

The officer finished scrutinising their ID's.

'We didn't stop the car *Sir*,' he said. 'Someone else did that. They stopped the driver too. You'd better come and see.'

He led the way around the stranded Touran where two other uniformed policemen and a paramedic stood impotently staring into the interior.

The driver was slumped over the steering wheel. Half of the back of his head had been blown away. The windscreen shattered.

'He's dead,' said the paramedic. 'He's been shot.'

'Did anyone see what happened?' said Caton.

'A woman in my traffic car,' the officer told him. 'My colleague is taking a statement. She was right behind them when it happened. So frightened she skidded up onto the kerb, and nearly hit that brick post.'

'What has she told you?'

'Just as she was entering the roundabout a big black 4x4 overtook her at speed on her right, and crashed into the VW forcing it onto the central reservation. That's when she skidded. She was about to get of her car to see if she could help when she saw a man leap out of the passenger side of the VW, and race back down the road in the direction from which she'd just come. At the same time the driver of the black car – it was a Mercedes by the way – ran to the driver's side of the VW. She assumed that he was going to help the driver, but instead he yanked open the door and fired three shots into the car. At that point she lost it. However, witnesses from cars that had stopped behind her say that the man got back into the Mercedes and drove off at speed around the roundabout and back in the direction in which the VW passenger had fled.'

He pointed back down the road to the A1063.

'Witnesses say the running man crossed the canal on the inside lane, and then ran down into the grounds of the crematorium. The Mercedes couldn't follow him because of the central barrier dividing the carriageways, so they pulled over in the entrance to the engineering works, and set off on foot, using the pedestrian crossing.'

'They?' said Caton. How many of them?'

'Two. Big buggers by the sound of it. Cropped hair, almost shaven, leather jackets.'

'How long ago?'

He looked at his watch.

'Nine minutes exactly.'

'Are your firearms team here yet?' said Caton.

'You'll be lucky,' he replied. 'But the Border police went after them three minutes since.'

'I need someone with local knowledge,' he told him. 'That knows this area, and the crematorium.'

The traffic cop waved over one of the uniformed officers controlling the traffic, and explained what was needed.

Caton, with Carter at his side, hurried across to the Firearms Team Commander standing beside the unmarked car.

'I need you,' he said. 'We have one suspect dead', and another being pursued by two men, one of them definitely armed.'

''We should leave this to the Humberside Force,' he replied.

'There's no time for that. If we don't act now we are going to lose possibly the only witness to a string of murders. Don't worry, I'll take full responsibility.'

'If only it were that simple,' said the Commander, signalling his men to follow them.

They jogged together down the slope, through iron gates, and onto a narrow path that ran along the wooded bank of the canal. After two hundred metres they reached another path at right angles to them.

'This takes you straight to the crematorium,' said the uniformed officer. 'There's a mixture of wooded copses, and open ground. It's bounded on our left by a factory with a high fence. When you get to the crem there's a dog leg that takes you down to the cemetery. Beyond the crem is a large area of woodland bisected by a railway line, over which more woods open out into the backs of a line of large semi-detached houses, and an estate. My guess is that your suspect will either have headed for the graveyard, or the railway line.'

'What makes you say that?' said the Firearms Team Commander.

'Because that's where the best cover lies.'

'I don't like it,' said the Commander. 'We have one presumably unarmed suspect, two presumably armed suspects, an unknown number of armed Border police, plus the six of us, blundering around in all this cover. It's a recipe for disaster.'

His argument was flawless.

'What do you suggest?' said Caton.

'That I proceed, cautiously, with my men. You three take cover, and wait here for the Humberside Tactical Team to arrive.'

Caton thought about it for a moment. It pained him to admit it, but he knew there was no logical alternative.

'Alright,' he said. 'Our Humberside colleague here can report to whoever is Gold Commander on this. That way we may be able to seal the perimeters of the cemetery before they get away.'

The firearms officers set off at a jog in the direction of the crematorium. The uniformed officer busied himself bringing his superiors up to date. Caton and Carter kicked their heels in frustration.

Suddenly there was the unmistakeable sound of challenges shouted, followed almost immediately by gun shots.

'Come on Nick,' said Caton sprinting down the path.' 'If they shoot our man we're stuffed!'

They ran pell-mell down the path, and out into the open. Ahead of them reared the four storey redbrick tower of the crematory church. There were more shouts from directly ahead of them, and another set of challenges to their left, followed by a volley of rifle shots, and what sounded like the reply of small arms fire.

'This way,' said Caton, setting off towards the sound of gunfire. He eschewed the path, and opted to run in a direct line, dodging the gravestones as he went. Carter found himself falling behind. The shouting grew louder.

'Armed Police! Throw down your weapon! Come out! Do it now!'

There was more rifle fire, and more shots returned. Then there was silence.

Caton burst into a clearing where there were several rows of graves beside a tarmac path. Three armed officers had their backs to him, all of them staring at a point on the ground ahead of them. One of them heard the sound of panting and whirled around his gun straight at Caton's chest.

'Armed Police!' he screamed. 'Stay where you are.'

The others turned to face him, and sighted their guns. Caton began to reach for his ID and instantly thought better of it.

'Don't move!' one of them yelled.

'Keep your hands where we can see them!' shouted another.

'Kneel down!' bellowed the third.

Caton sank to his knees. His heart was pounding, his legs felt like jelly. He had known of accidents in training, and in the field, when even the most experienced officers had adrenalin flowing through their veins.

'I'm a police officer,' he shouted. 'Pursuing suspects. This is my investigation.'

The officer, on the flanks moved to cover their colleague as he advanced cautiously towards Caton.

'In which case,' he said as he drew near. 'You'll know the drill. Lie face down with your arms out to the sides.'

Caton did as he was told.

The firearms officer drew level. Caton could see the barrel of the gun angled down towards him.

'Where do you keep your ID?'

Caton told him.

He reached down and took it from Caton's inside breast pocket. He was straightening up with it in his hand when Carter burst into the clearing.

'Armed Police!'

'Stand still!'

'Hold your fire! He's with me!' shouted Caton. 'He's a detective sergeant!'

'Bloody Hell!' said the officer scrutinising his warrant card. 'How many more of you are there?'

'Are you Border Agency support team?' said Caton, getting to his feet.

'That's right. We were the nearest armed response. What the hell was this all about?'

Caton brushed himself down.

'Where are my suspects?'

'One of them's over there,' he replied, pointing behind him. 'But you won't get anything out of him now.'

Fearing the worst, Caton walked towards the statue of a young female angel, wings outstretched. In her left hand she held a bunch of lilies. Her right arm, severed at the wrist, stretched up towards the sky. Rounding it he found that she was staring at a body lying, face down, at her feet.

It wasn't the two exit holes, one in the man's head and one in his back, that first caught Caton's attention; it was the black leather jacket, the shaven head, and the gun on the grass beside him.

He was still trying to decide if he was relieved or gutted when another shout disturbed the graveyard's solemn stillness.

'Armed Police! Stand still!'

He turned towards the sound. A man had stepped out from the cover of a tree, and stood beside it close to the margins of the path. His hands were behind his head. Given that there were three rifles pointing at him he didn't look anywhere near as worried as he should have done.

Chapter 38

They travelled back the way they had come, through bleak moorland hills, on the highest motorway in the country.

Carter sat in the back with Bowman. Ahead of them the unmarked car led the way at a steady but comparatively sedate pace. They drove in silence. Caton was in no hurry. Not now. He wanted Bowman to sweat it out. Nothing was going to compromise the interview. There was too much at stake.

He had left Helen Gates to sort it out over the phone with the Humberside Gold Commander. No doubt they would be unhappy that there were two dead bodies on their patch, one of their armed response units having to go through an IPCC investigation, an armed suspect on the loose, and none of the kudos of an arrest and conviction. Caton wouldn't be applying for a post that side of the Pennines anytime soon.

It was six in the evening when they reached Central Park. It was seven by the time Bowman had been processed. Caton had just had time to freshen up, have a hot drink, and a pastie from the canteen, ring Kate to explain yet again why he was going to be late, and go over the day's events with DS Gates.

'So Tom, have you got your interview strategy sorted?' she asked.

'I think so Ma'am,' he told her. 'Is there any news on Petrovic?'

'Not yet. We live in hope. At least if the forensics place the dead man – Hashim Dalca – at the scene of the murders, we've got a result. His gun is the right calibre for a start. Then we have the prints, and the DNA.'

'A partial result,' said Caton. 'We still need to know why they had to die.'

'That,' she said. 'Is what I'm hoping you're about to find out,'

'My client wants full immunity under Section 71 of the 2005 Act, as set out in the Undertakings and Agreements in the Serious and Organised Crimes Act 2007.'

It didn't come as a complete surprise to Caton, given the predicament Bowman now found himself in, and the barrister who had pitched up out of the blue. Alexis Hemmingford-Grey QC. No relative, to the commissioner thank God.

'Furthermore,' she continued 'He requires witness protection for himself and his immediate family, prior to, and during, any trials that should result from such statements as he may provide, and a change of identity, re-location, and re-settlement subsequent to those trials.'

'Doesn't want a lot, does he,' muttered Gordon Holmes.

Caton kicked him gently under the table.

Bowman stared back at them. He was shorter and slimmer than he had seemed in the photograph they had taken from his home. He had three day stubble on his face, his cheeks were sunken, and there were dark bags beneath his eyes. But he had recovered his composure; buoyed by the presence of his legal representative, and the get out of jail card she seemed to have thrown him. Nevertheless he looked suitably embarrassed, ashamed even. All of which bode well for the reliability of the information he might be willing to provide.

'You know that I can't promise anything without the approval of the Crown Prosecution Service,' Caton replied.

'And specifically the Attorney General,' she said, not that he needed reminding.

'And they are going to need to be convinced,' he continued. 'Not only that the information your client is willing to provide could not be obtained by other means, and that his part in any crime committed is of such a degree that it is in the public interest to set it aside from prosecution.'

She brushed imaginary dust from the lapels of her suit jacket.

'Are you teaching me to suck eggs Detective Chief Inspector?'

Touché, thought Caton.

'So, what exactly is it that you wish to tell us Mr Bowman?' he said.

Bowman looked at his brief. She answered for him.

'My client is willing to provide chapter and verse in relation to the circumstances surrounding the death of Okowu-Bello.'

'The *murder* of *Mr* Okowu-Bello,' said Caton. 'And his part in it?'

Her eyebrows arched.

'Come, come Mr Caton. This is an honest offer. There is no need to play games.'

Honest was not the word that Caton would have chosen.

'I can assure you,' she continued. 'That the information he is willing to provide, and to repeat in court, will be more than enough to secure the conviction of those responsible for Mr Okowu-Bello's death.'

'And what of those responsible for the deaths of Mr Ratten, Mr Gideon Jones, and Mr Holt?'

She smiled thinly.

'My client knows nothing of those. He can prove that he was in hiding with a friend in Leeds throughout the period in which those murders occurred. He never left the house.'

Caton didn't doubt it.

'I am terminating this interview,' he said. 'Your client will remain in custody pending a response from the Crown Prosecution Service.'

'My client,' she replied. 'Would not wish it any other way.'

'Lincolnshire Police have just detained Petrovic. He was trying to sneak on board a lolo at Immingham.' DS Gates informed him.

'Lolo?'

'Lift-on, lift-off, apparently. A container ship to you and me. Heading for the Baltic.'

Immingham, that's on the other side of the estuary from Hull?' he said.

'That's it. He stole a car from one the houses behind the cemetery, drove round the estuary, and dumped it. Then he mugged one of the crew from the vessel in an alley at the back of the Seafarers' Centre, and tried to blag his way onboard. I've sent DS Carter and DS Stuart to collect him.'

Caton was about to protest, but she forestalled him.

'It's alright Tom, they're only going to confirm the

ID, process him, and complete the paperwork. He's travelling back on his own in a prison van, with them and a traffic car riding shot gun.'

'We can't let Bowman or his Barrister know,' he said. 'He's only doing this because he's scared witless Petrovic will get to him or his family.'

He turned to Harry Spencer, who had proved to be a stickler for protocol on the Bluebell Hollow Case.

'How soon can we get a decision from the Attorney General?'

Spencer shook his head.

Here it comes, thought Caton, twenty reasons why not.

'This isn't going to the Attorney General,' he said. 'At least not on the terms that his barrister is seeking. The man is clearly implicated as an accessory to murder, before and after the event, even if he wasn't aware that murder had been intended. Now that you have one of your prime suspects in custody, Bowman's testimony may not be required.'

'Petrovic isn't going to give us anything,' Caton protested. 'I'd bet my life on it. At best he'll implicate Dalca. He was the one found with what we are assuming was the weapon used to murder the other four victims. All the really good trace evidence relates to the murders of Gideon-Jones and Holt. Petrovic will exercise his right to remain silent. You'll offer him a reduced sentence as an accessory if he pleads guilty to that. At best he'll get four concurrent life sentences, or a single minimum term, instead of five consecutive life sentences. He could be out within fifteen years.'

Spencer didn't bother to deny it.

'He will be deported on release from prison,' he said.

'There is something else Bowman isn't telling us,' Caton said. 'Not without immunity.'

The man from the CPS looked surprised.

'What precisely?' he said.

Caton looked at Helen Gates. She nodded her agreement. So Caton told him.

'Bloody Hell!' Spencer exclaimed. 'Does his barrister know?'

'I've no idea,' said Caton.

Spencer fiddled nervously with his tie. It cheered Caton up to see him so uncomfortable.

'This is political dynamite. The Attorney General will need to know about this. On the other hand, all you've got is your suspicions. You'd better find out what he has to say for himself first. This is how I suggest you proceed.'

'So that's it,' said Hemmingford-Grey. 'That's all you are prepared to offer?'

'Your client pleads guilty to accessory to murder, and the Crown Prosecution Service will guarantee a reduction of sentence under Section 73, protection for your client in a maximum security prison for the duration of his sentence, and witness protection for his family.'

'But without my client's evidence,' she began.

He cut her off.

'We no longer believe that we need to rely on your client's evidence.'

She was taken aback.

'What do you mean?'

Before Caton could reply Bowman slammed his hand down on the table.

'I'll give you Charles Grey!' he said.

They both stared at him.

Alexis Hemmingford-Grey fixed Caton with a steely stare.

'I need to speak with my client,' she said. 'In private.'

It had taken four hours. Helen Gates had gone direct to the Chief Constable; he had gone direct to the Attorney General. The Attorney General had agreed, with one proviso; no decision was to be taken about any prosecution of Charles Grey without consulting him. Now they were back in the interview room.

'Do you understand Mr Bowman,' said Caton. 'That I require a written agreement from you to assist with this investigation and subsequent prosecutions, on the understanding that if you do not fully disclose all relevant information known to you, or if you provide false evidence, the agreement will be void, and your immunity from prosecution will be revoked?'

'He understands,' said his barrister impatiently.

'I need to hear it from Mr Bowman.'

'I understand,' said Bowman. 'Now, can we get on with this?'

'It was back in December,' he began. 'Me and Shawcross were having a quiet drink in the Bent Brook. This guy came up to us. Said his name was Peter. Polish, we thought. He knew who we were, and where we worked. Anyway, he wanted to know if we were interested in some easy money.'

Caton was asking the questions. Helen Gates, Harry Spencer from the CPS, and the Chief Constable, watched and listened at the observation window.

'What did you say?'

'What do think? We said yes. Who wouldn't? Anyway it turned out he was offering £10,000 each for us to help some of the lads play a practical joke on Sunday Okowu-Bello.'

'Who did he mean by *the lads*?'

'Sunday's team mates. He was always playing practical jokes on them.'

'And you didn't think it strange that he was approaching you and not one of them?'

'Not especially. They wanted him to know who was behind it. He was capable of wilder tricks than any of them could think of.'

'And you didn't think it odd that you were being offered all that money to turn a blind eye?'

He shrugged.

'Not really. Do you know how much these guys are on? They blow that much on a weekend at the Races.'

Or at the Casino, Caton reflected.

'What exactly did this Peter want you to do,' he said.

'Make sure we were on outside duty for the area around the cryogenic unit, on a night of his choosing. He said the lads who were organising it would make sure Sunday turned up at the ground. It wasn't difficult because that was usually our job. I suppose he'd already sussed that out.'

'What else did he want you to do?'

'Let him know who would be responsible for monitoring the cameras that night.'

'And you told him.'

'That's right. Phil Ratten.'

'Did you discuss this with Mr Ratten yourselves?'

'No, he said not to. He'd deal with that.'

'Anything else?'

'Yeah. He wanted us to open the doors to the unit, switch it on, and switch it off. The idea was just to put the wind up Sunday.'

'You didn't think that odd?'

Bowman looked across at his barrister, and addressed himself to her as much as Caton.

'You wouldn't believe some of the things they get up to,' he said. 'Sunday stuck potatoes up the exhausts of Jacko's Lamborghini, and topped up the tank of Besty's Maserati with six cans of lager. It cut out in the outside lane of the M6 when he was doing a hundred miles an hour. Now *that's* dangerous.'

Caton was tempted to ask if he meant the lager, or the fact he was doing a ton on the motorway.

'Jacko and Besty are?'

Bowman turned back to face Caton.

'Joseph Azuku and Harvey Best. You must have heard of them.'

Okowu-Bello's best friend, and the team mate he was cheating on. Caton had interviewed the two of them.

'Tell me what happened on the night,' he said.

The tone of Bowman's voice changed dramatically, and he tensed visibly as he relived the events.

'We saw Sunday arrive at the stadium. He parked up, and waved to us on his way to the reception area. Then the Pole arrived in a black Mercedes 4x4. The same one that rammed us in Hull.'

He paused for a moment, steeling himself.

'He waved us over. Wanted one of us to check the monitors were off, the other one to wait by the van. Mark went to check; I went over and stood by the generator. Mark came back five minutes later, spoke to Peter the Pole, and came to join me.'

He reached for the beaker of water on the table, and had a drink.

'Ten minutes later these two guys appeared, carrying Sunday between them. Looked like he was pissed.'

He sensed Alexis Hemmingford-Grey shifting in her seat beside him.

'Sorry Miss,' he said. 'Drunk. Anyway, that's what the Pole said. *"No worry, he's a little drunk is all."*

Caton leaned forward.

'You still didn't think it strange that none of his team mates were there to capture it on their mobiles. Film it maybe?'

'I thought they'd turn up any minute.'

'What was Mr Okowu-Bello wearing?'

'The same clothes he had when he arrived.'

'Were his hands tied in any way?'

'No. If they had been we'd have been out of there.'

Hemmingford-Grey leaned forward towards Caton until there was just a foot between them.

'I would prefer it if you would allow my client to make his statement without interruption,' she said. 'There will be plenty of time for questions when he has finished.'

Caton was tempted to tell her what to do with her preferences, but having thought about it decided that on balance she was right. They could revisit this over and over again before he finally signed it off. What's more, there was a greater likelihood that Bowman would provide a more complete account uninterrupted.

'Very well,' he said. 'Please carry on Mr Bowman.'

The security guard folded his arms around his chest as though that would somehow protect him.

'We were both a bit worried at that point, but I sensed that these guys weren't gonna take no for an answer. Mark did too. The Pole told me to start up the generator and prepare to switch on. He told Mark to go and open the doors and lower the steps down. They took Sunday up the steps into the van, and sent Mark back to join me. Five minutes later they closed the doors, and I was told to switch on the controls in the cab, starting the cryogenic process. There's nothing to it you see. Flick two switches. Wait for the dial to reach -120. Wait two minutes, switch it off again.

Soon as I'd switched it on they made me get down from the cab. I told them I shouldn't leave it switched on. It was dangerous. Especially if Sunday was drunk. The Pole said we were to go and wait in the Transit van parked beside the 4X4.'

He looked across at his barrister again.

'We knew straight away we'd got mixed up in something really bad. I tried to get back in the cab. One of the other guys dragged me back down. His mate had a gun trained on Mark. They forced us over to the Transit and made us get in the back. I think the Pole got in the front. Then the engine started, and we set off.'

He looked down at the table. It came in a rush.

'Mark and me were scared witless. He said we had to get out of that van and disappear. The first time it stopped we pushed up the door release, flung the doors open, and leapt out. The Merc' was right behind us. We legged it over the central barrier, ran between the traffic on the other side, and into the Ordsall Estate. I used to live there. Expecting a bullet any moment, I ran down Coronation Street with Mark right behind me. I turned right into Huddart Close, and we hid in the gardens at the back of the Lads Club. We stayed there for ages. Then I took Mark to a mate's where we stayed the night. Soon as we heard the news the next morning we knew we had to get away. I got my mate to take us to Alex's place in Leeds. We were still there, keeping our heads down when that Merc' turned up at the front. We went out the back, took Alex's car and just drove. We'd heard about poor old Phil Ratten being found in Ship Canal. Reckoned we'd have to get out of the country. We didn't have our passports but we thought we might be able to get on the back of a lorry. Those immigrants seem to be able to get into the country that way; we thought it might be even easier to get out.'

He looked up, almost apologetic.

'We weren't thinking straight.'

No you weren't, Caton reflected, not from that very first moment back in the Bent Brook Pub.

'The rest,' Bowman said. 'You know.'

'Not in respect of how Charles Grey is involved,' said Caton.

Bowman looked momentarily confused.

'He's wasn't,' he said. 'Not with this.'

Hemmingford-Grey placed a hand on his arm.

'I don't think that was what Mr Caton was implying,' she said. She looked at Caton. 'I think it would be advisable Detective Chief Inspector if we had a little break, don't you?'

'It was Frank's idea,' he began.

'I'm sorry, said Caton, 'But could you please use their full names?'

Hemmingford-Grey raised her eyebrows, but let it go. She was as interested to know as Caton was.

'Frank Moston, Head of Manc Security Limited, Chief Executive of Dedicated Security Services Ltd. Our Boss. We used to be members of the same student club at Uni. '

'Thank you,' said Caton.

'Moston knew Grey wouldn't want the truth about his membership of Students For Britain to come out. He decided to give him a hand so he'd be even further in his debt. He said having someone like the Police Commissioner in your pocket was a real prize. A recommendation from him could get us all sorts of new business. All we had to do was dig up some dirt on his two rivals. If there wasn't any, we had to find a way of smearing either them or an immediate family member. It wasn't difficult at all.'

For the first time in the entire interview Caton felt real antipathy towards this man. It could be argued, and no doubt Hemmingford–Grey would have done so but for the immunity deal on the table, that his involvement in Okowu-Bello's death had been stupid and greedy. But his part in getting that innocent young girl hooked on crack cocaine, and landing her with a criminal conviction that would ruin her prospects, just to discredit her father, was pure evil.

'If it's alright with you Ms Hemmingford-Grey,' he said. 'There is one question I would like to ask?'

'Go ahead.'

'Mr Bowman, do you know at what point Mr Grey was made aware of the efforts made by you, Mr Shawcross, and Mr Moston to affect the election result?'

Bowman grinned.

'Straight after the election,' he said. 'He was hardly going to turn round and rat on us then was he? Even if he did, it was only his word against ours.'

Chapter 39

'So Grey didn't initiate it,' said Kate as she emptied the pasta into a bowl. 'But he profited from it, and concealed two crimes, and the fact that he'd been a member of that nasty pseudo-political organisation. What was it called?'

'Students For Britain,' said Caton, pulling the cork on a bottle of Ruffino 2007 Riserva Ducale, Chianti Classico. He had been looking forward to this, their first proper meal together in days.

'It's no wonder that he wanted the investigation over fast,' she said. 'I'd love to have seen his face when he used his one phone call to speak to the Chief Constable only to be told he couldn't help him.'

'It was a picture,' said Caton pouring the wine, and sitting down at the table. 'I'm just disappointed that he isn't going to be prosecuted.'

Kate placed the tomato and mozzarella salad on the table, and sat down facing him.

'Why ever not?'

'Because it would be too embarrassing for the Government. They're the ones who dreamt up the whole Police Commissioner thing. Grey claims he knew nothing about what Moston was up to. He says he was being blackmailed. Bowmen's statement confirms that.'

Caton had given up trying to find a politically

correct equivalent for blackmail. Gordon was right after all. There wasn't one. He knew the derivation wasn't racist so he'd just have to live with it.

Kate twisted some pasta on her fork.

'I saw his resignation statement on the news,' she said. 'What a weasel.'

'He hasn't heard the last of it though,' Caton told her. 'When Moston goes to trial it'll all come out. Moston was packing when Gordon arrived to arrest him. There was an airline ticket to Northern Cyprus in his bag.'

They ate and drank in silence for a moment, savouring the silky smoothness and ripe cherry flavour of the wine, and the fiery unctuous texture of the aglio olio e pepperoncino.

'The Pole got away though?' she said.

'Stasik Sakovich, we think,' he told her. 'A Russian Pole. Ismailov's right hand man in Manchester. According to Ismailov he went back to Russia because of a family bereavement, and he hasn't heard from him since.'

'Very convenient.'

She brushed a trickle of oil from her lips with the back of her hand.

'I see the Titans have lost again, you must be pleased?'

'It looks like a three horse race,' he said. 'City, United and Arsenal. The knives are out. Gerry Capper is already looking like a haunted man. The word on the street is that the Chinese owners are looking to sell.'

'They've only been there a couple of years.'

'A Russian consortium is firming up their bid apparently. Barbara Bryce at the National Crime Agency thinks that was what killing Okowu-Bello, and implicating the security team, was all about.

Softening up the club, and destabilising it for a takeover. Ismailov will probably have someone lined up to take over the security side as well.'

She put her glass down.

'That's appalling!'

'And the rest. It will probably prove impossible to trace it back to them though. Not unless the NCA manage to get their hands on Petrovic. Assuming he's still alive. Which I doubt.'

'So poor Sunday Okowu-Bello's gambling had nothing to do with it?'

'Not with his death. But they still believe he was on the take. Dave Munby says it's odds on there's an Asian betting consortium looking for new targets as we speak.'

'Gina Burman seems to have come out of it OK though?' she said. 'The papers will have paid her handsomely for the story she gave them. And I don't suppose it will have done her business any harm?'

'Far from it. She tells me business is booming. Though I think she'd much prefer to have still been in the Force.'

Kate tore off a piece of ciabbatta, and dipped it in her bowl.

'Nothing is ever as it seems, is it?' she said.

'No, it's not,' he replied, as he topped up their glasses.

'Speaking of which,' she said. 'Are you aware that your hair is thinning on the sides?'

He grimaced.

'I know. It's down to wearing helmets and caps all those years I was in uniform.'

'Never mind,' she told him. 'You're not the only one with body image issues.'

She patted her tummy.

'I'm going to have to get them to let the wedding

dress out a bit. By the way, did I mention that I've booked a place at the university crèche?'

'No you didn't. Don't you think we should have discussed it first?' He sounded peeved.

A twirl of pasta hung precariously from her fork, suspended in mid-air.

'Tom Caton! Don't tell me you're going sexist on me?'

'It's not that,' he protested.

'What then? Are you telling me you intend to become a house husband? Or will you take our child into work with you? You could always train it up to take over from Gordon.'

He put down his glass.

'Over my dead body. No son of mine is going into the police.'

'Who said anything about a he?'

'Are you saying it's a girl?'

'I don't know what sex our child is; I'm just saying you can't rule out the possibility.'

He pushed back his chair and stood up.

'Rule it out? Why would I want to do that? A girl would be amazing, if she's anything like you.'

As he started towards her, she jumped up and backed away, placing the table between them.

'Well I can think of several ways she's never going to be like you.' she teased.

'Baldy!'

The Author

Bill Rogers has written seven crime thriller novels to date – all of them based in and around the City of Manchester. His first novel *The Cleansing* received the ePublishing Consortium Writers Award 2011, and was short listed for the Long Barn Books Debut Novel Award. His Fourth novel, *A Trace of Blood, reached* the semi-final of the Amazon Breakthrough Novel Award in 2009.

Bill has also written *Breakfast at Katsouris,* an anthology of short crime stories, and a novel for teens, young adults and adults, called *The Cave.* He lives in Greater Manchester where he has spent his entire adult life.

www.billrogers.co.uk
www.catonbooks.com

If you have enjoyed **THE FROZEN CONTRACT**
Why not try the other novels in the series:

In order

The Cleansing
The Head Case
The Tiger's Cave
A Fatal Intervention
A Trace of Blood
Bluebell Hollow

All of his books are available as paperbacks from bookshops, or on Amazon and as Amazon Kindle EBooks

THE CLEANSING

The novel that first introduced DCI Tom Caton. Christmas approaches. A killer dressed as a clown haunts the streets of Manchester. For him the City's miraculous regeneration had unacceptable consequences. This is the reckoning. DCI Tom Caton enlists the help of forensic profiler Kate Webb, placing her in mortal danger. The trail leads from the site of the old mass cholera graves, through Moss Side, the Gay Village, the penthouse opulence of canalside apartment blocks, and the bustling Christmas Market, to the Victorian Gothic grandeur of the Town Hall. Time is running out: For Tom, for Kate...and for the City.

Awarded ePublishing Consortium Writers Award 2011.
Short listed for the
Long Barn Books Debut Novel Award

THE HEAD CASE

SOMETHING IS ROTTEN IN
THE CORRIDORS OF POWER.

Roger Standing CBE, Head of Harmony High Academy, and the Prime Minister's Special Adviser for Education, is dead. DCI Tom Caton is not short of suspects. But if this is a simple mugging, then why are MI5 ransacking Standing's apartment, and disrupting the investigation? And why are the widow and her son taking the news so calmly?

THE TIGER'S CAVE

A lorry full of Chinese illegal immigrants arrives in Hull. Twenty four hours later their bodies are discovered close to the M62 motorway; but a young man and a girl are missing, and still at risk. Supported by the Serious and Organised Crime Agency, Caton must travel to China to pick up the trail. But he knows the solution is closer to home – in Manchester's Chinatown - and time is running out.

TWELVE BODIES, NO MOTIVE, THE HUNT IS ON. A COLD CASE IS ABOUT TO GET HOT.

A FATAL INTERVENTION

A SUCCESSFUL BARRISTER, A WRONGFUL ACCUSATION, A MYSTERIOUS DISAPPEARANCE

It is the last thing that Rob Thornton expects. When he finds his life turned upside down he sets out on the trail of Anjelita Covas, his accuser. Haunted by her tragic history and sudden disappearance Rob turns detective in London's underworld. A series of rhyming messages arrive, each signalling a murder. Rob must find Anjelita and face a dark truth.

DEEP BENEATH THE CITY OF MANCHESTER LIES A HEART OF DARKNESS

BLUEBELL HOLLOW

DCI Tom Caton's world is rocked when he learns that he has a son by a former lover. Then the first of the bodies is discovered at the Cutacre Open Cast Mine. The victims appear to have addiction in common. Suspects include a Premiership footballer, a barrister, and just about everyone at the Oasis Rehab Clinic in leafy Cheshire. As Caton digs deeper his world begins to fall apart.

AND ALSO

THE CAVE

A TEST OF COURAGE
IN A RACE AGAINST TIME

A group of teenagers from a Manchester inner city academy set off for an adventure holiday in the Pennine Hills. Two days later tragedy strikes. Deep below the ground the six survivors struggle to stay alive until help arrives. The stories they tell about themselves will change their lives forever.

A rite of passage/coming of age novel, for teenagers, young adults, and adults. *The Cave* explores themes that affect the lives of young people in the modern multicultural city. Think the Cave by Plato, meets *The Canterbury Tales*, and a far more hopeful *Lord of The Flies.*

AND

BREAKFAST AT KATSOURIS

An anthology of three short stories and a novella.
A Caton's Quickies imprint of Caton Books

Breakfast at Katsouris
Adapted, as a short story, from *A Trace of Blood.*

The Wren Boy
Adapted, as a ghost story, from
A Trace of Blood

The Readers
A new Novella exploring the fragile barrier that separates the modern serial crime novelist from the serial killer.

To Die For
A Christmas Tale

Lightning Source UK Ltd.
Milton Keynes UK
UKOW042219241012

201149UK00003B/14/P